THE BEST
HORROR OF THE YEAR

VOLUME FIVE

Also Edited by Ellen Datlow

THE BEST
HORROR OF THE YEAR

VOLUME **FIVE**

EDITED BY **ELLEN DATLOW**

NIGHT SHADE BOOKS
SAN FRANCISCO

Night Shade books may be purchased in bulk at special discounts for sales promotion, corporate gifts, fund-raising, or educational purposes. Special editions can also be created to specifications. For details, contact the Special Sales Department, Night Shade Books, 307 West 36th Street, 11th Floor, New York, NY 10018 or info@skyhorsepublishing.com.

Night Shade Books™ is a trademark of Skyhorse Publishing, Inc. ®, a Delaware corporation.

Visit our website at www.nightshadebooks.com.

10 9 8 7 6 5 4 3 2

Library of Congress Cataloging-in-Publication Data is available on file.

ISBN: 978-1-59780-474-5

Cover art by Allen Williams
Interior layout and design by Amy Popovich
Photo of Ellen Datlow by Gregory Frost

Printed in the United States of America

ACKNOWLEDGMENTS

I'd like to thank Melody Chamlee for being my first reader. I'd like to thank Stefan Dziemianowicz for his generosity and his time, Charles Tan for bringing material from the Philippines to my attention, as well as Michael Kelly, and Laura Miller for recommendations. And thanks to Tamsyn Muir, who provided me with most unexpected yet welcome help in the last few days of putting this volume together.

I'd also like to thank and acknowledge the following magazines and catalogs for invaluable information and descriptions of material I was unable to obtain: *Locus*, *Publishers Weekly*, British Fantasy Society Journal, and S.F. Commentary. Thanks to the editors who made sure I saw their magazines during the year, the webzine editors who provided printouts, and the book publishers who provided review copies in a timely manner. Also, the writers who sent me printouts of their stories when I was unable to acquire the magazine or book in which they appeared.

Thanks to Merrilee Heifetz and Sarah Nagel at Writers House.

And a very special thank you to Jeremy Lassen, Jason Williams, Ross Lockhart, and Tomra Palmer.

TABLE OF CONTENTS

SUMMATION 2012

First some of the statistics: The twenty-eight stories and poems in this volume have been chosen from anthologies, collections, print magazine, webzines, and single story chapbooks. Unusually, I've taken three zombie stories this year, each very different from the other, and each dealing with the trope in unusual ways, showing there's still life (pun intended) in this staple of horror fiction that I would not have believed possible three years ago.

I took more and shorter stories this time around-only two came in over ten thousand words.

Thirteen of the stories and poems are by writers living in the United States, nine stories or poems are from the United Kingdom, three from Canada, two from Australia, and one from New Zealand. I've taken two poems by one poet and two stories by one author. The authors of the three poems and of twelve of the stories have never been in any of my *Best of the Year's* before. Eleven and a half of the stories and poems are by women. Seventeen and a half are by men.

Awards

The Bram Stoker Awards® for Achievement in Horror are given by the Horror Writers Association. The awards for material appearing during 2011 were presented at the organization's annual banquet held Saturday evening, March 31, 2012 in Salt Lake City, Utah, at the World Horror Convention, and marked the 25th Anniversary of the awards.

2011 Winners for Superior Achievement:

Novel: *Flesh Eaters* by Joe McKinney (Pinnacle Books); First Novel: *Isis Unbound* by Allyson Bird (Dark Regions Press); Young Adult Novel (tie): *The Screaming Season* by Nancy Holder (Razorbill) and *Dust and Decay* by Jonathan Maberry (Simon & Schuster Books for Young Readers); Graphic Novel: *Neonomicon* by Alan Moore (Avatar Press); Long Fiction: "The Ballad of Ballard and Sandrine" by Peter Straub (*Conjunctions: 56*); Short Fiction : "Herman Wouk Is Still Alive" by Stephen King (*The Atlantic Magazine*, May 2011); Screenplay: *American Horror Story*, episode #12: "Afterbirth" by Jessica Sharzer (20th Century Fox Television); Fiction Collection: *The Corn Maiden and Other Nightmares* by Joyce Carol Oates (Mysterious Press); Anthology: *Demons: Encounters with the Devil and his Minions, Fallen Angels and the Possessed* edited by John Skipp (Black Dog and Leventhal); Non-Fiction: *Stephen King: A Literary Companion by Rocky Wood* (McFarland & Company, Inc., Publishers); Poetry Collection: *How to Recognize a Demon Has Become Your Friend* by Linda Addison (Necon Ebooks).

HWA, in conjunction with the Bram Stoker Family Estate and the Rosenbach Museum & Library, also presented a special, one-time only Vampire Novel of the Century Award to Richard Matheson for his modern classic *I Am Legend*. This award was voted on by a jury chaired by Dracula expert Leslie S. Klinger and was sponsored by Jeremy Wagner.

HWA also presented its annual Lifetime Achievement Awards and its Specialty Press Award. Rick Hautala and Joe R. Lansdale were both on-hand to accept their Lifetime Achievement Awards. The Specialty Press Award went to Derrick Hussey of *Hippocampus Press* and Roy Robbins of *Bad Moon Books*. The Silver Hammer Award, for outstanding service to HWA, was voted by the organization's board of trustees to Guy Anthony DeMarco. The President's Richard Laymon Service Award was given to HWA co-founder Karen Lansdale.

The Shirley Jackson Award, recognizing the legacy of Jackson's writing, and with permission of her estate, was established for outstanding achievement in the literature of psychological suspense, horror, and the dark fantastic. The awards were announced at Readercon 23, July 14, 2012 held in Burlington, Massachusetts. Jurors were Laird Barron, Matthew Cheney, Maura McHugh, Kaaron Warren, and Gary K. Wolfe.

The winners for the best work in 2011: Novel: *Witches on the Road Tonight*, Sheri Holman (Grove Press); Novella: "Near Zennor," Elizabeth Hand (*A Book of Horrors*, Quercus/Jo Fletcher Books); Novelette: "The Summer People," Kelly Link (*Tin House 49/Steampunk! An Anthology of Fantastically Rich and Strange Stories*, Candlewick Press); Short Story: "The Corpse Painter's Masterpiece," M. Rickert (*The Magazine of Fantasy and Science Fiction*, Sept/Oct, 2011); Single-Author Collection: *After the Apocalypse: Stories*, Maureen F. McHugh (Small Beer Press); Edited Anthology: *Ghosts by Gaslight*, edited by Jack Dann and Nick Gevers (Harper Voyager).

The World Fantasy Awards were announced Sunday, November 4, 2012 at the annual banquet held at the World Fantasy Convention in Toronto, Canada. Lifetime Achievement recipients Alan Garner and George R. R. Martin were previously announced.

Winners for the best work in 2011: Novel: *Osama*, Lavie Tidhar (PS Publishing); Novella: "A Small Price to Pay for Birdsong", K.J. Parker (*Subterranean* Winter 2011); Short Story: "The Paper Menagerie", Ken Liu (*F&SF* 3-4/11); Anthology: *The Weird*, Ann & Jeff VanderMeer, eds. (Corvus; Tor, published May 2012); Collection: *The Bible Repairman and Other Stories*, Tim Powers (Tachyon and Subterranean Press); Artist: John Coulthart; Special Award Professional: Raymond Russell & Rosalie Parker, for Tartarus Press; Non-professional: Eric Lane, for publishing in translation for Dedalus Books.

NOTABLE NOVELS OF 2012

Zone One by Colson Whitehead (Doubleday) is an engrossing, realistic, horrific-with-a-touch of humor, and poignant zombie novel. The zombie plague is under control and the government headquartered in Buffalo is gung ho on reconstruction, especially down in New York City. The story unfolds from the point of view of Mark Spitz, a member of one of several civilian clean-up crews stationed in lower Manhattan, assigned to mop up any surviving zombie squatters after heavy duty artillery has stormed through. As the team does its sweeps, Spitz recalls how he ended up where he is.

The Company Man by Robert Jackson Bennett (Orbit) begins in 1919 as a trolley car filled with eleven factory workers dead inside of it rolls into a station. All were alive when they entered the trolley and all were union workers. The eponymous investigator works for the McNaughton Corporation, the powerful and mysterious entity running the United States from the capitol city of Evesden, located in a Pacific Northwest very different from the one we know. An engaging, noirish mystery, the book deservedly won the mystery and suspense field's Edgar Award in the original paperback category.

The Troupe by Robert Jackson Bennett (Orbit), the author's third novel, is a charming and occasionally harrowing dark fantasy about a sixteen year old pianist traveling from one vaudeville show to another, seeking information about the troupe of the mysterious Heironomo Silenus. Once the boy tracks down the troupe, he discovers that the odd assortment of performers comprise an act that does far more than just entertain.

The Rook by Daniel O'Malley (Little, Brown) is a marvelous first novel that is dark and violent yet laced with humor. It opens with one of the most engaging first lines I've read: "Dear You, The body you are wearing used to be mine." And so, a young woman comes to consciousness with two black eyes, dead people lying on the ground around her, and no memory of who she is or why she's in the situation in which she finds herself. The rest of the novel doesn't disappoint, with a secret agency protecting Great Britain from supernatural forces, conspiracies, and plenty of mayhem to keep the reader entertained throughout.

The Whisperer by Donato Carrisi and translated by Shaun Whiteside (Mulholland Books) is an impressive first novel by an Italian television writer, about a person able to persuade ordinary people to kill, serially or not.

The Croning by Laird Barron (Night Shade Books) is the author's first full-length novel (a novel of about 43,000 words was published in 2011) and the result has been worth the wait. Barron puts his poor innocent schmo of a protagonist through torturous paces in a smashing, horrific retelling of Rumpelstiltskin. The author is an expert at depicting Lovecraftian cosmic horror, and this book—with its echoes of places and characters from his short stories and novellas—is for every reader who has been devouring those works.

The White Forest by Adam McOmber (Touchstone) is a powerful gothic novel about a young woman living at the edge of Hampstead Heath in the mid-1800s with her widowed father. Having spent most of her childhood alone and unsuccessfully suppressing an ability to hear the souls of manmade objects, she's thrilled to develop a companionable friendship with two people her own age just as they all reach maturity. All seems well, until the young man becomes obsessed with her abilities, leading him to join a secret society in London. Then he disappears.

The Drowning Girl (A Memoir) by Caitlín R. Kiernan (Roc) is a complex story about ghosts, mermaids, sirens, insanity, cults, truth vs. fact, metamorphosis, and relationships. India Morgan Phelps (aka Imp) struggles for several years against her own inner demons to work out what really happened the night she stopped her car to pick up a naked woman walking along a deserted road. As Imp writes in her diary, her memories drift back and forth in time, introducing dreamy strands of possibilities. Kiernan expertly drives the narration through structural intricacies with apparent ease.

Devil Said Bang by Richard Kadrey (HarperVoyager) is the fourth novel in the Sandman Slim series about James Stark, a Nephilim (half angel/half human), the only live person ever sent to Hell who then broke out. In *Aloha From Hell*, Stark found God (literally) and when Lucifer left town was anointed the new Lucifer—which does not make him happy for a number of reasons, including the fact that there seems to be plot to kill him. Meantime, back in L.A. a serial killer ghost is loose and someone else might just be altering reality, such as it is.

Available Dark by Elizabeth Hand (Minotaur) is the sequel to *Generation Loss*, and both are excellent, compulsively readable contemporary dark suspense novels about Cassandra Neary, a brilliant photographer who lit up the 70s punk landscape briefly but quickly burned out with liquor and drugs. After escaping home to Manhattan after some real nastiness in Maine (*Generation Loss*), Neary is offered a great deal of money to fly all expenses paid to Helsinki and authenticate a series of five photographs purportedly taken by a famous photographer. Once there, she becomes embroiled in a Scandinavian death metal cult and sacrificial murder, ending up fighting for her life in economically destroyed Iceland. There are subtle elements of the supernatural threaded throughout this powerful novel.

Your House is on Fire, Your Children All Gone by Stefan Kiesbye (Penguin), is a disturbing novel about the inhabitants of the German village of Hemmersmoor, and is told through the multiple viewpoints of several children from the village, which seems to be entirely populated by psychopaths and sociopaths. For such a short novel, it's surprisingly jam-packed with incest, rape, revenge killings, murderous pranks, infanticide, and deadly accidents. There's nary an innocent or even sympathetic soul to be found. There are hints of the ghostly throughout but the creepiness is entirely due to the monstrousness of villagers.

Creole Belle by James Lee Burke (Simon & Schuster) is dark, with ghostly undertones, as the author continues to expertly weave the histori-cal and contemporary attitudes and circumstances of the rich and poor, multi-racial inhabitants of Louisiana and their crimes and vices into his fiction. One late night as Dave Robicheaux lies half asleep in a drug haze of painkillers recovering from gunshot wounds in a New Orleans hospital, he's visited by a young Creole barroom singer who brings him some of her music. Or does she? It turns out Tee Jolie Melton has been missing for several weeks and no one else can hear the music on Dave's iPod. Upon his recovery Dave's search for Tee Jolie embroils him in ugly, perverse, and violent conflicts. Burke has another winner in this nineteenth entry in the Dave Robicheaux series.

Long Lankin by Lindsey Barraclough (The Bodley Head-UK 2011/ Candlewick) is an excellent first novel marketed as a young adult. Although two of the three points of view are children's, this book should appeal to readers of any age. In the late 1940s, two young sisters from London are sent to stay with their great aunt in a small isolated village in rural England. Their aunt is strange and strict. The house is haunted, as are the grounds around it. The two children narrators overhear adult conversations and because it takes them longer to comprehend what's going on than the reader, we fear for them. There's a curse, a witch, ghosts, and a bog that can swallow a body without a trace. The unease creeps up on the reader slowly yet relentlessly but it's the individual voices of each character that makes this novel of fear and desperation so stand out. The last fifty pages are heart-grabbing.

Immobility by Brian Evenson (Tor) is an engrossing dystopic novel about a man who, upon being unfrozen after an indeterminate length of time, and despite the apparent paralysis of his legs, is instructed by a stranger to go out into the wastes and ruins of Earth to find and bring back a mysterious but important item about which he's told nothing. As Josef Horkai is carried to his destination by human "mules" he probes his circumstances and those of the world he has awakened into.

The Inquisitor by Mark Allen Smith (Henry Holt and Company) is an extraordinarily satisfying dark thriller debut about a mysterious man who makes his living from "information retrieval"—in this case not from computers but from humans. He's a skilled torturer for hire, one of the two best in the business. The book begins as a day in the life and as described for someone being tortured, the anticipation of what is to come is almost as terrifying as the actuality.

Some Kind of Fairy Tale by Graham Joyce (Doubleday) is another brilliant book by a writer who never repeats himself and rarely lets the reader down. Tara Martin appears at the door of an older couple's home one fall day announcing that she is their daughter, who disappeared twenty years earlier, at almost sixteen years of age. The husband gapes. The wife faints. Tara's disappearance broke her parents' and brother's heart and almost destroyed her musician boyfriend, who was accused of her murder and hounded by local police until he ended up in jail on an unrelated charge. Now Tara's back, telling a preposterous tale of where she's been. For anyone steeped in fantasy and the fairy tale tradition there's no doubt as to the truth of her claims, but that hardly matters in this dark, beautiful, satisfying read.

Motherless Child by Glen Hirshberg (Earthling Publications) is as heartbreaking as it is horrific. Natalie and Sophie, two single mothers who are lifelong friends living in a trailer park in North Carolina, are turned into vampires during a rare night out. The two young women are forced to leave behind their infants in order to protect them from the changes occurring. Think *Thelma and Louise* with vampires (the two women reference that movie). As they flee and try to ignore their growing hunger, the mystery man who changed them is on their trail for his own reasons.

Hide Me Among the Graves by Tim Powers (William Morrow) is a darkly engaging novel about Christina Rossetti, who is haunted by the vampiric ghost of her uncle, John Polidori, who she rashly accepted as her muse at the age of fourteen. The repercussions of this threaten her entire family and those they love.

Gone Girl by Gillian Flynn (Crown/Weidenfeld and Nicolson) is ingenious, engrossing, disturbing, and sometimes even very funny. Nick and Amy seem to be the perfect couple until Amy disappears, Nick is accused of her murder, and the walls come tumbling down. There's at least one human monster in this suspenseful, bestselling novel, perhaps two.

The Faceless by Simon Bestwick (Solaris) is a complex supernatural horror novel in which many dreadful things take place—possibly too many for the story to be completely coherent. In the Lancashire town of Kempforth, people disappear and creepy masked figures that the local children call "spindly men" are seen lurking. Outside town is a long abandoned hospital that once housed grievously wounded WWI veterans who were exploited by the greedy, dissolute son of the man who built the hospital. Throughout the story the ghosts of these mutilated men recite their awful and haunting litany of horrifying personal histories, until it becomes a cacophony of misplaced bitterness and hate, and a desire for revenge against the England that used them as cannon fodder. Meanwhile, in Manchester, a professional psychic has visions that draw him and his sister back to that same town where they had a miserable, abusive childhood. An engrossing and quick read, despite its length and many plot strands.

The Ravenglass Eye by Tom Fletcher (Quercus/Jo Fletcher Books) is a good, fast moving novel about Edie, the cook at a pub in the small town of Ravenglass, West Cumbria England. She's had seemingly harmless visions since she was a child but as an adult, those visions, combined with her alienation and discontent, accidentally initiate a series of events that threaten not only her town but all of Great Britain.

The Devil in Silver by Victor LaValle (Spiegel & Grau) is horrific, but the supernatural element takes backseat to the vivid, depressing, terrifying depiction of the United States mental-health system. Pepper is big, rough, and angry, and through a moment of misplaced gallantry, has ended up committed to and trapped in the New Hyde Mental Hospital, a place where the patients claim the Devil is stalking and murdering them.

Monster by Dave Zeltserman (Overlook Press) is an excellent and original reworking of Mary Shelley's *Frankenstein* from the point of view of the learned man whose brain was used to create the "monster."

ALSO NOTED

Zombies: *Horizon* by Sophie Littlefield (Harlequin/Luna) is the third in her Aftertime series. *I Saw Zombies Eating Santa Claus* by S. G. Browne (Gallery) is a sequel to his novel *Breathers*. *Zombies at Tiffany's* by Sam Stone (Telos Publishing) is about a shop girl at the famous jewelry emporium, who is forced to take on zombie hordes in New York. *Day by Day Armageddon: Shattered Hourglass* by J. L. Bourne (Gallery) is the third volume of a series. *A Mammoth Book of Zombie Apocalypse! Fightback* created by Stephen Jones (Running Press) is a "braided novel," with more than twenty writers contributing bits and pieces to create a whole. Included are eyewitness accounts, news reports, diaries, etc., documenting the struggle by the survivors of a world overrun by zombies. *Flesh and Bone* by Jonathan Maberry (Simon & Schuster), the third in his young adult zombie series. *Zombie Bake-Off* by Stephen Graham Jones (Lazy Fascist Press) is a humorous novel about what happens when a batch of donuts are infected during the annual Recipe Days Lubbock, Texas bake-off. *The Awakening* by Brett McBean (Tasmaniac Publications) is about the unlikely friendship that develops between a teenager and a strange man living in a small town in the American Midwest. Apocalyptic and post apocalyptic horror: *Revelations* by C. Dennis Moore (Necro Publications) is about a participant in a cryogenic project who awakens fifty years later into a "Hell on Earth" that might be the result of end times. *Apocalypse: Year Zero* by Sarah Langan, Sarah Pinborough, Rhodi Hawk, and Alexandra Sokoloff (self-published) is a series of novella length pieces by each writer, comprising a novel about four survivors of disasters who eventually come together, powerfully. *The Dog Stars* by Peter Heller (Knopf) is an engaging debut novel about a pilot who survives societal disaster but yearns to find the voice he hears on his radio. Not horror, but really excellent. *Edge* by Koji Suzuki, translated by Camellia Nieh and Jonathan Lloyd-Davies from the Japanese (Vertical), is an sf/horror novel about computer experimentation that somehow changes the value of Pi, and the disappearances this inexplicable change engenders. *The Flame Alphabet* by Ben Marcus (Knopf) is a post-apocalypse novel in which the speech of children mutates into a deadly virus. Vampires: *Me and the Devil* by Nick Tosches (Little, Brown) is about an aging writer who drinks blood to restore his sexual and creative vitality. Werewolves: *The Trouble with Hairy* by Hal Bodner (Phantom Hollow Publishing) is a humorous take on werewolves in West Hollywood. *Tallula Rising* by Glen Duncan (Alfred A. Knopf) is the disappointing sequel to the author's excellent *The Last Werewolf.* Witches and dark magic: *Nerves* by John Palisano (Bad Moon Books) is about two brothers who discover they have the power to kill or resurrect the dead with their magic. Rhodi Hawk's southern Gothic, *The Tangled Bridge* (Tor), is the second in her Twisted Ladder series. The artist Brom's *Krampus the Yule Lord* (HarperCollins) is about the long running feud between Santa Claus and his evil counterpart, Krampus. *A Cold Season* by Alison Littlewood (Quercus) is the first novel by a writer whose fiction I've reprinted in last year's *Best Horror of the Year.* *The Third Gate* by Lincoln Child (Doubleday) is an enjoyable but schematic tale of Egyptology, mummies, tombs, ghosts, and curses. *The Reckoning* (Gallery Books) follows up Alma Katsu's impressive debut novel in what will be the Taker trilogy. *The Chosen Seed* by Sarah Pinborough (Gollancz) is the fast-moving third volume of the Dog Faced Gods crime/horror trilogy about a London police detective who's been on the run after being framed for murder. *Tortured Spirits*, Greg Lamberson's (Medallion) fourth novel in his Jake Helman Files detective series. *The Curse of the Fleers* by Basil Copper (PS Publishing) restores the heavily edited gothic novel originally published in 1976 to its intended form. *A Tree of Bones* by Gemma Files (ChiZine Publications) is the third in her Hexslinger series. *Rasputin's Bastards* by David Nickle (ChiZine Publications) is about cold war shenanigans that threaten the world in the 1990s. *A Face Like Glass* by Frances Hardinge (Macmillan Children's books UK) is about a young girl who wears a mask to hide her terrifying face. *Odd Apocalypse*, the fifth volume of Dean Koontz's Odd Thomas series (HarperCollins). *The Last Final Girl* by Stephen Graham Jones (Lazy Fascist Press) is an absurdist, metafictional homage to slasher movies. Graham's *Growing Up Dead in Texas*, a fictionalized memoir/mystery, was also out in 2012, from M.P. Publishing. *In Delirium's Circle* by Stephen J. Clark (Egaeus Press) is about a man in postwar England who seeks the truth about a group of sinister game-players. Stephen King's *The Dark Tower: The Wind*

Through the Keyhole (Scribner), is the eighth in his Dark Tower series but fits chronologically between volumes four and five. *The Apocalypse Codex* is the fourth volume of Lovecraftian dark fantasy in Charles Stross's Laundry Files series (Ace).

ANTHOLOGIES

Night Terrors II edited by Theresa Dillon and Marc Ciccarone (Blood Bound Books) is a non-genre horror anthology with twenty-eight stories. The strongest are by Angela Bodine, Danny Rhodes, Patricia Russo, Maria Alexander, and John Morgan.

Corrupts Absolutely edited by Lincoln Crisler (Damnation Books) features twenty stories about people with superpowers and the negative effects those powers have. Because the book title states flat out that no one gets out untarnished, the stories begin to have a similar feeling to them as they move toward their inexorable march toward negativity. The most interesting stories are by Weston Ochse, A. D. Spencer, and Jason M. Tucker.

A Season in Carcosa edited by Joseph S. Pulver, Sr. (Miskatonic River Press) has twenty-one new stories written in tribute to Robert W. Chambers's series about a "monstrous and suppressed book, whose perusal brings fright, madness, and spectral tragedy." [H. P. Lovecraft]. The reader doesn't need to be familiar with the original tales in order to appreciate this volume. There are fine stories by Anna Tambour, Cody Goodfellow, Gemma Files, Richard Gavin, Kristin Prevallet, and Laird Barron.

Four for Fear edited by Peter Crowther (PS Publishing) is an excellent mini anthology commissioned for the annual Humber Mouth Literature Festival held in Hull, England. The contributors are Nicholas Royle, Alison Littlewood, Christopher Fowler, and Ramsey Campbell. The Campbell is reprinted herein.

The First Book of Classical Horror Stories edited by D. F. Lewis (Megazanthus Press) is a fascinating anthology of twenty-one darkly weird stories on the theme of classical music. Many of the stories are subtle and dense. There were notable stories by D. P. Watt, Adam S. Cantwell, S. D. Tullis, M. Sullivan, Aliya Whiteley, and Nicole Cushing.

The Ghosts & Scholars Book of Shadows edited by Rosemary Pardoe (Sarob Press) is an attractive little hardcover of prequels and sequels to some of M. R. James's most famous stories. The twelve stories were written in response to Pardoe's contest in tribute to the 150th anniversary of the birth of James. One appeared earlier in 2012 in *The Ghost & Scholars, M.R. James Newsletter* #21. There were notable stories by John Llewellyn Probert and David A. Sutton.

Dark Faith: Invocations edited by Maurice Broaddus and Jerry Gordon (Apex Publications) is a second volume of new horror stories loosely themed around religion and faith. The best are by Laird Barron, Nick Mamatas, Elizabeth Twist, W. Tempest Bradford, Gemma Files, Lucy A. Snyder, and Jeffrey Ford. The Snyder is reprinted herein.

Black Wings II edited by S. T. Joshi (PS Publishing) is the second volume of new stories inspired by H. P. Lovecraft edited by the premier expert on the author. The eighteen stories are an interesting mixed bag. My favorites were by Donald Tyson, Rick Dakan, Tom Fletcher, Richard Gavin, Caitlín R. Kiernan, John Langan, and Melanie Tem.

Worlds of Cthulhu edited by Robert M. Price (Fedogan & Bremer) is another Lovecraftian anthology of mostly original material but this one is aimed at fans of Lovecraftian pastiche. Other readers will find the slavishness to the originals in style and substance less interesting.

The Book of Cthulhu II edited by Ross Lockhart (Night Shade Books) is a nicely varied, mostly reprint anthology of twenty-four stories, four of them new. The best of the new ones is the Laird Barron novella.

Torn Realities edited by Paul Anderson (Post Mortem Press) seems to be an attempt to jump on the Lovecraftian bandwagon, but I discerned minimal influence on the stories either thematically or stylistically. All but one story appear for the first time.

Urban Cthulhu: Nightmare Cities edited by Henrik Sandbeck Harksen (H. Harksen Productions) features ten new stories of urban estrangement as filtered through a Lovecraftian lens. Thankfully, none of the stories are pastiches, and while not all are successful, the anthology is an interesting one. My favorites are by Joseph S. Pulver, Sr. and Jayaprakash Satyamurthy.

Night Shadows: Queer Horror edited by Greg Herren and J. M. Redman (Bold Strokes Books) is an anthology of one reprint, twelve original stories, and one brilliant, sucker punch of a novella. In addition to the novella, by Victoria A. Brownworth, there are notable stories by Lee Thomas and Steve Berman.

The Thirteen Ghosts of Christmas edited by Simon Marshall-Jones (Spectral Press) is an entertaining revival of the British tradition of telling ghost stories around Christmas time. All but one of the thirteen stories is new and some of the more notable ones are by Adrian Tchaikovsky, John Forth, Richard Farren Barber, and William Meikle.

Danse Macabre edited by Nancy Kilpatrick (Edge) has twenty-six new stories about death, and humanity's interaction with the great leveler. There are strong stories by Tanith Lee, Edward M. Erdelac, Suzanne Church, Lisa Morton, and Brian Hodge.

The Ninth Black Book of Horror edited by Charles Black (Mortbury Press) is a British, un-themed horror anthology with sixteen new stories, and although there were a few with not enough plot and few surprises, some of the more notable stories were by John Llewellyn Probert, John Forth, Paul Finch, Thana Niveau, and Simon Bestwick.

The Screaming Book of Horror edited by Johnny Mains (Screaming Dreams) is another un-themed horror anthology out of England, this one featuring twenty-one new stories, including never previously published work by the late John Brunner and the late John Burke, plus notable stories by Charles Higson, Alison Moore, Janine Langley-Wood, Paul Finch, Craig Herbertson, Rhys Hughes, Alison Littlewood, David Riley, Bernard Taylor, and Steve Rasnic Tem.

The Burning Maiden edited by Greg Kishbaugh (Ex Hubris Imprints) features sixteen stories and poems that purport to combine horror and literature, as if that's something unusual and even daring. Despite the pretentious introduction there are some very good dark stories by Joe R. Lansdale, Louis Bayard, Lyndsay Faye, and Orrin Grey.

Fungi edited by Orrin Grey and Silvia Moreno-Garcia (Innsmouth Free Press) takes an unusual idea and runs with it, with twenty-three new stories, one original poem, and two reprints about fungi, a collection of organisms that includes mushrooms, yeasts, and molds. The stories are weird and/or horrific and grotesque, but not as diverse in style or content as they could be. That said, there are notable stories by Laird Barron, Nick Mamatas, Chadwick Ginther, A. C. Wise, Ian Rogers, Richard Gavin, John Langan, and Paul Tremblay, with a strong poem by Ann K. Schwader. The jacket cover and interior illustrations are divine.

Visions Fading Fast edited by Gary McMahon (Pendragon Press) is a very readable non-themed horror anthology of five stories and novelettes, one a reprint. The originals are by Kaaron Warren, Joel Lane, Paul Meloy, and Nathan Ballingrud. The reprint is by Reggie Oliver. Nathan Ballingrud's story is reprinted herein.

Dark Tales of Lost Civilizations edited by Eric J. Guignard (Dark Moon) features twenty-five new stories updating the pulp tropes of yesteryear with some success. There are notable stories by Joe E. Lansdale, Michael G. Cornelius, and Deskin C. Rink.

Hauntings edited by Ian Whates (NewCon Press) has fifteen original ghost stories. The best of the darkest stories are by Robert Shearman, Adrian Tchaikovsky, Mark West, Amanda Hemingway, Tanith Lee, and Mark Morris.

Zombies vs Robots: Women on War! is a volume of ten stories from this series of themed anthologies, with notable stories by Rachel Swirsky and Amber Benson. Also *Zombies vs Robots: This Means War!* with good stories by Steve Rasnic Tem and Nick Mamatas. Both anthologies are edited by Jeff Connor (IDW).

Psychos: Serial Killers, Depraved Madmen, and the Criminally Insane edited by John Skipp (Black Dog & Leventhal) is a hefty volume of thirty-eight stories, almost half new. Readers will be better off dipping into this one than reading straight through. A majority of the stories are depressing rather than horrifying or chilling. Some of the better originals are by Violet Levoit, Steve Rasnic Tem, Cody Goodfellow, and Leslianne Wilder.

Tales From the Yellow Rose Diner and Fill Station (no editorial credit) (Sideshow Press) is a linked anthology connected by the six responses to one question asked in a roadside diner: What's the worst thing that you've done?

Dangers Untold edited by Jennifer Brozek (Alliteration Ink) is an un-themed horror anthology of seventeen new and reprinted stories.

A Feast of Frights From the Horror Zine edited by Jeani Rector (The Horror Zine) includes fiction, poetry, articles, and interviews originally published on the website. There are three new stories in the book, including one by Graham Masterton.

Terror Tales of the Cotswolds edited by Paul Finch (Gray Friar Press) has fourteen stories, twelve new, plus vignettes about true atrocities/hauntings in the Cotswolds, before each fictional tale. Some of the stories are very strong, particularly those by Simon Clark, Christopher Harmon, Alison Littlewood, Steve Lockley, Gary McMahon, Thana Niveau, Reggie Oliver, and Simon Kurt Unsworth.

Terror Tales of East Anglia edited by Paul Finch (Gray Friar Press) has thirteen stories, all but three new, with the strongest originals by Reggie Oliver, Alison Littlewood, Simon Bestwick, Christopher Harmon, and Paul Finch. As usual in the series, the stories are each broken up by a "true" vignette about the region.

The Devil's Coattails: More Dispatches from the Dark Frontier edited by Jason V. Brock and William F. Nolan (Cicatrix Press) is a non-themed, all-original anthology. Oddly, although Brock proudly asserts that: "We are excited by the large number of offerings by female writers, a group we feel are often under-represented," I'm guessing he means submissions because there are only four and a half out of twenty-one stories by women in the actual volume. There are notable stories by Paul Bens, Jr. and Ramsey Campbell.

21ˢᵗ Century Dead edited by Christopher Golden (St. Martin's Press) is an anthology of nineteen new zombie stories. The strongest and most original are by Dan Chaon, Jonathan Maberry, Mark Morris, Stephen Susco, Daniel H. Wilson, and a collaboration by Stephanie Crawford and Duane Swierczynski, this last reprinted herein.

Exotic Gothic 4 edited by Danel Olson (PS Publishing) is an impressive and varied volume of twenty-four new gothic stories taking place outside the traditional gothic traditions of the UK, France, and Germany. All the stories are good, but those that really stood out are by Terry Dowling, Adam Nevill, Lucy Taylor, Simon Kurt Unsworth, and Kaaron Warren. The Taylor, Dowling, and Nevill are reprinted herein.

Darker Minds (no editorial credit) (Dark Minds Press) is an anthology of fifteen new stories about the power of the mind. Although there are some excellent writers in the book, few are at the top of their form, or perhaps it's just the sameness of tone throughout that creeps over the reader because so many of the stories internalize the theme. Only Gary McMahon's powerful story breaks away from the pack.

Attic Toys edited by Jeremy C. Shipp (Evil Jester Press) is an all original anthology of eighteen stories about toys found in attics. The best are by Gary McMahon and Mae Empson.

Slices of Flesh edited by Stan Swanson (Dark Moon Books) is a flash fiction anthology created to fund several charities from the net proceeds. Of the approximately ninety stories, all but eleven are originals. The best of the originals are by Jacob Ruby, Tim Lebbon, Matthew Warner, Erin Eveland, Susan Palwick, and Sandy DeLuca.

Horror for Good edited by Mark C. Scioneaux, R. J. Cavender, and Robert S. Wilson (Cutting Block Press) is a charity anthology of reprints and original stories, with proceeds going to amfAR, the Foundation for Aids Research. There are notable new stories by Stephen Bacon, Ian Harding, and Lisa Morton,

Postscripts to Darkness 2 edited by Sean Moreland and Aalya Ahmad (Ex Hubris imprint) is a Canadian volume of sixteen supernatural, very brief stories—usually too brief. Daniel Lalonde has a good story in it.

Siblings edited by Stuart Hughes (Hersham Horror Books) features five new stories about siblings with a dark secret. The best of the batch is by Richard Farren Barber.

Fogbound From 5 edited by Peter Mark May (Hersham Horror) is a mini anthology of five original stories taking place in fog. The best are by Neil Williams and Adrian Chamberlain.

Fading Light: An Anthology of the Monstrous edited by Tim Marquitz (Angelic Knight Press) presents thirty stories on the theme of monsters, with a preponderance of those monsters bringing about the end of the world. In any case, there are notable stories by Stephen McQuiggan and D. L. Seymour.

Hell Comes to Hollywood edited by Eric Miller (Big Time Books) has twenty original stories set in the film and television capitol. There are good stories in it by Andrew Helm, Joseph Dougherty, and John Schouweiler.

The Big Book of Ghost Stories edited by Otto Penzler (Black Lizard) is a massive volume of seventy-nine reprints by writers ranging from August Derleth, Conrad Aiken, and H. P. Lovecraft to M. Rickert, Albert E. Cowdrey, and Chet Williamson.

Blood Stones edited by Amanda Pillar (Ticonderoga Press) has seventeen original dark stories themed around myths and legends. The most interesting are by Dirk Flinthart, Joanne Anderton, Thoraiya Dyer, Kat Otis, and Dan Rabarts.

Terror Scribes edited by Adam Lowe and Chris Kelso (Dog Horn Publishing) brings together twenty-four stories (most new) by a loose group of writers from the United States and the United Kingdom. There's a notable story by Rachel Kendall.

Zombies for a Cure edited by Angela Charmaine Craig (Elektrik Mil Bath Press) is a charity anthology with forty three stories and poems, most published for the first time. Jay Wilburn's story is reprinted herein.

Prime Books brought out a number of big reprint anthologies in 2012, all edited by Paula Guran, including *Extreme Zombies*, which reprints twenty-five graphic violent zombie stories by well-known and newer writers. *Ghosts: Recent Hauntings* with thirty stories by writers such as Neil Gaiman, Elizabeth Hand, Glen Hirshberg, Richard Bowes, Margo Lanagan, Peter Straub, and Barbara Roden (with one original by Stephen Graham Jones). *Obsession: Tales of Irresistible Desire* has nineteen reprints ranging from classic stories by Edgar Allan Poe and Fritz Leiber to work by contemporary masters such as Elizabeth Hand, Tanith Lee, Lawrence Block, and others.

Kaiki: Uncanny Tales From Japan volume 3: Tales of the Metropolis selected and introduced by Higashi Masao (Kurodahan Press) with a foreword by Robert Weinberg is a worthy successor to the earlier volumes of this series. It presents eleven stories and one manga, all originally published in Japan between 1921 and 1981, most never previously appearing in English. The strongest were by Murayama Kaita and Akutagawa Ryūnosuke.

The Mammoth Book of Body Horror edited by Paul Kane and Marie O'Regan (Robinson, UK) has twenty-five stories, seven original (not seen) ranging from Mary Shelley to Conrad Williams.

Surviving the End edited by Craig Bezant (Dark Prints Press) is a very good anthology of post-disaster stories with interludes by the "storyteller" who has recorded them from survivors. All of the eight stories are impressive and all are quite dark.

The Spirit of Poe edited by W. J. Rosser and Karen Rigley (Literary Landmark Publishing and Angelic Knight Press) is a charity anthology of reprint and original stories and poetry with profits from its sale donated to the Poe House in Baltimore, Maryland. Notable stories and poetry by M. Bennardo and Melissa Dollahon Eyler.

Chiral Mad: An Anthology of Psychological Horror edited by Michael Bailey (Written Backwards) has twenty-eight stories, all but five published.

for the first time. The proceeds go to Down Syndrome charities. The best originals are by Monica J. O'Rourke and Gary McMahon. The McMahon is reprinted herein.

Dark Light edited by Carl Hose (MARLvision Publishing) is a non-themed horror anthology created to benefit the Ronald McDonald House Charities. More than half the forty-two stories are reprints (all those by the better-known writers).

The Horror Hall of Fame: The Stoker Winners edited by Joe R. Lansdale (Cemetery Dance) was knocking around for fifteen years before finally seeing the light of day. During that time, HWA went from being named the Horror Writers of America to the Horror Writers Association, and since the original publication of the most recent winning story in the book (1996) there have been double the number of winners. Nonetheless, there are thirteen wonderful stories and novellas presented here.

The Century's Best Horror Fiction Volumes One and Two edited by John Pelan (Cemetery Dance) is another long delayed reprint volume. In this one, the editor chose one story per year from 1900–2000, with no author represented more than once, which actually precludes the word "best," as the editor might very well be constrained from choosing a better story by a specific author. Surprisingly, there's no Harlan Ellison nor Clive Barker, both of whom have produced powerful horror stories. With those caveats, it's still an impressive achievement, with one hundred stories from one hundred writers, and over 700,000 words.

The Mammoth Book of Best New Horror Volume 23 edited by Stephen Jones (Robinson/ Running Press) reprints twenty-six stories, a summary of the year, and a necrology. There are no story overlaps with *The Best Horror of the Year Volume Four*. (Datlow).

MIXED-GENRE ANTHOLOGIES

The Weird: A Compendium of Strange and Dark Stories edited by Ann and Jeff VanderMeer (Corvus-UK 2011, Tor 2012) deservedly won the World Fantasy Award last year. It represents an enormous undertaking, with the VanderMeers casting a wide net, reprinting 110 stories from around the world, some published in English for the first time. This is a feast for readers. *Wilde Stories: The Year's Best Gay Speculative Fiction* edited by Steve Berman (Lethe Press) presents fifteen reprints of stories from 2011. Its companion volume, *Heiresses of Russ 2012: The Year's Best Lesbian Speculative Fiction* edited by Connie Wilkins and Steve Berman (Lethe Press), has fourteen reprints of stories originally published in 2011. *Dark Currents* edited by Ian Whates (Newcon Press) is a loosely themed all original anthology of science fiction and horror, with fifteen stories and one poem, the strongest are by Emma Coleman, Sophia McDougall, and Adam Nevill. *The Monster Book for Girls* edited by Terry Grimwood (theEXAGGERATEDpress) is an intriguing mix of thirty-two stories and poems in different genres (all but three original). The strongest darker stories and poems are by David Rix, Tony Lovell, Jessica Lawrence, Gary McMahon, Shay Darrach, and Gary Fry. Akashic continued its Noir series: *Kansas City Noir* edited by Steve Paul was relatively weak but had some strong work by J. Malcolm Garcia, Kevin Prufer, Daniel Woodrell, and Nancy Pickard. *Mumbai Noir* edited by Altaf Tyrewala. *Staten Island Noir* edited by Patricia Smith. *Long Island Noir* edited by Kaylie Jones with an excellent story by Nick Mamatas that's been picked up for *The Best American Mystery Stories*. *Venice Noir* edited by Maxim Jakubowski. *Kingston Noir* edited by Colin Channer. *St. Petersburg Noir* edited by Julia Goumen and Natalia Smirnova. *Shadow Show: All-New Stories in Celebration of Ray Bradbury* edited by Sam Weller and Mort Castle (William Morrow) features a very mixed bag of twenty-six stories inspired by the master. The best of the darker stories are by Dan Chaon, Kelly Link, Jay Bonansinga, John McNally, and Alice Hoffman. Chaon's is reprinted herein. *An Anthology of the Esoteric and Arcane Magic* edited by Jonathan Oliver (Solaris Books) features sixteen new stories of mostly dark fantasy, with some horror. The best stories are by Alison Littlewood, Gemma Files, Will Hill, Thana Niveau, and Robert Shearman. The Files is reprinted herein. Jurassic London, a new press run by Anne C. Perry and Jared Shurin, plans to publish limited edition print anthologies and chapbooks plus e-book versions of the same books. Each anthology will be produced with a cultural partner, and a portion of the proceeds goes to a charity of their choice. The first publication was *Pandemonium: Lost Souls*, a book of all reprints with one original, mostly classics. *Pandemonium: Stories of the*

Smoke was the second publication—all original sf/f/h stories inspired by Charles Dickens' London. The best dark stories are by Kaaron Warren, Sarah Anne Langton, and David Thomas Moore. And there's a charming non-horror story by Lavie Tidhar. *Unfit for Eden* edited by Peter Crowther and Nick Gevers (PS Publishing) is Postscripts 26/27 and has twenty-seven new sf/f/h stories. The strongest horror stories were by George Hulseman and Simon Unsworth. *The Mammoth Book of Ghost Stories by Women* edited by Marie O'Regan (Running Press) is a hefty volume of twenty-five stories ranging from classics by Mary E. Wilkins-Freeman and Edith Wharton to notable new darker stories by Muriel Gray, Kim Lakin-Smith, Sarah Langan, Elizabeth Massie, and others. Many of the stories however, are not dark. *Carnage: After the End volumes 1 and 2* edited by Gloria Bobrowicz (Sirens Call publications) is an interesting pair of dark post-apocalypse anthologies that show no hope whatsoever for the human race, There are monsters, but the real monsters are the survivors in this hell on earth. *Lauriat: A Filipino-Chinese Speculative Fiction Anthology* edited by Charles A. Tan (Lethe Press) is a refreshing, varied anthology of fourteen original stories, most of them dark fantasy, with a few stories verging on horror. The best of the dark ones are by Gabriela Lee, Kristine Ong Muslim, Margaret Kawsek, Yvette Tan, Ysabel Yap, and Christine V. Lao. *Damnation and Dames* edited by Liz Grzyb and Amanda Pillar (Ticonderoga Publications) presents sixteen, mostly lightweight paranormal detective stories that are all too similar in feel. Despite describing itself as "noir" there's nothing noirish about the tone, attitude, or detectives, who are more often schlubs—not cynical, corrupt, or even seducible. Despite this, there are some good, darkish stories by Dirk Flinthart, Joseph L. Kellogg, Karen Dent, Pete Kempshall, and a collaboration by Alan Baxter and Felicity Dowker. *Four in the Morning* by Malon Edwards, Edward M. Erdelac, Lincoln Crisler and Tim Marquitz (self-published) contains a novella each of mixed genre fiction. *Ocean Stories* edited by Angela Charmaine Craig (Elektrik Milkbath Press) has twenty-five new, mixed genre stories about the sea. As silly as the theme is, *Walrus Tales* edited by Kevin L. Donihe (Eraserhead press) actually has a pretty interesting line-up of twenty-two original tales, including notable ones by Bentley Little, Ekaterina Sedia, and Nick Mamatas. *Where Are We Going?* edited by Allen Ashley (Eibonvale) is a fascinating anthology of all new stories about journeys: internal and external, mysterious, odd, and sometimes dangerous. Notable darker stories are by Joel Lane, Ian Shoebridge, Ralph Robert Moore, and Alison J. Littlewood. *Fear the Abyss* edited by Eric Beebe (Post Mortem Press) has twenty-two science fiction and horror stories (two reprints) about fear of the unknown with strong dark stories by S. C. Hayden, Gary A. Braunbeck, and Jeyn Roberts. *Don't Read This Book: 13 Tales From the Mad City* edited by Chuck Wendig (Evil Hat Productions) is an intriguing original anthology about the insomniacs of a nightmare city. The best of the darkest tales are by Stephen Blackmore, Mur Lafferty, Harry Connolly, and Richard Dansky.

A couple Best of the Year anthologies include horror with science fiction or fantasy. *The Year's Best Dark Fantasy & Horror 2012* edited by Paula Guran (Prime) has thirty stories, with no story overlap with my own *The Best Horror of the Year Volume Four*. *The Year's Best Australian Fantasy and Horror 2011* edited by Liz Grzyb and Talie Helene (Ticonderoga Publications) contains thirty-two stories and poems plus a genre overview and a list of honorable mentions. Margo Lanagan's "Mulberry Boys" is reprinted both in their volume and in my own.

SINGLE-AUTHOR COLLECTIONS

Remember Why You Fear Me is Robert Shearman's (Chizine Publications) fourth collection of stories and the only one he categorizes as "horror" (although many of his earlier tales are dark). This volume includes twenty-one stories, ten of them new. Enjoy the feast—Shearman's one of the best of the newer prose writers in the field (his World Fantasy Award winning first collection *Tiny Deaths* was published in 2008). Before that he was best-known as the *Doctor Who* writer who reintroduced the Daleks into the series. In addition to this collection, Shearman has been posting stories on his blog since 2011—some reprints, most for the first time (but some have since been published). The idea was, in his own words: "I wrote a book of short stories, called *Everyone's Just So So Special*. And to celebrate its release, I proposed that everyone who bought the one hundred special leatherbound editions would receive an entirely unique story of their own, featuring their name, of at least 500 words in length. And to prove that the stories really *were* unique, I'd post them all online, for all the world to see. The problem is, they're not 500 words. They're a bit longer than that. But, hey, I like a challenge." As of February 2013 Shearman had forty more to go. Enjoy what comes out of this guy's brain at: http://justsosospecial.com

Through Splintered Walls by Kaaron Warren (Twelve Planets) features three fierce stories and one novella inspired by different aspects of the Australian landscape.

At Fear's Altar by Richard Gavin (Hippocampus Press) is an all-around excellent gothic and weird collection, the fourth by this Canadian. About half of the thirteen stories are new and one, "The Word-Made Flesh" is reprinted herein.

Where Furnaces Burn by Joel Lane (PS Publishing) is another consistently terrific collection by a writer often named in the same breath as Conrad Williams, whose new collection I mention below. The twenty-three reprints and three original stories in the Lane volume are never less than very good, and always readable.

Born with Teeth by Conrad Williams (PS Publishing) is another excellent volume of short fiction by this author. It has seventeen diverse horror stories originally published between 1997 and 2012 in various magazines and anthologies, including one excellent new story, "The Pike," which is reprinted herein.

The Signal Block and Other Tales by Frank Duffy (Gallows Press) is the author's impressive debut collection, featuring thirteen stories, nine published for the first time. Duffy's language is expressive, and although the occasional slip in coherence indicates that he's not always in total control of his craft, his work is well worth seeking out.

Confessions of a Five Chambered Heart: 25 Tales of Weird Romance by Caitlín R. Kiernan (Subterranean Press) follows Kiernan's acclaimed *The Ammonite Violin & Others* and showcases twenty-five of Kiernan's erotic horror stories, all previously published, with most originally appearing in her subscription based *Sirenia Digest*.

W. H. Pugmire had two fine collections published in 2012: *Uncommon Places* (Hippocampus Press) has twenty-two stories and prose poems, a number of them published for the first time. Many are written in the decadent style, most are tinged with darkness, and all are weird. *The Strange Dark One: Tales of Nyarlathotep* (Miskatonic Press) is a collection of what Pugmire considers his best fiction about Lovecraft's creation, *Nyarlathotep*. The title story is new.

Never Bet the Devil and Other Warnings by Orrin Grey (Evileye) is one of the first two publications brought out by a new horror press (along with the anthology *The Burning Maiden*). This is Grey's debut collection and showcases ten very good and varied supernatural stories, two published for the first time.

Nothing As It Seems by Tim Lebbon (PS Publishing) features fifteen stories and novellas, three appearing for the first time. Lebbon's a master of voice, whether he's telling a story from a child's point of view or a dying enforcer, and his stories are engrossing. With an introduction by F. Paul Wilson.

Ian Rogers had two collections out in 2012: *Every House Is Haunted* (ChiZine Publications) was his debut collection, with twenty-two stories, seven published for the first time. His best stories are suffused with the perfect creepiness so many horror aficionados crave. One is reprinted herein. *SuperNOIRtural Tales* (Burning Effigy Press) collects four reprints and an original novella about Felix Renn, a paranormal investigator. Mike Carey provides a brief introduction and Rogers gives a history of his creation, the Black Lands, a parallel dimension to ours, darker and inhabited by all sorts of supernatural creatures.

Busy Blood: Combo Stories by Stuart Hughes and D. F Lewis (theEXAG-GERATEDpress) contains eleven reprinted weird and dark stories by these two British writers.

Shadow Plays by Reggie Oliver (Egaeus Press) contains ten stories previously published in two of the author's earlier collections. Included is a new preface and new, individual introductions for each story by the author, plus a previously unpublished two-act play. This new small press out of the UK has created a lovely object, in addition to the volume's admirable content.

Selected Stories by Mark Valentine (The Swan River Press) brings together eleven stories originally published in several, hard to find limited editions by Ex Occidente Press. More strange than horrific, these tales represent a good selection of Valentine's work.

Still Life: Nine Stories by Nicholas Kaufmann (Necon E-Books) is a digital collection with eight varied horror stories written over eleven years. Two are new.

The Secret Life by James Ulmer (Nortex Press) is a fine volume of ghost stories by a writer-poet previously unknown to me. All but four of the ten stories are new, and those four were previously published in literary journals. The best is also the longest, a novella about a man who renovates an abandoned house that survived the murderous Galveston flood of 1900.

Indignities of the Flesh by Bentley Little (Subterranean Press) collect ten stories from throughout the author's career, each with a snippet on the genesis of the story.

Where the Summer Ends: The Best Horror Stories of Karl Edward Wagner volume 1 and *Walk on the Wild Side: The Best Horror Stories of Karl Edward Wagner volume 2* (Centipede Press) is a comprehensive retrospective of Wagner's short fiction. The books contain the entire contents of *In a Lonely Place* and *Why Not You and I?* plus most of the contents of *Exorcisms and Ecstasies*, a compilation of Wagner's previously uncollected short fiction that editor Stephen Jones assembled in 1995.

Festival of Fear by Graham Masterton (Severn House) is entertaining, as is all of the author's short work. This new collection has twelve stories, one published for the first time in 2012.

Baubo's Kiss: The Best of Lucy Taylor (Constable & Robinson) presents five horror stories by a writer who made a reputation for herself in the 1990's, for her hard-hitting depictions of erotic horror.

Creeping Stones by Cullen Bunn (Evileye Books) is a debut collection with fourteen impressive horror stories published between 1999 and 2012, one new.

Ghostwriting by Eric Brown (Infinity Plus Books) is an anomaly for the author, who, during his twenty-five year career, has only written a handful of horror and ghost stories—all eight of them in this collection. Judging from these reprints, published in venues including *Cemetery Dance*, *The Third Alternative*, and several anthologies, he should be writing more of them.

The Red Empire and Other Stories by Joe McKinney (Redrum Horror) features seven crime and horror stories and a horror novella. Three of the stories appear for the first time.

Party Pieces: The Horror fiction of Mary Danby edited by Johnny Mains (Noose & Gibbet/ Airgedlámh Publications) has over thirty stories (one written specifically for the volume) by this once prolific contributor to several long-running horror series published in the UK during the 1970s to mid-80s.

Portraits of Ruin by Joseph S. Pulver, Sr. (Hippocampus Press) won't be for everyone. As in his first two collections, the prose in these thirty-nine stories, vignettes, and poems is always evocative, but the thread of his fictions are occasionally difficult to follow. What most impresses is the cumulative effect on the reader.

The Female of the Species by Richard Davis (Shadow Publishing) is the first collection of all eleven of the late author's stories in one volume. Most of the stories, published between 1963 and 1978, still pack a punch. In addition, two rare essays and a 1969 interview provide an excellent introduction to the writer/anthologist who in 1971 started *The Year's Best Horrors Stories* series for Sphere in the UK and DAW in the US.

Living with the Dead by Martin Livings (Dark Prints Press) features twenty-three stories by this Australian horror writer, all but three reprints originally published since 1992.

A surprising number of British writers had more than one collection of their fiction published in 2012: Peter Bell's *Strange Epiphanies* (The Swan River Press) features seven gothic stories, two published for the first time, including a lengthy, beautifully realized vampire story. The hardcover book is beautifully produced with a striking dust jacket designed by Meggan Kehrli from art by R. B. Russell. *A Certain Slant of Light* (Sarob Press) is comprised of eight ghost stories and three new ones influenced by M. R. James. I found the stories in this collection a bit less satisfying than those in *Strange Epiphanies* although the production, as with all Sarob Press books, is topnotch.

R. B. Russell had *Ghosts* (The Swan River Press), a collection comprised of a collection and short novel previously published by Ex Occident Press. It includes six stories, one the World Fantasy Award nominated "In Hiding." The good-looking new package comes with Russell's debut album of the same title as a bonus, presenting a selection of tracks composed and arranged by the author. *Leave Your Sleep* (PS Publishing) is another good-looking volume, this one with twelve stories, five appearing for the first time. There is no overlap in the two books' table of contents.

The longtime writing partners L.H. Maynard and M.P.N Sims published *Flame and Other Enigmatic Tales* (Sarob Press), containing six original stories and novellas. Also, *A Haunting of Ghosts*, a self-published book under their Enigmatic Press imprint, featuring six traditional English ghost stories.

Gary McMahon had an extraordinarily productive 2012, with two single author collections out and another half dozen topnotch stories in various anthologies and magazines. *Tales of the Weak & the Wounded* (Dark Regions Press) is a very impressive collection of seventeen stories, seven new. The book uses the framing device of a skeptical television ghost hunter scoping out a deserted insane asylum for his show who finds files of old case studies. These are the stories. *To Usher, the Dead* (Pendragon Press) features Thomas Usher, McMahon's protagonist from two of his novels, a man who can "see" the recently dead and is often called upon to use his skill in murder detection. The psychic detective is a traditional trope in supernatural fiction and it takes talent and care to render it fresh, which McMahon does. Seven of the fourteen stories are new, and each is very well told.

Curious Warnings: The Great Ghost Stories of M. R. James: 150th Anniversary Edition (Quercus/Jo Fletcher) edited by Stephen Jones is an omnibus of *Collected Ghost Stories*, James's children's novel *The Five Jars*, in addition to essays and uncompleted work. Also, with an historical Afterword by Jones.

Bread and Circuses by Felicity Dowker (Ticonderoga Publications) presents fifteen horror and dark fantasy stories from this Australian writer. Two appear for the first time.

Vampires and Gentlemen: Tales of Erotic Horror by A. R. Morlan (Borgo Press) features twelve stories (one new) by this vastly underrated writer of horror fiction.

Windeye by Brian Evenson (Coffee House Press) presents twenty-five dark and sometimes weird stories by a writer who has been consistently praised by the mainstream despite the fact that he mostly writes horror fiction. He's one of the few writers in the field today whose work, even in a very few pages, can pack a punch and not seem gimmicky doing so.

From Hell to Eternity by Thana Niveau (Gray Friar Press) presents sixteen stories, half new half reprints published since 2009. Two of the stories were reprinted in Stephen Jones' series, *The Mammoth Book of New Horror*.

Peel Back the Sky by Stephen Bacon (Gray Friar Press) is this promising newcomer's first collection and features fifteen stories reprinted from mostly small press magazines and websites and six originals. He's a writer to keep an eye on.

The Function Room: the Kollection by Matt Leyshon (no publisher) is a series of sixteen interconnected vignettes taking place in the imaginary Welsh town of Leddenton. The pieces are as strange as they are horrific.

Urn & Willow by Jeffrey Thomas (Ghost House) contains twenty all new ghost tales and vignettes wonderfully illustrated in black and white by Erin Wells.

Hell & Damnation II by Connie Corcoran Wilson (The Merry Blacksmith Press) features eleven new stories inspired by the nine circles of Hell in Dante's *Inferno*.

Wailing and Gnashing of Teeth by Ray Garton (Cemetery Dance) is a very limited edition not offered for sale but for members of the publisher's "Collectors Club." It featured six of the author's most controversial religious horror short stories.

More Than Midnight by Brian James Freeman (Cemetery Dance) reprints five stories, all originally published between 2001 and 2011.

Ad Nauseum by C. W. LaSart (Dark Moon) features thirteen new stories of gruesome horror.

Little Deaths by John F. D. Taff (Books of the Dead Press) has nineteen stories, about half new.

No Sharks in the Med and Other stories: The Best Macabre Stories of Brian Lumley (Subterranean Press) features twelve of Lumley's creepiest non-Lovecraftian stories.

Enemies at the Door by Paul Finch (Gray Friar Press) is the author's fourth collection. The twelve stories, three published for the first time, are all vivid and disturbing in their depiction of ugly sexual politics and exceedingly dark criminal acts.

Dark Melodies by William Meikle (Dark Regions Press) has eight horror stories related to music, some Lovecraftian. Six of the stories are published for the first time.

Vampyric Variations by Nancy Kilpatrick (Edge) has ten stories and novellas about vampires, one new. With an introduction by Tanith Lee.

MIXED-GENRE COLLECTIONS

Jagannath: Stories by Karin Tidbeck (Cheeky Frawg Press) presents thirteen quirky stories by a rising star in Swedish literature. Most of the stories are being published in English for the first time. Only a few are dark enough to be considered horror but the collection is definitely worth a look. *The Edge of Waking* by Holly Phillips (Prime) is the author's second collection of stories. Ten of the eleven stories are reprints, most are dark fantasy with a few edging over into horror. Peter Beagle introduces the book and Phillips provides story notes. *The Woman Who Married a Cloud: The Collected Short Stories* by Jonathan Carroll (Subterranean Press) is only the second collection by the multi-award winning American expatriate over a thirty year career, and it contains thirty-eight stories and novellas that beautifully showcase Carroll's unique, rich, dark imagination. He's better known for his fifteen novels such as *Land of Laughs*, *A Child Across the Sky*, *Outside the Dog Museum*, *The Wooden Sea*, and most recently *The Ghost in Love*, all exemplars of a quirky magic realism, possibly influenced by residing for decades in Vienna. Many of Carroll's stories and novels begin with lighthearted plots and situations but veer into dark territories, bridging into horror. Although his work is sexy and romantic, he doesn't allow those elements to keep him from putting his characters (and the reader) through the wringer. *Beautiful Sorrows* by Mercedes M. Yardley (Shock Totem Publications) is a quirky collection of mostly very brief stories and vignettes. Some of the stories appear for the first time and a few are pretty dark. *All-Monster Action*! by Cody Goodfellow (Swallowdown Press) is slaphappy and fun, with its six stories and one novella (this last new) but nothing in the volume creeps up on the reader to provide the frisson of horror. *Crackpot Palace* by Jeffrey Ford (William Morrow) is this talented and eclectic writer's fourth collection of short fiction. These twenty stories, five of which I originally published, range from quirky and strange to dark and utterly creepy. The one original is a winner. *Stay Awake* by Dan Chaon (Ballantine Books) is a very good, mostly non-genre collection of twelve stories by a writer primarily known outside our field, but who has written some excellent horror stories for genre anthologies. One story was in the horror half of the *Year's Best Fantasy and Horror* series. *Cracklescape* by Margo Lanagan (Twelfth Planet Press) is a powerful mini-collection of four stories by a four-time winner of the World Fantasy Award. The excellent, all new stories are fantasy, dark fantasy, and horror. One, "Bajazzle," is reprinted herein. *Midnight and Moonshine* by Lisa L. Hannett and Angela Slatter (Ticonderoga) is a series of thirteen dark fantasy stories, all but one new, featuring the Norse gods in their different forms, playing havoc with humanity. *Attic Clowns* by Jeremy C. Shipp (Redrum Horror) contains thirteen mostly new stories. They're original and weird and occasionally dark, but rarely provide the frisson of horror. *A Pretty Mouth* by Molly Tanzer (Lazy Fascist Press) is all over the place with four stories and a short novel that show the influence of writers from P. G. Wodehouse to H. P. Lovecraft. *Monsoon and Other Stories* by Arinn Dembo (Kthonia Press) collects eighteen short stories and poems of science fiction, erotica, and horror. Two stories appear for the first time. *Shoggoths in Bloom* by Elizabeth Bear (Prime) is a gorgeous collection of twenty science fiction and fantasy (with a bit of dark fantasy) stories, including a couple of award-winners. One original. *Hair Side, Flesh Side* by Helen Marshall (ChiZine Publications) is a remarkable debut collection featuring fifteen stories of the weird, the dark, and the quirky. *Glory & Splendour: Tales of the Weird* by Alex Miles (Karōshi Books) has eight weird stories by a new writer, all published for the first time, none particularly horrific. *Shoebox Train Wreck* by John Mantooth (Chizine Publications) is an excellent debut collection, with sixteen stories published since 2006 (seven in 2012). Few of the stories are horror, but many of them provide glimpses into the darkness of human soul. *Flying in the Heart of the Lafayette Escadrille* by James Van Pelt (Fairwood Press) is the author's fourth collection of science fiction, fantasy, and horror stories originally published from 1991–2012. *Back Roads & Frontal Lobes* by Brady Allen (Post Mortem Press) is an interesting mixture of twenty-three science fiction, dark fantasy, and horror stories, more than half published for the first time. With some pruning of the weaker tales, this could have been a better collection than it is. *Black Dahlia & White Rose* by Joyce Carol Oates (Ecco) is the prolific author's twenty-fifth collection of short stories. Oates is totally in control of voice, style, structure as she easily shifts gears from story to story, starting with the brilliant tale about two infamous women of 1940s Los Angeles who might have met: Elizabeth Short (Black Dahlia) and Marilyn Monroe (White Rose). *Ugly Behavior* by Steve Rasnic Tem (New Pulp Press) is an excellent collection of nineteen noir stories that often slip over into horror, with one story published for the first time. *Bedtime Stories for Carrion Beetles* by Adrian Ludens (self-published) has nineteen stories of mystery and horror published between 2009 and 2012. *Stabs at Happiness* by Todd Grimson (Schaffner Press) collects thirteen stories over thirty years by a writer better known for his horror novels *Stainless* and *Brand New Cherry Flavor*. The stories (most previously published in literary magazines) are strange and sometimes dark, but too often unsatisfying. *Salsa Nocturna* by Daniel José Older (Crossed Genres Publications) is the debut collection of a very promising writer. Several of the thirteen ghostly stories are written from the point of view of a Cuban guy who died and has been partially resurrected in order to work for the bureaucratic New York Council of the Dead, cleaning up some of the nastiest jobs. Readers of urban fantasy should take a look. *Errantry: Strange Stories* by Elizabeth Hand (Small Beer Press) showcases ten recent pieces of fantasy, dark fantasy, and horror by one of our best stylists, including Hand's brilliant, award-winning novellas "Near Zennor" and "The Maiden Flight of McCauley's Bellerophon" (this latter not horror). Hand writes beautifully and elegiacally about the dark, relentlessly drawing the reader into her worlds. *Black Horse and Other Strange Stories* by Jason A. Wyckhoff (Tartarus Press) is a strong debut collection of sixteen supernatural tales by an accomplished new voice in weird literature. The stories are varied, sometimes but not always dark. *The Back of Beyond: New Stories* by Alan Peter Ryan (Cemetery Dance Publications) is, along with the novella chapbook *Amazonas* (see under chapbooks), likely the last new work we'll be seeing by the late writer. The author of four novels and two collections of short stories and novellas and the editor of five anthologies, Ryan lived in Rio de Janeiro the last several years of his life. He died in 2011. The new collection contains four stories, two of them excellent: one brilliantly melancholic with a fantastical element and a truly frightening and creepy western horror story about demonic possession. *Eater-of-Bone: and Other Novellas* by Robert Reed (PS Publishing) is a collection of three reprints and one original novella. Reed's science fiction often is quite dark (including the eponymous, published for the first time piece). *Lotteria* by Cynthia Pelayo (Burial Day Books) presents fifty-four mostly original short shorts inspired by Mexican and Latin American superstitions and urban myths. *Secret Europe* by John Howard and Mark Valentine (Ex Occidente Press) features twenty-five stories (ten by

Howard, fifteen by Valentine) of weird and decadent fiction. *Requiems & Nightmares: Selected Short Fiction of Guido Gozzano* translated by Brendan and Anna Connell (Hieroglyphic Press) contains twelve weird stories by an Italian writer who was born in 1883 and died of consumption at the age of thirty-five in 1916. He was better known for poetry and nonfiction than his fiction and only a collection of his children's short stories were published during his lifetime. *On the Hill of Roses* by Stefan Grabinski translated by Miroslav Lipinski (Hieroglyphic Press) collects seven stories by this unheralded Polish author of weird tales, now translated into English for the first time. His champion, Miroslav Lipinski, has previously published other collections of Grabinski's work. This volume includes a foreword and an introduction to Grabinski, (1887–1936) and his work. *In Dark Corners* by Gene O'Neill (Genius Publishing) presents twenty-five sf/h and suspense stories published since 1983, with one new. *Moscow But Dreaming* by Ekaterina Sedia (Prime) is a debut collection of twenty-one stories by this talented Russian-born writer, whose (often dark) short fiction is inspired by and about her homeland. Two of the stories were originally published in 2012 anthologies and two are original to the collection. *Trapped in the Saturday Matinee* by Joe R. Lansdale (PS Publishing) brings together some of the author's early favorites plus those he felt missed their audience the first time around. Also included are essays and two previously unpublished stories. *A Bottle of Storm Clouds* by Eliza Victoria (Visprint) is the first collection by this award-winning Filipino writer of fantasy and dark fantasy. *May We Shed These Human Bodies* by Amber Sparks (A Curbside Splendor Book) is a debut collection of strange tales, most very brief, some inhabited by monsters. *The Tainted Earth* by George Berguño (Egaeus Press) is the author's third collection and presents eight stories and one novella of weird and sometimes dark fiction, all published in 2012 (six of them in the collection for the first time). *The Pottawatomie Giant and Other Stories* by Andy Duncan (PS) is the brilliant second collection of twelve science fiction, fantasy, and dark fantasy stories (one new) by this award-winning writer who is a genre unto himself. *Intimations of Unreality: Weird Fiction and Poetry* by Alan Gullette (Hippocampus Press) is an omnibus of all the author's Cthulhu Mythos stories, two new novellas, and fifty-eight of his poems. *At the Mouth of the River of Bees* by Kij Johnson (Small Beer Press) is the first collection of this amazing cross-genre writer. She writes sf/f/dark fantasy, some of which can be very dark indeed. A few of the eighteen stories in the book have won multiple awards.

MAGAZINES, JOURNALS, AND WEBZINES

It's important to recognize the work of the talented artists working in the field of fantastic fiction, both dark and light. The following artists created art that I thought especially noteworthy during 2012: Ellen Jewett, Tessa Chuddy, Dag Jørgensen, Aurélien Police, Jim Burns, Nicolas Delort, Ben Baldwin, Danielle Tunstall, Glenn Chadbourne, Elena Vizerskaya, Eleanor Finch, Vincent Sammy, Steve Upham, Bernie Gonzales, Linda Saboe, Silvia Moreno-Garcia, Sandro Castelli, Erin Wells, David Gentry, Mark Pexton, Svetlana Sukhorukova, Erik Mohr, Danny Evarts, Sara Richard, Eric Lacombe, Paul Lowe, Richard Wagner, Dave Senecal, Kirk Alberts, Matt Mills, David Rix, Sarolta Bán, David Grilla, Tomislav Tikulin, Steven Archer, Mariusz Siergiejew, Mark Crittenden, David Whitlam, Oliver Wetter, Antonello Silverini, Victor Bravo, Stephen James Price, Bryan Prindiville, Katie Rose Pipkin, Elizabeth Heller, Vincent Chong, and George Cotronis.

Some of the most important magazines/webzines are those specializing in news of the field, market reports, and reviews. *The Gila Queen's Guide to Markets*, edited by Kathryn Ptacek, emailed to subscribers on a regular basis, is an excellent fount of information for markets in and outside the horror field. *Market Maven*, edited by Cynthia Ward is a monthly email newsletter specializing in professional and semi-professional speculative fiction market news. Ralan.com and Duotrope.com are *the* web sites for up-to-date market information. *Locus*, edited by Liza Groen Trombi and *Locus Online*, edited by Mark Kelly specialize in news about the science fiction and fantasy fields, but include horror coverage as well.

The only major venues specializing in reviewing *short* genre fiction are *Tangent Online*, *Locus* Magazine, and *Locus* Online, but none of them specialize in horror.

Ghosts & Scholars M.R. James Newsletter is edited by Rosemary Pardoe and continues to be published periodically. There was one issue out in

2012, and it contained a chilling, contest-winning sequel by Christopher Harman to James's "Oh, Whistle and I'll Come to You, my Lad," in addition to scholarly essays and discussions of Jamesian work.

The Silent Companion edited by António Monteiro is an annual fiction magazine that comes as part of the subscription price to "A Ghostly Company," an informal literary society devoted to the ghost story in all its forms. The group produces a quarterly, non-fiction newsletter containing articles, letters, and book reviews. The fiction magazine featured six stories. http://www.aghostlycompany.org.uk/

Fangoria edited by Chris Alexander and *Rue Morgue* edited by Dave Alexander (no relation as far as I know) are where the horror movie aficionado can find superficial but up-to-date information on most of the horror films being produced. Both magazines include interviews, articles and lots of gory photographs. For in-depth coverage of older movies of all types, *Video Watchdog*, a bi-monthly edited by Tim Lucas, is a gem. It's erudite yet entertaining. In addition to movie reviews, the magazine runs a regular audio column by Douglas E. Winter, a book review column, and a regular column by Ramsey Campbell. *Headpress* 2.6 is a quarterly edited by David Kerekes, published as a hardcover book and webzine. The first half of the issue is about the contemporary Grand Guignol—limited run performances by theater companies in London around Halloween. This section is generously illustrated with blood-soaked photographs and illustrations. Included are interviews with the producers of such events and a bit of history. The second half of the issue features a piece on Philip K. Dick, an interview with one of the co-founders of Re/Search, the publisher that produced books such as *Modern Primitive, We Who are Not as Others*, and *Industrial Culture Handbook*. And an interview with Adam Parfrey, publisher of *Apocalypse Culture*.

Supernatural Tales edited by David Longhorn is an excellent biannual magazine of supernatural fiction. In addition to the generous helping of stories, there are book reviews. The stories that most impressed me were by Adam Golaski, Stephen J. Clark, Derek John, Ian Rogers, S. M. Cashmore, and Steve Rasnic Tem.

Shadows & Tall Trees edited by Michael Kelly published two issues in 2012. This consistently good-looking magazine of low-key but usually potent fiction featured eight stories, the strongest by Stephen Bacon,

Gary McMahon, Kirsty Logan, Laura Mauro, David Surface, V. H. Leslie, Robert Shearman, Ralph Robert Moore, and Nina Allan. In addition, there were book and movie reviews although Kelly has decided to drop both and instead included two pieces of criticism, interviews, or commentary. Stories by Gary McMahon and Stephen Bacon are reprinted herein.

Phantasmagorium, a promising quarterly webzine began with Laird Barron editing the first issue. Joseph S. Pulver, Jr. took over after that, editing the final three issues. During the year it featured notable work by Nadia Bulkin, Stephen Graham Jones, and Mike Allen during its brief existence.

Nightmare Magazine edited by John Joseph Adams, a new monthly sister webzine to *Lightspeed*, launched in October and mixes originals with reprints. The first three issues had notable originals by Sarah Langan, Jonathan Maberry, Daniel H. Wilson, and Laird Barron, the last reprinted herein.

Weird Fiction Review edited by S. T. Joshi had one fat issue in 2012, which a wonderful *Mad Magazine* parody cover featuring icon Alfred E. Neuman as Cthulhu. The journal has over 230 pages of original fiction, poetry, and nonfiction. There was strong dark fiction and poetry by Tom Fletcher, Ann K. Schwader, and a collaboration by Maryanne K. Snyder and W. H. Pugmire.

Lovecraft e-zine edited by Mike Davis is a monthly that's available online and for e-readers and publishes Lovecraftian fiction and poetry. Some very good work was published in 2012, including stories and poems by Tracie McBride, Joseph Pulver, Sr., Simon Kurt Unsworth, and Joshua Reynolds.

Innsmouth Magazine edited by Silvia Moreno-Garcia and Paula R. Stiles, another e-zine specializing in Lovecraftian fiction published three issues in 2012, with notable stories by Fritz Bogott, William Meikle, Colin Leslie, L. Lark, and L. T. Patridge.

Black Static edited by Andy Cox always publishes excellent horror fiction. The stories that impressed me the most in 2012 were by Stephen Bacon, Simon Bestwick, Jon Ingold, Carole Johnstone, David Kotok, Susan Kim, Daniel Mills, Daniel Kaysen, Joel Lane, Jacob Ruby, Priya Sharma, Nina Allan, Tim Lees, and Ray Cluley. The Priya Sharma is reprinted herein.

Cemetery Dance edited by Richard Chizmar published four issues in 2012, trying to catch up after publishing none in 2011—unfortunately some of the reviews published in the first half of 2012 (this includes my own) were dated and some of the fiction bought as "original" were reprints by the time they came out in CD. But by the end of the year, the magazine had caught up. Of the new stories published during 2012 the best were Graham Masterton, Jeremy C. Shipp, Terry Dowling, Bruce McAllister, Sophie Littlefield, Bill Pronzini, Steve Rasnic Tem, and David Bell. The McAllister is reprinted herein.

Morpheus Tales edited by Adam Bradley brought out four issues in 2012. There were notable stories by Harley Campbell, Deborah Walker, and Kyle Hemmings.

Lamplight edited by Jacob Haddon is a promising new horror quarterly available as an inexpensive e-book for various formats. The first two issues, published in 2012, featured several new stories, a classic or two, and essays about anthologies by J. F. Gonzales. I discovered the magazine too late (early 2013) to cover it adequately in this volume.

Polluto 9 ¾ : Witchfinders vs. the Evil Red edited by Victoria Hooper had a generous helping of dark fiction and poetry. The more notable pieces were by Richard Thomas, Nicole Cushing, and Kiik Araki-Kawaguchi.

Albedo One edited by John Kenny, Peter Loftus, Frank Ludlow, David Murphy, and Robert Neilson is the only genre magazine I'm aware of that's published in Ireland. The one issue out in 2012 had some very good dark fiction by Priya Sharma, Craig Saunders, and Lawrence Wilson.

Nameless: A Biannual Journal of the Macabre, Esoteric and Intellectual edited by Jason V. Brock is a new magazine devoted to horror and dark fantasy including fiction, articles, interviews, reviews, comics, and art. The first issue is a good looking, promising start.

Not One of Us edited by John Benson is a reliably interesting long-running magazine of weird fiction and poetry that often has material dark enough to be considered horror. There were two issues published in 2012, with good stories by Erik Amundsen, F. J. Bergmann, and Mark Rigney. Also, Benson's annual one-off was out, and called *Under Review*.

Dark Discoveries edited by James Beach has been bought by Christopher C. Payne, owner of JournalStone Publications. Beach remains editor in chief. The magazine, mixing fiction, articles, reviews, and interviews, had two issues out in 2012. It's now in full color and has expanded its page count. There was good dark fiction by Benjamin Kane Ethridge, Paul Melniczek, Lisa Morton, and Stephen Mark Rainey.

Shock Totem edited by K. Allen Wood brought out one good-looking issue in 2012. In it are reviews, fiction, and an interview with Jack Ketchum. There's notable fiction by Anaea Lay and Darrell Schweitzer.

The Sirenia Digest is a long-running email newsletter by Caitlín R. Kiernan. For ten dollars a month, the reader might read a preview of a new work, a fragment of an old rare one, or a brand new story or poem, usually by Kiernan, occasionally by one of her friends.

MIXED-GENRE MAGAZINES AND WEBZINES

Interzone edited by Andy Cox, is the bi-monthly science fiction sister magazine of *Black Static*, and as such has less horror. But in 2012 there were notable dark stories by Carole Johnstone, Tyler Keevil, Stephen Bacon, Jon Ingold, Priya Sharma, Jacob Ruby, Daniel Kaysen, and Joel Lane. *Asimov's Science Fiction* edited by Sheila Williams, specializes in science fiction but occasionally includes some very dark themed stories. The strongest in 2012 were by Robert Reed, Paul McAuley, Ekaterina Sedia, Alan Smale, and Zachary Jernigan. There was also an excellent poem by Jane Yolen. *The Magazine of Fantasy & Science Fiction* edited by Gordon Van Gelder publishes a variety of science fiction, fantasy, and horror bi-monthly. There was notable dark fiction by Albert E. Cowdrey, Dale Bailey, Jeffrey Ford, Matthew Johnson, and Rachel Pollack. The Jeffrey Ford is reprinted herein. *Shimmer* edited by E. Catherine Tobler is a quarterly, publishing mostly fantasy and dark fantasy, occasionally spilling over into horror. The best horror stories appearing in 2012 were by Dustin Monk and K. M. Ferebee. *On Spec*, a Canadian magazine edited by The Copper Pig Writers' Society, is published quarterly and is a mix of sf/f/h. In 2012 there were notable dark stories by David K. Yeh and Daniel Moal. The British Fantasy Society now combines its journal of fantasy and horror, called BFS Journal, with poetry, prose, and nonfiction into one entity edited by Peter Coleborn, Lou Morgan, and Ian Hunter. The three issues published in 2012 had notable dark stories and poetry by Deborah Walker, James Brogden, Garry Kilworth,

Richard Farren Barber, Fiona Moore, Jonathan Oliver, Marie O'Regan, and Ray Cluley. *Lore* edited by Rod Heather has been revived after more than ten years and its one issue had a good story by Patricia Russo. *Andromeda Spaceways Inflight Magazine* edited by the ASIM Hivemind had strong dark fiction by Debbie Moorhouse, Belinda Crawford, R. P. L. Johnson, Nike Sulway, Dirk Flinthart, B. G. Hilton, Stephen Gallagher, Deborah Kalin, Nicole M. Taylor, David Tallerman, and Tamlyn Dreaver. *Tin House* edited by Rob Spillman has published fiction by a variety of genre names and every once in awhile has some knockout dark fiction, During 2012 the magazine had strong dark stories by Amy Hempel, Karen Russell, Susan Minot, and Bennett Sims. *Rosebud* edited by Roderick Clark is a fifteen year old literary magazine that occasionally publishes dark work. In 2012 there were interesting dark pieces by Sheldon Gleisser, Andrew Bourelle, and Cameron Witbeck. *Sacrum Regnum* is a new magazine edited by Daniel Corrick and Mark Samuels dedicated to publishing and promoting weird literature. The first issue is promising, with four short stories, several essays, and reviews. *Weird Tales* #359 was the last issue edited by Ann VanderMeer, the editor who dragged the venerable magazine into the twenty-first century. In that issue there were notable stories by Stephen Graham Jones, Joel Lane, Tom Underberg, and Tamsyn Muir. The Muir is reprinted herein. New publisher Marvin Kaye brought out one issue, #360 dubbed "The Elder Gods" issue, combined with a special Ray Bradbury tribute section. There was a generous helping of fiction and poetry along with a few book reviews, and an essay about Lovecraft's use of the state of Vermont in his fiction. *Phantom Drift* edited by David Memmott, Leslie What, and Matt Schumacher has some good dark fiction and poetry by Helen Marshall, Elizabeth Schumacher, Robert Guffey, and Jacob Rakovan. The Australian magazine *Aurealis*, edited by Dirk Strasser, is one of the best long-running mixed-genre magazines. In 2012 there were good dark stories by Robert N. Stephenson, Daniel Baker, Jenny Blackford, and Jason Nahrung. *Abyss & Apex Magazine of Speculative Fiction* had notable poetry (edited by Stephen M. Wilson) by Tina Connolly, Sandra Kasturi, Nandini Dhar, and Helen Marshall. *Subterranean*, a website run by publisher William Schafer of Subterranean Press, regularly publishes short stories and novelettes. There were notable dark stories in 2012 by

Maria Davhana Headley, Caitlín R. Kiernan, Hal Duncan, and Terry Dowling. *Conjunctions* edited by Bradford Morrow, is a well-known literary magazine that occasionally publishes fantasy and/or horror. There was notable dark work by Gabriel Blackwell, Bernadette Esposito, and Joyce Carol Oates. *Conjunctions 59: Colloquy* has a section edited by Peter Straub inspired by a panel held at the 2012 International Conference of the Fantastic in the Arts. Essays by China Miéville, Theodora Goss, James Morrow, and Straub himself make up *A Portfolio on the Monstrous*. *Clarkesworld Magazine* edited by Neil Clarke and Sean Wallace regularly publishes science fiction and fantasy fiction with the occasional horror story. In 2012 there were good horror stories by Lisa L. Hannett, Xia Jia, and Kij Johnson. The Johnson is reprinted herein.

POETRY JOURNALS, WEBZINES, AND CHAPBOOKS

Goblin Fruit, the quarterly webzine edited by Amal El-Mohtar, Jessica P. Wick, and Oliver Hunter, is easily the best publisher of dark poetry around, consistently publishing varied quality material. My favorites during 2012 were by Kelly Rose Pflug-Back, Jennifer Crow, Sonya Taaffe, Mike Allen, F. J. Bergmann, Lynn Hardaker, Sandy Leibowitz, Foz Meadows, Amanda Reck, and Dominik Parisien. The Leibowitz is reprinted herein.

Mythic Delirium edited by Mike Allen is a reliable little magazine for good dark poetry. In 2012 there were notable dark poems by Sonya Taaffe and Sandi Leibowitz.

Star*Line edited by F. J. Bergmann is the bi-monthly journal of the Science Fiction Poetry Association and publishes science fiction, fantasy and horror poetry. During 2012 the strongest dark poems were by Marcie Lynch Tentchoff, Ann K. Schwader, Mike Allen, and Kurt Newton.

Dwarf Stars 2012 edited by Geoffrey A. Landis and Joshua Gage (Science Fiction Poetry Association) is a selection of the best speculative poems of ten lines or fewer from the previous year. The SFPA members vote for the Dwarf Stars Award, from the works in this anthology.

The 2012 Rhysling Anthology: The Best Science Fiction, Fantasy, and Horror Poetry of 2011 Selected by the Science Fiction Poetry Association edited by Lyn C. A. Gardner (Science Fiction Poetry Association/ Hadrosaur Productions) is used by members to vote on the best short poem and the best long poem of the year.

Anthropomorphisms by Bruce Boston (Elektrik Milkbath Press) contains twenty-five reprinted poems themed under "people" and describing how crow people, gargoyle people, and many others would behave. Witty, but only one or two pieces of horror.

Come Late to the Love of Birds by Sandra Kasturi (Tightrope Books) has forty-one mostly original poems, some of them dark. *Dark Duet* by Linda D. Addison and Stephen M. Wilson (Necon E-Books) features science fiction, fantasy, and dark fantasy poems written solo and together by Addison and Wilson. *The Monstrance* by Bryan D. Dietrich (Needfire Poetry) takes Dr. Frankenstein's monster on a journey of discovery in this interesting take on James Whale's movie version of Mary Shelley's novel. *Vampires Zombies and Wanton Souls* by Marge Simon & Sandy DeLuca (Elektrik Milkbath Press) has about seventy short, mostly amusing rather than horrific poems, the majority published for the first time. *Notes from the Shadow City* by Gary William Crawford and Bruce Boston (Dark Regions Press) has over forty-five dystopian poems, a number of them published for the first time. *Loves & Killers* by Mary Turzillo (Dark Regions Press) is an excellent mixed-genre collection of over thirty-five poems, new and reprints.

NONFICTION

Real Wolfmen: True Encounters in Modern America (Tarcher/Penguin) is a book of mostly anecdotal evidence about the existence of werewolves and/or dogmen. The author reports on her many first person interviews of witnesses but comes to no conclusions as to the actual existence of such creatures. *Real Ghosts, Restless Spirits, and Haunted Houses* by Brad Steiger (Visible Ink) is an updated edition of the 2003 book. The twenty-nine chapters cover topics ranging from "Spirit Parasites That Possess" to "Animal Ghosts—Domesticated and Wild." *An Epicure in the Terrible: A Centennial Anthology of Essays in Honor of H. P. Lovecraft* edited by David E. Schultz and S. T. Joshi (Hippocampus Press) is an updated and revised edition of an invaluable book of essays about Lovecraft originally published in 1991. *That's Disgusting* by Rachel Herz (W. W. Norton) is a book that explores the nature of disgust—"what it is, how, where, and why it is elicited psychologically and neurologically, what its dark sides are, our perverse attraction to it, and its consequences of us as individuals and for our society." Note such delicacies as Iceland's hákarl (Greenland shark left to decompose then dried) and Sardinian casu marzu (sheep cheese riddled with live maggots) and then fill out the questionnaire showing where you rank on the "disgust scale." *Popular Revenants: The German Gothic and Its International Reception, 1800–2000* edited by Andrew Cusack and Barry Murnane (Camden House) is the first book in English dedicated to the German Gothic in over thirty years. *Raising Hell: Ken Russell and the Unmaking of the Devils* by Richard Crouse (ECW Press) includes interviews with the late Ken Russell, cast, crew, and historians about Russell's controversial 1971 movie about a charismatic (and oversexed) priest blamed for the apparent possession of an order of nuns, led by the sexually repressed Sister Jeanne. Graphically violent, sexually explicit, and for some blasphemous, the movie has been edited, banned, and buried by Warner Brothers. *Gothicka: Vampire Heroes, Human Gods, and the New Supernatural* by Victoria Nelson (Harvard University Press) is a readable but narrow exploration of what the author refers to as "literary shock genre"—"gothicka." She begins with the intriguing premise that authors of possession and exorcism fiction and movies—whether written by believers or not—have created a "faux Catholicism" that gives an enormous power to the rituals and symbols of the Catholic Church, and speculates as to why that may be. From there she analyzes a range of popular titles including the vampire novels of Bram Stoker, Anne Rice, Chelsea Quinn Yarbro, Laurell Hamilton, and Stephenie Myer; the religious conspiracy books of James Redfield, Dan Brown, and Umberto Ecco; Lovecraftian fiction; and international movies including examples of J-Horror and Guillermo del Toro's *Pan's Labyrinth*. This is all quite entertaining, but only after reading most of the book does one realize that her entire point is to speculate on how religion is evolving in the twenty-first century by using all these pop cultural examples, rather than an actual exploration of the horror genre. If the reader is interested in a strictly religious interpretation of the gothick, this is for you, but otherwise the book is terribly limited in illuminating the mystery and wonder of the supernatural movies and literature. *The Forgotten Writings of Bram Stoker* edited by John Edgar Browning (Palgrave Macmillan) is an important resource for those interested in other writings by the author of *Dracula*, even though the material is not dark. Elizabeth Miller provides a brief preface about Stoker's life and works. The book features twelve previously unknown published works of fiction, poetry, and nonfiction writing. *The Mammoth Book of Slasher Movies: An A–Z Guide to More Than 60 Years of Blood and Guts* by Peter Normanton (Running Press) is a lively compendium covering slasher movies, alphabetically from 1959 through 2011. First, there's a fascinating overview of the history of the visceral in movies, including sections on US and UK movie censorship, on the rise of Hammer films, the dramatic development of cinematic horror in the sixties (with *Psycho*, *Peeping Tom*, *Les Yeux Sans Visage*, etc), the promulgation of grindhouse and exploitation, the video nasties campaign in the 1980s, up to where we are today. But the meat is the more than 250 reviews, with release dates, running times, cast and production notes, and splats ranging from 0–5 denoting the amount of gore and splatter. *Trick or Treat: A History of Halloween* by Lisa Morton (Reaktion Books) provides context for one of the United States' favorite holidays, looking at its precursors in Ireland and the United Kingdom, the related Day of the Dead in Mexico, and contemporary customs and costumes in the US. She also examines the holiday's influence on popular culture in film, literature and television. *Reel Terror* by David Konow (St. Martin's Press/ Thomas Dunne Books) is a hundred year history of horror films. *The Walking Dead and Philosophy* edited by Wayne Yuen (Carus Publishing/ Open Court) has twenty critical essays about the comics and television show. *The Zombie Movie Encyclopedia: Volume 2* by Peter Dendle (McFarland) follows up the author's first book, which took the zombie from 1932 through the 1990s. The new volume covers movies features and short films made in the 2000s. *The Vampire Film: Undead Cinema* by Jerry Weinstock (Wallflower) is an excellent entry in a series called "Short Cuts: Introductions to Film Studies." The author compresses a lot into a mere 130 pages of text and does it in an entertaining and readable style. *The Undead and Theology* edited by Kim Paffenroth and John W. Morehead (Pickwick Publications) covers vampires, zombies, and in a third section, the golem, gothic subculture, and the cenobites of Clive Barker but the bulk of the book is taken up with zombies. *Insufficient Answers: Essays on Robert Aickman* edited by Gary William Crawford (Gothic Press) contains three essays about Aickman's work by Philip Challinor, Rebekah Memel Brown, and Isaac Land. *Character Actors in Horror and Science Fiction Films, 1930–1960* by Laurence Raw (McFarland) is a biographical dictionary of ninety-six entries about the character actors who regularly appeared in Hollywood's Golden Age, including in depth analyses of their best performances. *European Nightmares: Horror Cinema in Europe Since 1945* edited by Patricia Allmer, David Huxley, and Emily Brick (Wallflower) features essays about British, French, Spanish, Italian, German, Northern European, and Eastern European horror cinema. *Unutterable Horror: A History of Supernatural Fiction Volume 1 and 2* by S.T. Joshi (PS Publishing) comprises more than seven hundred pages beginning with Gilgamesh and ending with a discussion of the works of Laird Barron and Joe Hill. Joshi's always been opinionated and he certainly doesn't hold back here. Readers might be by turns nodding their heads in approval or squeaking their outrage, but they will always be entertained. *Speaking of Monsters: A Teratological Anthology* edited by Caroline Joan S. Picart and John Edgar Browning (Palgrave Macmillan), while academic, is still of interest to the general reader interested in the subject. The book is broken down into seven topics. *Horror and the Horror Film* by Bruce F. Kawin (Anthem Press) is an extremely readable book for anyone interested in horror films. In it, the author views "their narrative strategies, their relations to reality and fantasy, and their cinematic power." (taken from copy). *Trucker Ghost Stories* edited by Annie Wilder (Tor) is a compilation of "true" stories of ghostly encounters experienced by truckers around the U.S.

Chapbooks and Limited Editions

Spectral Press published several single story chapbooks: *Rough Music* by Simon Kurt Unsworth is a haunting, well-done tale about a man who cheated on his wife in the past but is currently attempting to make up for it. *The Eyes of Water* by Alison Littlewood is a smart, nicely-told creepy tale of two young men who thrive on the exploration of Mexican cenotes (flooded caves) in the Yucatan. *The Nine Deaths of Dr. Valentine* by John Llewellyn Probert is about a serial killer in Bristol murdering doctors in ingeniously grisly ways borrowed from Vincent Price horror movies. *The Way of the Leaves* by David Tallerman is a moving tale about two young friends who discover and explore a local barrow and how it changes their lives. The press also published the novella *The Respectable Face of Tyranny* by Gary Fry about a man, who having lost most of his money in the stock market, moves into a caravan (trailer) with his daughter near a stretch of ancient, deserted beach. Nightjar Press continued to publish single story chapbooks: *Marionettes* by Claire Massey is a disturbing tale about a married couple returning to Prague for vacation seven years after their first visit. *Into the Penny Arcade* by Claire Massey is about a mysterious lorry parked on a quiet street down which a young girl must go to get home from school. (reprinted herein). *Puck* by David Rose is about a divorced painter who lives in an isolated cottage with his daughter. *Small Animals* by Alison Moore is a very creepy story about two women visiting a third woman who lives in isolation with her child. Peter Atkins and Glen Hirshberg through Earthling Publications, created their annual chapbook in conjunction with the reading series, The Rolling Darkness Review. This year's volume is called *The Raven of October* and includes a play, a reprint by Atkins, a collaboration by Atkins and Hirshberg, and originals by Hirshberg and the two authors' alter-ego Thomas Bartlett. This is Horror is a horror website that has launched a series of chapbooks in 2012, edited by Michael Wilson. The first two are *Joe & Me*, a tense science fiction story by David Moody about biowarfare experimentation, and the second "Thin Men with Yellow Faces" is a creepy collaboration by Gary McMahon and Simon Bestwick about what happens when a social worker attempts to help a young girl under her supervision. Cemetery Dance published "Amazonas" by Alan Peter Ryan, a marvelous lush and sinister exploration into the heart of darkness of Brazil. In 1906, a married couple are led up the Amazon River by a guide who knows of the "slave tree," a tree that grows slaves, that the husband wants to exploit. Also, from Cemetery Dance came the controlled, chilling, moving novella "I'm Not Sam" by Jack Ketchum and Lucky McKee about a happily married couple who wake up one day to a shocking change that affects their lives and their marriage. Lee Thomas's *Torn* is a chilling story about what happens when a child gone missing is found in the woods around the town of Luthor's Bend. Bad Moon Books published Lisa Morton's *Hell Manor*, about a guy whose first love is the haunted·house he and his business partner develop for Halloween. Trouble enters the picture in the person of an unearthly blonde who applies for a job. The Dalkey Archive Press published *Vlad*, a new novella by Carlos Fuentes, about the Count in contemporary Mexico City. *Delphine Dodd* by S. P. Miskowsi (Omnium Gatherum) is a powerful novella about what happened to the two young sisters who are taken in by their grandmother after being left on a roadside by their mother.

ODDS AND ENDS

The Art of Luke Chueh: Bearing the Unbearable (Titan Books) is a coffee table book, the first about the work of this contemporary artist, whose simple, cartoon-like style has been picking up enthusiasts for the past ten years. He's known as "the bear guy" because most of his paintings feature bears—not realistic bears but comic like teddy bears. These are not happy-go-lucky, charming bears, but bears that suffer and self-harm, bears that are beaten, cut and burned and otherwise abuse themselves, bears with bloodied eye sockets, burning paws, targets painted on their chests. Chueh's work is deeply personal, as he works out his demons of self-identity and depression.

Graphic Horror: Movie Monster Memories by John Edgar Browning (Schiffer), with a foreword by David J. Skal and an Afterword by Chelsea Quinn Yarbro, is an entertaining coffee table book made up of loads of colorful classic horror movie posters, stills from the films, and brief tidbits or reactions to each film by well-known enthusiasts from the sparse 1920s through the 2000s. The entertaining commentary is by writers, anthologists, scholars, and editors including Mort Castle, Brian Stableford, Katherine Ramsland, Ramsey Campbell, Nancy Kilpatrick, and Tony Timpone. This is very much for the casual browser, not for those in the know but it's still quite enjoyable to dip into. Included is "A Selection of Readings in Horror and the Supernatural" that's more interesting for the anthologies it leaves out than for what it includes (there are at least eight science fiction anthologies listed), not one horror anthology edited by either Stephen Jones or by myself.

Halloween Classics: Graphic Classics Volume Twenty-Three edited by Tom Pomplum (Eureka Publications) is an enjoyable compilation of five classic stories (and a screenplay) adapted for the contemporary reader by several talented writers and comic artists. Mort Castle and Kevin Atkinson's brief but colorful introduction to the horror aficionado's favorite holiday sets the mood for the five tales by Washington Irving, Arthur Conan Doyle, H. P. Lovecraft, Mark Twain, and Hans Janowitz and Carl Mayer. The art is uniformly excellent, the adaptations smartly done. Among the illustrators and writers who've done a bang-up job are Ben Avery, Nick Miller, Tom Pomplum, Rod Lott, Simon Gane, Craig Wilson, and Matt Howath.

Inner Sanctum: Tales of Mystery, Horror & Suspense by Ernie Colón (NBM) adapts six stories from the popular radio show, which aired from 1941–1952 (and regularly opened with a creaking door). The stories are illustrated in black and white, and are heavily influenced by the pulp horror era. The only story credited in the book is an original by Colón. The other five, including "The Horla" by Guy de Maupassant, Robert Sloane, and Fred Maytho (and two others I couldn't track down) are all uncredited.

The Vampire Combat Manual: A Guide to Fighting the Bloodthirsty Undead by Roger Ma (Berkley) follows up on the fun, high concept Zombie Combat Manual and will appeal to those vampire lovers with a sense of humor.

Witch Hunts: A Graphic History of the Burning Times by Rocky Wood and Lisa Morton, illustrated by Greg Chapman (McFarland & Company) covers the history of the witch hunt, those who introduced the practice and those who later supervised the accusations, torture, and executions of thousands of victims over a period of three centuries.

Mirror Mirror: The Burns Collection Daguerreotypes by Stanley Burns, MD (Burns Archives Press) is the third volume in the series of 5x6 inch hardcover mini books being published irregularly by the Burns Archive. Dr. Stanley B. Burns started collecting vintage photographs in late 1975. He specialized in medical daguerreotypes, and since then has accumulated over one million images. This specific volume is not focused on medical curiosities. Instead, it's "intended as a reference for collectors, photographers, and historians . . . and contains 250 daguerreotypes representing a wide range of American, British, and French images." Even so, there are plenty of unintentionally strange images to be appreciated by horror aficionados—there's something about the dead-eyed stares of live portrait subjects that is often as creepy as the posed dead.

The Oopsatoreum: Inventions of Henry A. Wilcox by Shaun Tan (Powerhouse Publishing) should make new fans for the Australian artist and filmmaker, whose short animated film, *The Lost Thing* won an Oscar in 2011. It's a look at the unsuccessful inventions of the fictional Wilcox, with descriptions and illustrations of real but obscure objects from Sydney, Australia's Powerhouse Museum.

◀◦▶

NIKISHI

LUCY TAYLOR

Seasick and shivering, Thomas Blacksburg peered out from beneath the orange life boat canopy, watching helplessly as the powerful Benguela current swept him north up the coast of Namibia. For hours, he'd been within sight of the Skeleton Coast, that savage, wave-battered portion of the west African shore stretching between Angola to the north and Swakopmund to the south.

Through ghostly filaments of fog that drifted around the boat, Blacksburg could make out the distant shore and the camel's back outline of towering, buff-colored dunes. To his horror, the land appeared to be receding. Having been brought tantalizingly close to salvation, the current was now tugging him back out into the fierce Atlantic.

A leviathan wave powered up under the boat, permitting Blacksburg a view of houses strung out like pastel-colored beads. Impossible, he thought. This far north, there was nothing but the vast, inhospitable terrain of the Namib desert, an undulating dunescape stretching inland all the way to the flat, sun-blasted wasteland of the Etosha Pan.

Blacksburg calculated his options and found them few. So suddenly and fiercely had the storm struck the night before that no distress call had gone out from the ill-fated yacht Obimi. With the captain knocked overboard and the boat taking on water, Blacksburg and his employer,

Horace DeGroot, had been too busy trying to launch the life boat to radio for help. The Obimi wasn't expected in Angola until the following Friday. No one was looking yet. When they did look, there would be nothing to find. He was the sole survivor.

The settlement in the dunes appeared to be his only chance.

Checking to make sure the leather pouch strapped across his chest was still secure, he dove into the water.

◄◦►

Hours passed before finally he hauled himself ashore and collapsed, half-dead, onto the sand. The fog had lifted, revealing a narrow beach hemmed in between two vast oceans—to the west, the wild Atlantic and, to the east, an unbroken sea of dunes that rose in undulating waves of buff and ochre and gold. Silence reigned. The hiss and thunder of the surf was punctuated only the cries of cormorants and the plaintive lamentations of gulls.

Believing that he'd overshot the settlement he'd glimpsed from the boat, Blacksburg trudged south.

Fatigue dogged him and acted on his brain like a psychedelic drug. Retinues of ghost crabs, fleet translucent carrion-eaters with eyes on stalks, seemed to scurry in his footprints with malevolent intent. Once he thought he glimpsed a spidery-limbed figure traversing the high dunes, but the image passed so quickly across his retina that it might have been anything, strands of kelp animated by the incessant wind or a small, swirling maelstrom of sand that his exhausted mind assigned a vaguely human form.

The hyena slinking toward him, though, was no trickery of vision. A sloping, muscular beast with furrowed lips and seething, tarry eyes, it angled languidly down the duneface, its brown and black fur hackled high, its hot gaze raw and lurid.

Blacksburg took in the clamping power of those formidable jaws, and dread threaded through him like razor wire.

He bent and scooped up a stone.

"Bugger off!" he shouted—or tried to shout. What emerged from his parched throat was a wretched, sandpapery croak, the sound a mummy entombed for thousands of years might make if resurrected.

The hyena edged closer. Blacksburg hurled the rock. It struck the hyena with a muted thunk, laying open a bloody gash on the tufted ear.

The hyena's lips curled back and it uttered a high pitched whooping sound so eerie and wild that the temperature on the windswept beach seemed to go ten degrees colder. He heard what sounded like a Range Rover trying to start on a low battery, but this false rescue was only the guttural cough out of the spotted hyena's broad muzzle. With a final saw-toothed snarl, the pot-bellied creature—which was 70 kilos if it was 10—wheeled around and loped back into the dunes that had spawned it.

◀◦▶

Exhaustion had so blunted Blacksburg's senses that he almost sleepwalked past the grey, wind-scoured facade of a two-story house whose empty window frames and doorway stared down from atop a dune like empty eye sockets above a toothless mouth. Climbing up to investigate, he found a gutted shell, the bare interior carpeted with serpentines of sand, roof beams collapsed inward to reveal a square of azure sky. Gannets nested in the eaves. On the floor, a black tarantula held court atop a shattered chandelier.

Spurred by a terrible intuition, he struggled up another dune until he could look down at the entire town—a pathetic row of derelict abodes, a sand-blasted gazebo where lovers might have lingered once, a church whose steeple had toppled off, the rusted carcass of a Citroen from some forgotten era.

The hoped for sanctuary was a ghost town. A graveyard of rubble and stones.

Stunned, despairing, he roamed amid the wreckage.

The wind shifted suddenly and he inhaled the mouth-watering aroma of cooking meat. The hot, heady aroma banged through his blood stream like heroin. Saliva flooded his mouth. Half-dead synapses danced.

Stumbling toward the scent, he crested another dune and looked down upon the beach to see a sinewy, dark-skinned old man using a stick to stir the enormous cast-iron potije that rested atop a fire. The old fellow wore frayed trousers, a yellow ball cap, and a short-sleeved pink shirt. His left hand did the stirring. The right one, flopping by his side, was lacking all its fingers.

Behind him, a girl in her late teens or early twenties was pulling a bottle of water from a canvas backpack on the ground. She uncapped the bottle and poured it into the potije. She wore an ankle-length tan skirt, battered high-tops, and a billowy red blouse. A brown bandanna around her head held back a crown of windblown dreads. An old scar zigzagged like a lightning bolt between her upper lip and the corner of one eye.

With feigned heartiness, Blacksburg slid and trotted down the dune, crying out, "Uhala po". It meant good afternoon in the Oshiwambo tongue, but judging from the old man's reaction, it might as well have been a threat to lop off his remaining fingers. The old man's eyes bulged and he let loose a shriek of mortal fear. The woman had considerably more sang-froid. She held her ground, but snatched up a sharpened stick.

"My name is Blacksburg," he croaked, holding up his hands to show he meant no harm. "I need help."

The old man commenced a frenzied jabbering. The woman chattered back, and an animated exchange took place, virtually none of which Blacksburg understood. Finally the old man fell silent, but he continued to appraise Blacksburg like a disgruntled wildebeest.

"Excuse my uncle," the woman said, in meticulous, school book English. "You frightened him. He thought you were an evil spirit come to kill us."

"No, just a poor lost wretch." He gestured at the empty water bottle. "You wouldn't have another of those, would you?"

The woman took another bottle of water from the backpack and handed it to Blacksburg, who gulped greedily before eyeing the potije. "Fine smelling stew there," he said. "What is it, some kind of wild game, stock, chutney, maybe an oxtail or two?"

Using her stick, she speared a dripping slab of wild meat. Blacksburg fell upon it like a wolf. The meat was tough and stringy as a jackal's hide, but, in his depleted state, he found it feastworthy.

Between mouthfuls, he gave a version of his plight, detailing the sinking of the Obimi and the loss of her captain, but speaking only vaguely of the one who had chartered the boat, his boss Horace DeGroot. The woman told him that her name was Aamu, that she and the old man were from an Owambo village to the east. "We'll take you there tomorrow. A tour bus stops by twice a week. You can get a ride to Windhoek."

DeGroot's largest diamond store was in Windhoek. Blacksburg had no intention of showing his face there.

"But what are you doing in a ghost town cooking up a feast," he said to redirect the conversation. "Did you know that I was coming? What are you, witches?"

The girl snorted a bitter laugh. "If I were a witch, I'd turn myself into a cormorant and fly up to Algiers or Gibraltar. I'd never come back."

Something in her vehemence intrigued Blacksburg, who was no stranger to restlessness and discontent. "Why do you stay?"

The bite in her voice was like that of a duststorm. "Do my uncle and I look rich to you? We live in a tiny village where the people raise cattle and goats. A good year means we get almost enough to eat. A bad year. . ."

Blacksburg saw no evidence of food shortage in the overflowing potije, but saw no need to point that out.

With greasy fingers, he gestured toward the forlorn remnants of the town. "This place, what is it? What *was* it?"

Aamu foraged deeper inside the backpack, bringing out a couple of Windhoek Lagers. "No ice," she said. "You drink it warm?"

He grinned. "I'll manage."

"Come walk with me. I'll tell you about the town." She took off at a brisk pace, high-tops churning up small clouds of sand, hips fetchingly asway.

Walking was the last thing he wanted to do, but Blacksburg wiped his hands on his trousers and headed up the dune behind her. It was a star dune, one of those sandy forms created by wind blowing from all directions, and it had Blacksburg's eye. Suddenly, with an agility and vigor that caught him by surprise, the old man lunged and seized his biceps in a fierce, one-handed grip, babbling wildly while pumping his mutilated hand.

"Nikishi!" he repeated urgently.

Blacksburg, a head taller and twenty kilos heavier, shook him off like a gnat.

"What's wrong with him?" he asked, catching up to Aamu.

"He's warning you about the evil spirits, the ones that take animal and human form. They like to call people by name to lure them out and kill them." She rolled her eyes. "My uncle's yampy. In our village, people laugh at him. Last week he grabbed a tourist lady's iPod and stomped it in the dirt, because he thought that evil spirits called his name from the earbuds." She took a swig of Lager, grimaced. "Can't stand this stuff warm."

She took off abruptly again, climbing nimbly while Blacksburg labored to keep up. They navigated a surreal dunescape, where decaying buildings pillaged by time and the unceasing wind stood like remnants of a bombing. The larger buildings, the ones the desert hadn't yet reclaimed entirely, indicated a degree of bourgeois prosperity that must have, in its heyday, seemed incongruous, perched as the town was on the edge of nothing, caught between the hostile Namib Desert and the pounding surf.

Aamu must have read his thoughts. "Forty years ago," she said, "this was a busy diamond town called Wilhelmskopf. Water was trucked in once a week. There was a hospital, a school, plans for a community center, even a bowling alley. Everybody lived here—Afrikaners, Germans, Damara and Owambo tribesmen."

"What happened?" Blacksburg said, although he could guess. Many of the smaller diamond towns had petered out by the middle of the previous century, eclipsed by the huge discovery of diamonds in Oranjemund to the south. Of these, Kolmanskopf, a ghost town just outside Luderitz, and now a major tourist attraction, was the most well-known.

Aamu's answer shocked him. "In the late 60s, there were a lot of violent deaths, people found with their throats ripped out, torn apart by animals."

Blacksburg thought of the hyena that had menaced him on the beach. "Hyenas? Jackals?"

"Certainly. But fear spread that a nikishi and its offspring lived among these Wilhelmskopf people, changing into animal form at night to prey on them. A few superstitious fools panicked and turned on one another, accusing each other of sorcery. Eventually the town was abandoned. Can you believe such bosh? Now it belongs to the ghost crabs and the hyenas."

Blacksburg finished off his beer and flung the empty bottle across the threshold of a faded cobalt house with sand piled inside up to the turquoise wainscoting. Lizards stern and still as ancient gods stared down from a piano's gutted innards and perched atop a cracked and broken set of shelves. A shiver rustled his spine. He looked away. Down below, in the purpling twilight, he could see the old man reaching into the potije with his stick, stabbing slabs of bloody meat and flinging them out across the sand.

"Hey, he's throwing away the food!"

Aamu looked away, embarrassed. "I told you he's mad. Years ago, my uncle was here collecting driftwood after a storm when he was attacked by what he thought was a nikishi. He claims it called his name, and when he answered, it bit his fingers off and ate them while he begged for mercy. His mind hasn't been right since. He says the nikishi told him he must come here after every storm and make a spirit offering of meat and beer. To thank the nikishi for not eating all his fingers."

"Waste of good food," scoffed Blacksburg. "This transforming rot, you believe it, too?"

She looked affronted. "Of course not. I'm educated. I was sent to Swakopmund Girls' School. I studied German and English, some science, learned about the world. That's why it's hard for me to live in an Owambo village. I know something bigger's out there."

Blacksburg bit back a sarcastic jibe. What would someone who considered schooling in Swakopmund to be a cosmopolitan experience know about the wider world? This Owambo girl inhabited the most barren region of one of Africa's least populated countries. In Blacksburg's view, she was a half-step above savagery.

"How did you and your uncle get here? Trek across the desert?"

She arched a kohl-black brow. "No, we rode our camels. Look!" Grabbing his hand, she pulled him along a passageway between a debris-strewn house and a derelict pavilion and laughed.

For a second he almost expected to see two tethered dromedaries. But it was a black Toyota Hilux, sand-caked and mud-splattered, that was angled on the slope behind the buildings.

Blacksburg gave the Hilux a covetous once-over.

"Nice-looking camel, this. Where do you gas it up?"

"There's a petrol station for people going to the Etosha Pan about forty kilometers from here. And the safari companies that fly rich tourists in from Cape Town and Windhoek, they have way stations through the desert. Before he became ill, my uncle used to guide for one. That's how he got the jeep."

"I need to get to Angola," Blacksburg said. "What say I buy it from you?"

She eyed him scornfully, his ragged, salt-caked clothes, bare feet, disheveled hair. "And use what for money? Shark's teeth? Ghost crabs?"

"No need to mock me. Let me explain. . ." He felt a sudden, irresistible urge to touch her, as though some electrical energy pulsed inside her skin that his own body required for its sustenance. A few strands of hair had whipped loose from under the bandanna and he used that as an excuse, reaching out to tuck the hair back into place. To his dismay, she flinched as though he'd struck her.

"Sorry." He held up his hands, contrite. "Look, about the jeep, I can pay you well."

"The jeep isn't mine. It belongs to the village."

"Loan it to me then. Go with me as far as Luanda. After that, I'm on my own."

"But why should I help you?"

"A fair question that I'd expect of you, a graduate of Swakopmund Girl's School. Here, let me show you something," His smile was confident, but his stomach corkscrewed at what he was about to do – betting everything on this girl's gullibility and greed.

"You say you want to see the wider world. What if I told you you could go anywhere you wanted and live like a movie star? What would you say to that?"

"I'd say maybe you swallowed too much seawater, Blacksburg. That you're as crazy as my uncle."

"Crazy, huh? Look here."

With a showman's flair, he reached inside his shirt, unhooked some clasps and pulled out a leather wallet protector. Unzipping it, he produced two plastic baggies.

"Cup your hands."

He unzipped one baggy and spilled into her palms a treasure trove of uncut stones. Even in the dimming light, they glittered like a fairy king's ransom. Aamu's breath caught. She cradled the diamonds as though she held a beating heart. Her voice, when she finally spoke, was a reverential whisper.

"*Ongeypi?* What are you, a jewel thief?"

"I'm a diamond dealer," he corrected brusquely. "I was transporting these to a buyer in Luanda."

He scooped the stones back into the baggy and opened up the next. These were a few museum quality pieces from DeGroot's private collection, several of which had been loaned out over the years to South African celebrities headed to New York and Cannes. Enjoying himself now, warming to his role, he plucked out a dazzling yellow diamond on a platinum chain. When he held it up, the sunlight put on a fire show, the facets blazed.

Aamu's dark eyes widened as he fastened it around her neck. In her inky irises were gold glints, a few grains of sand out of the Namib desert.

"It must be worth a fortune!"

"A bit more than a used jeep, I imagine. If you get me to Luanda, it's yours to sell. Do we have an arrangement?"

She frowned and chewed her lower lip. "What about my uncle? We can't let him go back to the village. Everyone will know I took the jeep and went off with an *oshilumbu*."

Blacksburg cringed a little at being called "white man," and looked down onto the beach, where the flames under the potije still danced. The old man paced a furious circle around the pot, raising his arms in wild supplication to whatever dark gods fueled his imagination. Silhouetted against the blood red sun, the mutilated hand looked like a misshapen club.

He took Aamu's hand and brought her fingers to his lips, tasting the meat and salt under the nails. "Right then, let's leave your uncle to his demons."

She laughed and pulled away, trotting along an alleyway between a half-dozen tumbled-down buildings, beckoning him to follow. When he caught up with her, she was framed in the empty doorway of a small stone house where, with a dancer's grace and the lewdness of a seasoned whore, she slowly peeled off the scarlet top and beige skirt.

"At the school in Swakopmund," she said, letting the blouse fall, "the priest said I was too wild—too hungry for excitement, for boys and beer, for freedom. He said it's wrong to want too much, that it's a sin to be too hungry." In the fading light, her black eyes made promises both heartfelt and indecent. "What about you, Blacksburg? Are you too hungry?"

For the first time in months, Blacksburg permitted himself a laugh of real delight. For a giddy moment, he actually romanced the notion of the two of them leaving Namibia together, a fantasy that Aamu's reckless passion only fueled.

She rode him with a mad abandon Blacksburg had experienced in only a few women—and then always prostitutes high on serious street drugs. If it was sex she'd been talking about when she asked him if it was a sin to be too hungry, then both were surely hellbound.

Their rutting was as much attack as ardour. Blacksburg, glorying in pain both given and received, devoured her. Past and future fell away, until all that remained was her thrashing body and feral moans, the sea-salt scent of her, and the fierce and biting sweetness of her teeth and tongue. He drank in the musky sweat that ran between her breasts and down her prominent ribs and tangled his hands in the lush snarls of her dread-locked mane. And when they rested, panting, sated, Blacksburg knew only that he wanted more.

Later, she spooned her limber body around his and chuckled in his ear, "Where will you go after you sell your diamonds? Don't lie to me. I know you're running. You wouldn't be so quick to trade a diamond for a jeep if you weren't a desperate man."

He was surprised when truth slipped out. "England, maybe. My mother always said we had relatives in Cornwall. I might go there."

"Cornwall." She pronounced the word like one uttering an incantation. "Maybe I'll go with you, my handsome Blacksburg."

And, for a few ecstatic moments, the idea of an impromptu adventure with this exotic woman moved Blacksburg deeply, fed into his desire to see himself as noble, heroic even, a survivor conquering the world by dint of ruthlessness and valor and self-will. The man he truly was, rich and powerful like DeGroot.

Later, as he drifted toward sleep, he saw filaments of moonlight slant through the empty window and spill across her face. She was lovely, even with the scar, but what mesmerized him, what he could not tear his eyes from, was how the yellow diamond glimmered around that dark as bitter-chocolate throat.

Blacksburg dreamed about his mother. She stood outside the cottage in Cornwall before a running stream that he had seen in photographs. No longer gaunt, used-up and grey as he remembered her, but young and spirited. Her voice was high and lilting, clear as birdsong, infused with a calm serenity that in her life he'd never known her to possess. She called to him, not in the sharp haranguing style that in life had been her nature, but with a serenity and sweetness. Blacksburg almost loved her then, an alien emotion he had seldom felt for her in life, for this woman who had been an Afrikaner whore.

He woke up to the unholy cackling of hyenas and the taste of charred meat on his tongue.

Aamu was gone. For a second panic gripped him. But the diamonds, still secure in their plastic baggies, were undisturbed.

He pulled his pants on and went outside into a night no longer flecked with stars, but murky, swimming with long, damp tresses of fog. He felt like a diver floating along the bottom of the sea, enveloped in an endless, choking school of pale grey, tubular fish.

Peering down onto the beach, he tried to spot the old man's fire and thought he glimpsed the orange flare of a few remaining embers, but no sooner had he started to descend the dune, than a low, contralto rumbling halted him. The sound came from a dozen yards away, where the fog-swathed columns of the pavilion jutted from the gloom like a ghostly Parthenon.

As he approached, he saw a nest of shadows, low to the ground, diverge and reconfigure, then caught a glimpse of a pink shirt and let himself exhale. The old man was asleep in the pavilion, the noise he'd heard undoubtedly was snoring. More movement—undulating, languid. He saw what looked to his uncertain eyes to be a wild crown of Medusa dreads whipped back and forth—a host of unwelcome images besieged his mind—but it was the hyena's glaring eyes and not its mane-like, ruffled tail that finally made the scene before him recognizable.

The hyena's eyes flashed, then vanished into the fog only to reappear a few feet away. The grumbling, growling intensified. Blacksburg, shocked motionless, counted five sets of eyes.

A frightful snarling commenced as two of the hyenas, snapping wildly, fought over a choice morsel. Bits of skin and gristle flew. Blacksburg glimpsed a ragged nub of bone attached to a scrap of pink cloth.

His breath caught in a stifled gasp. A hyena's head jerked up, and it raised its gory snout to test the wind.

Blacksburg shoved away from the pavilion and plunged headlong into the fog. He tried to remember the location of the jeep, thinking he might be able to lock himself inside, but the drifting mist cast a surreal opaqueness across the dunescape. Nothing that he saw was recognizable, the blank facades of the buildings as alike as weathered tombstones.

Ahead the murky outline of a crumbling two-story building floated up out of the fog. An empty window gaped. He hurled himself through it, tripped, and landed atop the piano he'd seen earlier—its ancient keys produced a wheezing bleat.

Behind him a sagging door led into a low hallway. The darkness was crypt black. He groped his way along, stumbling over obstacles—a plank, an empty drum of some kind—until he half fell into a small enclosed space, a storage room or closet. He huddled there, heart galloping, listening for the murderous whoops of the converging pack.

Blacksburg?

His own name sounded suddenly as alien and frightful as a curse. It floated on the hissing wind, at once as distant as the moon and close as his own breath, Aamu's voice or maybe just the scrape of windswept sand. He cleared his throat to answer and found that he was mute.

They call people by name to lure them out.

Although never in his life had Blacksburg been superstitious, now some atavistic fear crawled out of his reptilian brain and commandeered all else.

He tried to tell himself his frantic mind was playing tricks, but an older knowledge told him what he feared the most, that what called to him was no hyena but a shape shifter, a nikishi, that would split him open like the old man, from groin to sternum and feed while he lay dying.

Blacksburg!

The piano suddenly coughed out a great, discordant cacophony, as though four clawed feet had leaped onto the keyboard and bounded off.

The door he'd come through creaked, and then a single animal sent forth its infernal wail into the hollow building. At once a clan of hyenas, some inside, others beyond the walls, took up the ungodly cry.

Knowing he was seconds from being found and trapped, he bolted from his hiding place, raced up the hallway and hurled himself through a window that was partially intact, crashing to the sand amidst a biting drizzle of shattered glass.

Without pause, he got up and pounded down the duneface, arms pinwheeling, skidding wildly.

The hyenas converged around him.

The largest, boldest of the beasts feinted once before going for his throat. Its teeth snagged his shirt, taking with the fabric a strip of flesh from Blacksburg's ribs. He fell to one knee, one arm up to guard his jugular, the other to protect the pouch across his chest—even knowing, beyond all doubt, that both were lost to him.

The ecstatic yips of the hyenas were suddenly drowned out by the roar of an approaching motor. The Hilux teetered at the top of the dune, then careened straight down the face, sand spewing out behind the tires, high beams punching through the fog. It slammed onto beach, suspension screaming, bounced off the ground, and veered toward the hyenas. The pack scattered. Blacksburg staggered to his feet, as the jeep skidded to a halt beside him.

"Get in!"

Aamu flung the door wide, and Blacksburg launched himself inside, the jeep lurching into motion while his legs still dangled out the door. A hyena leaped, jaws snapping. He screamed and kicked out. The hyena twisted in mid-air and fell away. Blacksburg muscled the door closed.

Aamu gunned the engine and the jeep tore away through the fog.

She drove like a witch, outdistancing the pack by many miles, before she turned to Blacksburg and said gravely, "I looked for you on foot at first. I called your name. I knew you were close by, but you didn't answer."

"I didn't hear you," Blacksburg lied, shame making him curt, resentful of her. They both knew he'd been afraid to answer, that in that desperate moment, rationality had failed him. He'd believed the hyena pack to be nikishis and one of them was mimicking her voice. He was a fool and a coward, just as all along he knew his boss DeGroot had judged him privately to be. In that moment, when he felt as though she'd seen into his soul and found him wanting, he made a harsh decision.

He told her to stop the vehicle and switch places. He would drive.

◂◦▸

Later, when the mid-day sun was high and blazingly hot, Blacksburg decided they'd come far enough. He'd been driving for hours while Aamu slept. Now he halted the Hilux in the middle of a sun-blasted stretch of desert bleak and desolate as a medieval rendition of hell, shook her by the shoulder, and said, "Get out."

She sat up, blinking groggily. "What . . . what are you talking about?"

"It's simple. End of the line. Get out."

"I don't understand." She looked around at the miles of barren, retina-searing whiteness. "Is this a joke?"

He barked a bitter laugh. "Did you really think I was taking you with me? I can get to Angola on my own."

"But . . . I'll die out here."

"Yes, I imagine so."

For a woman contemplating her very short future, she appeared strangely unmoved. "But we are going to Luanda."

"One of us. Not you." He held his hand out. "And by the way, I want my diamond back."

"Then take it and be damned!" Before Blacksburg could stop her, she yanked the diamond from around her neck and hurled it out the window as casually as if she were discarding a wad of gum.

He swore and struck her across the head. The bandanna came off. He saw the dried blood in her hair, and the fresh blood flowing from the wound at the top of her ear. He stared at his hand, where her blood stained it.

She dragged a finger pensively along the scar that ran along her cheek. "You know how I got this? My uncle cut me with a knife. But I was merciful and let him live. Last night I was merciful again. I killed him before I fed his flesh to the hyenas."

Using sheer force of will, Blacksburg hauled himself back from the brink of panic. "You think you scare me? You're crazier than your uncle was. If I can kick my old boss out of a dingy and into the sea, I can damn sure get rid of you. Now get the hell out of my jeep."

She didn't budge. Wild hunger, wanton and insatiable, raged in her eyes. Her lips curled in a soulless smile. "Yesterday I could have killed you on the beach, but I was curious about what kind of man you were, about what was in your heart. Now I know. And now, you know me."

Her voice was lush with malice. Her face, as she commenced her changing, was radiant with cruelty.

"See me as I am," shrilled the nikishi.

At once, her slashing teeth cleaved the soft, white folds of his belly. She thrust her muzzle inside the wound, foraging for what was tastiest. The salty entrails were gobbled first, then the tender meat inside the bones, his life devoured in agonizing increments.

Hours later, a hyena pup following a set of jeep tracks came across a human skull. It seized the trophy in its strong young jaws and headed back denward to gnaw the prize at leisure.

◄O►

LITTLE AMERICA

DAN CHAON

First of all, here are the highways of America. Here are the states in sky blue, pink, pale green, with black lines running across them. Peter has a children's version of the map, which he follows as they drive. He places an X by the names of towns they pass by, though most of the ones on his old map aren't there anymore. He sits, staring at the little cartoons of each state's products and services. Corn. Oil wells. Cattle. Skiers.

Secondly, here is Mr. Breeze himself. Here he is behind the steering wheel of the long old Cadillac. His delicate hands are thin, reddish as if chapped. He wears a white shirt, buttoned at the wrist and neck. His thinning hair is combed neatly over his scalp, his thin, skeleton head is smiling. He is bright and gentle and lively, like one of the hosts of the children's programs Peter used to watch on television. He widens his eyes and enunciates his words when he speaks.

Third is Mr. Breeze's pistol. It is a Glock 19 nine millimeter compact semi-automatic handgun, Mr. Breeze says. It rests enclosed in the glove box directly in front of Peter, and he imagines that it is sleeping. He pictures the muzzle, the hole where the bullet comes out: a closed eye that might open at any moment.

‹○›

Outside the abandoned gas station, Mr. Breeze stands with his skeleton head cocked, listening to the faintly creaking hinge of an old sign that advertises cigarettes. His face is expressionless, and so is the face of the gas station storefront. The windows are broken and patched with pieces of cardboard, and there is some trash, some paper cups and leaves and such, dancing in a ring on the oil-stained asphalt. The pumps are just standing there, dumbly.

"Hello?" Mr. Breeze calls after a moment, very loudly. "Anyone home?" He lifts the arm of a nozzle from its cradle on the side of a pump and tries it. He pulls the trigger that makes the gas come out of the hose, but nothing happens.

Peter walks alongside Mr. Breeze, holding Mr. Breeze's hand, peering at the road ahead. He uses his free hand to shade his eyes against the low late afternoon sun. A little ways down are a few houses and some dead trees. A row of boxcars sitting on the railroad track. A grain elevator with its belfry rising above the leafless branches of elms.

In a newspaper machine is a *USA Today* from August 6, 2012, which was, Peter thinks, about two years ago, maybe? He can't quite remember.

"It doesn't look like anyone lives here anymore," Peter says at last, and Mr. Breeze regards him for a long moment in silence.

—◇—

At the motel, Peter lies on the bed, face down, and Mr. Breeze binds his hands behind his back with a plastic tie.

"Is this too tight?" Mr. Breeze says, just as he does every time, very concerned and courteous.

And Peter shakes his head. "No," he says, and he can feel Mr. Breeze adjusting his ankles so that they are parallel. He stays still as Mr. Breeze ties the laces of his tennis shoes together.

"You know that this is not the way that I want things to be," Mr. Breeze says, as he always does.

"It's for your own good."

Peter just looks at him, with what Mr. Breeze refers to as his "inscrutable gaze."

"Would you like me to read to you?" Mr. Breeze asks. "Would you like to hear a story?"

"No, thank you," Peter says.

◄○►

In the morning, there is a noise outside. Peter is on top of the covers, still in his jeans and T-shirt and tennis shoes, still tied up, and Mr. Breeze is beneath the covers in his pajamas, and they both wake with a start. Beyond the window, there is a terrible racket. It sounds like they are fighting or possibly killing something. There is some yelping and snarling and anguish, and Peter closes his eyes as Mr. Breeze gets out of bed and springs across the room on his lithe feet to retrieve the gun.

"Shhhh," Mr. Breeze says, and mouths silently: "Don't. You. Move." He shakes his finger at Peter: *no no no!* and then smiles and makes a little bow before he goes out the door of the motel with his gun at the ready.

Alone in the motel room, Peter lies breathing on the cheap bed, his face down and pressed against the old polyester bedspread, which smells of mildew and ancient tobacco smoke.

He flexes his fingers. His nails, which were once long and black and sharp, have been filed down to the quick by Mr. Breeze—*for his own good,* Mr. Breeze had said.

But what if Mr. Breeze doesn't come back? What then? He will be trapped in this room. He will strain against the plastic ties on his wrist, he will kick and kick his bound feet, he will wriggle off the bed and pull himself to the door and knock his head against it, but there will be no way out. It will be very painful to die of hunger and thirst, he thinks.

After a few minutes, Peter hears a shot, a dark firecracker echo that startles him and makes him flinch.

Then Mr. Breeze opens the door. "Nothing to worry about," Mr. Breeze says. "Everything's fine!"

◄○►

For a while, Peter had worn a leash and collar. The skin-side of the collar had round metal nubs that touched Peter's neck and would give him a shock if Mr. Breeze touched a button on the little transmitter he carried.

"This is not how I want things to be," Mr. Breeze told him. "I want us to be friends. I want you to think of me as a teacher. Or an uncle!

"Show me that you're a good boy," Mr. Breeze said, "And I won't make you wear that anymore."

In the beginning, Peter had cried a lot, and he had wanted to get away, but Mr. Breeze wouldn't let him go. Mr. Breeze had Peter wrapped up tight and tied in a sleeping bag with just his head sticking out—wriggling like a worm in a cocoon, like a baby trapped in its mother's stomach.

Even though Peter was nearly twelve years old, Mr. Breeze held him in his arms and rocked him and sang old songs under his breath and whispered *shh shhh shhhh*. "It's okay, it's okay," Mr. Breeze said. "Don't be afraid, Peter, I'll take care of you."

◄•►

They are in the car again now, and it is raining. Peter leans against the window on the passenger side, and he can see the droplets of water inching along the glass, moving like schools of minnows, and he can see the clouds with their gray, foggy fingerlings almost touching the ground, and the trees bowed down and dripping.

"Peter," Mr. Breeze says, after an hour or more of silence. "Have you been watching your map? Do you know where we are?"

And Peter gazes down at the book Mr. Breeze had given him. Here are the highways, the states in their pale primary colors. Nebraska. Wyoming.

"I think we're almost halfway there," Mr. Breeze says. He looks at Peter and his cheerful children's-program eyes are careful, you can see him thinking something besides what he is saying. There is a way that an adult can look into you to see if you are paying attention, to see if you are learning, and Mr. Breeze's eyes scope across him, prodding and nudging.

"It's a nice place," Mr. Breeze says. "A very nice place. You'll have a room of your own. A warm bed to sleep in. Good food to eat. And you'll go to school! I think you'll like it."

"Mm," Peter says, and shudders.

They are passing a cluster of houses now, some of them burned and still smoldering in the rain. There are no people left in those houses, Peter knows. They are all dead. He can feel it in his bones; he can taste it in his mouth.

Also, out beyond the town, in the fields of sunflowers and alfalfa, there are a few who are like him. Kids. They are padding stealthily along the rows of crops, their palms and foot soles pressing lightly along the loamy earth, leaving almost no track. They lift their heads, and their golden eyes glint.

◄○►

"I had a boy once," Mr. Breeze says.

They have been driving without stopping for hours now, listening to a tape of a man and some children singing. *B-I-N-G-O*, they are singing. *Bingo was his name-o!*

"A son," Mr. Breeze says. "He wasn't so much older than you. His name was Jim."

Mr. Breeze moves his hands vaguely against the steering wheel.

"He was a rock hound," Mr. Breeze says. "He liked all kinds of stones and minerals. Geodes, he loved. And fossils! He had a big collection of those!"

"Mm," Peter says.

It is hard to picture Mr. Breeze as a father, with his gaunt head and stick body and puppet mouth. It is hard to imagine what Mrs. Breeze must have looked like. Would she have been a skeleton like him, with a long black dress and long black hair, a spidery way of walking?

Maybe she was his opposite: a plump young farm girl, blond and ruddy-cheeked, smiling and cooking things in the kitchen like pancakes.

Maybe Mr. Breeze is just making it up. He probably didn't have a wife or son at all.

"What was your wife's name?" Peter says, at last, and Mr. Breeze is quiet for a long time. The rain slows, then stops as the mountains grow more distinct in the distance.

"Connie," Mr. Breeze says. "Her name was Connie."

◄○►

By nightfall, they have passed Cheyenne—*a bad place,* Mr. Breeze says, *not safe*—and they are nearly to Laramie, which has, Mr. Breeze says, a good, organized militia and a high fence around the perimeter of the city.

Peter can see Laramie from a long way off. The trunks of the light poles are as thick and tall as sequoias, and at their top, a cluster of halogen lights, a screaming of brightness, and Peter knows he doesn't want to go there. His arms and legs begin to itch, and he scratches with his sore, clipped nails, even though it hurts just to touch them to skin.

"Stop that, please, Peter," Mr. Breeze says softly, and when Peter doesn't stop he reaches over and gives Peter a flick on the nose with his finger. "*Stop*." Mr. Breeze says. "*Right. Now.*"

There are blinking yellow lights ahead, where a barrier has been erected, and Mr. Breeze slows the Cadillac as two men emerge from behind a structure made of logs and barbed wire and pieces of cars that have been sharpened into points. The men are soldiers of some kind, carrying rifles, and they shine a flashlight in through the windshield at Peter and Mr. Breeze. Behind them, the high chain fence makes shadow patterns across the road as it moves in the wind.

Mr. Breeze puts the car into park and reaches across and takes the gun from its resting place in the glove box. The men are approaching slowly and one of them says very loudly: "STEP OUT OF THE CAR PLEASE SIR," and Mr. Breeze touches his gun to Peter's leg.

"Be a good boy, Peter," Mr. Breeze whispers. "Don't you try to run away, or they will shoot you."

Then Mr. Breeze puts on his broad, bright puppet smile. He takes out his wallet and opens it so that the men can see his identification, so that they can see the gold seal of the United States of America, the glinting golden stars. He opens his door and steps out. The gun is tucked into the waistband of his pants, and he holds his hands up loosely, displaying the wallet.

He shuts the door with a thunk, leaving Peter sealed inside the car.

There is no handle on the passenger side of the car, so Peter cannot open his door. If he wanted to, he could slide across to the driver's seat, and open Mr. Breeze's door, and roll out onto the pavement and try to scramble as fast as he could into the darkness, and maybe he could run fast enough, zig-zagging, so that the bullets they'd shoot would only nip the ground behind him, and he could find his way into some kind of brush or forest and run and run until the voices and the lights were far in the distance.

But the men are watching him very closely. One man is holding his flashlight so that the beam shines directly through the windshield and onto Peter's face, and the other man is staring at Peter as Mr. Breeze speaks and gestures, speaks and gestures like a performer on television who is selling something for kids. But the man is shaking his head no. *No!*

"I don't care what kind of papers you got, mister," the man says. "There's no way you're bringing that thing through these gates."

⟨◦⟩

Peter used to be a real boy.

He can remember it—a lot of it is still very clear in his mind. "I pledge allegiance to the flag" and "Knick knack paddy whack give a dog a bone this old man goes rolling home" and "ABCDEFGHIJKLMNOPQRSTU-VWXYZ now I know my ABCs, next time won't you sing with me?" and "Yesterday . . . all my troubles seemed so far away" and . . .

He remembers the house with the big trees in front, riding a scooter along the sidewalk, his foot pumping and making momentum. The bug in a jar—cicada—coming out of its shell and the green wings. His mom and her two braids. The cereal in a bowl, pouring milk on it. His dad flat on the carpet, climbing on his Dad's back: "Dog pile!"

He can still read. The letters come together and make sounds in his mind. When Mr. Breeze asked him, he found he could still say his telephone number and address, and the names of his parents.

"Mark and Rebecca Krolik," he said. "Two one three four Overlook Boulevard, South Bend, Indiana four six six oh one."

"Very good!" Mr. Breeze said. "Wonderful!"

And then Mr. Breeze said, "Where are they now, Peter? Do you know where your parents are?"

⟨◦⟩

Mr. Breeze pulls back from the barricade of Laramie and the gravel sputters out from their tires and in the rearview mirror Peter can see the men with their guns in the red taillights and dust.

"Damn it," Mr. Breeze says, and slaps his hand against the dashboard. "Damn it! I knew I should have put you in the trunk!" And Peter says nothing. He has never seen Mr. Breeze angry in this way, and it frightens him—the red splotches on Mr. Breeze's skin, the scent of adult rage—though he is also relieved to be moving away from those big halogen lights. He keeps his eyes straight ahead and his hands folded in his lap, and he listens to the silence of Mr. Breeze unraveling, he listens to the highway moving beneath them, and watches as the yellow dotted lines at the center of the road are pulled endlessly beneath the car. For a while, Peter pretends that they are eating the yellow lines.

After a time, Mr. Breeze seems to calm. "Peter," he says. "Two plus two."

"Four," Peter says softly.

"Four and four."

"Eight."

"Eight and eight."

"Sixteen," Peter says, and he can see Mr. Breeze's face in the bluish light that glows from the speedometer. It is the cold profile of a portrait, like the pictures of people that are on money. There is the sound of the tires, the sound of velocity.

"You know," Mr. Breeze says at last. "I don't believe that you're not human."

"Hm," Peter says.

He thinks this over. It's a complicated sentence, more complicated than math, and he's not sure he knows what it means. His hands rest in his lap, and he can feel his poor clipped nails tingling as if they were still there. Mr. Breeze said that after a while he will hardly remember them, but Peter doesn't think this is true.

"When we have children," Mr. Breeze says, "they don't come out like us. They come out like you, Peter, and some of them even less like us than you are. It's been that way for a few years now. But I have to believe that these children – at least *some* of these children—aren't really so different, because they are a part of us, aren't they? They feel things. They experience emotions. They are capable of learning and reason."

"I guess," Peter says, because he isn't sure what to say. There is a kind of look an adult will give you when they want you to agree with them, and it is like a collar they put on you with their eyes, and you can feel the little nubs against your neck, where the electricity will come out. Of course, he is not like Mr. Breeze, nor the men that held the guns at the gates of Laramie; it would be silly to pretend, but this is what Mr. Breeze seems to want. "Maybe," Peter says, and he watches as they pass a green luminescent sign with a white arrow that says EXIT.

He can remember the time that his first tooth came out, and he put it under his pillow in a tiny bag that his mother had made for him which said *"Tooth Fairy,"* but then the teeth began to come out very quickly after that and the sharp ones came in. Not like Mother or Father's teeth. And the fingernails began to thicken, and the hairs on his forearms and chin and back, and his eyes changed color.

"Tell me," says Mr. Breeze. "You didn't hurt your parents, did you? You loved them, right? Your mom and dad?"

◄◦►

After that, they are quiet again. They are driving and driving and the darkness of the mountain roads closes in around them. The shadows of pine trees, fussing with their raiments. The grim shadows of solid, staring boulders. The shadows of clouds lapping across the moon.

You loved them, right?

Peter leans his head against the passenger window and closes his eyes for a moment, listening to the radio as Mr. Breeze moves the knob slowly across the dial: Static. Static—static—man crying—static—static—very distant Mexican music fading in and out—static—man preaching fervidly— static—static. And then silence as Mr. Breeze turns it off, and Peter keeps his eyes closed, tries to breathe slow and heavy like a sleeping person does.

You loved them, right?

And Mr. Breeze is whispering under his breath. A long stream of whisps, nothing recognizable.

◄◦►

When Peter wakes, it's almost daylight. They are parked at a rest stop— Peter can see the sign that says "WAGONHOUND REST AREA" sitting in a pile of white rocks, he can see the outlines of the little buildings, one for MEN, one for WOMEN, and there is some graffiti painted against the brick, *FOR GOD SO LOVED THE WOLRD HE GAVE HIS ONLY BEGONTEN SON,* and the garbage cans tipped over and strewn about, the many fast food bags ripped open and torn apart and licked clean, and then the remnants licked again later, hopefully, and the openings of the crushed soda cans tasted, hopefully, and the other detritus examined, sniffed though, scattered.

There is a sound nearby. Sounds. A few of them creeping closer.

An old plastic container is being nosed along the asphalt, prodded for whatever dried bit of sugar might still adhere to the interior. Peter hears it. It rolls—*thok thok thok*—then stops. One has picked it up, one is eying it, the hardened bit of cola at the bottom. He hears the crunch of teeth against the plastic bottle, and then the sound of loud licking and mastication.

And then one is coming near to the car, where he and Mr. Breeze are supposed to be sleeping.

One leaps up onto the front of the Cadillac, naked, on all fours, and lets out a long stream of pee onto the hood of the car. The car bounces as the boy lands on it, and there is the thick splattering sound, and then the culprit bounds away.

That shakes Mr. Breeze awake! He jerks up, scrabbling, and briefly Peter can see Mr. Breeze's real face, hard-eyed and teeth-bared—nothing kindly, nothing from television, nothing like a friendly puppet—and Mr. Breeze clutches his gun and swings it in a circle around the car.

"What the fuck!" Mr. Breeze says.

For a minute, he breathes like an animal, in tight, short gasps. He points his gun at the windows: Front. Back. Both sides. Peter makes himself small in the passenger seat.

Afterward, Mr. Breeze is unnerved. They start driving again right away, but Mr. Breeze doesn't put his gun in the glovebox. He keeps it in his lap and pats it from time to time, like it is a baby he wants to stay asleep.

It takes him a while to compose himself.

"Well!" he says, at last, and he gives Peter his thin lipped smile. "That was a bad idea, wasn't it?"

"I suppose so," Peter says. He watches as Mr. Breeze gives the gun a slow, comforting stroke. *Shhhhhhh. There, there.* Mr. Breeze's friendly face is back on now, but Peter can see how the fingertips are trembling.

"You should have said something to me, Peter," Mr. Breeze says, in a kindly but reproachful voice.

Mr. Breeze raises an eyebrow.

He frowns with mild disappointment.

"You were asleep," Peter says, and clears his throat. "I didn't want to wake you up."

"That was very thoughtful of you," Mr. Breeze says, and Peter glances down at his map. He looks at the dots: Wamsutter. Bitter Creek. Rock Springs. Little America. Evanston.

"How many of them were there, do you think, Peter?" Mr. Breeze says. "A dozen?"

Peter shrugs.

"A dozen means twelve," Mr. Breeze says.

"I know."

"So—do you think there were twelve of them? Or more than twelve of them?"

"I don't know," Peter says. "More than twelve?"

"I should say so," Mr. Breeze says. "I would venture to guess that there were about fifteen of them, Peter." And he is quiet for a little while, as if thinking about the numbers, and Peter thinks about them too. When he thinks about *one dozen,* he can picture a container of eggs. When he thinks about *fifteen,* he can picture a 1 and a 5 standing together, side by side, holding hands like brother and sister.

"You're not like them, Peter," Mr. Breeze whispers. "I know you know that. You're not one of *them.* Are you?"

What is there to say?

Peter stares down at his hands, at his sore, shaved fingernails; he runs his tongue along the points of his teeth; he feels the hard, broad muscles of his shoulders flex, the bristled hairs on his back rubbing uncomfortably against his T-shirt.

"Listen to me," says Mr. Breeze, his voice soft and stern and deliberate. "Listen to me, Peter. You are a special boy. People like me travel all over the country, looking for children just like you. You're different, you know you are. Those *things* back there at the rest stop? You're not like them, you know that, don't you?"

After a time, Peter nods.

You loved them, right? Peter thinks, and he can feel his throat tighten.

He hadn't meant to kill them. Not really.

Most of the time, he forgets that it happened, and even when he *does* remember he can't recall *why* it happened.

It was as if his mind was asleep for a while, and then when he woke up there was the disordered house, as if a burglar had turned over every object, looking for treasure. His father's body was in the kitchen, and his mother's was in the bedroom. A lot of blood, a lot of scratches and bites on her, and he put his nose against her hair and smelled it. He lifted her limp hand and pressed the palm of it against his cheek and made it pet him. Then he made it hit him in the nose and the mouth.

"Bad," he had whispered. "Bad! Bad!"

"It's going to be better once we get to Salt Lake," Mr. Breeze says. "It's a special school for children like you, and I know you're going to enjoy it so much. You're going to make a lot of new friends! And you're going to learn so much, too, about the world! You'll read books and work with a calculator and a computer, and you'll do some things with art and music! And there will be counselors there who will help you with your . . . feelings. Because the feelings are just feelings. They are like weather, they come and go. They're not *you*, Peter. Do you understand what I'm saying?"

"Yes," Peter says. He stares out to where the towering white-yellow butte cliffs have been cut through to make room for the road, and the metal guard rail unreels beside them, and the sky is a glowing, empty blue. He blinks slowly.

If he goes to this school, will they make him tell about his mom and dad?

Maybe it will be all right, maybe he *will* like it there.

Maybe the other children will be mean to him, and the teachers won't like him either.

Maybe he *is* special.

Will his fingernails always hurt like this? Will they always have to be cut and filed?

"Listen," Mr. Breeze says. "We're coming up on a tunnel. It's called the Green River Tunnel. You can probably see it on your map. But I want to tell you that there have been some problems with these tunnels. It's easy to block the tunnels from either end, once a car is inside it, so I'm going to speed up, and I'm going to go very, very fast when we get there. Okay? I just want you to be prepared. I don't want you to get alarmed. Okay?"

"Okay," Peter says, and Mr. Breeze smiles broadly and nods and then without another word they begin to accelerate. The guard rail begins to slip by faster and faster until it is nothing but a silver river of blur, and then the mouths of the tunnels appear before them—one for the left side of the road, one for the right, maybe not mouths but instead a pair of eyes, two black sockets beneath a ridged hill, and Peter can't help himself, he tightens his fingers against his legs even though it hurts.

When they pass beneath the concrete arches, there is a soft *whuff* sound as if they've gone through the membrane of something, and then suddenly there is darkness. He can sense the curved roof of the tunnel over them, a rib cage of dark against dark flicking overhead, and the echo of the car as it speeds up, faster and faster, a long crescendo as the opening in the distance grows wider and wider, and the opening behind them grows smaller.

But even as the car quickens, Peter can feel time slowing down, so that each rotation of tire is like the click of the second hand of a clock. There are kids in the tunnel. Twenty? No, thirty maybe, he can sense the warm bodies of them as they flinch and scrabble up the walls of the tunnel, as they turn and begin to chase after the car's taillights, as they drop stones and bits of metal down from their perches somewhere in the tunnel's concrete rafters. "Yaaah!" they call. "Yaaah!" And their voices make Peter's fingers ache.

In front of them, the hole of daylight spreads open brighter, a corona of whiteness, and Peter can only see the blurry shadow-skeletons of the kids as they leap in front of the car.

They must be going a hundred miles an hour or more when they hit the boy. The boy may be eight or nine, Peter can't tell. There is only the imprint of a contorted face, and the cry he lets out, a thin, wiry body leaping. Then, a heavy thump as the bumper connects with him, and a burst of blood blinds the windshield, and they hear the clunking tumble of the body across the roof of the car and onto the pavement behind them.

Mr. Breeze turns on the windshield wipers, and cleaning fluid squirts up as the wipers squeak across the glass. The world appears through the smeared arcs the wipers make. There is a great expanse of valley and hills and wide open sky.

<o>

"We're getting very low on gas," Mr. Breeze says, after they've driven for a while in silence.

And Peter doesn't say anything.

"There's a place up ahead. It used to be safe, but I'm not sure if it's safe anymore."

"Oh," Peter says.

"You'll tell me if it's safe, won't you?"

"Yes," Peter says.

"It's called Little America. Do you know why?"

Mr. Breeze looks at him. His eyes are softly sad, and he smiles just a little, wanly, and it's tragic, but it's also okay because that boy wasn't special, not like Peter is special. It is something to be left behind us, says Mr. Breeze's expression.

Peter shrugs.

"It's very interesting," Mr. Breeze says. "Because there once was an explorer named Richard Byrd. And he went into Antarctica, which is a frozen country far to the south, and he made a base on the Ross Ice Shelf, south of the Bay of Whales. And he named his base 'Little America.' And so then later—much much later—they made a motel in Wyoming, and because it was so isolated they decided to call it by the same name. And they used a penguin as their mascot, because penguins are from Antarctica, and when I was a kid there were a lot of signs and billboards that made the place famous."

"Oh," Peter says, and he can't help but think of the kid. The kid saying, "Yaaah!"

They are driving along very slowly, because it is still hard to see out of the windshield, and the windshield wiper fluid has stopped working. It makes its mechanical sound, but no liquid comes out anymore.

⤙◦⤚

It is a kind of oasis, this place. This Little America. A great, huge parking lot, and many gas pumps, and a store and beyond that a motel, with a green concrete dinosaur standing in the grass, a baby brontosaurus, a little taller than a man.

It is the kind of landscape they like. The long, wide strip-mall buildings with their corridors of shelves; the cave-like concrete passageways of enormous interstate motels, with their damp carpets and moldering beds, the little alcoves where ice machines and tall soda vendors may still be inexplicably running; the parking lots where the abandoned cars provide shelter and hiding places, better than a forest of trees.

"There are a lot of them around here, I think," Mr. Breeze says, as they settle in next to a pump. Above them, there is a kind of plastic-metal canopy, and they sit for a while under its shade. Peter can sense that Mr. Breeze is uncertain.

"How many of them are there, do you think?" Mr. Breeze says, very casually, and Peter closes his eyes.

"More than a hundred?" Mr. Breeze says.

"Yes," Peter says, and he looks at Mr. Breeze's face, surreptitiously, and it is the face of a man who has to jump a long distance, but does not want to.

"Yes," he says. "More than a hundred."

He can feel them. They are peering out from the travel center building and the windows of the boarded-up motel and old abandoned cars in the parking lot.

"If I get out of the car and try to pump gas, will they come?" Mr. Breeze says.

"Yes," Peter says. "They will come very fast."

"Okay," Mr. Breeze says. And the two of them are silent for a long time. The face of Mr. Breeze is not the face of a television man, or a skeleton, or a puppet. It is the elusive face that adults give you when they are telling you a lie, for your own good, they think, when there is a big secret that they are sorry about.

Always remember, Peter's mother said. *I loved you, even . . .*

"I want you to hold my gun," Mr. Breeze says. "Do you think you can do that? If they start coming . . . ?"

And Peter tries to look at his real face. Could it be said that Mr. Breeze loved him, even if . . .

"We won't make it to Salt Lake unless we get gas," Mr. Breeze says, and Peter watches as he opens the door of the car.

Wait, Peter thinks.

Peter had meant to ask Mr. Breeze about his son, about Jim, the rock hound. "You killed him, didn't you?" Peter had wanted to ask, and he expected that Mr. Breeze would have said *yes.*

Mr. Breeze would have hesitated for a while, but then finally he would have told the truth, because Mr. Breeze was that kind of person.

And what about me? Peter wanted to ask. *Would you kill me too?*

And Mr. Breeze would have said yes. *Yes, of course. If I needed to. But you would never put me in that situation, would you, Peter? You aren't like the others, are you?*

Peter thinks of all this as Mr. Breeze steps out of the car. He can sense the other kids growing alert, with their long black nails and sharp teeth, with their swift, jumping muscles and bristling hairs. He can see the soft, slow movement of Mr. Breeze's legs. How easy it would be to think: *Prey.*

How warm and full of pumping juice were his sinews, how tender was his skin, the cheeks of his face like a peach.

He knew that they would converge down upon him so swiftly that there wouldn't be time for him to cry out. He knew that they could not help themselves, even as Peter himself could not help himself. His mom, his dad. *Wait,* he wanted to say, but it happened much faster than he expected.

Wait, he thinks. He wants to tell Mr. Breeze. *I want . . .*

I want?

But there isn't really any time for that. *Oh, Mom, I am a good boy*, he thinks. *I want to be a good boy.*

⊶⊶⊶

A NATURAL HISTORY
OF AUTUMN

JEFFREY FORD

On a blue afternoon in autumn, Riku and Michi drove south from Numazu in his silver convertible along the coast of the Izu Peninsula. The temperature was mild for the end of October, and the air was clear, the sun glinting off Suruga Bay. She wore sunglasses and, to protect her hair, a yellow scarf with a design of orange butterflies. He wore driving gloves, a black dress shirt, a loosened white tie. The car, the open road, the rush of the wind made it impossible to converse, and so for miles she watched the bay to their right and he the rising slopes of maple and pine to their left. Just outside the town of Dogashima, a song came on the radio, "Just You, Just Me," and they turned to look at each other. She waited for him to smile. He did. She smiled back, and then he headed inland to search for the hidden onsen, Inugami.

They'd met the previous night at The Limit, an upscale hostess bar. Riku's employer had a tab there and he was free to use it when in Numazu. He'd been once before, drunk and spent time with a hostess. Her conversation had sounded rote, like a script; her flattery grotesquely opulent and therefore flat. The instant he saw Michi, though, in her short black dress with a look of uncertainty in her eyes, he knew it would be a different experience. He ordered a bottle of Nikka Yoichi and two glasses. She introduced herself. He stood and bowed. They were in a private room at a polished table of blond wood. The chairs were high-backed and upholstered like thrones. To their right was an open-air view of pines and the coast. She waited for him to smile and eventually he did. She smiled back and told him, "I'm writing a book."

Riku said, "Aren't you supposed to tell me how handsome I am?"

"Your hair is perfect," she said.

He laughed. "I see."

"I'm writing a book," she said again. "I decided to make a study of something."

"You're a scientist?" he said.

"We're all scientists," she said. "We watch and listen, take in information, process it. We spin theories by which we live."

"What if they're false?"

"What if they're not?" she said.

He shook his head and took a drink.

They sat in silence for a time. She stared out past the pines, sipping her whisky. He stared at her.

"Tell me about your family," said Riku.

She told him about her dead father, her ill mother, her younger sister and brother, but when she inquired about his parents, he said, "Okay, tell me about your book."

"I decided to study a season, and since autumn is the season I'm in, it would be autumn. It's a natural history of autumn."

"You've obviously been to the university," he said.

She shook her head. "No, I read a lot to pass the time between clients."

"How much have you written?"

"Nothing yet. I'm researching now, taking notes."

"Do you go out to Thousand Tree Beach and stare at Fuji in the morning?"

"Your sarcasm is intoxicating," she said.

He filled her glass.

"No, I do my research here. I ask each client what autumn means to him."

"And they tell you?"

She nodded. "Some just want me to say how big their biceps are but most sit back and really think about it. The thought of it makes all the white-haired ojiisans smile, the businessmen cry, the young men a little scared. A lot of it is the same. Just images—the colorful leaves, the clear cold mornings by the Bay, a certain pet dog, a childhood friend, a drunken night. But sometimes they tell me whole stories."

"What kind of stories?"

"A very powerful businessman—one of the other hostesses swore he was a master of the five elements—once told me his own love story, about a young woman he had an affair with. It began on the final day of summer, lasted only as long as the following season, and ended in the snow."

"What did you learn from that story? What did you put in your notes?"

"I recorded his story as he'd told it, and afterward wrote, 'The Story of a Ghost'."

"Why a ghost?" he asked.

"I forget," she said. "And I lied—I attended Waseda University for two years before my father died."

"You didn't have to tell me," he said. "I knew when you told me you called the businessman's story, 'The Story of a Ghost'."

"Pretentious?" she asked.

He shrugged.

"Maybe," she said and smiled.

"Forget about that," said Riku. "I will top that makeinu businessman's exquisite melancholy by proposing a field trip." He sat forward in his chair and touched the tabletop with his index finger. "My employer recently rewarded me for a job well done and suggested I use, whenever I like, a private onsen he has an arrangement with down in Izu. I need only call a few hours in advance."

"A field trip?" she said. "What will we be researching?"

"Autumn. The red and yellow leaves. The place is out in the woods on a mountainside, hidden and very old-fashioned, no frills. I propose a dohan, an overnight journey to the onsen, Inugami."

"A date," she said. "And our attentions will only be on autumn, nothing else?"

"You can trust me when I say, that is entirely up to you."

"Your hair inspires confidence," she said. "You can arrange things with the house on the way out."

"I intend to be in your book," he said and prevented himself from smiling.

After hours of winding along the rims of steep cliffs and bumping down tight dirt paths through the woods, the silver car pulled to a stop in a clearing, in front of a large, slightly sagging farmhouse—minka style, built of logs with a thatched roof. Twenty yards to the left of the place there was a sizeable garden filled with dying sunflowers, ten-foot stalks, their heads bowed. To the right of the house there was a slate path that led away into the pines. The golden late-afternoon light slanted down on the clearing, shadows beginning to form at the tree line.

"We're losing the day," said Riku. "We'll have to hurry."

Michi got out of the car and stretched. She removed her sunglasses and stood still for a moment, taking in the cool air.

"I have your bag," said Riku and shut the trunk.

As they headed for the house, two figures appeared on the porch. One was a small old woman with white hair, wearing monpe pants and an indigo Katazome jacket with a design of white flames. Next to her stood what Michi at first mistook for a pony. The sight of the animal surprised her and she stopped walking. Riku went on ahead. "Grandmother Chinatsu," he said and bowed.

"Your employer has arranged everything with me. Welcome," she said. A small, wrinkled hand with dirty nails appeared from within the sleeve of the jacket. She beckoned to Michi. "Come, my dear, don't be afraid of my pet, Ono. He doesn't bite." She smiled and waved her arm.

As Michi approached, she bowed to Grandmother Chinatsu, who only offered a nod. The instant the young woman's foot touched the first step of the porch, the dog gave a low growl. The old lady wagged a finger at the creature and snapped, "Yemeti!" Then she laughed, low and gruff, the sound at odds with her diminutive size. She extended her hand and helped Michi up onto the porch. "Come in," she said and led them into the farmhouse.

Michi was last in line. She turned to look at the dog. Its coat was more like curly human hair than fur. She winced in disgust. A large flattened pug face, no snout to speak of, black eyes, sharp ears, and a thick bottom lip bubbling with drool. "Ono," she said and bowed slightly in passing. As she stepped into the shadow beyond the doorway, she felt the dog's nose press momentarily against the back of her dress.

In the main room there was a rock fireplace within which a low flame licked two maple logs. Above hung a large paper lantern, orange with white blossoms, shedding a soft light in the center of the room. The place was rustic, wonderfully simple. All was wood: the walls, the ceiling, the floor. There were three ancient carved wooden chairs gathered around a low table off in an alcove at one side of the room. Grandmother led them down a hallway to the back of the place. They passed a room on the left, its screen shut. At the next room, the old lady slid open the panel and said, "The toilet." Further on, they came to two rooms, one on either side of the hallway. She let them know who was to occupy which by mere nods of her head. "The bath is at the end of the hall," she said.

Their rooms were tatami style, straw mats and a platform bed with a futon mattress in the far corner. They undressed, put on robes and sandals, and met in the hallway. As they passed through the main room of the house, Ono stirred from his spot by the fireplace, looked up at them, and snorted.

"Easy, easy," said Riku to the creature. He stepped aside and let Michi get in front of him. Once out on the porch, she said, "Ono is a little scary."

"Only a little?" he asked.

Grandmother appeared from within the plot of dying sunflowers and called that there were towels in the shed out by the spring. Riku waved to her as he and Michi took the slate path into the pines. Shadows were rising beneath the trees and the sky was losing its last blue to an orange glow. Leaves littered the path and the temperature had dropped. The scent of pine was everywhere. Curlews whistled from the branches above.

"Are you taking notes?" he called ahead to her.

She stopped and waited for him. "Which do you think is more autumnal—the leaves, the dying sunflowers, or Grandmother Chinatsu?"

"Too early to tell," he said. "I'm withholding judgment."

Another hundred yards down the winding path they came upon the spring, nearly surrounded by pines except for one spot with a view of a small meadow beyond. Steam rose from the natural pool, curling up in the air, reminding Michi of the white flames on the old lady's jacket. At the edge of the water, closest to the slate path, there was ancient stonework, a crude bench, a stacked rock wall covered with moss, six foot by four, from which a thin waterfall splashed down into the rising heat of the onsen.

"Lovely," said Michi.

Riku nodded.

She left him and moved down along the side of the spring. He looked away as she stepped out of her sandals and removed her robe, which she hung on a nearby branch. He heard her sigh as she entered the water. When he removed his robe, her face was turned away, as if she were taking in the last light on the meadow. Meanwhile, Riku was taking Michi in, her slender neck, her long black hair and how it lay on the curve of her shoulder, her breasts.

"Are you getting in?" she asked.

He silently eased down into the warmth.

When Michi turned to look at him, she immediately noticed the tattoo on his right shoulder, a vicious swamp eel with rippling fins and needle fangs and a long body that wrapped around Riku's back. It was the color of the moss on the rocks of the waterfall.

Riku noticed her glancing at it. He also noticed the smoothness of her skin and that her nipples were erect.

"Who is your employer?" she asked.

"He's a good man," he said and lowered himself into a crouch, so that only his head was above water. "Now, pay attention," he said and looked out at the meadow, which was already in twilight.

"To what?" she asked, also sinking down into the water.

He didn't respond and they remained immersed for a long time, just two heads floating on the surface, staring silently and listening, steam rising around them. At last light, when the air grew cold, the curlews lifted from their branches and headed for Australia. Riku stood, moved to a different spot in the spring, and crouched down again. Michi moved closer to him. A breeze blew through the pines, a cricket sang in the dark.

"Was there any inspiration?" he asked.

"I'm not sure," she said. "It's time for you to tell me your story of autumn." She drew closer to him and he backed up a step.

"I don't tell stories," he said.

"As brief as you want, but something," she said and smiled.

He closed his eyes and said, "Okay. The autumn I was seventeen, I worked on one of the fishing boats out of Numazu. We were out for horse mackerel. On one journey we were struck by a rogue wave, a giant that popped up out of nowhere. I was on deck when it hit and we were swamped. I managed to grab a rope and it took all my strength not to be drawn overboard, the water was so cold and powerful. I was sure I would die. Two men did get swept away and were never found. That's my Natural History of Autumn."

She moved forward and put her arms around him. They kissed. He drew his head back and whispered in her ear, "When I returned to shore that autumn, I quit fishing." She laughed and rested her head on his shoulder.

They dined by candlelight, in their robes, in the alcove off the main room of the farmhouse. Grandmother Chinatsu served, and Ono followed a step behind, so that every time she leaned forward to put a platter on the table, there was the dog's leering face, tongue drooping. The main course was thin slices of raw mackerel with grated ginger and chopped scallions. They drank sake. Michi remarked on the appearance of the mackerel after Riku's story.

"Most definitely a sign," he said.

They discussed the things they each saw and heard at the spring as the sake bottle emptied. It was well past midnight when the candle burned out and they went down the hall to his room.

Three hours later, Michi woke in the dark, still a little woozy from the sake. Riku woke when she sat up on the edge of the bed.

"Are you alright?" he asked.

"I have to use the toilet." She got off the bed and lifted her robe from the mat. Slipping into it, she crossed the room. When she slid back the panel, a dim light entered. A lantern hanging in the center of the hallway ceiling bathed the corridor in a dull glow. Michi left the panel open and headed up the hallway. Riku lay back and immediately dozed off. It seemed only a minute to him before Michi was back, shaking him by the shoulder to wake up. She'd left the panel open and he could see her face. Her eyes were wide, the muscles of her jaw tense, a vein visibly throbbing behind the pale skin of her forehead. She was breathing rapidly and he could feel the vibration of her heartbeat.

"Get me out of here," she said in a harsh whisper.

"What's wrong?" he said and moved quickly to the edge of the bed. She kneeled on the mattress next to him and grabbed his arm tightly with both hands.

"We've got to leave," she said.

He shook his head and ran his fingers through his hair. It wasn't perfect anymore. He carefully removed his arm from her grip and checked his watch. "It's three a.m.," he said. "You want to leave?"

"I demand you take me out of this place, now."

"What happened?" he asked.

"Either you take me now or I'll leave on foot."

He gave a long sigh and stood up. "I'll be ready in a minute," he said. She went across the corridor to her room and gathered her things together.

When they met in the hallway, bags in hand, he asked her, "Do you think I should let Grandmother Chinatsu know we're leaving?"

"Definitely not," she said, on the verge of tears. She grabbed him with her free hand and dragged him by the shirtsleeve down the hallway. As they reached the main room of the house, she stopped and looked warily around. "Was it the dog?" he whispered. The coast was apparently clear, for she then dragged him outside, down the porch steps, to the silver car.

"Get in," he said. "I have to put the top up. It's too cold to drive with it down."

"Just hurry," she said, stowing her overnight bag. She slid into the passenger seat just as the car top was closing. He got in behind the wheel and reached over to latch the top on her side before doing his.

Michi's window was down and she heard the creaking of planks from the porch. She leaned her head toward her shoulder and looked into the car's side mirror. There, in the full moonlight, she could see Grandmother Chinatsu and Ono. The old lady was waving and laughing.

"Drive," she shrieked.

Riku hit the start button, put the car in gear, and they were off into the night, racing down a rutted dirt road at fifty. Once the farmhouse was out of sight, he let up on the gas. "You've got to tell me what happened," he said.

She was shivering. "Get us out of the woods first," she said. "To a highway."

"I can't see a thing and I don't remember all the roads," he said. "We might end up lost." He drove for more than an hour before he found a road made of asphalt. His car had been brutalized by the crude paths and branches jutting into the roadway. There would be a hundred scratches on his doors. During that entire time, Michi stared ahead through the windshield, breathing rapidly.

"We're on a main road. Tell me what happened," he said.

"I got up to use the toilet," she said. "And I did. But when I stepped back out into the hallway to return, I heard a horrible grunting noise. I swear it sounded like someone was choking Grandmother Chinatsu to death in her room. I moved along the wall to the entrance. The panel was partially open, and there was a light inside. The noise had stopped so I peered in, and there was the shriveled old lady on her hands and knees on the floor, naked. Her forearms were trembling, her face was bright red, and she began croaking. At first I thought she was ill, but then I looked up and realized she was engaged in sexual relations."

"Grandmother Chinatsu?" he said and laughed. "Who was the unlucky gentleman?"

"That disgusting dog."

"She was doing it with Ono?"

"I almost vomited," said Michi. "But I could have dealt with it. The worst thing was Ono saw me peering in and he smiled at me and nodded."

"Dogs don't smile," he said.

"Exactly," she said. "That place is haunted."

"Well, I'll figure out where we are eventually, and we'll make it back to Numazu by morning. I'm sorry you were so frightened. The field trip seemed a great success until then."

She took a few deep breaths to calm herself. "Perhaps that was the true spirit of autumn," she said.

"The Story of a Ghost," he said.

The silver car sped along in the moonlight. Michi was leaning against the window, her eyes closed. Riku thought he was heading for the coast. He took a tight turn on a narrow mountain road and something suddenly lunged out of the woods at the car. He felt an impact as he swerved, turning back just in time to avoid the drop beyond the lane he'd strayed into.

Michi woke at the impact and said, "What's happening?"

"I think I grazed a deer back there. I've got to pull over and check to see if the car is okay."

Michi leaned forward and adjusted the rearview mirror so she could look out the back window.

"Too late to see," he said. "It was a half-mile back." He eased down on the brake, slowing, and began to edge over toward the shoulder.

"There's something chasing us," she said. "I can see it in the moonlight. Keep going. Go faster."

He downshifted and took his foot off the brake. As he hit the gas, he reached up and moved the mirror out of her grasp so he could see what was following them.

"It's a dog," he said. "But it's the fastest dog I ever saw. I'm doing forty-five and it's gaining on us."

They passed through an area where overhanging trees blocked the moon.

"Watch the road," she said.

When the car moved again into the moonlight, he checked behind them and saw nothing. Then they heard a loud growling. Each searched frantically to see where the noise was coming from. Swerving out of his lane, Riku looked out his side window and down and saw the creature running alongside, the movement of its four legs a blur, its face perfectly human.

"Kuso," he said. "Open the glove compartment. There's a gun in there. Give it to me."

"A gun?"

"Hurry," he yelled. She did as he instructed, handing him the sleek nine millimeter. "You were right," he said. "The place was haunted." He lowered his side window, switched hands between gun and wheel. Then, steadying himself, he hit the brake. The dog looked up as it sped past the car—a middle-aged woman's face, bitter, with a terrible underbite and a beauty mark beneath the left eye, riding atop the neck of a mangy gray mutt with a naked tail. As soon as it moved a foot ahead of the car, Riku thrust the gun out the window and fired. The creature suddenly exploded, turning instantly to a shower of salt.

"It had a face," he said, maneuvering the car out of its skid. "A woman's face."

"Don't stop," she said. "Please."

"Don't worry."

"Now," she said, "who is your employer? Why would he send you to such a place?"

"Maybe if I tell you the truth it'll lift whatever curse we're under."

"What is the truth?"

"My employer is a very powerful businessman, and I have heard it said that he is also an Onmyoji. You know him. In a moment of weakness he told you a story about an affair he had. Afterward, he worried that you might be inclined to blackmail him. If the story got out, it would be a grave embarrassment for him both at home and at the office. He told me, spend time with her. He wanted me to judge what type of person you are."

"And if I'm the wrong kind of person?"

"I'm to kill you and make it look like an accident," he said.

"Are you trying to scare me to death, you and the old woman?"

"No, I swear. I'm as frightened as you are. And I couldn't harm you. Believe me. I know you would never blackmail him."

She rested back against the car seat and closed her eyes. She could feel his hand grasp hers. "Do you believe me?" he said. In the instant she opened her eyes, she saw ahead through the windshield two enormous dogs step onto the highway thirty yards in front of the car.

"Watch out," she screamed. He'd been looking over at her. He hit the brake before even glancing to the windshield. The car locked up and skidded, the headlights illuminating two faces—a man with a thin black mustache and wire-frame glasses, whose mouth was gaping open, and a little girl, chubby, with black bangs, tongue sticking out. On impact, the front of the car crumpled, the air bags deployed, and the horrid dogs burst into salt. The car left the road and came to a stop on the right-hand side, just before the tree line.

Riku remained conscious through the accident. He undid his seatbelt and slid out of the car, brushing glass off his shirt. His forehead had struck the rearview mirror, and there was a gash on his right temple. He heard growling, and pushing himself away from the car, he headed around to Michi's side. A small pot-bellied dog with the face of an idiot, sunken eyes, and swollen lower lip was drooling and scratching at Michi's window. Riku aimed, pulled the trigger, and turned the monstrosity to salt.

He opened the passenger door. Michi was just coming around. He helped her out and leaned her against the car. Bending over, he reached into the glove compartment and found an extra clip for the gun. As he backed out of the car, he heard them coming up the road, a pack of them, speeding through the moonlight, howling and grunting. He grabbed her hand and they made for the tree line.

"Not the woods," she said and tried to free herself from his grasp.

"No, there's no place to hide on the road. Come on."

They fled into the darkness beneath the trees, Riku literally dragging her forward. Low branches whipped their faces and tangled Michi's hair.

Although ruts tripped them, they miraculously never fell. The baying of the beasts sounded only steps behind them, but when he turned and lifted the gun, he saw nothing but night.

Eventually they broke from beneath the trees onto a dirt road. Both were heaving for breath, and neither could run another step. She'd twisted an ankle and was limping. He put one arm around her, to help her along. She was trembling; so was he.

"What are they?" she whispered.

"Jinmenken," he said.

"Impossible."

They walked slowly down the road, and stepping out from beneath the canopy of leaves, the moonlight showed them, a hundred yards off, a dilapidated building with boarded windows.

"I can't run anymore," he said. "We'll go in there and find a place to hide."

She said nothing.

They stood for a moment on the steps of the place, a concrete structure, some abandoned factory or warehouse, and he tried his cell phone. "No reception," he said after dialing three times and listening. He flipped to a new screen with his thumb and pressed an app icon. The screen became a flashlight. He turned it forward, held it at arm's length, and motioned with his head for Michi to get close behind him. With the gun at the ready, they moved slowly through the doorless entrance.

The place was freezing cold and pitch black. As far as he could tell there were hallways laid out in a square, with small rooms off it to either side.

"An office building in the middle of the woods," she said.

Each room had the remains of a western-style door at its entrance, pieces of shattered wood hanging on by the hinges. When he shone the phone's light into the rooms, he saw a window opening boarded from within by a sheet of plywood, and an otherwise empty concrete expanse. They went down one hall and turned left into another. Michi remembered she had the same app on her phone and lit it. Halfway down that corridor, they found a room whose door was mostly intact but for a corner at the bottom where it appeared to have been kicked in. Riku inspected the knob and whispered, "There's a lock on this one."

They went in and he locked the door behind them and tested its strength. "Get in the corner under the window," he said. "If they find us, and the door won't hold, I can rip off the board above us and we might be able to escape outside." She joined him in the corner and they sat, shoulders touching, their backs against the cold concrete. "We're sure to be safe when the sun rises."

He put his arm around her and she leaned into him. Then neither said a word, nor made a sound. They turned off their phones and listened to the dark. Time passed, yet when Riku checked his watch, it read only 3:30. "All that in a half-hour?" he wondered. Then there came a sound, a light tapping, as if rain was falling outside. The noise slowly grew louder, and seconds later it became clear that it was the sound of claws on the concrete floor. That light tapping eventually became a clatter, as if a hundred of the creatures were circling impatiently in the hallway.

A strange guttural voice came from the hole at the bottom corner of the door. "Tomodachi," it said. "Let us in."

Riku flipped to the flashlight app and held the gun up. Across the room, the hole in the bottom of the door was filled with a fat, pale, bearded face. One eye was swollen shut and something oozed from the corner of it. The forehead was too high to see a hairline. The thing snuffled and smiled.

"Shoot," said Michi.

Riku fired, but the face flinched away in an instant, and once the bullet went wide and drilled a neat hole in the door, the creature returned and said, "Tomodachi."

"What do you want?" said Riku, his voice cracking.

"We are hunting a spirit of the living," said the creature, the movement of its lips out of sync with the words it spoke.

"What have we done?" said Michi.

"Our hunger is great, but we only require one spirit. We only take what we need—the other person will be untouched. One spirit will feed us for a week."

Michi stood up and stepped away from Riku. He also got to his feet. "What are you doing?" she said. "Shoot them." She quickly lit her phone and shone it on him.

Instead of aiming the gun at the door, he aimed it at her. "I'm not having my spirit devoured," he said to her.

"You said you couldn't hurt me."

"It won't be me hurting you," he said. She saw there were tears in his eyes. The hand that held the gun was wobbling. "I'm giving you the girl," he called to the Jinmenken.

"A true benefactor," said the face at the hole.

"No," she said. "What have I done?"

"I'm going to shoot her in the leg so she can't run, then I'm going to let you all in. You will keep your distance from me or I'll shoot. I have an extra clip, and I'll turn as many of you to salt as I can before you get to me."

Turning to Michi, he said, "I'm so sorry. I did love you."

"But you're a coward. You don't have to shoot me in the leg," she said. "I'll go to them on my own. My spirit's tired of this world." She moved forward and gave him a kiss. Her actions disarmed him and he appeared confused. At the door, she slowly undid the lock on the knob. Then, with a graceful, fluid motion, she pulled the door open and stepped behind it against the wall. "Take him," he heard her call. The Jinmenkin bounded in, dozens of them, small and large, stinking of rain, slobbering, snapping, clawing. He pulled the trigger till the gun clicked empty, and the room was filled with smoke and flying salt. His hands shook too much to change the clip. One of the creatures tore a bloody chunk from his left calf and he screamed. Another went for his groin. The face of Grandmother Chinatsu appeared before him and devoured his.

The following week, in a private room at The Limit, Michi sat at a blond-wood table, staring out the open panel across the room at the pines and the coast. Riku's employer sat across from her. "Ingenious, the Natural History of Autumn," he said. "And you knew this would draw him in?"

She turned to face the older man. "He was a unique person," she said. "He'd faced death."

"Too bad about Riku," he said. "I wanted to trust him."

"Really, the lengths to which you'll go to test the spirit of those you need to trust. He's gone because he was a coward?"

"A coward I can tolerate. But he said he loved you, and it proved he didn't understand love at all. A dangerous flaw." He took an envelope from within his suit jacket and laid it on the table. "A job well done," he said. She lifted the envelope and looked inside.

A cold breeze blew into the room. "You know," he said, "this season always reminds me of our time together."

As she spoke she never stopped counting the bills. "All I remember of that," she said, "is the snow."

◂◦▸

MANTIS WIVES

KIJ JOHNSON

"As for the insects, their lives are sustained only by intricate processes of fantastic horror."—John Wyndham.

Eventually, the mantis women discovered that killing their husbands was not inseparable from the getting of young. Before this, a wife devoured her lover piece by piece during the act of coition: the head (and its shining eyes going dim as she ate); the long green prothorax; the forelegs crisp as straws; the bitter wings. She left for last the metathorax and its pumping legs, the abdomen, and finally the phallus. Mantis women needed nutrients for their pregnancies; their lovers offered this as well as their seed.

It was believed that mantis men would resist their deaths if permitted to choose the manner of their mating; but the women learned to turn elsewhere for nutrients after draining their husbands' members, and yet the men lingered. And so their ladies continued to kill them, but slowly, in the fashioning of difficult arts. What else could there be between them?

The Bitter Edge: A wife may cut through her husband's exoskeletal plates, each layer a different pattern, so that to look at a man is to see shining, hard brocade. At the deepest level are visible pieces of his core, the hint of internal parts bleeding out. He may suggest shapes.

The Eccentric Curve of His Thoughts: A wife may drill the tiniest hole into her lover's head and insert a fine hair. She presses carefully, striving for specific results: a seizure, a novel pheromone burst, a dance that ends in self-castration. If she replaces the hair with a wasp's narrow syringing stinger, she may blow air bubbles into his head and then he will react unpredictably. There is otherwise little he may do that will surprise her, or himself.

What is the art of the men, that they remain to die at the hands of their wives? What is the art of the wives, that they kill?

The Strength of Weight: Removing his wings, she leads him into the paths of ants.

Unready Jewels: A mantis wife may walk with her husband across the trunks of pines, until they come to a trail of sap and ascend to an insect-clustered wound. Staying to the side, she presses him down until his legs stick fast. He may grow restless as the sap sheathes his body and wings. His eyes may not dim for some time. Smaller insects may cluster upon his honeyed body like ornaments.

A mantis woman does not know why the men crave death, but she does not ask. Does she fear resistance? Does she hope for it? She has forgotten the ancient reasons for her acts, but in any case her art is more important.

The Oubliette: Or a wife may take not his life but his senses: plucking the antennae from his forehead; scouring with dust his clustered shining eyes; cracking apart his mandibles to scrape out the lining of his mouth and throat; plucking the sensing hairs from his foremost legs; excising the auditory thoracic organ; biting free the wings.

A mantis woman is not cruel. She gives her husband what he seeks. Who knows what poems he fashions in the darkness of a senseless life?

The Scent of Violets: They mate many times, until one dies.

Two Stones Grind Together: A wife collects with her forelegs small brightly colored poisonous insects, places them upon bitter green leaves, and encourages her husband to eat them. He is sometimes reluctant after the first taste but she speaks to him, or else he calms himself and eats.

He may foam at the mouth and anus, or grow paralyzed and fall from a branch. In extreme cases, he may stagger along the ground until he is seen by a bird and swallowed, and then even the bird may die.

A mantis has no veins; what passes for blood flows freely within its protective shell. It does have a heart.

The Desolate Junk-land: Or a mantis wife may lay her husband gently upon a soft bed and bring to him cool drinks and silver dishes filled with sweetmeats. She may offer him crossword puzzles and pornography; may kneel at his feet and tell him stories of mantis men who are heroes; may dance in veils before him.

He tears off his own legs before she begins. It is unclear whether The Desolate Junk-land is her art, or his.

Shame's Uniformity: A wife may return to the First Art and, in a variant, devour her husband, but from the abdomen forward. Of all the arts this is hardest. There is no hair, no ant's bite, no sap, no intervening instrument. He asks her questions until the end. He may doubt her motives, or she may.

The Paper-folder. Lichens' Dance. The Ambition of Aphids. Civil Wars. The Secret History of Cumulus. The Lost Eyes Found. Sedges. The Unbeaked Sparrow.

There are as many arts as there are husbands and wives.

The Cruel Web: Perhaps they wish to love each other, but they cannot see a way to exist that does not involve the barb, the sticking sap, the bitter taste of poison. The Cruel Web can be performed only in the brambles of woods, and only when there has been no recent rain and the spider's webs have grown thick. Wife and husband walk together. Webs catch and cling to their carapaces, their legs, their half-opened wings. They tear free, but the webs collect. Their glowing eyes grow veiled. Their curious antennae come to a tangled halt. Their pheromones become confused; their legs struggle against the gathering web. The spiders wait.

She is larger than he and stronger, but they often fall together.

How to Live: A mantis may dream of something else. This also may be a trap.

-‹o›-

TENDER AS TEETH

STEPHANIE CRAWFORD AND
DUANE SWIERCZYNSKI

"Is it true that the cure made all of you vegetarians?" Carson asked.

Justine was staring at the road ahead, but could see him toying with his digital recorder in her peripheral vision. He was asking a flurry of questions, but at the same time, avoiding The Big Question. She wished he'd just come out with it already.

"Why are you asking me?" she replied. "I'm not the mouthpiece for every single survivor."

Carson stammered a little before Justine glanced over and gave him a wide grin.

"Oh yes, I referred to former zombies as survivors. Make sure to include that. Your readers will love it."

As they drove across the desert the sun was pulling the sky from black to a gritty blue-grey. The rented compact car held a thirty-three-year-old man named Carson with enough expensive camera equipment to crowd up the backseat, and Justine, a woman two years younger, who kept her own small shoulder bag between her feet.

The rest of her baggage was invisible.

◄○►

49

Some said as far as apocalyptic plagues went, it could have been a lot worse.

The dead didn't crawl out of their graves. Society didn't crumble entirely. The infection didn't spread as easily as it did in the movies—you had to either really *try* to get infected, or be genetically predisposed to it.

Justine happened to be one of the latter.

After work one night, Justine was nursing a Pabst at her local generic, suburban sports bar while half-listening to the news about a virus that would probably quiet down like H1N1 and texting her late friend Gina. She was just raising the bottle's mouth to her lips when a thick, dead weight fell against her and knocked her out of her bar stool and onto the sticky, peanut shell covered floor. Too fucking enraged to wait for a good Samaritan to jump up and give a *Hey, Pal*, Justine started blindly kicking out her heels and thrusting out fists at the drunk bastard. That's how it played out until the drunk started gnawing at her fists until his incisors connected with the actual bone of her fingers while his mouth worked to slurp up and swallow the shredded meat of her knuckles.

After that, Justine remembered little until the cure hit her bloodstream.

That had been six months after the attack in the bar. And in the meantime . . .

⭒

Carson tried to look at Justine without full-on *staring* at her. Like much of the time he'd spent with her so far, he was fairly certain he was failing miserably. The miracle vaccine seemed to have left Justine with little more damage than a scarred face, a lean-muscled body that bordered on emaciation, and an entire planet filled with people who actively wanted her dead. That was called "being one of the lucky ones."

Keep her talking, he reminded himself. Carson asked, "I understand your mom paid for the cure?"

Justine kicked the glove compartment while crossing her legs. "Sadly, yes. I guess she meant well."

"Aren't you glad to be alive?"

"If you call this living."

"Better than being dead."

She turned to face him, squinting and twisting her lips into a pout. "Is it?"

Asking questions was the problem, Carson decided. He wasn't a real journalist. He'd only brought the digital recorder to please his editor, who couldn't afford to send both a photographer *and* a reporter.

Just keep her talking as much as possible, the editor had said. *We'll make sense of it later.*

But most important, his editor added, *we want her to talk about what it's like.*

What what *is like?* Carson had asked.

His editor replied: *What it's like to go on living.*

A year ago today he'd been out in Las Vegas for one of the most inane reasons of all: a photo shoot for a celebrity cookbook. The celebrity in question was a borderline morbidly obese actor known for both his comedic roles as well as his darker turns in mob flicks. Right before he'd left on that trip the first outbreaks had been reported, but the virus seemed to be contained to certain parts of the country, and Carson thought he'd come to regret it if he turned down the assignment over the latest health scare. Especially if that would leave him stuck in his Brooklyn apartment for months on end while this thing ran its course. They were saying it could be as bad as the 1918 flu pandemic.

Oh, if he had only known.

The outbreak had happened mid-shoot. A pack of zombies had burst in just as the food stylist had finished with the chicken scarpariello. They weren't interested in the dish. They wanted the celebrity chef instead. Carson kept snapping photos before he quite realized what was happening. He escaped across Vegas, continuing to take photos as the city tore itself apart.

And then he saw Justine, though he didn't know her name then.

Back then, she was just . . .

Carson heard his editor's impatient reminder in his head:

Keep her talking.

Yeah.

Not talking was the reason he'd become a photographer. He preferred to keep the lens between himself and the rest of the world, speaking to subjects only when he absolutely *had* to.

He was struggling to formulate a new inane question when she spoke up.

"Do you remember the exact place?"

Carson nodded.

"So where was it?" Justine asked.

That surprised him. He assumed she would have just . . . known. Maybe not when she was in that state, because the former zombies—the *survivors*—were supposed to have blanked memories. The photo, though . . . surely she had to have seen the photo at some point.

Or did she?

"Outside of Vegas. Almost near Henderson."

"Huh," Justine said. "Makes sense."

"Does it?"

"That's not far from where I used to live. So come on. Where did you . . . um, *encounter* me?"

Carson pulled onto the 5, which would take them out of the Valley and out through the desert. "I'm hoping I'll be able to find it again once we're out there," he said.

"Don't count on it, buddy boy," she said. "My mom tells me they've razed a lot of the old neighborhood. There's even been talk of abandoning Vegas altogether. Clear everyone out, then drop an H-bomb directly on it. Wipe the slate clean."

Carson, still fumbling, heard the question tumble out of his mouth before he could stop himself.

"Have you, um, *seen* the photo?"

◄o►

Justine had woken up in the hospital, still spoiling for a fight. After about a minute her eyes registered that she was in a hospital bed, and she felt her mom squeezing her hand through layers of aching pain and a wooziness that could only be coming from the IV attached to her arm—so she'd assumed. So the bastard actually put her in the hospital?

Justine's first lucid words were spent reassuring her mom, who herself looked like she'd been put through the wringer.

"Hey ma, it's alright . . . you should see the other guy."

That's what she attempted to say, at any rate. It came out sounding more like "ACK-em, aight . . . shouldas . . . other guy." Her voice sounded cracked and enfeebled . . . almost as if her actual esophagus was bruised and coated in grime.

Her mother teared up and went in for the most delicate hug Justine could remember ever having experienced.

"Thank God . . . He finally showed up. Thank God you're back, and thank Him that you don't remember."

It was only then that Justine noticed that the doctors and nurses surrounding her had what could only be taken as unprofessional looks of pure, barely disguised looks of disgust on their faces. All this for a fucking bar fight she didn't even start?

Before Justine could ask what exactly was going on, her mom cupped her palm against her daughter's cheek: Justine couldn't help realizing how hollowed out it felt against her mom's warm hand.

"Sweetie . . . I have a lot I need to tell you. It's not when you think it is, and you're not exactly who you think you are anymore. The world got infected and wormed you worse than anyone. You're going to need to prepare yourself. Just know I love you, always."

And then her mom told her what the world had been up to.

-◦-

Justine stared at the passing power lines with an interest they didn't exactly warrant. "Is this professional curiosity?"

"No," Carson said. "I'd really like to know."

Justine glanced over at Carson, who gave her a tight-lipped smile. She had done her research on him, and she was almost personally insulted by what she found. A small part of her was hoping she'd get a gonzo journalist-type that would end the interview with him trying to hunt her in a "most dangerous game" scenario. Carson was, at best, a mid-level photog—his writing credits adding up to captions under his glossy photos of celebrities she had never heard of. There were a few dashes of pretension, but he was clearly paying the bills.

Except for those unexpected, dramatic moments every photographer lives for. He had a few absorbing shots.

The main one starring her ownself.

"My mom kept it from me for as long as possible. She acted a bit as if seeing it would trigger me, somehow. But . . . eh."

Justine started absently gnawing on a fingernail with more vigor that she realized.

"I'll see little thumbnails on Google and squint my eyes to blur it out. I've been told about it enough that my taste to see the actual money shot has long been sated."

Justine glanced over at Carson to see how that landed. She was sleep deprived and barely knew the guy, but he somehow looked . . . puzzled.

⟨◦⟩

Was she serious? How could she have *not* looked?

Carson knew he'd created that photo by pure accident. Even the framing and lighting and composition were a happy accident—a trifecta of the perfect conditions, snapped at exactly the right moment. He admitted it. He'd lucked into it. He couldn't even claim to have created that photo. He'd merely been the one holding the camera, his index finger twitching. That image wanted to exist; he was simply the conduit.

The photo wasn't his fault, just like her . . . sickness . . . wasn't her fault. They were like two car accident victims, thrown together by chance, and left to deal with the wreckage.

He got all that.

Still . . . how could she *not* want to see? How could you ever hope to recover if you didn't confront it head-on?

"Pull over," she said suddenly.

"Are you okay?"

"Unless you want to clean chunks of puke out of this rental, pull over now. Please."

Carson was temporarily desert-blind. He couldn't tell where the edge of the broken road ended and the dead, dry earth began. Blinking, he slowly edged to the right as Justine's hands fumbled at the door handle. He saw—*felt*—her entire body jolt. He applied the brake, kicking up a huge plume of dust. Justine flew out of the passenger seat even before the car had come to a complete halt. She disappeared into the dust. Within seconds, Carson could hear her heaving.

He knew this was what the Cure did to you. It took away the zombie, but left you a very, very sick person.

Should he get out? Did she maybe want a little water, or her privacy? He didn't know. For a moment, Carson sat behind the wheel, watching the dust settle back down. There were a lot of dust storms out here, he'd read. The Southwest hadn't seen them this bad since the 30s Dust Bowl days. Some people thought it was nature's way of trying to wipe the slate clean, one sharp grain of sand at a time.

All was quiet; she'd stopped heaving.

"Justine?" he called out. "You okay?"

He opened the door just as the truck pulled up behind them. Damnit. Probably a good Samaritan, thinking they needed help.

"Justine?"

Car doors slammed behind Carson. He turned off the ignition, pulled the keys from the steering column, pushed open the door with his foot, stepped out into the hot, dry air. There were three people standing there. Carson was struck at first by how familiar they looked, but couldn't immediately place them. Not until one of them said,

"Where's the babykiller?"

Fuck me, he thought. It was the protesters.

They'd followed them out into the desert.

◄·►

When Carson arrived at Justine's Burbank apartment just a few hours earlier, he was stunned to see them there, carrying placards and pacing up and down the front walkway. They must have been at it all night, and towards the end of some kind of "shift," because they look tired, haggard and vacant eyed. Ironically enough, they kind of looked like you-know-whats.

Carson was equally stunned by the things coming out of their mouths, the sheer hate painted on their signs.

An Abomination Lives Here.

That Baby Had A Future.

Kill Yourself Justine.

Delusional people who had to seize on something, he supposed. There was a whole "Disbelief in the Cure" movement going on now, with a groundswell of people who brought out these pseudo-scientists claiming that the Cure was only temporary, that at any moment, thousands of people could revert to flesh-eating monsters again. There was not a lick of scientific evidence to back this up, mind you. But when has that stopped zealots before?

Carson had parked the car a block away, in the rubble of a lot in front of an old 50s-style motel that had promptly gone out of business a year ago during the chaos. He wiped the sweat from his brow—wasn't California supposed to be cooler this time of year? At first he grabbed his small digital camera and locked everything else in the trunk, figuring that if he tried to run that gauntlet with his full gear there was a strong chance he'd be molested. Carson was prepared for anything, but wasn't in the mood to lose ten grand worth of gear that he *knew* the paper wouldn't replace.

But then again, when the going gets weird, the weird turn pro . . . wasn't that what Hunter S. Thompson said? Carson donned his vest (he hated it, but people associated it with being a pro, so . . .) and walked right up to the nutcases, smiling. That's right, he thought. Just a happy photojournalist on assignment, here to take your picture.

That's the thing: you don't ask. You keep your camera low and just start shooting. Ask, and there's a strong chance they'll think, Hey, wait a minute, maybe I shouldn't agree to this. But if you act like God Himself sent you down here to record the moments for posterity, most people will step out of your way and let you do His Holy Work. Carson snapped away from waist level. Sometimes you want that feeling of looking up from a child's POV, right up into the faces of these lunatics, the sun bouncing from their hand-painted signs. Carson was feeling good about the assignment when something hard slammed into the center of his back and he tumbled forward into someone's fist.

These things happen so fast—your ass getting kicked. In the movies there's always an explanation. Your antagonists go to great pains to tell you exactly *why* you're going to receive a brutal beating right before the beating actually happens. Not in reality. When a mob attacks you, and blood's filling your mouth, and someone's kicking you in the back and you can feel your internal organs convulsing . . . there there are no explanations.

But Carson heard one thing. The most chilling thing he could possibly hear, actually. And that was his name.

They know who I am, he thought. *They know I'm the one who had made Zombie Chick famous.*

Which was when said Zombie Chick saved Carson from hospitalization.

She didn't rush down and start growling at the crowd, asking for brains. She merely opened her window and stared down at them. Carson didn't notice it at first; all he sensed was that the kicks came slower, and then tapered off entirely.

The crowd backed away from Carson and focused on her, up in her window. Cursing at her. Gesturing at her. Spitting. Picking up tiny chunks of broken sidewalk and hurling them at her. Only then did she duck inside and slide the window shut.

Carson wanted to get the hell out of there . . . *pronto*. But then he imagined stepping into his boss's office empty-handed, without a single photo. That simply wasn't an option. Not if he wanted to eat. So he pushed himself, ribs and legs screaming, and took advantage of the temporary distraction, jogging right up through the center of the crowd, pushing his way past them, blasting through the front door of the apartment complex. By the time they noticed, it was too late—Carson had flipped the deadbolt behind him. As he scanned the mailboxes with the call buzzers he could hear them yelling, threatening to kill him for real . . .

Looked like they wanted to make good on that promise now, out here in an empty stretch of desert, with no one to interrupt them.

◄⊙►

Justine looked down at what she evacuated, noting it was pretty much pure water. She started to straighten up but stopped herself when she noticed the long shadows stumble over themselves.

"Shit."

Justine stayed bent over, hands on her knees, mind racing. She could hear muffled angry voices and some half-hearted pounding on a car. She figured it was road warriors, insanely persistent Latter-Day Saints missionaries, or they were being followed by her own personal Raincoat Brigade. Whoever it was, she was going to need a decent-sized rock at the very least, and she needed to look as fucked up as possible. The latter was covered, and her eyes scanned quickly for the former.

Jackpot.

Eyes up. Take it slow.

Most of the brigade (biggest bunch of vultures this desert has ever produced, Justine thought) was standing back from the car, attempting to look casual but barely pulling off "vaguely gassy." There were three men in their mid-forties actually on the car. One was playing the lean-against-the-windshield cop move, with the other two settling for leaning against the side.

Justine crouched in the warm dirt, obscured by a large grouping of banana yucca. If Carson had left the passenger seat unlocked she could probably jump in, he could floor it and ride like hell until they got to a gas station.

Fake cop had just cocked some kind of gun. Seriously? Fuck this. Fuck all of it. She should have never agreed to this interview. She was probably going to be one of those survivors who ended up dead—for real this time—at the hands of a frightened mob.

Unless she could use their fear against them.

Justine stood up, stretched . . . and moaned. Moaned like some kind of unholy undead piece of hell would yawn after centuries of hungry slumber—or whatever these assholes believed.

"There she is!"

"Why didn't anyone see her get out?"

"Weren't you supposed to be watching that patch, Dana?"

"There's the babykiller! I bet they don't prosecute in Nevada and he's smuggling her!"

But the crowd quickly lost interest in Carson and his compact car, and moved en masse towards Justine. Just a yard down was a van with a flat tire facing the road.

Clever dumb bastards, Justine thought. That'll keep the passing cars moving.

"I'd ask if you didn't have anything better to do," Justine called out. "But after watching you all for months out my window I know you don't."

Justine found bravado sometimes worked when the rocks weren't up to snuff.

One of the guys leaning against the car gave a grimace that bordered on a grin at Justine.

"You have served no jail time for killing the most innocent of our Savior's creations. We just want to . . . talk to you about it. Maybe get you to turn yourself in. There's no reason for you to get your bowels in an uproar."

Some of the gang nodded in agreement, others just eyed Justine as if she was about to leap out like a cat in a closet in a bad slasher movie.

Fake Cop kept his fingers moving on the gun that he was holding close to his thigh.

Justine glanced over to the car. Carson was standing there quietly. Now that their little "freak" was front and center, nobody bothered to keep an eye on him. He had his cell phone in his hand. He made eye contact and gave a short nod.

Please, Justine thought. *Don't come to my rescue, photo boy. From the looks of you, you've got the muscle strength of warm butter.*

Moving her eyes back to the group, Justine took a deep breath and tried to make eye contact with as many as possible.

"Look, I really understand. I hate myself too," Justine said. "But I really, truly was not myself when that happened, and believe me they would have found out if I was. I'm cured now and my life is a living hell, so can you just leave me alone to fester it out, please? You guys will just go to jail and I'm really not worth it."

"Maybe we can just shoot 'er here," one of them said.

Another: "Shut up. Just shut up. You weren't even invited here, you dumb psycho."

Fake Cop and the one that had been talking had a tension between them that made Justine more nervous than the pure hatred that was being leveled at her.

The man turned back to her.

"I'm sorry, this was stupid. My name is Mike. How about you let your friend leave, and you come with us and we can talk to my brother—he's a police officer—and we can get you right. . . ."

Mike stopped himself. Justine could see that he had just spotted the phone in Carson's hand.

"Well shit, son," Mike said. "I really wish you hadn't done that."

Justine, strangely enough, wished the same thing.

◄•►

For an awful moment there, Carson thought that Justine's "cure" hadn't fully taken.

His fevered imagination put together the sequence of events this way: *She's riding along, in the sun, next to a living human being. She doesn't get out much. She's not around people much. Something in her breaks down.*

She senses the flesh, the blood beating through his veins. It's all too much. It makes her sick. She thinks she has to puke. She asks him to pull over and she scrambles from the car when it hits her. She can't help it, can't control it. Suddenly she's acting like a zombie again. . . .

Because suddenly, she *was*.

A zombie again.

Forcing this unholy sound out of her throat, clawing at invisible enemies, eyes rolling up in the back of her head . . .

The protest mob jolted, taking a step away from each other, as if collectively hoping the crazy baby-killing zombie bitch would attack the person standing next to them. Carson jolted, too, from the shock of it, but also the thought that just a few minutes ago, he'd been inside a speeding car with this woman. *Thing.*

He instantly regretted that it was a cell phone in his hand and not his camera, which was still packed up in the backseat. He hated himself for even thinking it, but . . . c'mon! The impact of a photo like that would be seismic. Proof that the cure doesn't work! As shown by its most infamous poster child. . . .

But those fantasies were dashed the moment he heard Justine scream, in perfect English:

"Carson—the car—NOW!"

◦

The best Justine could hope for was not getting shot.

She dove into the crowd and just started shoving. There was no telling how many other guns were hiding in this group, but she was counting on the stark raving fear factor and element of surprise to keep the men from using them. For a few seconds at least. Until fucking Carson got the car revved up. . . .

"Carson, goddamnit!'

She couldn't keep herself from picturing how, if Carson wasn't here, she'd probably just have gone for it. Her anger and annoyance were burning so hot that she could easier have chosen this day as her last—as long as she took these assholes out along with her.

Baby-Eating Zombie Desert Rampage; 8 Dead!

Justine smiled at the imagined headline; she should have been the journalist.

But no, Justine felt oddly protective towards Carson. He wasn't much, but right at this moment he was the only one listening. One last blind elbow to what felt like a butt, and Justine scrammed it to the passenger door.

"GO GO GO!" she screamed at Carson as she locked her door, screaming in laughter as Carson fishtailed it out of there with white knuckles. "All we need is some banjo chase music, compadre!"

Once they'd cleared the first quarter mile, Justine patted the shoulder of the poor, shaking Carson.

"The fuck," Carson sputtered. "The fuck was that?"

"The usual," Justine said.

"Are you okay? I mean . . . shit, did they . . ."

Justine looked behind them, seeing only a random semi-truck. "I'm fine. Actually, no. I'm not fine. I'm hungry. *Starving* even."

Carson looked at her, wide-eyed. Justine noticed the stare also contained a bit of apprehension. "What?"

"And in an answer to your earlier question," she said, "no. I'm not a vegetarian."

-<o>-

Justine had Carson stop at a roadside barbecue joint a handful of miles outside Barstow. She assured him it was the best obscure, outdoor barbecue you could get in the southwest, not to mention that she was pretty sure the owner was a Hell's Angel and therefore coated the area with a kind of grimy aura of protection.

Carson sat at a picnic table while Justine ordered them two orders of the works. She had put on a pair of large-framed glasses and affected an uneven Texan drawl, claiming it was a disguise while Carson suspected it was mostly to amuse herself.

Roughly half an hour had passed since they were accosted, but in that short span of time Justine had seemed to come alive. Bouncing in her seat, looking behind them in her sun visor's mirror and squeezing his shoulder every few minutes—she was as enthusiastic as he imagined she might have been on a regular road trip in her life before infection had made her somber and shifty-eyed. Her skin also seemed to take on what he could only describe as a glow, and her stone grey eyes seemed to skew closer to silver.

"How much for one rib?"

Carson sat up straight and turned to see Justine laughing with the barbecue proprietor before shaking her head and walking to their table. She smiled at him before laying down a stack of white sandwich bread and two Styrofoam boxes in front of him.

"Is everything ok? Did you need more money?" Carson asked while he peeked under one of the lids.

"What? Are you not familiar with the comedic stylings of Chris Rock?" Justine was still putting on her weird drawl, which was toeing the line between cute and unsettling pretty aggressively. "*I'm Gonna Git You Sucka?* No? Boy, we need to hook you up with a movie marathon."

Justine took the bench across from Carson, popped open her lid, and proceeded to stare at the meat. The only motion she made was to follow in the tradition of countless customers before her in leisurely picking at the peeling red paint of the table with a fingernail. Carson couldn't help indulging himself in a mouthful of brisket before asking her if everything was okay.

Justine sighed.

"No. Sure. Everything is fine. This is the first time I had even the desire to eat meat since you-know-what, let alone actually ate the stuff. Before that I was a stone cold carnivore."

She never took her eyes off her meal, but had worked up to poking it around with her spork.

Carson raised his eyebrows and took a long sip of his lukewarm Mountain Dew. He became aware of a weird undercurrent that had seemed to sit itself at their table, but couldn't place it.

Justine stabbed at a piece of pork until the weak teeth of the spork finally speared it enough to lift. He eyed the meat and her mouth, wishing he had his camera out. She caught him staring. He flashed her a quick, reassuring half smile when their eyes met. Justine saluted him with her spork full of pork, and took it in one bite.

She chewed. Carson took another mouthful of his meal in camaraderie. He waited until they both swallowed and took sips of their respective drinks before asking her how it was.

"Tastes good, but just that one bite already made my jaw ache."

"Does eating hurt?"

"Aren't you forward? But no; the little I eat just sits with me funny and makes my tongue feel coated in something like wax. I probably brush my teeth about 10 times a day. I don't care enough about my check-ups with the therapist or doctor to find out if it's mostly in my head or if human veal just forever fucked up my stomach."

Carson coughed in surprise, choking a bit as Justine's words hit him. She gave him a sad shrug and continued eating the meat.

"This is good though. No coated-tongue feeling, either."

"Maybe you just needed time. Just try to take it slow."

Carson took out his camera, nodded as if to ask, Is this okay? Justine paused for a moment before nodding in return. He snapped a few photos of her eating with the large, faded MOOSE's BBQ sign behind her.

Suddenly he noticed a man moving at a leaden pace a few feet behind Justine. Carson lowered his camera. The man was gaunt, with gnarled hands reminiscent of arthritic joints and old tree branches. He worked his mouth around hungrily; almost like an infant eyeing a nipple just out of reach. Only when he noticed the old, slow-shambling man pull out a Black & Mild cigar and chomp it between his grinning teeth did he relax.

"I'll be right back," Justine said, and put a hand on his shoulder as she passed. Carson thought she might be feeling sick again, but when he glanced across the way a few minutes later he saw that she was on her cell phone.

-◦-

They rode in mostly companionable silence for about ninety more minutes, until the suburban sprawl of Henderson appeared. Carson felt a thrumming work its way up his spine, plucking at his nerves until his skin physically itched. Here was the moment he'd been dreading: setting up a shot where you ask someone to hunker down in a place where they'd experienced the darkest moment of their life.

"You, uh, feeling okay?" Carson asked.

Justine rustled a bit in her seat, looking tiny and weird from the corner of Carson's eye.

"Yeah. Was worried about all that food I ate, but it's staying down."

Carson cleared his throat, and Justine hurried over the sound. "I know that's not what you're asking about, but I'm putting off any reaction to this as long as I can. Is that okay with you?"

Carson nodded as he squeezed his hands tighter around the wheel. Justine crammed some more gum into her mouth. She had told him that with her stomach working with rarely any food in it had given her "death breath." He hadn't noticed any of it personally, but when she also divulged how often and obsessively she brushed her teeth, he understood that the situation went a little deeper than oral hygiene.

Carson fumbled at the radio dials until he heard Sam Cooke's voice. He told himself to stop feeling guilty. Everyone in this car was there by choice, right? Of course they were.

Except they really weren't.

Carson had been there by chance.

Justine had been there because of a fluke of a disease. She didn't know what she was doing, where she'd gone, who she'd hurt.

And it was only because Carson happened to be there, with his camera, that Justine—and the rest of the world—knew that while she'd been a zombie, she had eaten an infant child.

◄◦►

The area had been cleaned up more than Carson expected. Imported palm trees stood perfectly distanced from each other, as pretty and welcoming as well-trained showgirls. As they pulled into the parking lot of the grocery store, his memory replaced the newly built structures with the way he remembered the place looking the last time he was here—a looted out, broken shell of a place crawling with cops, zombies and "reporters" like himself. There was a rumor that the area was harboring a building full of people who had taken over a grocery store after raiding a gun store, but the virus had gotten in there with them. Carson had been unable to confirm any of this at the time. He was mostly walking around in the area in a horrified daze, snapping photos to give himself a sense of purpose in all of the chaos.

"So, where were you?" Justine asked.

Carson shook himself mentally into the present. "I was walking around the barricades at the back of the lot. I guess luckily nobody was paying much attention to me. My editor just told me to snap anything interesting or fucked up that might pop out."

Justine turned to him. "And then out I popped, all interesting and fucked up with bells on?"

Carson tried to smile. "Yeah."

Justine laughed in surprise but it quickly died in her throat.

They slowly pulled themselves out of the car, groaning and stretching as they squinted into the sun. A nervous and false jovial energy permeated the air between them, as if they decided by an unspoken vote to act as if they were here to recreate a photo from a first date rather than an amnesiac murder.

Justine wandered the half-full parking lot while Carson started gathering and preparing his gear. Once he was fully kitted up he inhaled deeply and started towards her.

Keeping her back to him, she said, "I thought maybe standing here there'd be . . . something. A fragment of memory. But no."

"In all honesty it's almost hard to remember it happening myself. It happened so quickly and there was so much chaos . . ."

"Did anyone try to stop me? Did you?"

Carson stopped fidgeting before answering.

"Stop? I mean . . . the cops tackled you. The thing is, I think the baby was already dead. I didn't hear crying."

"How did I get it?"

"Uh . . ." Carson wished for a cigarette more than he had wished for anything else in the entirety of his life. "There was a huge crush of people running out of the shopping center when the police smoked them out. They think the baby was inside, and got . . . trampled. There was a broken stroller nearby."

It was, in fact, in the photograph.

He heard Justine exhale shakily.

"Fuck me, fuck you, and fuck this. What's the point of us being here? I'd want me dead, too. Let's just get this done so I can crawl back to my hole."

Carson silently worked his mouth open and closed, platitudes at the ready on his tongue. They didn't want to come out, though; every fiber of his being fully agreed with her that being here was wrong. In for a penny, in for a pound, though. The texts he had been getting from his editor were becoming increasingly insistent.

"Yeah, alright."

The photojournalist considered the parking lot around them, trying to avoid looking at the photo again on his iPhone and going solely by memory.

"The pile of rubble . . . I'm pretty sure it was over there."

He pointed at a grouping of empty parking spaces, completely indistinguishable from any other in the world. Apparently not everything required a plaque.

They made their way over, the cloud of unease silencing them. Everything was so generic and bright around them that it the entire assignment the feel of some kind of ill-planned playacting. The only piece of reality that didn't seem a part of their make-believe was a small murder of crows nearby that were effectively edging any pigeons out of their territory.

It seemed easier to just mumble and gesture the whole thing. In the back of his mind Carson supposed he had hoped returning here might summon up at least an emotional memory for Justine, but it was clear that whatever breakthrough he had been hoping for was doomed to die the quiet death of simply going through the motions.

Carson pointed and shot, getting the majority of his pictures framing Justine in front of the rapidly setting sun. She crouched, stood and even sat in a few, looking pensive and disconnected in each one. The stark contrast of a traumatized woman in a new parking lot made the whole thing feel a dust-in-the-blood kind of dirty to Carson. The look in her eyes, though . . .

"Alright, I think we got it. We can go."

She didn't move.

"What's wrong?" Carson asked.

"Aren't you going to ask me?"

"Ask you what?"

"All this time together, and you're too timid to ask the question. I know you want to ask. It's been all over your face since we met."

Carson opened his mouth, then closed it and shook his head.

"Go ahead," Justine said, hands on her hips. "Ask me, how can I possibly go on living after something like that? How can I make jokes and drop stupid pop culture references and eat ribs and laugh and listen to music? Isn't that what you want to know? Isn't that what you've been dying to ask me this whole time?"

Carson didn't know how to respond, mainly because she was dead right. It was the question he'd wanted to ask ever since he'd heard the news a month ago that the Famous Baby Eater—the subject of a photo that had won him fame he didn't want and acclaim he didn't deserve—was still alive.

How *do* you go on living after something like that?

Justine sighed and walked past him, muttering: "Let's get to a hotel with a bar."

-◦-

"Thanks for being less of a dick about this than I thought you'd be," she said.

They were sitting at the bar in some sports-themed joint on the ground floor of a chain hotel on the edge of Henderson, knees almost touching. Carson stared into his beer, already thinking about the new set of photos he'd just made. Wondering if it was going to do more harm than good. Of course he'd sold it to Justine as a way to show the world that she wasn't a monster, that the Cure *did* work. But now he wasn't so sure.

Justine laid her hand over his and gave a gentle squeeze. Her other hand fiddled with her cell phone on the bar top.

"Hey."

Carson met her gaze. Said nothing. What could he say? That he was about to ruin her life all over again?

The photo of Justine eating ribs alone . . . ugh. She had no idea what she'd agreed to.

"Look, I'm serious," Justine said. "You've been good to me, despite everything. Which is why I feel bad about doing this."

"Doing what?"

Without warning she leaned forward and pressed her lips to his.

To a passerby it would have looked like a couple doing a parody of a cover of a historical romance novel, except with the man in the submissive stance. Right in the thick of it, however, was a demented sincerity. Justine used her tongue to pry open his lips. What the hell was she doing?

Justine didn't have "death breath." He could taste peppermint and beer; her lips were warm. But still, all he could think about was where her lips had been, and about the chunks of flesh her tongue had once licked away from her teeth . . .

Before he could break the embrace he heard the sound of a fake camera shutter snapping closed.

Oh God, Carson thought as his eye popped open and saw the cell in her hand. *She's taken a photo of her own.*

"Wait," he said. "Please . . ."

But Justine's fingers were already working the keypad, and the photo was already on its way to a wireless cell tower, and from there... who knew? She glanced up at him.

"Sorry, I grabbed your boss's number when you left your cell alone at the BBQ place. He's just one, though. I guess I could have sold this as an exclusive, but that felt a little tacky."

Carson pulled back from the table and just stared. His eyes felt feverish as they flitted from Justine's face to the phone, to the staring bar patrons surrounding them.

"You want to know what it was like, to have your worst moment broadcast to the world?" Justine asked. "Buddy, you're about to find out."

She smiled, and reached back to hold his shaking hand. "But at least we have each other, right?"

◄◦►

THE CALLERS

RAMSEY CAMPBELL

Mark's grandmother seems barely to have left the house when his grandfather says "Can you entertain yourself for a bit? I could do with going to the pub while I've got the chance."

Mark wonders how much they think they've entertained him, but he only says "Will grandma be all right coming home on her own?"

"Never fret, son. They can look after theirselves." The old man's hairy caterpillar eyebrows squirm as he frowns at Mark and blinks his bleary eyes clear. "No call for you to fetch her. It's women's stuff, the bingo." He gives the boy's shoulder an unsteady squeeze and mutters "You're a good sort to have around."

Mark feels awkward and a little guilty that he's glad he doesn't have to meet his grandmother. "Maybe I'll go to a film."

"You'd better have a key, then." His grandfather rummages among the contents of a drawer of the shaky sideboard—documents in ragged envelopes, rubber bands so desiccated they snap when he takes hold of them, a balding reel of cotton, a crumpled folder stuffed with photographs—and hauls out a key on a frayed noose of string. "Keep hold of that for next time you come," he says.

Does he mean Mark will be visiting by himself in future? Was last night's argument so serious? His mother objected when his grandfather offered him a glass of wine at dinner, and then her mother accused her of not letting Mark grow up. Before long the women were shouting at each other about how Mark's grandmother had brought up her daughter, and the men only aggravated the conflict by trying to calm it down. It continued after Mark went to bed, and this morning his father informed him that he and Mark's mother were going home several days early. "You can stay if you like," she told Mark.

Was she testing his loyalty or hoping he would make up for her behaviour? While her face kept her thoughts to itself his father handed him the ticket for the train home like a business card, one man to another. Mark's mother spent some time in listing ways he shouldn't let anyone down, but these didn't include going to the cinema. Wearing his coat was among the requirements, and so he takes it from the stand in the hall. "Step out, lad," his grandfather says as Mark lingers on the pavement directly outside the front door. "You don't want an old crock slowing you down."

At the corner of the street Mark glances back. The old man is limping after him, resting a hand on the roof of each car parked with two wheels on the pavement. Another narrow similarly terraced street leads into the centre of the small Lancashire town, where lamps on scalloped iron poles are stuttering alight beneath a congested late April sky. Many of the shops are shuttered, and some are boarded up. Just a few couples stroll past deserted pristine kitchens and uninhabited items of attire. Most of the local amusements have grown too childish for Mark, though he might still enjoy bowling or a game of indoor golf if he weren't by himself, and others are years out of bounds—the pubs, the clubs waiting for the night crowds while doormen loiter outside like wrestlers dressed for someone's funeral. Surely the cinema won't be so particular about its customers. More than one of Mark's schoolmates has shown him the scene from *Facecream* on their phones, where the girl gets cream squirted all over her face.

As he hurries past the clubs he thinks a doorman is shouting behind him, but the large voice is down a side street full of shops that are nailed shut. At first he fancies that it's chanting inside one of them, and then he sees an old theatre at the far end. While he can't distinguish the words, the rhythm makes it clear he's hearing a bingo caller. Mark could imagine that all the blank-faced doormen are determined to ignore the voice.

The Frugoplex is beyond the clubs, across a car park for at least ten times as many vehicles as it presently contains. The lobby is scattered with popcorn, handfuls of which have been trodden into the purple carpet. A puce rope on metal stilts leads the queue for tickets back and forth and twice again on the way to the counter. When Mark starts to duck under the rope closest to the end of the queue, a man behind the counter scowls at him, and so he follows the rope all the way around, only just heading off two couples of about his own age who stoop under. He's hoping to avoid the disgruntled man, but the queue brings Mark to him. "*Facecream*, please," Mark says and holds out a ten-pound note.

"Don't try it on with me, laddie," the man says and turns his glare on the teenagers who have trailed Mark to the counter. "And your friends needn't either."

"He's not our friend," one of the boys protests.

"I reckon not when he's got you barred."

Mark's face has grown hot, but he can't just walk away or ask to see a film he's allowed to watch. "I don't know about them, but I'm fifteen."

"And I'm your sweet old granny. That's it now for the lot of you. Don't bother coming to my cinema." The manager tells his staff at the counter "Have a good look at this lot so you'll know them."

Mark stumbles almost blindly out of the multiplex. He's starting across the car park when somebody mutters behind him "He wants his head kicked in."

They're only words, but they express his feelings. "That's what he deserves," Mark agrees and turns to his new friends.

It's immediately clear that they weren't thinking of the manager. "You got us barred," says the girl who didn't speak.

"I didn't mean to. You oughtn't to have stood so close."

"Doesn't matter what you meant," she says, and the other girl adds "We'll be standing a lot closer. Standing on your head."

Mark can't take refuge in the cinema, but running would look shameful and invite pursuit as well. Instead he tramps at speed across the car park. His shadow lurches ahead, growing paler as it stretches, and before long it has company, jerking forward to catch up on either side of him. He still stops short of bolting but strides faster. He's hoping passers-by will notice his predicament, but either they aren't interested or they're determined not to be. At last he reaches the nightclubs, and is opening his mouth to appeal to the nearest doorman when the fellow says "Keep walking, lad."

"They're after me."

The doorman barely glances beyond Mark, and his face stays blank. "Walk on."

It could be advice, though it sounds like a dismissal. It leaves Mark feeling that he has been identified as an outsider, and he thinks the doormen's impassive faces are warning him not to loiter. He would make for the police station if he knew where it is. He mustn't go to his grandparents' house in case they become scapegoats as well, and there's just one sanctuary he can think of. He dodges into the side street towards the bingo hall.

The street looks decades older than the main road and as though it has been forgotten for at least that long. Three streetlamps illuminate the cracked roadway bordered by grids that are clogged with old leaves. The glow is too dim to penetrate the gaps between the boards that have boxed up the shopfronts, because the lanterns are draped with grey cobwebs laden with drained insects. The only sign of life apart from a rush of footsteps behind Mark is the amplified voice, still delivering its blurred chant. It might almost be calling out to him, and he breaks into a run.

So do his pursuers, and he's afraid that the bingo hall may be locked against intruders. Beyond the grubby glass of three pairs of doors the foyer is deserted; nobody is in the ticket booth or behind the refreshment counter. His pursuers hesitate as he sprints to the nearest pair of doors, but when neither door budges, the gang closes in on him. He nearly trips on the uneven marble steps as he stumbles along them. He throws all his weight, such as it is, against the next set of doors, which give so readily that he almost sprawls on the threadbare carpet of the foyer.

The caller seems to raise his voice to greet him. "Sixty-three," he's announcing, "just like me." The pursuers glare at Mark from the foot of the shallow steps. "You can't stay in there," one girl advises him, and the other shouts "Better not try."

All the gang look determined to wait for him. If they don't tire of it by the time the bingo players go home, surely they won't dare to let themselves be identified, and so Mark shuts the doors and crosses the foyer. The entrance to the auditorium is flanked by old theatrical posters, more than one of which depicts a plump comedian with a sly schoolboyish face. Mark could imagine they're sharing a joke about him as he pushes open the doors to the auditorium.

The theatre seats have been cleared out, but the stage remains. It faces a couple of dozen tables, most of which are surrounded by women with score cards in front of them and stumpy pencils in their hands. The stage is occupied by a massive lectern bearing a large transparent globe full of numbered balls. Mark might fancy that he knows why the posters looked secretly amused, because the man in them is behind the lectern. He looks decades older, and the weight of his face has tugged it piebald as well as out of shape, but his grin hasn't entirely lost its mischief, however worn it seems. Presumably his oversized suit and baggy shirt are meant to appear comical rather than to suggest a youngster wearing cast-off clothes. He examines a ball before returning it to the globe, which he spins on its pivot. "Three and three," he says as his eyes gleam blearily at Mark. "What do you see?" he adds, and all the women eye the newcomer.

At first Mark can't see his grandmother. He's distracted by a lanky angular woman who extends her speckled arms across the table nearest to him. "Lost your mammy, son?" she cries. "There's plenty here to tend to you."

For an uneasy moment he thinks she has reached for her breast to indicate how motherly she is, but she's adjusting her dress, her eagerness to welcome him having exposed a mound of wrinkled flesh. Before he can think of an answer his grandmother calls "What are you doing here, Mark?"

She's at a table close to the stage. He doesn't want to make her nervous for him if there's no need, and he's ashamed of having run away. The uncarpeted floorboards amplify every step he takes, so that he feels as if he's trying to sound bigger than he is. All the women and the bingo caller watch his progress, and he wonders if everybody hears him mutter "I went to the cinema but they wouldn't let me see the film."

As his grandmother makes to speak one of her three companions leans forward, flattening her forearms on the table to twice their width. "However old are you, son?"

"Mark's thirteen," says his grandmother.

Another of her friends nods vigorously, which she has been doing ever since Mark caught sight of her. "Thirteen," she announces, and many of the women coo or hoot with enthusiasm.

"Looks old enough to me," says the third of his grandmother's table-mates, who is sporting more of a moustache than Mark has achieved. "Enough of a man."

"Well, we've shown you off now," Mark's grandmother tells him. "I'll see you back at home."

This provokes groans throughout the auditorium. The woman who asked his age raises her hands, and her forearms sag towards the elbows. "Don't keep him to yourself, Lottie."

The nodding woman darts to grab a chair for him. "You make this the lucky table, Mark."

He's disconcerted to observe how frail his grandmother is by comparison with her friends, though they're at least as old as she is. The bingo caller gives him a crooked grin and shouts "Glad to have another feller here. Safety in numbers, lad."

Presumably this is a joke of some kind, since quite a few women giggle. Mark's grandmother doesn't, but says "Can he have a card?"

This prompts another kind of laughter, and the nodding woman even manages to shake her head. "It's the women's game, lad," the caller says. "Are you ladies ready to play?"

"More than ever," the moustached woman shouts, which seems some-how to antagonise Mark's grandmother. "Sit down if you're going to," she says. "Stop drawing attention to yourself."

He could retort that she has just done that to him. He's unable to hide his blazing face as he crouches on the spindly chair while the bingo caller elevates the next ball from the dispenser. "Eighty-seven," he reads out. "Close to heaven."

The phrase earns mirth and other noises of appreciation as the women duck in unison to their cards. They chortle or grunt if they find the number, grimacing if they fail. Nobody at Mark's table has located it when the man at the lectern calls "Number forty, old and naughty."

"That's us and no mistake," the moustached woman screeches before whooping at the number on her card.

"Number six, up to tricks."

"That's us as well," her friend cries, but all her nodding doesn't earn her the number.

"Forty-nine, you'll be fine."

The third woman crosses out the number, and flesh cascades down her arm as she lifts the pencil. "He's that with bells on," she says, favouring Mark with a wink.

He has to respond, though the smile feels as if his swollen lips are tugging at his hot stiff face. "Three and twenty," the man at the lectern intones. "There'll be plenty." Mark's grandmother hunches over the table. He could think she's trying to evade the phrase or the coos of delight it elicits from the rest of the players, but she's marking the number on her card. She seems anxious to win, staying bent close to the card as the bingo caller consults the next ball. "Six and thirty," he says, and a roguish grin twists the left side of his mouth. "Let's get dirty."

He pokes at the grin with a finger as if he wants to push the words back in, although they've raised appreciative squeals throughout the auditorium. The fleshy woman falls to her card so eagerly that every visible part of her wobbles. "That'll do me," she cries.

Presumably she means his suggestion, since she hasn't completed her card. Mark sees his grandmother glance nervously at it and then stare at her own as though striving to conjure up a number. "Four and four," the caller says and almost at once "There's the door."

The moustached woman rubs her upper lip so hard that Mark fancies he hears the hairs crackle. "Never mind that," she tells the caller.

He blinks at her and stares around the hall. Mark feels more out of place than ever, as though he's listening to jokes too old for him—beyond his comprehension, at any rate. The caller's drooping face grows defiant as he identifies the next ball. "Ninety-five," he says. "Leave alive."

This brings no laughter, just a murmur that falls short of words. At least Mark's grandmother has found the number on her card. She needs three more to win, and he's surprised by how much he hopes she will. He puts the wish into his eyes as he gazes up at the stage. "Number fifty," the caller says in a tone that seems almost as mechanical as the dispenser. "He'll be nifty."

"Aye," several women respond, and the quivering woman gives Mark another wink.

"Eighty-one, nearly done."

"That's me," the nodding woman agrees, bowing to her card as if the motion of her head has overtaken the rest of her.

Perhaps she means her age, since the irregular cross she makes doesn't finish off the card. "Twenty-nine," the caller says, keeping his eyes on the ball he's raised between the fingertips of both hands. "See the sign."

If the players do so, they keep quiet about it, not even greeting the number or bemoaning their luck. The caller displays the next ball like a magician and puts a finger to the edge of a grin that's meant to appear mysterious. "Sixty-three," he says. "Time to flee."

The murmur this provokes is unamused, and he concentrates on the ball that rolls out of the dispenser. "Twenty-four," he says. "Can't do more."

His gaze is drifting towards Mark when the fleshy woman emits a shriek that jabs deep into the boy's ears. "We're done," she cries. "It's mine."

The caller shuts the globe and extends a hand. "Give us a look."

As she mounts the steps to the stage a series of tremors passes through her body, starting at her veinous legs. Having checked her numbers against those that came up, the caller says "We've a winner."

She snatches the card and plods back to the table, where Mark sees how the crosses resemble sketches of gravestones, at least until she turns the card the right way up. She lowers herself onto her creaking chair and says "I claim the special."

The caller doesn't look at her or anywhere near her. "It's not time yet," he tells whoever needs to hear.

While he leans on the lectern to say so he puts Mark in mind of a priest in a pulpit, though the comparison seems wrong in some way Mark doesn't understand. He's distracted by his grandmother, who lays down her pencil next to the card scattered with the kind of crosses all the women have been drawing. "I'll do without my luck tonight," she says and grasps his arm to help her stand up. "Time someone was at home."

"Don't be like that," the fleshy woman says. "You can't just go running off."

"I won't be running anywhere." As Mark wonders whether that's defiance or the painful truth his grandmother says "I'll see you all another night."

"See us now and see yourself." The speaker nods so violently that her words grow jagged. "You're still one of us."

"I'm not arguing," Mark's grandmother says and grips his arm harder. "Come along now, Mark."

He doesn't know how many women murmur as she turns towards the exit. While he can't make out their words, they sound unhappy if not worse, and all of them are closer than the exit. Nobody moves as long as he can see them, and he finds he would rather not look back. His grandmother has almost led him out, clutching his arm so tightly that it throbs, when the lanky woman who first greeted him plants a hand on her breast again. Though she could be expressing emotion, Mark has the unwelcome fancy that she's about to bare the wizened breast to him. His grandmother hurries him past, and the doors to the foyer are lumbering shut behind them when a woman says "We aren't done."

Mark hopes she's addressing the man on the stage—urging him to start the next game—but he hasn't heard the caller by the time he and his grandmother emerge onto the steps. The street is deserted, and he suspects that the couples who followed him from the cinema are long gone. Outside the clubs the doormen keep their faces blank at the sight of him and his escort, who is leaning on him as much as leading him. She's quiet until they reach the shops, where she mutters "I wish you hadn't gone there tonight, Mark. We're meant to be responsible for you."

He feels guiltier than he understands. She says nothing more while they make their increasingly slow way home. She's about to ring the doorbell with her free hand when Mark produces the key. "Isn't he in?" she protests.

"He went to the pub."

"Men," she says so fiercely that Mark feels sentenced too. She slams the door by tottering against it and says "I think you should be in your bed."

He could object that it isn't his bedtime—that he doesn't know what offence he's committed—but perhaps he isn't being punished, in which case he isn't sure he wants to learn her reason for sending him to his room. He trudges up the narrow boxed-in stairs to the decidedly compact bathroom, where every item seems too close to him, not least the speckled mirror that frames his uneasy face. The toothpaste tastes harsher than usual, and he does his best to stay inaudible while spitting it into the sink. As he dodges into the smaller of the two front bedrooms he sees his grandmother sitting at the bottom of the stairs. He retreats under the quilt of the single bed against the wall beneath the meagre window and listens for his grandfather.

He doesn't know how long he has kept his eyes shut by the time he hears the front door open below him. His grandmother starts to talk at once, and he strains to catch her words. "Did you send Mark to fetch me tonight?"

"I told him to stay clear," Mark's grandfather says not quite as low. "What did he see?"

"It isn't what he saw, it's what they did."

"Are you still up to that old stuff? Makes you all feel powerful, does it?"

"I'll tell you one thing, Len—you don't any more." Just as righteously she says "I don't remember you crying about it too much when it was your turn."

"Well, it's not now."

"It shouldn't be our house at all." This sounds accusing, especially when she adds "If there's any talking to be done you can do it."

Apparently that's all. Mark hears his grandparents labour up the stairs and take turns to make various noises in the bathroom that remind him how old they are. He finds himself wondering almost at random whether they'll take him to the celebrations tomorrow on the town green; they have on other May Days. The prospect feels like a reward if not a compensation for some task. The door of the other front bedroom shuts, and he hears a series of creaks that mean his grandparents have taken to their bed.

For a while the night is almost quiet enough to let him drift into sleep, except that he feels as if the entire house is alert. He's close to dozing when he hears a distant commotion. At first he thinks a doorman outside a club is shouting at someone, perhaps a bunch of drunks, since several people respond. There's something odd about the voice and the responses too. Mark lifts his head from the lumpy pillow and strives to identify what he's hearing, and then he realises his efforts are unnecessary. The voice and its companions are approaching through the town.

Mark does his best to think he's misinterpreting what he hears. The voices sound uncomfortably close by the time he can't mistake them. "Seventy-four," the leader calls, and the ragged chorus answers "Knock on his door." Mark is additionally disconcerted by recognising that the caller isn't the man who was on the stage. However large and resonant it is, it's a woman's voice.

"Number ten," it calls, and the chant responds "Find the men." The chorus is nearly in unison now, and the performance puts Mark in mind of a priest and a congregation—some kind of ritual, at any rate. He kicks the quilt away and kneels on the yielding mattress to scrag the curtain and peer through the window. Even when he presses his cheek against the cold glass, all of the street that he can see is deserted. His breath swells up on the pane and shrinks as the first voice cries "Sweet thirteen" and the rest chant "While he's green."

They sound surer of themselves with every utterance, and they aren't all that troubles Mark. Although he knows that the houses opposite are occupied, every window is dark and not a single curtain stirs. Is everyone afraid to look? Why are his grandparents silent? For a few of Mark's breaths the nocturnal voices are too, but he can hear a muffled shuffling—the noise of a determined march. Then the caller announces "Pair of fives," and as her followers chant "We're the wives" the procession appears at the end of the road.

It's led by the fleshy woman. As she advances up the middle of the street she's followed by her moustached friend and the nodding one, and then their fellow players limp or trot or hobble in pairs around the corner. The orange glow of the streetlamp lends them a rusty tinge like an unnatural tan. Mark doesn't need to count them to be certain that the parade includes everybody from the bingo hall except the man who was onstage and Mark's grandmother. As his grip on the windowsill bruises his fingers the fleshy woman declares "Ninety-eight."

She has a handful of bingo cards and is reading out the numbers. "We're his fate," the procession declares with enthusiasm, and Mark sees eyes glitter, not only with the streetlight. The moustached woman wipes her upper lip with a finger and thumb while her partner in the procession nods so eagerly that she looks in danger of succumbing to a fit. "Eighty-nine," their leader intones as if she's reading from a missal, and the parade almost as long as the street chants "He'll be mine."

They're close enough for Mark to see the fleshy woman join in the response. He sees her quivering from head to foot with every step she takes towards him, and then his attention is caught by the lanky woman in the middle of the procession. She's by no means alone in fumbling at a breast as though she's impatient to give it the air. That's among the reasons why Mark lets go of the curtain and the windowsill to huddle under the quilt. Once upon a time he might have believed this would hide him, but it doesn't even shut out the voices below the window. "Twenty-four," the caller shouts and joins in the chant of "Here's the door."

This is entirely too accurate for Mark's liking. It's the number of the house. As he hugs his knees with his clasped arms and grinds his spine against the wall he hears a muffled rumble close to him. Someone has opened the window of the next bedroom. Mark holds his breath until his grandfather shouts "Not here. Like Lottie says, you've been here once."

"That was a long time ago, Len." Mark can't tell whether this is reminiscent or dismissive, but the tone doesn't quite leave the fleshy woman's voice as she said "It's either you or him."

After a pause the window rumbles shut, and Mark finds it hard to breathe. He hears footsteps padding down the stairs—whose, he doesn't know—and the front door judders open. This is followed by an outburst of shuffling, first in the street and almost at once to some extent inside the house. As it begins to mount the stairs Mark hears the caller's voice, though it's little more than a whisper. "Number one," she prompts, and a murmuring chorus responds "Let's be mum." Is it proposing a role to play or enjoining secrecy? Mark can't judge, even when the procession sets about chanting in a whisper "Mum, mum, mum . . ." The repetition seems to fill the house, which feels too small for it, especially once the front door closes behind the last of the procession. The chorus can't blot out the shuffling, which sounds like the restlessness of an impatient queue. All Mark can do is squeeze his eyes so tight that the darkness throbs in time with his pulse, and he manages not to look until he hears a door creep open.

-◄o►-

TWO POEMS FOR HILL HOUSE

KEVIN McCANN

ANSWERED AN AD

Pulls the apartment door
Towards her, slowly clicks
It shut, picks up her bag
Packed for who knows,
Pads down backstairs, slips
On her shoes, clack-taps
Echoing the basement car
Park, finds her old Ford,
Still starts first time, drives
Up the ramp, checks right
And left, *No traffic yet*,
Re-reads the directions
That came with his note,
Rolls down her window,
Grips the wheel gulping,
At long last sets off,
Chalked my name
On the sidewalk,

Watched that night
As rain washed it away
Reaches the Freeway,
Still early, still quiet
But takes a Highway
Instead as her sister
Wakes up crying, makes
Coffee until it's late enough
To phone *A shower of stones*
Cracked our roof tiles. Mother
Said it was neighbours who've
Never liked us at all Mid-morning
She stops at a diner, drinks coffee,
Has doughnuts for breakfast,
Smokes openly as she leaves
Brushing some man *Beery breath*
Who whistles *And the wheels on*
The car go round and round and
Past a cop, parked by some billboard,
Asleep *Round and round and round*
Overtakes a school bus, jaundiced,
Empty *Round and reaches* her turn off,
Checks herself in the mirror,
Smiles, practicing.

I AM THE ONE

Who set out that morning,
Instructions laid out
On the passenger seat.

I am the one
Who, after driving all day,
Slowed through that town

But when I wound down my window
To ask last minute directions
Had my *pardon me sir*
Or *'scuse me there mam*
Get no more response
Than some panhandling bum.

I am the one
Who was last to arrive
(So the gatekeeper told me
Then smiled at his wife)
I am the one Who followed the slowly
Last curving stretch
And when the house pounced
As I rounded the curve
Just past the tree stump

Hung in a vacuum Head in a vice

Cold freshly scalped

I am the one whose mind changed right there.

I am the one who turned back

◄◦►

MARINERS' ROUND

TERRY DOWLING

t started small, as these things do, with a cheap glass jewel pried from the rump of a genuine Charles Carmel merry-go-round horse at Sydney's Luna Park one cool autumn evening in 1977. A blue glass jewel set into a gold-painted wooden harness, many faceted, the size of a king's thumbnail, a queen's ransom, big enough to be easily visible and look so precious to kids watching the carousel turn.

Easy to pry off, too, in a small enough act of vandalism by one of three fourteen-year-old schoolboys on a cool, just past summer evening.

Davey Renford wanted it, yearned for it, loved the idea of having a precious blue-glass jewel from the haunch of the magnificent white wooden horse he'd chosen. *Lysander*, the chest blazon said, and it was on the outermost of the three rings, a smooth-turning stander, not like the favoured lift-and-fall jumpers on the two inner rings that most boys preferred. The fixed ones were not as exciting to ride but, being on the outside, they had the armour and bright fish-scale saddle cloths, the mirrors and the jewels. And this, to Davey, was the finest mount of them all, picked from the forty-two others, chosen over the two chariots, the lion and the fabulous (oh-so-tempting) griffin.

There was something about its dark gaze, the arch of the neck, the way the splendid creature lunged forward to seize the night, Davey couldn't explain exactly. Stallion or mare, it didn't matter. This was his horse, his jewel, something to mark the time.

Riley Trencher couldn't have cared less, not yet. He was on an inner ring jumper, four horses ahead, yelling something back to Frank Coombs who was busy swapping horses mid-ride when the operator wasn't looking. And it was just as Davey's cousin, Frank, was swinging between a second-ring jumper and the outer-ring fixed black behind Davey's that he saw Davey reach back to run his finger yet again over the blue gem in the golden harness.

"You want it, take it!" Frank said. "It's just glass!"

Which it was, of course, yet could never be.

"Take it!" Frank said again.

Davey couldn't.

But for Frank Coombs it wasn't an issue. He glanced at Riley Trencher sailing on ahead, then at the operator, whose back was still turned, then in seconds had his penknife out and open and the blade in under the jewel. In seconds, he was cupping the cool hard thing as it came away, then passing it forward to Davey, who took it, gaping in shock and wonder.

"What's that you're doing?" Riley called, which made the operator turn, shout an automatic "Behave yourselves, you boys!" and ended conversation until the ride was over.

By the time the platform had glided to a halt and all the horses were fixed and still, Riley and Frank had forgotten the jewel. They were too busy hurrying off to the Ghost Train, leaving Davey to follow on, lost in a buzz of wondering if it had really happened.

It was on the way home that Riley became the closest thing to an enemy Davey had ever known. The three of them were off the train at Hornsby, walking down Sutter's Lane with the backyards of homes to one side and the vast open spread of the railway lines to the other. There was a streetlight ahead, just before the pedestrian underpass, and in the thin yellow light Frank saw how distracted Davey was.

"Hey, Davey-boy! Why the long face? You got the jewel."

Which had Riley immediately demanding to see it. "Hey, yeah! I wondered what you two were doin'. Show me!"

Davey would've refused, but it wasn't worth setting Riley off about anything. He was like a spring on its first flex, a firework teased with fire.

Davey took the jewel from his pocket and passed it over.

Maybe it looked precious in the light. Maybe it triggered something in Riley Trencher that had never existed before. For in a flash, mere seconds, his arm was back and he was flinging the stone out across the tracks.

For Davey it was a frozen moment, an eternity of alarm, dismay, rage beyond telling. He couldn't speak, couldn't move.

Not so Frank. An instant more and Frank had his own arm back and was punching Riley full in the face, spinning him off balance, sending him careening down the embankment. The chain-link fence should have caught him, but other kids had loosened the mesh for a short-cut and Riley went plunging through, scrambling and yelling, landing hard at the bottom on a standing length of pipe that went through his left thigh.

The yelling roused the neighbours. Suddenly there were adults there, and police and an ambulance soon afterwards. But by then Davey and Frank had been led aside, questioned and taken home.

So it is that things happen, lives are turned, debts left owned and owing.

-o-

Twenty-five years later, David Renford—Dave to his close friends, still Davey to his closest—knew so much more about the jewel, or rather the horse and the merry-go-round they had ridden that fateful night. Even before becoming a free-lance heritage analyst, even before being called in to do insurance appraisals on two different Luna Park gates and associated vintage attractions by various state governments, he had learned its origins: how it was an American three-row menagerie carousel in the Coney Island style purchased in England by Herman Phillips and brought to Sydney in 1910. How the horses had been carved by Charles Carmel, one of the greatest of the American carousel horse carvers of the early twentieth century, a student of Charles Looff himself, and who, as an independent competitor, had specialised in splendid armoured mounts, fish-scale saddle blankets and feather-pattern, jewelled harnesses.

And twenty-five years to the day of that momentous evening (though he wasn't to know *that* for another hour or so), Davey was sitting in the Trebarin in Dublin at 1:45 on an overcast Saturday afternoon listening to a five-piece band playing 'Whiskey in the Jar.' There was a petite, redheaded woman with a winsome, heart-shaped face drinking with friends and singing along who kept catching his eye and smiling the right way. Losing on-again off-again Tina had made him cautious, even shy, and he meant to wait before attempting any kind of overture. What if he were wrong?

Still, it was the first time he'd been really, truly, unequivocally happy in the five years since Annie died, and it had started with winning the lucky door prize at the local RSL: the return trip to Ireland with three weeks' accommodation and three thousand dollars spending money. He felt his life re-making itself at last.

But then—sheer astonishment!—Frank Coombs walked in, Frank or a time-worn lookalike. There was no mistaking him, though it had been ten years since he'd last seen his long-lost cousin, well before Annie.

"Frank!" Davey called above the singing, and Frank heard and turned, eyes widening in recognition, mouth falling open in an amazement to match Davey's own.

"Davey? What on earth?"

For the next thirty minutes they huddled over beers in that corner of the Trebarin just off O'Connell Street, though the surprise and delight turned to a different, darker sort of astonishment after the first few minutes.

For Frank had won his own prize at another RSL, the three weeks' accommodation, the three thousand dollars. It was unbelievable, impossible.

But more. On his way out of his hotel just forty minutes ago, Frank had been handed a most intriguing message at reception.

Your next surprise. The bar of the Trebarin Hotel, 2 p.m.

It had all been planned: the strictly fixed-term plane tickets, the proximity of their hotels, the meeting.

"What's going on, Dave?" Frank asked, more to the universe than his one-year-younger cousin. "I thought *you* must've arranged the whole thing."

"How I'm seeing it too, Frank. But what are the chances? Someone saw I was here and phoned your hotel."

They spoke on, matched lives, found they had even more in common than they'd first thought.

Davey had lost Annie five years before in a car accident in Royal National Park. Frank's wife Marguerite had left him a year ago, taking their remaining child to her parents' property at Calloway Point after a house fire had caused the death of their six-year-old son Mark.

The more they talked about their lives, the more alarming the symmetry became.

Several years back, Davey had looked like becoming a favoured heritage analyst for the Australian Museum in Sydney until an elaborately staged hoax had led first to his being sidelined, then sidestepped altogether. Frank, on the other hand, had been forced to close a promising rural medical practice when a lawsuit from a woman whose cancer had been misdiagnosed led to a malpractice investigation. The pathology lab had ended up being held accountable but, country towns being what they were, Frank's reputation in the district had been effectively ruined.

"Believe in conspiracy theories, Davey?" Frank asked.

"Starting to," Davey answered. "It's too weird."

The timing of this "discovery phase" had been planned as well. Forty-five minutes after their meeting, the waitress who came to clear the glasses handed them a business card.

"A gentleman upstairs asked me to give you this," she said. "He's in the private lounge on the first floor. Room 10."

No, she didn't know his name, just what was on the card. He'd booked the room, seemed a bit of a big spender. Then she hurried off about her duties before they could quiz her further.

The card gave no other identification than Blue Circle International, with a downtown New York address and contact details. On the reverse someone had written in a neat script:

There are things to discuss. Please join me for 3:00 p.m.

Davey and Frank checked their watches, saw that it was five minutes of that.

All of it planned.

But answers. Answers now at least.

They left their table and took the stairs to the first floor, continued along the hallway to the polished mahogany door of Room 10. Davey and Frank exchanged glances, then Frank knocked and they entered.

The spacious room was unoccupied but for a tall man sitting in a leather armchair before the fire. He was their age, late forties, early fifties, and had a full head of greying hair, a neatly trimmed beard. There was a walking stick by his left hand and his suit looked expensive. Two more armchairs were arranged near his, and a small table was set with an ice bucket and a bottle of champagne, three glasses, a modest if ample plate of sandwiches and cakes.

The man turned in his chair, smiled. "Gentlemen, good afternoon. Excuse me if I don't get up. An old injury."

"We got your card," Davey said, settling in one of the armchairs.

"And your plane tickets," Frank added, taking the other. "An explanation would be appreciated."

"Of course, Frank," the bearded man said. "And please help yourselves to the sandwiches. Davey, do the honours and pour us each a glass. You've come a long way and we have things to celebrate."

"We do?" Frank asked, even as Davey twigged to it.

"Riley? It's you!"

"Indeed it is, Davey-boy. Good to see you. You too, Frank. Good of you to come."

There was a strange silence then, absurd under the circumstances, and Davey eased them through it by opening the bottle, filling the champagne flutes and passing them out.

"Thought we should catch up," Riley said when they all had glasses. "Twenty-five years ago today. *Today*, you realise!"

Frank had lost things from his life. He needed to gain control here. "Riley, none of that was meant to happen."

"Of course, it wasn't, Frank. We were kids. I was a jerk. But twenty-five years! Different hemisphere, different country but *this* date, and here we are!"

Davey returned the bottle to the ice bucket. It was vintage Krug. "You seem to have done well."

"Based in New York now. Married into old money. Spend my time running Blue Circle. Mainly antiquities auctions. One of the top five auction houses on the east coast. Who would've thought? But here's to your health!"

They all drank the toast.

"So why the beat-up, Riley?" Frank said when it was done. "It's a long way for an anniversary drink. Afraid we wouldn't come?"

Riley set down his glass and laced his fingers. "Frank, it's more to do with completing an old formula, an old incantation, if you can believe it."

"An incantation!" Frank was first puzzled, then annoyed. As he'd just told Davey down in the lounge, ever since the lawsuit, ever since Markie died, he'd sworn never to put up with bullshit again.

Riley smiled. "All right. A protocol, if you prefer. How something has to be done. Davey, you're in the trade. Ever hear of something called the Chinder Commission?"

"The name's familiar. A carousel?"

"Exactly. A menagerie merry-go-round. Charles Carmel worked on it after the fire destroyed his own new carousel in 1911. His was uninsured and he lost nearly everything. But before he died in 1933, he did some work for Horace Chinder."

Frank set his glass on the table. "Davey, Riley, how about you talk shop some other time. I want to know why we're here."

Riley raised a hand in a placating gesture. "Frank, please. What happened *that* night definitely has a place in this. That jewel you got for Davey."

Davey was restless too but saw that the best way to get answers was to play it as Riley wanted. He turned to his cousin. "Frank, the carousel we rode back in 1977 was a Charles Carmel merry-go-round. Brought to Sydney from the US, sold back to a US company after the 1979 Ghost Train fire. We might want to hear this."

Frank settled back, let Davey top up his glass. "All right. But make it the five-dollar version, okay?"

Riley grinned. "The five-dollar version it is. Chinder was a stage magician, grandson and great-grandson in a family of very successful stage magicians. He was into puzzles and tricks, creating mysterious objects and events. A bit like that Kit Williams fellow."

"Like who?" Frank asked.

"Kit Williams. Back in the 70s he made a hare out of gold, set it with jewels, and buried it in the countryside, then published a picture book with clues to its whereabouts so a lucky treasure hunter could find it. *Masquerade.* Do a net search. Chinder was like that, only he did it with a carousel."

"Oh, and why is that?"

For all Davey knew Frank might have been trying to behave but his words came over as sarcasm.

Riley seemed not to notice. "Well, it's a sacred shape, isn't it? The wheel of life. Like the Round Table. No beginning or end. Anyway, you can't stoppeth one of three unless you have three to start with, yes. Just like in '77."

"That's a Coleridge reference," Davey said for Frank's benefit, in case his cousin didn't know the allusion. "The Rime of the Ancient Mariner."

"Gee, I was just going to say that," Frank added. "Five-dollar version, Riley."

"Gotcha. But it was Chinder's favourite poem," Riley continued. "And his favourite line was the first one: 'It was an Ancient Mariner, And he stoppeth one of three.' He had it inscribed on the marquee on *Mariners' Round*, the carousel he had made for him, all fancy curlicue so you can barely read it. At least it's supposed to be there, hidden in plain sight. And it's a clue."

"To what?" Frank asked.

"Exactly, Frank." It was comical. Riley was ignoring Frank's impatience and irritation, was treating him as if he were a fellow devotee, an interested colleague and ally. "To what indeed? That's where you can help. I've located the Chinder Carousel. Now it's a matter of solving the clues. All I need is an hour of your time."

Frank shook his head in amazement. "That's it? We're here to solve a puzzle?"

Riley remained unshakeably charming and enthusiastic. "I've done a lot of work already. I'm nearly there. It has to do with the real purpose behind the Chinder Commission. Why these particular mounts. What they were intended to do."

"To do?"

"To make possible."

Incredibly, there was another silence then, just the sound of the fire crackling and of traffic out in the street. Quite possibly the champagne and the warmth were having their effect, for when Frank next spoke, it was as if he had worked through the absurdities and the impossibility, had found other things to settle on for a time, other memories, possibly a clearer sense of the reality of this unique moment in their lives. "Never thought of people having careers carving carousel horses," was all he said.

Riley seized on the change of mood, handled Frank as he was no doubt handling them both. "I know. And you can't imagine what a competitive, quirky bunch they were, Frank. One of them, Marcus Illions, had highly trained assistants but insisted on carving every horse head himself. Just the heads, think of it. Solomon Stein and Harry Goldstein turned out really quite frightening mounts with big heads and large teeth, quite ferocious-looking, like they were deliberately trying to frighten the children they were meant to attract. But most manufacturers just did the frames and hired carvers to provide what was needed. That one we rode as kids was a real beauty. Bit of a hybrid, not quite the usual Carmel menagerie. Mostly horses but there was a lion, a griffin and two chariots for variety."

"We remember," Frank said, the edginess returning.

Riley picked up his glass of Krug, though barely drank. "Right. How can we forget? Something else was there to 'stoppeth one of three' that night."

"Riley, we were kids," Davey reminded him in case it was needed. "Let it go."

"Hey, they saved the leg. I've done well." Riley became thoughtful again. "But it's strange, Davey. You seem to know Carmel's work, but nothing about the Commission."

"Just heard the name somewhere."

"Right. But you probably know that when the fire destroyed his own carousel, Carmel was a broken man. He had to take whatever work he could get. I'm not saying it was arson, but suddenly Chinder comes along wanting a special menagerie unlike any Carmel had worked on before."

"All conveniently omitted from the biographies," Davey said. "I get piecework, diabetes, worsening arthritis, dead of cancer in his mid-sixties."

"Strict secrecy was part of the brief. Carmel went to a dockside location in Brooklyn, used only the most trusted assistants. We know so little about it, just that it had a nautical theme and took two years to complete. Chinder was very specific about what had to be included. He also provided the materials. Can you guess what they were?"

"Just tell us," Frank said.

"The timbers from wrecked sailing ships, Frank. Every single sea-mount for the Chinder Commission was made from the bulwarks and ribbing of old trading ships, from wrecks washed ashore, buried or never appraised properly. Timbers from storm-damaged vessels or hulks turned in for salvage."

Frank had reached his patience limit again. "Great. So how does the jewel fit in?"

"Precisely the right word, Frank. Fit. Something being fitted. And since it has to do with the three of us, *re-fitted*. All three involved, like in the poem."

It wasn't what Coleridge had meant at all, Davey wanted to remind him, but he was looking out for Frank. "*One* of three, that poem says, Riley. Every three people, the Mariner would stop one to tell his story to."

"Right, Davey-boy. A bit melodramatic pushing the image, I know, but circumstances make it relevant. You wanted the jewel back then. Frank took it. I ended up with it. Only fitting, don't you think?"

Ended up with it! was Davey's immediate thought, but his cousin spoke first.

"You threw it away!" Frank's words were too loud in the otherwise empty room.

Riley's eyes flashed in the firelight. "Did I now?" He gave a strange, somehow nasty, possibly exulting grin; Davey wasn't sure how to read it. "Time to put this on again, I think."

He took a silver ring from his jacket pocket and slipped it onto his right ring finger. It was handsome but too large, too overdone. And set into the crown was the blue glass jewel pried loose all those years ago.

Davey sat stunned. Blue Circle International. That name, of course. "But how—?"

"You bastard, Trencher," Frank muttered, even as Riley answered.

"I palmed it! What did you think I did?"

Davey and Frank glanced at each other. The implications spun out before them.

"Riley . . ." Davey began. *He never got to tell them he had it! It happened so quickly. Too quickly. All the violence for nothing*!

"You two nearly ruined my life," Riley continued. "For a while I even got to thinking that maybe I should ruin yours a bit."

"Say again?" Frank demanded.

"What's that?" Davey said.

But Riley had regained whatever composure the rush of feeling had brought undone. He reached down and laid a hand on his walking stick, then regarded the cousins again. "Still, that was then. This afternoon I have something important to show you."

Frank was leaning forward, hands on his knees. "Finish what you were saying!"

"Frank, bear with me a bit longer, please. You've come a long way. The Blue Circle offices are in New York. You should be asking yourselves why here. Why Dublin?"

"The carousel's here," Davey said, before Frank could speak.

"Right on, Davey-boy! So think back to that night. Those horses had names. What was the one you rode? The one Frank took the jewel from? Do you remember?"

How could Davey forget? *"Lysander."*

Now it was Riley whose face showed surprise, more than that: astonishment. He went very still, not blinking for ten, twenty, thirty seconds. Then he reached up and stroked his beard with one hand, almost absentmindedly. He probably didn't know he was doing it.

"Riley, what?" Davey asked.

"Lysander," Riley said at last. His manner had changed. He was still distracted, but now seemed shrewd and calculating as well.

"Yes, so?"

Riley brought his attention back to the cousins. "Part of what got me into this. The auctions, maritime archaeology, all of it. There was a seventeenth century spice trader with that name. Ninety-eight footer. Three masts. Went missing at sea in 1704 by all reports." He took out a pen and notebook. "Davey, how is that spelt, please?"

He wrote the name as Davey spelled it, then, saying "Excuse me a moment," took out his mobile and called a pre-set number. "Beverley, I have the name. It's *Lysander*. Spelled L-Y-S-A-N-D-E-R. Within half an hour please." He broke the connection.

Frank was still sitting forward as if preparing to leave. "Riley, something important to show us, you were saying. I assume it's this carousel."

"Gents, just one more hour, that's all I ask." Riley was not only back in control but seemed to have reconsidered how much he would reveal. "Davey, it may help to see it as Chinder must have. He pondered the old questions. What is the role of magic in a life? Not necessarily *real* magic, *working* magic, as they say, but our relationship to magic as an idea, a constant, something wished for."

"Magic?" Davey was thrown by the sudden change of topic, then realised that the coincidence with the names had changed everything, saw too that Riley was probably working to a schedule, filling time.

"I know. Crazy stuff. But as a historical, cultural, personal thing we keep yearning for, keep returning to. The *possibility* of it."

Frank made a disgusted sound. "Riley, what *are* you going on about? Real magic! Working magic! What is all this?"

But Davey raised a hand this time, urging patience. "You're saying Chinder sought more than just the conceptual kind?"

"Davey, he did. We're talking *real* magic here, I promise you. The real deal." He turned back to Frank. "Chinder made his career exploiting the other kind, Frank, the conceptual kind, pandering to our yearnings, manipulating our need to believe. He was an entertainer, but his papers show he actually did believe in working magic as well. He spent much of his life finding ways to use it."

Frank breathed out heavily. "Oh, for Pete's sake!"

But he too saw the glint in Riley's eyes, no doubt grasped that it *was* quite likely from exultation at a quest nearly completed, something about to reach its end.

"The Chinder Commission was the culmination of his efforts," Riley said. "Some ancient cabbalistic, shamanistic way of reaching his goal."

Davey had to ask it. "Which was?"

"Why, finding the heart's desire, of course. Nothing less. That's how his papers put it."

"Which for him was what?"

Riley shrugged. "Chinder doesn't say. And if I'm right, he never completed the process. But that's what it was. Finding his heart's desire."

Frank shook his head in disbelief. "Which for you would be locating this old ship. Using the bloke's carousel."

"An indulgence, Frank. We all have them."

Though much more than that, Davey knew, fascinated in spite of himself. After the long flight, after winning the prize that wasn't a prize, the shock of meeting first Frank and now Riley again, this was something familiar, something to anchor him. "Riley, the Commission was never displayed. Never seen."

"Right. It was packed up and shipped. Even Carmel never saw it re-assembled."

"But you've located it."

"Davey, I have. It's out in the docklands, and I've bought it. Humour me, please. Come and see it now is all I ask. Then you can both go on your way. Enjoy your holiday."

Frank stood, stepped away from his armchair. "Riley, I've heard enough!"

"Frank, one thing for old time's sake, please! All I ask. Just ten minutes from here."

Frank looked down at his one-time friend. "Oh, Jesus! For old time's sake then."

⟨◦⟩

The afternoon outside was bleak and wintry and Davey wasn't surprised to see a hire car waiting for them at the curb. They climbed in and were driven, mostly in silence, through late afternoon traffic out to a dockland, warehouse district, finally pulled over near a large brick building beside a chainlink fence.

Davey could easily imagine a menagerie being hidden away in such a structure, but the building itself wasn't to be their destination. When they were standing in the road and the hire car had driven off, Riley used a key to unlock a gate in the fence, then led them down a pass-through by a construction yard to a high fenced enclosure of a more traditional kind, a barricade of old wooden palings, sturdy and close-fitting. All about them could be heard the sounds of the Liffey.

Riley unlocked a gate in that fence as well and held it open while they all stepped through. The cousins found themselves in a large dim precinct formed by paling fences on all sides, even facing the river so there was no view at all, just the sounds of gulls, with the smell of estuarine mudflats strong on the breeze.

At first, Davey wasn't certain what he was seeing; then, as his eyes adjusted in the last light of day, he saw that it was indeed a derelict carousel. *Mariners' Round*, the faded letters on the canopy said. And, sure enough, all the worn and time-damaged mounts he could make out were things of the deep, lunging, looming, crowding over each other.

Some were based on real animals: sharks with gaping mouths, dolphins in mid-leap, whales sounding, spouting, a great squid with out-thrust tentacles, a brace of seahorses side by side, the impressive spiral of a nautilus. But others were fanciful, wonderfully, disturbingly strange: a wild-eyed kraken, a sea-serpent with a tabard of old mirrors scrolling down its chest, half-human tritons and mermaids, all with heads that seemed larger than life, more in the style of Stein and Goldstein than Carmel, with bared teeth, rolling eyes, a manic, frantic, restless quality, like gasping things dragged from the depths before their time and against their wills.

Davey couldn't help but be impressed. It did indeed seem to be the Chinder Carousel, Riley's lost Carmel merry-go-round, seized, landed and trapped here in this sad enclosure beside the Liffey.

"Not as derelict as it looks," Riley assured them. "There's a new electric motor installed, though the musical accompaniment will be turned right down this evening. Mustn't draw too much attention. But it'll work well enough for a little ride."

Frank wasn't having any of it. "And why would we want to do that?"

"Frank, please. Choose a mount and take the one ride. Just one."

"Riley, what's to be gained?" Davey asked. "Why does it matter so much?"

"This jewel." He raised his ring. "It was never meant to go to the carousel we rode in Sydney that night. Bet you never knew that, Davey. It was meant for *this* special hybrid, the Commission. There was a mix-up. Just the one jewel and it all went wrong for Chinder. Maybe a mischievous assistant palmed it, passed it on." Riley's grin was fierce. "Maybe it was an honest mistake. Maybe the carousel itself wasn't ready. But that's why it never worked as far as we can know. Never fulfilled its function."

"Delivering the heart's desire," Davey said, echoing Riley's words from the hotel, even as his mind locked on what else Riley had just now said. *Maybe the carousel itself wasn't ready!*

"The heart's desire," Riley continued. "Something like that. But *we* found the jewel that night. I palmed it, had it in my pocket at the accident. And there was blood. It was blooded. Maybe that's it, you tell me. But the three of us were involved then; it seems right that all three have to be involved now. Chinder's papers put it like that: 'All that is intended,' the line goes. Well, all this was intended—*is* intended, as I see it! What we did then means it should be that way now. I'd already been tinkering with your lives a bit, getting even for what happened."

There it was again, the hint of threat and reprisal. Frank seized on it. "Wait! Wait! What's that supposed to mean?"

And again Riley ignored the question. "Last year I finally located the carousel here, arranged to buy it."

"Wait up, Riley!" Frank's eyes flashed with anger. This wasn't a hotel lounge with torpor brought on by alcohol and a cosy fireside. This was a chill, naked evening with a fine drizzle beginning to fall. "What do you mean 'tinkering with our lives a bit'?"

"Then I brought you all this way. Now we take the ride, restore the jewel one way rather than another and it's done. You can go."

"Go fuck yourself, Trencher!" Frank said. "What sort of tinkering?"

All through Frank's outburst, Riley seemed patient, even unnaturally calm, but Davey sensed the old Riley Trencher danger waiting there. "Forget it, Riley," he said, more gently than he felt. "We've seen enough."

Riley gave a strange smile. "Gents, you don't understand. I have more fun and games planned if you don't co-operate. Frank, right now Marguerite is at Calloway Point with your daughter and your parents, yes? Davey, your parents are still living in Chatswood. There are things in place. I need only say the word. I think one quick ride will be worth all the inconvenience. So, please, choose a mount, finish what we started. What Chinder started."

He left a silence then, rather something of one for it was filled with the soughing of wind about the transoms and the canopy, getting in between the palings of the enclosure. Time seemed distended, every second stretched, laden. Davey and Frank stood in the growing gloom numb with loss and grief all over again, feeling the helplessness, the rage and fury, the old embers smouldering now, re-kindled.

For the first time, Davey saw his life as something *deliberately* spoiled. Not just the hoax but—hell and Jesus, no!—the accident! Annie! Other things that had been at least bearable as part of the burden of hazard in any life. But no longer. No longer.

Frank had to be feeling the same: seeing Markie's death anew, the malpractice suit, losing Marguerite. What else had *she* been told in the careful, spiteful workings of Riley Trencher's plan?

And Riley read that moment for precisely what it was, knew where it had to lead. He reached inside his jacket, produced a handgun and aimed it their way.

"Think carefully about what you do now, gents. My associates are close by. Refuse to take the ride and you'll be shot. You'll be strapped to a mount. We'll take the ride anyway. You don't have to be alive for it. Inside or out, the blood is still there. All that is intended."

"You killed my son," Frank said in a whisper, a ghost's voice drawn thin.

Riley just tilted his head in a way that might have said: *Collateral damage, Frank. I merely requested a house fire.*

Davey couldn't speak at all. The thought of Annie's death, of Riley's abiding hatred, that order of single-mindedness, brought the familiar weight, the exhaustion.

Only the search for this old carousel had stayed his hand, Davey realised, had brought this respite, this interlude, this whole parody of charm and civility. There'd be no going their own way once this was done, he was sure of it.

And dying here wouldn't just end his own life, Davey saw, that was the thing. It would end Annie as well somehow, the chance to keep her in the world in some way, *any* way. Just as Frank surviving, continuing, kept Markie's memory as something at least. We end, those things end. More forgotten things, the world moving on.

The bleakness of the thought, the hour, this cold, too early evening hour, made it possible. Why not take the ride? Move it along. Bring more hazard to the mix. Why not?

He moved towards the carousel. As if on cue, three proximity floods switched on, ghost-lighting the whole macabre display. Now glass eyes glittered in the time-struck faces, teeth gnashed, flashed off-white and worn silver, tongues lolled, mouths silently screamed. Old mirrors gave the barest glints and gleams, ancient brightwork showed in swatches, snatches, hints of fraught primary colours that had not been visible before.

Davey didn't dare stop. The great squid impaled on its brass pole rolled a baleful eye, watched him approach, move past. Three mermaids offered scarred breasts, mouths flecked with old enamel.

Mount us! Mount us! Ride!

Sirens heaved, rolled, lolled in their meagre twists of surf.

No fish tails here, fancy-boy! Press close. We can be Annie! Annie!

Davey saw them through tears: flaunting, writhing, limbering.

Tritons glared, daring, warning off. One lunged—no, no it was Frank, Frank there with him now, circling the zodiac too, this wheel of lost and forsaken things.

"Davey—" his cousin began to say.

"Just do it!" Davey said with a voice, a forthrightness neither Davey nor Frank had ever heard from him before. "Move it along!"

"But we have to—"

"Frank, he has others with him. We've no choice."

"We don't know that! We don't know that at all!"

"Doesn't matter which ones we choose. Just pick one near mine, okay? Stay close!"

"Davey, we have to—"

"Frank, there's been enough harm. Let it go! Get through this."

And Frank did let it go then, like a balloon deflating, emptying, moved with Davey around this ancient wheel sea-changed—no, land-changed—into a base pathetic thing. Only one mount had a legible name-plate, a *new* plate newly fitted, *Lysander*. Riley's mount this time, not his. Not now. Never his now.

Davey moved clear of it, well beyond, climbed atop a leaping dolphin on the outermost ring, one that looked less manic and blighted than the rest. Frank took the wild-eyed shark next in the row, climbed up and settled, gripped the pole.

Riley must have already been in place back there behind them for the platform began creaking, heaving, easing forward like a tide on the turn, moving faster and faster, girding itself like a king tsunami reaching to take on the world.

The music would be playing, that was part of the equation too, but was turned right down as Riley had said it would be. There was just the creaking, the straining, the flapping of the old torn canopy, just the on-shore breeze, laving, pushing, growing stronger, smelling of tidal flats, sea-wrack and early rain. So, too, set running out there was the turn, turn of the city lights a way off, and more lights from the river, scant, precious, locked in time, those things shifting to a blur as the great wheel gained speed, completing itself by the act of moving forward: animals, grotesques and halflings thrown, lunging, plunging into flickering night, snatching the life of the flow, wheeling, rushing, flinging into time and chance, purest hazard.

And caught in the sweep, that relentless rush, Davey almost saw it happen!

◄○►

He came back to it, to everything, with a song, to words that went like this—

> Hoist away and make some sail,
> We'll have a toast for England.
> Tomorrow we're away to Spain or off to Araby.
> A man has many chains on shore
> But Davy Jones has many more.
> He has no home, his wits are foam,
> He cannot leave the sea.

—found himself in a corner of the Trebarin in Dublin on a wintry Saturday afternoon, woke to an old sea-shanty being sung as a round—a round, yes!—by two, three dozen men and women who were laughing, many with arms linked, raucously singing their parts. The pretty woman he'd seen before was still among them, smiling at him, coaxing, inviting, daring—he couldn't be wrong!—so clear now through the refrain.

Mariners' Round. Of course. Davey spared a thought for Frank and, unexpectedly, for Riley Trencher, wondering what had befallen them in this astonishing sleight-of-hand, sleight-of-mind, sleight-of-time.

Because look where he was! Just look! And look at what he had! Davey laughed, found his feet, and went to join the chorus.

◄○►

Frank Coombs woke under the trees in the sea-meadow above Calloway Point, looking out across the headland to the sparkling Pacific. When he heard laughter, the sound of children singing, he leant up on his elbows like some hayseed farm-boy, saw the old farmhouse under its sheltering Moreton Bay figs. Before it there were adults dancing in a circle with ten, eleven children—a reel it was—while other parents and friends watched, smiling, singing along, clapping in time.

A round, Frank realised. It's a celebration, probably a birthday, and they're dancing a round!

"Come on, Frank!" one of the spectators called, leaving the group, approaching. It was Marguerite, worn, dishevelled from the festivities and another handful of years, but Marguerite! "You took the trouble to come," she said. "Least you can do is join in. Unless you're too old for it!"

"As if!" Frank cried.

For he wasn't. You never were. While you lived, you did what you could.

Frank laughed. There was no Markie, no, that lasting bruise on the perfect day, but there was this and, surprisingly, it was enough. He scrambled to his feet and went to join in, wanted Marguerite to see him doing that. Just that.

-◇-

And Riley Trencher? Why, Riley found himself on the ship of his dreams, of course, on the deck of the late seventeenth century spice trader *Lysander* circling, endlessly circling, on the inner slope of a mighty maelstrom, a vast yawning gulf in the sea, at least two thousand metres across, five hundred deep, turning, roaring under a wild, leaden sky.

The decks were canted at an alarming forty degrees above that terrible drop, but a crewman used sea-lines to haul himself along the upper rail, finally arrived drenched by rain and spray. He wore the foul-weather oilskins of an older time.

"You made it!" he shouted above the roar of the vortex. "They said you would! *You've got the ring?*"

"What?" Riley could barely hear his own voice. The roar numbed everything. "What's that?"

"*The ring, man! You've got the bloody ring?*"

And when Riley raised his hand to show it, the man nodded, actually managed a ragged grin.

"Thank God! We can end this!"

"End what?" Riley asked, but knew, knew, even as the seaman gestured out at the gloom, the churning murk below.

All that is intended.

And after so many, too many, wasting, wearying years, the old ship leant harder into the wind, doors to crew quarters blew open, maps flew from the captain's cabin like doves, the twin mirrors of a sextant floated in a half-silvered sky, and *Lysander* began its final descent.

-⟨o⟩-

NANNY GREY

GEMMA FILES

OH LOW ESTATE, *my love my love*, the song's hook went, or seemed to, through the wall of the Ladies'. Bill Koslaw felt it more than heard it, buzzing in his back teeth through the sweaty skin of his jaws as he pushed into this toff tart—Sessilie, he thought her name was, and the rest began with a K—from behind with her bent over the lav itself, hands wide-braced, each thrust all but mashing that great midnight knot of hair against the cubicle's tiling. And he could see her lips moving, too, half-quirked in that smile he'd literally never seen her lose thus far: *Oh low estate, the threat is great, my love my love (my love) . . .*

Tiny girl, this Sessilie K., almost creepily so. She looked barely legal, though he'd touched a cupcake-sized pair of breasts beneath that silky top of hers as she pulled him inside the Ladies', nipples long enough to tent the material and one apparently bar-pierced, set inside a shield like a little silver flame which pricked his hand when he'd tried to flick it, drawing blood. "Oh, never mind that," she'd said, that smile intact, opaquely unreadable even as she'd leaned forward with her hips hiked high, flipping her skirt up to show her thong already moved neatly aside for easier penetration.

"Bit cruel to your knickers," he'd commented. "Bet those cost a pretty penny."

"No doubt," she'd replied, bum still in the air and both legs wide-spread, aslant on her too-high heels, completely shameless. "But then, it all ends up in the fire eventually. Doesn't it?"

Punctuating it with a bit of a shimmy, like: *Well, get a wiggle on. Don't waste my time, groundling; better things to do, you know. Better classes of fools to fuck.*

That airy contempt of hers, especially when delivered in those plummy tones, engorged him. But . . .

He should be liking this better than he was, he reckoned. Some sort of aristocrat, perpetually drunk and perpetually talking, always with her credit card out like it was glued to her palm and no apparent impulse control to speak of; what *wasn't* to like, for Christ's sake?

Just her, he supposed. Her, and almost everything about her.

He slid one hand up to ruck her blouse over her shoulder blades, and flinched from what he encountered there: Something halfway between a grey-on-grey tattoo of uncertain design and a brand with scabby edges, so rough it took on a Braille-like texture beneath his fingers. As though if he knew how, he could read it, but only in the dark.

"That a birthmark?"

"Oh, we all have one."

"Your family?"

"Some of them too, yes."

"Who was it you meant, then?"

"Oh, Billy, silly Billy. Does it really matter?"

And here she rammed back against him unexpectedly, throwing him off his beat. Singing once more, this time out loud, as she took control of their rhythm: *Ohhhh low estate, the threat is great . . .*

(*my love*)

"Am I boring you?"

"No, no. Do carry on."

"What's that, then?"

"Quite like this song, is all. I'll stop if you'd like. Wouldn't want to, mmm . . . put you *off*."

She shot him a glance back over her shoulder, with that, and reached back down between her legs to run one long nail over the seam of his sack—inch-long nails she had, white with black tips like some odd parody of a French manicure, each with a small black bedazzlement down where the cuticle should be. Pressing just hard enough to make him jump, so she could clamp around him and milk him so fiercely it began to hurt as she tossed a loose forelock out of her eyes and winked at him.

Winked.

Jesus wept.

That, right there—as he grunted and came, listening to her give out a rippling laugh in reply, her own orgasm seeming very much like an afterthought—probably marked the exact point at which Bill stopped feeling anything like bad about always having planned to slip her a Rohypnol and rob her house, later on.

BILL HAD COME to London on a Kon-Tiki packet, planning to round-trip Europe before moving on to the next leg of his pre-Uni world tour. But that'd all been put paid to when this arsehole, Gary, from Tasmania decided he'd cheated him out of the proceeds from reselling a bag of weed they'd both gone in on and took off with his stuff in revenge—passport, money, tickets, the whole deal.

Now it was three months later, and Bill still hadn't quite worked himself up to the point where he was willing to tell the Old Man what had happened—just kept on moving from place to place, bed to bed, sofa to sofa. Squatted here and there, took under-the-counter jobs, and tried to build up some sort of pad. Going to clubs had become about the next ride home, the next overnight, and then—slowly but surely—about whatever he could pick up around the flat or the house, or wherever, before they woke up: Small items of value, gold and silver, electronics; stuff non-specific enough to pawn or fence without being traced, but nice enough they'd bring a fair turnaround.

Girl like Sessilie, wherever she lived, it had to be just *full* of stuff like that—a spread of hockable trinkets peppered in and between the *Lock, Stock & Two Smoking Barrels*-type stuff: antique firearms, paintings and knick-knacks with nice pedigrees, etcetera. That was the assumption, anyhow.

He'd long since learned to trust his instincts when it came to such matters, and it had paid off, literally. Hadn't been wrong once, thus far.

So: "Shouldn't there be somebody home, this time of night?" Bill asked as he half-walked, half-lifted her up the stairs. The place was dark, like nineteenth century dark; it was the sort of towering three-story house that should really be lit with oil-lamps, not cunning little sodium bulbs on dimmer switches. "Place is a bloody tomb."

Sessilie's constant smile skewed a bit to the left, those horrifying nails making a slithery noise on the banister as she dragged them along its curve. "Oh, there's very little staff left, you know—family holidays, all that. Most of them have already gone down to air out the summer house, for when I'm done with End-of-Term."

"What about your parents?"

"Hmmm, be *quite* the surprise if *they* were here; they've both been dead since I was eight."

" . . . sorry."

"Oh, no need. Papa crashed a car and killed himself, but Mama held on a few days in hospital, at least. And ever after, it's just been me and Nanny Grey."

As she spoke this last name, Bill almost thought he heard something drop in the dark above them—on the next landing, maybe, or higher up yet. A stealthy noise like a single clock-tick, or the sound of a hairpin falling to the floor. Not footsteps, not exactly. But the dim stairwell and its adjacent hallways took on an air of waiting, of watchfulness, even though absolutely nothing which might be qualified to fill such a role evinced itself.

"You . . . still have a nanny?" Bill asked, pushing Sessilie up onto what he thought was the second floor, where she laid a finger against her lips and shook her head, drunkenly. Then tottered over to a side-table in those ludicrous heels, their clacking muffled by a thick oriental rug, and took out a long candle the colour of bone that she fitted onto a nearby holder with an absurd little flourish, before rummaging in her purse for a cigarette and lighting it. She took a long drag, then pressed the tip against the candle's wick, which flared into life.

"*Governess* would be the proper term. That's what Nanny would say, anyhow. Such an old *bulldog*, Nanny Grey. So protective! She's always been with our family, you see . . ."

And here she paused, wavering back and forth, her eyes unfocused—yet still retained presence of mind enough to stub the smoke out in the candle-holder's dish and blink over at Bill, rather sweetly. "Scuse me," she said. "I feel . . . rather off-colour, all of a sudden. Might I rely on you to get me to bed?"

Slowest-to-take-effect Rohypnol in all creation, Bill thought, amazed by her stamina. *Ought to check my supply, once this is over with . . .*

"My pleasure," was what he said, though, giving her a leg-out bow, fairytale prince-style. To which she tittered and made him a practiced curtsy, so well-learnt she barely even stumbled; he slung a hand under either armpit and caught her up with ridiculously little effort (so light, her bones like a bloody bird's), letting her fold into him, apparently too tired to yawn. Sleeping bloody Beauty.

The bedroom in question, which she directed him towards with a series of slurry, chest-muffled murmurs, looked almost exactly the way he'd pictured it would—big canopied bed, choked with pillows and fluffy plush dolls: cute versions of un-cute animals, emo *anime* characters. He set her down in their embrace, and watched her curl into a foetal position, tucking a particularly infectious-looking teddy-bear—the size of a two-year-old, chenille-furred and shedding worn lace in leprous swathes—down tight between those hungry thighs.

Strange little girl, he thought. Well, he was right to want to be rid of her, and not just for the obvious reasons; best to get to it, then flee this damn place. Nothing so big should be so empty, so quiet. . . .

And there it was again, from somewhere: that *sound.* A dog's nails clicking on the floor, one leg at a time. A mouth opening, pop-gasp, only to shut once more, without even an exhaled breath.

Get going, son, Grab what you can find, and scarper.

If only he could tell which direction the sounds were coming from.

Closer, now. To his left; no, right.

Bill shut the door behind him with excruciating slowness, tensed for the latch's click, and once he heard it, turned left so hard he thought he might twist an ankle. The candle—left abandoned, with only Sessilie's crumpled cigarette-butt for company—gave just enough light to navigate by, and Bill took the stairs upwards in loping strides, two by two by two. His heart hammered fast in his throat.

The third floor was smaller than it had seemed, from below. Just a door on either side, master bedroom versus guest-room, or maybe office. Forcing himself not to wonder what might be on the other side, Bill twisted the closest knob and slid in sidelong, trying to keep it open just the bare minimum allowable to admit his frame.

Within, he crept across the floor, tai chi tread, heel rolling straight and narrow to toe with every touch-down, to at least keep the creaks even. This had to be where Sessilie's dearly departed Mum and Dad once slept—hung with tapestry like some set for *Hamlet*; a strange mixture of blue velvet and purple trim that shone all the darker in what little moonlight leaked in under drawn blackout shades. Dark like club lighting without the natter of crowds and the underfoot thunder of feet, pulse of music seeping in from everywhere at once as though it were a swarm of tiny biting flies.

(*oh low estate*)

(*the threat*)

(*my*)

Bill felt his way forwards, in search of drawers, cupboards, some sort of indication that anything had ever been kept in this damnable room besides memories and a place for wrinklies to shag. Something pushed forward under his fingers, a slick surface impossible to hold onto. Something hit the ground with a crunch, right in the midst of a bright stripe of moonlight: a presumably happy couple trapped under a fresh lattice of cracks, taken someplace sunny enough their faces were almost impossible to make out in detail, except that the man might have had Sessilie's hair-colour, while the woman's smile cut the exact same angle as her darling daughter's. . . .

Bill froze, waiting in vain for another of those . . . no-sounds; those weird, unidentifiable lack-of-noises, but none came. So he just kept staring down as though hypnotised, finding himself trying to make out what that was there, on the inside crook of dead Mrs. K's arm, just angled so the camera barely registered it; grey on grey, uneven edges. It couldn't be . . . no, stupid idea.

No one gets a tattoo—or whatever—just like their Mum's, you twat.

Not even someone as odd as Sessilie, surely. Or—That *was* it, goddamnit. And *that* . . . he realized, at pretty much the very same instant . . .

. . . was the *noise*.

It's right behind me.

Before he could tell himself not to, he'd already turned.

At first, he genuinely didn't recognize her without all that high-gloss cack on her face. She'd taken her hair down, proving it to be far longer than it had seemed when knotted up—brushing her thighs in one thick, glossy, dead-straight fall, shiny-black as her own nail-tips. She'd changed, too, into an actual honest-to-God cotton nightie with long, ruffled sleeves and a button-down front, whose collar went up to her jawline. With skin thus mainly hidden yet feet left bare, she looked both younger than before—enough to make him seriously question his own judgement, in terms of where he'd chosen to stick his tackle—and sexier than ever in a still freakier way.

"Do you like the rest of my home, Billy?" she said, fluttering her lashes. "It's a bit of a dump, but one does what one can. Still, it must've exerted quite a pull on you, for you to go stumbling around here in the dark while you thought I was asleep."

"Well, uh . . . I was just looking around for . . ."

"The loo? I do know how you appreciate a nice bathroom, after all. One on every floor, dear; two, sometimes. One wonders how you missed them."

Oh, does *one?* That tone of hers was maddening; not simply the way in which she spoke, but the sentiment—or lack thereof—behind it. And so difficult to listen to as well. Slipped away whenever the ear tried to fasten on it, pig-greasy with happy idiocy, as though nothing said '*like that*' could be worth paying attention to, even with only half an ear.

Which was why he found himself trying to focus on the light she held, instead, using its soft flicker to steady himself. "That's from . . . downstairs, isn't it?"

"Why yes, it is. Funny you should notice."

"Why? I was there when you lit it."

"Course you were, I knew that. But, you see—this is rather a *special* candle."

She took a moment to run her finger over its uppermost quarter, hot wax slopping onto her in a way that anyone else would find unbearable, and made an odd little fiddly gesture that seemed to make a perfect little approximation of somebody's features emerge from the unburnt portion. Not just somebody's, though—for as she did, Bill heard a fold of tapestry pull back, revealing a long, narrow oval of mirror, and glanced automatically towards its surface. There, hanging inside like a drowned corpse under glass, he recognized himself; his blood congealed, the air itself becoming slow, difficult to move through. He could barely think, barely breathe; his chest heaved painfully, a landed fish yearning for water.

"Whuh . . ." was all he could say by way of reply, and Sessilie smirked.

"Oh, it's an *awfully* amusing story. You see, when one of my Mama's great-great-whatevers was clapped in durance vile over having been accused of merry-dancing with Old Sir 'S', she smuggled this candle into the clink to make a dolly out of it. And where she put it, I can't possibly say; a very secret place indeed, if you take my meaning. But . . ."

With a frighteningly massive effort, Bill managed to half-turn himself back towards the door, though his feet seemed snared in treacle, his Achilles tendons shot full of novocaine. He fell to his knees, clutching for Sessilie's ankles, but she skipped back out of range as though playing hop-scotch, content to let his own weight carry him down onto all fours. And even then, practically parallel with the floor, he couldn't manage to keep upright everything hurt, impossible to support. His hands gave way, knees bowed inwards, joints unsteady.

"It's special, you see," Sessilie went on, "because it can burn all night, and still never quite be consumed. The wax grows back like flesh, so that every new woman of my blood may re-shape the face to their liking, light it, and use it like a Hand of Glory to trap our enemies. Though it has other uses too, of course. Summoning the one who first gave it us, for example, and who is sworn to do our bidding just as we, in turn, swear to eventually pay for that long and faithful service."

Behind her, a stirring. A wind ruffling those tapestries' as *something* passed behind them, dropped pin-quiet, clicking dog's nails-distinct. A lip-pop with every step.

"As for *you*, meanwhile," Sessilie added, "how long d'you intend to make me wait, exactly? And after all this trouble I've gone to, on your behalf."

The answering voice seemed to come from everywhere and nowhere at once, soft as fallen leaves. Saying, without haste: "A moment's rest is always pleasant, my lady. You do keep me so very busy."

"Really, Nanny, you're *very* lazy, all things considered; greedy, too. But then, Mama always warned me you were. *Rule with an iron hand,* and all that."

"Yes, my lady. Your lady mother was a perceptive woman, with—very good taste."

"You aren't being impertinent, are you, Nanny?"

"Only a trifle, my lady. Will you deny me that, too?"

"No, Nanny. You may be as impertinent as you like, so long as you do what you're told."

"Yes, my lady."

She rose up then, manifesting from what might have been the bottom of the tapestries, the dark under Sessilie's parents' bed, or a pile of rags in the corner. Thirty at the most, slim and straight and taller than Sessilie yet bent, willow-graceful; coloured white and black and grey like Sessilie's room, with the occasional hint of red at her mouth, her ears, her distressingly long fingers. The dress she wore might've been modelled on Sessilie's nightgown but copied in negative, its fabric less cotton than bombazine, giving off a distinctive swish of underskirts as she stepped forward in her neat little black patent shoes.

The click, the pin-drop, that was the sound of each movement—not a creak, not a sigh, nothing human. As Bill goggled at the realization, she dipped her head as though he'd spoken out loud, projecting: *Yes, I fooled you. I am sorry to play such games. They are the only pleasures left to me, I'm afraid. . . .*

(*Well—almost. I do not mean to lie. Lying is the provenance of your species, not mine.*)

(*But we will talk further of such things, soon enough.*)

"Where'd you . . . come from?" He asked her, barely able to raise what voice remained to him. She simply regarded him silently while Sessilie frowned, tapping her nails so that the candle-holder rang dully. Replying, impatiently—

"Really, Billy, don't you *listen*? I told you already, she's always here. This is Nanny Grey."

It was a dream—had to be. How else could they have moved from one room to another, on whose walls an array of photos gave way to prints, giving way in turn to portraits, etchings, watercolours, oils? And somewhere in each composition—lurking patient and anonymous, behind or beside the centrepiece arrangement of well-dressed men, women, girls and even some boys who all shared Sessilie's dead-straight ink-fall of hair, her grey-blue eyes, her cruelly slanted smile—a version of Nanny Grey was present in her long black dress, her sensible footwear, no matter what the era.

"Nanny is my governess, as I said," Sessilie told Bill as she pressed him back onto what felt like a nest of sheets. "My servant, my lady-in-waiting. She's my helpmeet, the head of my household; she keeps all of this running, and whatever she does, she does at *my* pleasure." Raising her voice slightly here, a coiled lash, brandished rather than used: "Isn't that so, Nanny?"

"It is, my lady."

"Since—oh, I forget the year. Thirteen-oh-oh something, Mama said . . ."

"1346, my lady. When the very fount of your blood was almost cut off in full flower, for—was it treason? Yes. You Kytelers are treasonous by nature, I believe. And to kill one's husband, then, no matter what provocation might have preceded such a desperate act, was considered just as bad as conspiring to kill the king himself. They burnt women at the stake for it just as surely as for witchcraft, soaked in oil and pitch with no hope of merciful strangulation, whilst crowds screamed and pelted them with garbage."

"Better by far to turn to the Devil than God, under such circumstances," Sessilie chimed in, with an air of quoting something learned by rote. "Or easier, anyhow."

"Down there in the dark, yes, amongst the rats and bones. A bad place for any pretty woman to end. But then again, that *is* where your ancestor Lady Alyce eventually found me, after all—where we found each other, more accurately."

"Quite. But the promise behind our contract isn't enough to satisfy Nanny, you see, not always. And though it's *such* a bother to arrange for boys like you to come visit every once in a while, Nanny does *so* much work on our behalf that she really must be kept happy. It's only good manners."

"I do value good manners, you see. Courtesy, common or otherwise. The little gestures."

"'Manners maketh man', and all that."

"A party-dress on an ape, that's all they are, when everything is said and done. But since there's no alternative, they simply have to do."

"Given it must've been God who deeded you to us in the first place, directly or in-, do you think perhaps we might be part of *your* Hell, Nanny?"

"I often ask myself that very question, my lady."

"But to no avail?"

"None, my lady."

"That's prayer for you, Nanny."

"Yes, my lady."

Nanny Grey eddied forward with one long white hand on her breast, head bent down submissively. And when she looked up, eyes pleasantly crinkled, she smiled so wide that Bill could see how her teeth were packed together far too numerously for most human beings, bright as little red eyes in the wet darkness of her mouth. While her eyes, on the other hand, were white—white as real teeth, as salt, as a blank page upon which some unlucky person's name had yet to be inscribed.

"Little master," she murmured. "You wished a tour, I believe, and no one knows this house better than I. Come with me, please."

"I don't—"

"Oh, it will be no trouble; what my lady orders, I do. For as she told you, this is the bargain between us—the terms of my employment."

"Yes, and I do hope you were finally paying attention, silly Billy. Because with so little time left, I'd hate to have to repeat myself."

Sessilie leant down then, pressing one ear to Bill's chest, in a vile parody of post-coital relaxation. But when Nanny Grey laid one of those too-long hands on his forehead a moment later, he felt his heart lurch and stutter as though he were about to have a heart attack, pounding double, triple, quadruple-time. Sessilie must've heard it, for she gave yet another of those rippling laughs, and he wanted nothing more than to be able to rouse his limbs enough to tear her soft white throat open with his thumbs. She drew back and pouted.

"I'm going to tell you something now, Billy," she said, "because I actually quite like you, all things considered. One day, when I turn Nanny over to *my* daughter the way Mama turned her over to me, she will take me wherever she's taking you—wherever she took my Mama, and hers before her, so on, etcetera. Back to the first of us, great Lady Alyce in her shit-filled cell. So there; that might help."

Bill swallowed hard, barely scraping enough air to whisper: "It . . . really . . . doesn't."

"Mmm, s'pose not; shouldn't think it would. But then, I did only say 'might'."

He sank down further then, excruciatingly slow, into a deep, deep blackness. Only to hear them still arguing, as he went—

"Do this, Nanny Grey; do that, Nanny Grey. Eat up, Nanny Grey. You'll expect me to digest him completely as well, I'm sure, just to save you the trouble of having to cover up your own indiscretions."

"Well, I could simply take him away now, if you'd prefer—but what on earth would be the use of that, considering? There are limits to even your perversity, I'm sure."

"Really, it's you Kytelers who are the lazy ones. Never doing anything for yourselves . . . what sort of example do you think that sets, for everyone else?"

"Oh, pish-tosh, Nanny. Why should we have to make the effort, when we have *you* to do it for us?"

". . . crazy . . ." Bill told them both, through stiffening lips, to which Sessilie only smiled, as ever. While Nanny Grey raised a single perfectly-arched eyebrow, expressionless as a cast pewter mask, and murmured, in return: "I had *wings* once, little master. You'd be disappointed too, I'd venture, if you found yourself where I find myself now."

"Poor Nanny. Quite the come-down, wasn't it?"

"A fall, yes, both long and hard. And at the end of it—"

"Me," Sessilie supplied, brightly. "Wasn't that nice?"

A pause, infinite as some gigantic clock's gears turning over, millennial, epochal. Deep time caught in the shallowest of all possible circuits, and only digging itself deeper. After which Bill heard the thing that called itself Nanny Grey reply, with truly terrible patience—

". . . even so, my lady."

◄◦►

THE MAGICIAN'S APPRENTICE

TAMSYN MUIR

When she was thirteen, Mr. Hollis told her: "There's never more than two, Cherry. The magician and the magician's apprentice." That was the first year, and she spent her time sloo-o-owly magicking water from one glass to another as he read the newspaper and drank the coffee. Magician's apprentice had to get the Starbucks. Caramel macchiato, no foam, extra hot, which was a yuppie drink if you asked her (but nobody did). "Quarter in," he'd say, and she'd concentrate on the liquid shivering from cup to cup. "Now half. Slower."

For Cherry Murphy, the water always staggered along. She'd seen him make it dance with a twitch of his fingers. "When do I get to stop bullets? My hypothesis is that stopping bullets would be friggin' sweet."

"Maybe when you do your homework," said Mr. Hollis, and so she'd take out her homework. It wasn't even magic homework. It was stuff like *Catcher In The Rye*. Mr. Hollis was big on literature, so after they cleared the table of glasses he'd trick her into arguing about Holden Caulfield. Could've been worse—to make her feel better he'd given her *Catch-22*, and Cherry had read it approximately a million times. He said she easily read at college level, though he also said that didn't amount to much these days.

"All right," said her master magician, when her chin had started to droop. "Now you eat."

Magic wore terrible holes in you. Just shunting water around would give her a headache and throbbing nosebleeds, so he'd fry up a steak or fresh brown eggs and watch her gobble them down while saying, "Elbows off the table." The steak was always bloody. The eggs were always softboiled. Food would take the edge off, but not enough. Second lesson: magic feeds off your soul, said Mr. Hollis. There's only two ways to not be hungry, Cherry. I'm sorry.

"Two ways? How?"

"One, quit magic, Harriet Potter," he said, but then he pushed the plate of eggs at her. Her master magician never seemed hungry like she was. "Second's simple: eat more."

After dinner they usually had a little time. She'd told him over and over that Mark wouldn't notice if she came home at midnight covered in blood, but he always said: "Don't disrespect your dad," which was why she thought he was kind of a stiff. Then he'd follow it up with, "He does that enough on his own," which was why she loved him. So until six-thirty hit they'd watch the last fifteen minutes of a *Golden Girls* rerun—or listen to some Led Zeppelin, his iPod strung earbud to earbud between them both. Only then was she really content.

Mr. Hollis was a bachelor with a girlfriend downtown, so his apartment always kind of smelled like Old Spice and dead body, only she would have knocked back neat bleach before saying so.

When six-thirty came he'd say, "Put on your jacket," even if outside it was the average surface temperature of the Sun and she'd die of heatstroke. Then he'd say, "See you later, alligator," and she'd say, "In a while, crocodile," or if the day had been crappy she'd just make a series of grunts. Then she'd skip home through the dusk to her empty house or her passed-out, empty father, and read *Catch-22* until she fell asleep.

◀◦▶

There were spells on which everything hinged, he said; to *move, stop* and *make*. The spell that year was 'move'. Cool, fine; she was always on the move. Cherry had long spindly limbs like a juvenile spider, and before she'd been an apprentice she'd taken track and baseball. Her fingers did drum solos if she wasn't given things to do with them. All of that nervous energy went into her spells, and she worried her lips skinless as her water dripped, her winds scattered and any attempt to lift stuff embedded it in the far-off wall. Mr. Hollis primly mopped tables dry and set her to roll a marble around on the slick linoleum.

But he made it look so easy. There was not a flicker in those paper-grey eyes as a curl of his hand coaxed a hairbrush out of his drywall, beckoning it to remove itself and have the plaster rework to pre-Cherry wholeness. Objects put themselves back in his hands, ashamed. *His* marble rolled in perfect madman's circles.

Once—wild with frustration and knees scored with tile lines—she ignored him when he said: "Leave it. Stop." Her marble wobbled in a wide spiral. "Cherry." She feigned deafness. Her head suddenly spun towards him, yanked by invisible iron fingers, and worst of all her marble rolled away lost under the fridge forever.

"Cherry," he said evenly, "I don't ask twice."

"I can do this! Screw you!"

That got her grounded for a week before she realised he technically didn't have the authority to do so. Cherry sulked to bed each night at nine o'clock anyway.

June. In the summer evenings Mr. Hollis went off with his girlfriend, so they'd spend three brilliant breakfast hours down at the beach rolling grains of sand from palm to palm. Her skinny arms and legs grew browner if not less skinny, and he made her wear a one-piece instead of a bikini ("Nice try, but no cigar") but each of those days was more perfect than the last. Homework was John Knowles's *A Separate Peace* ("You could give me something with a good movie, Mr. H") and he sat shirtless under the beach umbrella as she read aloud.

Mr. Hollis had rangy bones and a nerdy fishbelly farmer's tan, lots of crisp dark hairs on his arms and his chest. It was possible that somebody found him hot, but only theoretically so; the fact that he had a girlfriend was mystifying. Possibly being a magician and the ensuing squillions of dollars, or at least the squillions as was her understanding, sweetened the deal. That summer she also rolled marbles until her nostrils squirted blood and she found herself eating raw hot dogs from the freezer. It was pretty gross. Cherry was hungry until her mouth hurt.

After August she struggled at his kitchen table, pushing ball bearings. Her head hurt. Sometimes he would ignore her and it was a kindness, as she had her pride even if she was in seventh grade, and sometimes he would briefly ruffle his hand through her short dark hair and say: "Be zen."

"I'm never going to get this."

"You're going to get it, emo kid."

"If I die, I leave you all my stuff."

"Try 'bequeath.' You *bequeath* me all your stuff."

When she did start to get the magic, in-between Knowles and *A Separate Peace*, Mr. Hollis gave her a single brief smile that made the rest of it a cinch. The marble rolled its circle. The water halved into its glass. As a test, he set his Honda Civic in first gear and she pushed it inch by burning inch nine feet forward: she puked bloodied bile afterwards like a champ, him holding her hair, but once her stomach settled he took her out for lobster. It was the kind where you picked your sacrifice out of its tank and were eating ten minutes later. It tasted incredible.

"Congratulations, cadet," said Mr. Hollis, gesturing with the fork. "Here's my toast: I'm proud of you. First we take Manhattan, Cherry, then we take Berlin."

Her joy was wild, and her Coke sweet like imagined champagne.

◄◦►

When she was fourteen, Mr. Hollis told her: "The apprenticeship only ends when you know everything the magician knows, and understand everything the magician understands."

Cherry took this to mean that she'd be an apprentice until she was like thirty. He switched from caramel macchiatos to skinny vanilla lattes, which this year she pointed out was "totally gay," and earned her a long, indifferent look. Mr. Hollis was an award winner at indifferent looks. He could scratch you with a word, or by flicking his pale aluminum eyes away at any place but you. The hunger still boiled low in her belly as she jumped water from cup to cup to cup, but crushingly all he'd say now was, "Cute one trick, pony."

Instead he got her to empty the glass out over the sink and try to divert it upwards. Cherry spent most of her time on her feet and mopping at her t-shirt when this proved to be a son of a bitch, and all he did was sit at the kitchen table reading his newspaper. That had started to drive her a little crazy too. Mr. Hollis was a slob who left the Sports section lying around and never dusted, but when she started scrubbing his stove and looking for his Dustbuster he said: "Don't go there. Jen doesn't even go there."

He'd been dating Jennifer Blumfield over a year now. Cherry had been introduced as his niece. Jen did accounting and was sweet without being patronizing, but she hated her a little anyway and bullshitted her best smile to hide it. Only complete dumbasses weren't nice to the girlfriend. Mr. Hollis wasn't prehistoric, and even though his five driver's licences showed four different ages he was allowed to date.

"Are you going to tell her about the magic thing?"

Cherry hadn't expected the cold shoulder. "You never tell *anyone* about what we do, Charlene. I didn't think you capable of being this big an imbecile."

Her eyes had smarted, and his were turned away.

They went from Knowles to Dickens, *David Copperfield*. She'd argued it was abuse. That was the year of many long arguments: she liked Marlowe, he liked Shakespeare, he liked Austen and she liked American Lit. Mr. Hollis set her to tossing M&Ms up in the air and slowing their descent, staring down his narrow nose in impatience at any cracks in their hard candy carapaces. It sucked.

And she might have been prodigious for fourteen, but not in science. That was the year she also had to stay half an hour after school for remedial physics, which was stupid, but Mr. Hollis was calmly unsympathetic: "Suck it down. You can't pass high school with just one subject." He was equally unsympathetic to the notion that, as a magician's apprentice, physics was beneath her: "I still have a day job, Cherry."

"You do not have a day job. Every so often a car comes around and you get in and then you come back with a suitcase full of cash. I'm not judging, I'm just saying that I bet you my whole life you are not making money off a David Copperfield Quiz Olympics."

Whatever he was doing he wouldn't tell her. A big black car would pull up outside and he'd be waiting in a suit, and the driver would even open the door for him and he'd nod coolly like the guy was toilet paper attached to his heel. Cherry would hang around outside for hours and hours until he came back, and even then he'd only let her get a whiff of that new-money smell before the case shut and disappeared. She hoped all the time this meant Disneyland instead of college.

"I don't care. I'm not countenancing your future ignorance if I have to live with it." She asked furtively about higher education. "Ivy League, champ." Oh, Jesus.

On the brighter side, that was also the year Callum asked her to the dance. He was older and wore seriously skinny jeans. Tenth graders usually weren't all that interested in eighth graders, but they liked the same bands and she'd graduated to a real bra with an underwire and wore short shorts starting May. The first and last time she'd worn them to Mr. Hollis's his eyebrows shot up to his hairline.

"You seem to be *sans pants.*"

"They're daisy dukes, old man. I am trying to maximise my coolness, okay?"

A newspaper page got flipped. "They looked better on Daisy Duke. Put on my gym pants before you go home."

"That suggestion is completely horrifying."

"Yes, Cherry?" Definitely not amused. His professor voice always turned into sharp, hard-edged vowels when he was pissed, like a movie villain. "Are you suffering hearing trouble? You're a little slow with my lesson of not always getting your way."

"But—"

"Cherry," he said. "There are rapists out there. Serial killers. Look at the news for once: girls get kidnapped constantly, and there are dead joggers in every alleyway. And for the bottom line, I made a request of my apprentice and I don't ask twice."

She wore his gym pants home. Wearing short shorts at school didn't seem a blast any more either, and after the dance in the back seat Callum put his hand on her knee and she felt weird about it. The hunger gnawed at her stomach, and she made his car lurch forward in the parking lot each time his hand moved up her leg. "Wow!" she said. "Ghost car!" Callum dumped her the next day. Mr. Hollis handed her Kleenex when she cried.

⊸◦⊶

The spell that year was 'stop'. She knew enough now to dread it. Mr. Hollis sat with her in meditative Yoga poses on the floor of her living room as the scent of rot and old washing tickled her nose: she sneezed, she fidgeted, she popped her knuckles one by one until he came to show her how to hold her hands and then it was easy.

It was stupid easy, really. The trick was understanding gravity (thanks, remedial physics) and that she was working magic to oppose a force, not flow with one as she did rolling ball bearings. Cherry could make marble after marble hang in midair like tiny spaceships. Water shivered to a halt as Mr. Hollis upended a glass over the rug. Her master magician watched her progress over his newspaper or with an eye on a TiVo'd episode of *Seinfeld* while she tossed up handful after handful of flour to stop dead as fine white mist: the downside was that you got even hungrier than before.

That was the year of the accident. Some douchebag in a Ford came screaming out of the intersection as Mr. Hollis made a June-morning car ride to the beach. Cherry rode shotgun with the umbrella. Brakes squealed as the guy saw his mistake too late, about to plough right into the driver door, and she Stopped his car so hard that her fingernails twisted. Most of the tiny veins in her eyeballs popped. Blood leaked from her mouth and ears and nose as she gave everything, fed everything into the furnace of her magic as a starving body fed on tissue when out of options. The last thing she thought she saw were his hands, raised above the steering wheel, and then she blacked out.

When she woke up it was on his couch, to the smell of food. Every breath made her lungs scream. Mr. Hollis knelt next to her with a bowl and a forkful of gamey meat liberally covered in teriyaki sauce, and that meat smelled like fried chicken, like fudge sundaes and candyfloss, like everything that used to make her mouth water. The first bite she choked on in her eagerness. "For the love of God, slower," he said, and, "Chew. Please. I've long forgotten how to Heimlich, Cherry."

Each morsel of that meal warmed her from the tips of her toes to the crown of her skull. It was almost enough that she didn't look at the expression on his face, the grim and painful tenderness, sweat sweeping back his dark hair. There were little sprays of grey at the temples. He wasn't even forty, and the grey made her terribly sad somehow. But she was less sad than she was starving. "Whash *ish* thish."

"Chew, swallow, rinse, wash, repeat," he said, but the taut line of his mouth was softening. Cherry opened her mouth like a little baby bird for the next forkful. Her master magician hesitated uncharacteristically: "An hour ago this was real live goat."

"That is literally disgusting," she said. "Goats are adorable." Mr. Hollis loaded up the fork again and she licked all the tines. The bloodied crust at her nose and eyes didn't matter anymore. She could have run a marathon. "Is goat always this good? Because this is awesome."

"I'll let you in on a little secret, as your mentor." The texture of the pale teriyaki fry-up was a little weird, a little dry, but he was mashing his fork against the side of the bowl to get her every last delicious bit. "When something dies, Cherry, it leaves a little bit of itself behind. That part, and I'll call it life force, starts to dissipate out the body immediately. But if we get it and we get it fresh—well, we're not hungry after that."

"So we should just be fruitarians," she said, wiping her tongue around the corners of her mouth. The hunger had eased, and the pain had driven a couple blocks away. "Pick apples off the trees, eat them right there."

"If it was that easy I'd be dismembering broccoli plants."

"What *do* you do?"

"Terrible things to God's own creatures, for you," her master magician said, which struck her as a little evasive. The bowl went away. Cherry looked at the fine bones of his face as he cleaned up hers, his dignified jaw, his slash of a nose. His eyes: the unbelievably pale grey of snow three days old, with faint crow's feet. Mr. Hollis was old before his time. Now he was dabbing her forehead, her ears, and he said, "You should have trusted me to take care of that car. Don't you ever do that to me again, Charlene Murphy, or so help me I don't know what I'll do."

She felt drunk, or at least what drunk probably felt like. "'Cherry.'"

"You're a brat." He was touching her hair. "'Charlene' never did suit."

"I like how you always called me Cherry." She really was drunk. "Like *ma chérie*, am I right?"

Mr. Hollis's expression smoothed into something careful and polite, and he took his hand away from her hair. "Get some rest," he said, and he laid his jacket over her legs as he stood up and took the bowl. There was neutral kindness in his voice, the type which made her burn with teen humiliation; or would've, if she hadn't been high off feeling full and sleepy for the first time since forever. "No more magic for a while."

Before she dozed off she thought she heard him eating in the kitchen, cramming something into his mouth and chewing before frantic wet swallows.

◄◦►

When she was fifteen, Mr. Hollis told her, "We've come this far, you and I. You can call me John."

Cherry slipped up on it all the time, and called him 'Mr. Hollis' more than she called him 'John'. She practiced in the mirror with it: John, John, Johnny, Jack, John. John Hollis. John Hollis, the magician. Cherry Murphy, the apprentice. John and Cherry, Charlene and John.

She was too old and experienced to be in love with him, seriously, only stupid kids did that with their teachers—and as he said, she wasn't stupid. He damned with faint praise. Cherry had come a long way: he was a God-King, but she was his lieutenant, his right hand and left, his Holy Ghost. She read Vonnegut and Faulkner without needing his recommendation. Cherry could also drive between the hours of twelve-thirty a.m. and five p.m., which was cool.

This was the year of the cappuccino, and they sat around his kitchen table sipping them as they swapped sections of the newspaper. It was also the year of the world's most disappointing growth spurt. She'd made five foot one and stopped, resigned to Smurfitude until the next spurt hit, doomed to skinny legs and arms and brown hair that had never gone blonde. It was depressing. Even her eyes were heading more beigewards than chocolate. To cheer herself up Cherry wore hipster scarves and bobby socks, and she gave all her daisy dukes to the Salvation Army.

"When are you going to move in with Jen?" she said. "This apartment smells like leprosy. I can't believe how much you pay for it."

"One day I may want to pick up and leave."

"So you abide in this creepy shack instead? Are you this afraid of commitment?"

John was a champ with non-responses. "Wouldn't you like to know?"

"Yes, I would. No rhetorical."

"Leave my love life alone, Cherry," he said. "I won't ask twice."

He still set her bedtimes: twelve o'clock on weeknights, two o'clock on Saturday and Friday. Her dad was having a mid-life fatherhood AA crisis and kept having family dinners with her, telling her awkwardly she was looking more like Mom each day. To get through those meals Mr. Hollis sometimes even set her menu. Like: eat all your green vegetables, but nothing else. They both knew that table food was a joke.

The hunger was an old sickness. Eating the goat ruined her for everything else. Sometimes she and John went down to the sea where he shore fished, gutting his catch in record time, and they sat there gorging themselves on fresh raw perch squirted with hot sauce—but it was never really the same.

When they read together, she found herself leaning in so that their faces were nearly touching. Cherry let her bare shoulder touch the thin polyester of his shirt, imagining the hot blood going through his veins that made his skin warm through the fabric. She sat on the kitchen table and swung her legs from side to side as he worked at his laptop, completely ignored in a way that was nearly acknowledgement.

"Well, fifteen is a gulf away from fourteen," said John one day, shoulders slumped back in his chair. "I think you're old enough to have this."

It was Vladimir Nabokov. *Lolita*. Cherry turned the book over and over, feeling the weight of it in her hands like it was lead. "His novel about pedophilia," she said, and regretted how dumb that sounded.

"That's the obvious reading." The chair tipped back and forth, his gaze on the ceiling in contemplation. "The other one is about devouring somebody's life."

It took her a while to get up the courage to read it. When she cracked open the cover she broke his rule to spend three sleepless nights finishing the thing, reading it at lunchtimes, reading it in study hall in another dustcover, skipping gym and reading it in the park. When she tried to talk about it he was so removed on the subject that she stopped, angry somehow like he'd breached the terms of their contract—and he shook away her hand when she rested her fingers over his own.

"For someone so clever, you can be an unbelievably stupid kid," he said abruptly.

That shot told. "I haven't been a kid in a while, John."

"You're a child, Charlene. Don't fool yourself. You don't know anything."

So she stopped touching him. That was the year she felt very tired.

◄○►

The spell that year was 'make'. If she'd still been riding high on last year's successes, it would have killed her; as it was she spent her time mechanically breathing life back into dead matches, watching the blackened wood burst into flame that spluttered out as quickly as it flared. Cherry spent long nights trying to coax water to ice and ice to water again with red raw hands. 'Make' was a double-edged sword. Creating things was easy enough, but sustaining them was like eating soup with a fork, and after the most half-assed attempt she'd be so hungry that she'd chew her hair and her nails trying to make the feeling go away. Sometimes she thought about eating Styrofoam peanuts just to fill up the space in her gut.

Mr. Hollis withdrew from her into an armoured shell, emerging only sporadically like he was guilty for the absence. Cherry was good at absences, the best, and it hardly hurt unless you thought about it suddenly. He sat across the kitchen table with a crossword, a great wall of silence spanning between master and apprentice as she tried to make a bud unfurl on his spider plant. Sometimes he'd stand by the window and make tiny incisions in the air with his fingers, and then Jen would suddenly show up and she'd be kicked out and flipping the bird at his closed door. She was pretty surprised when that summer came and she got dragged off to the beach as per usual; she almost thought he'd cancel summer due to lack of goddamned interest.

There was no comment on her bikini that long, hot July. She kicked around in the tidal pools trying to make starfish grow back their legs, slathered with sunscreen and visceral disappointment. John spent his time under the umbrella with the newspaper, and she spent her time talking to dusty blond surfer boys with loud-patterned board shorts.

Seagulls cawed. He was fiddling with his sunglasses, saying nothing. The crow's feet were tracking deeper indents at his eyes and mouth than they had when she'd first met him; back then she'd never noticed his age, only that he was old. Now he just looked young with premature crow's feet. "You need some Botox," she added, and unnecessarily reached out her hand to touch his cheek.

John flinched, then pretended he hadn't. "God only knows, Cherry," he said, with a little bit of the old humour. "Sometimes I feel there's nothing left to teach you. Maybe it's time to move on."

That made her a little bit crazy, and with hunger it made her frantic. Matches, spider plants and ice cubes lost all appeal, June lost its sunshine. She threw herself down on her bed and cradled her head like her thoughts would pop off the top of her skull. Fuelled by his retreat and his distance, the specter of that idea haunted her like Casper the Friendly Ghost on meth.

When she turned up on his doorstep at 2 a.m. he didn't look surprised, just tired. "You can't send me away any more," she said. "You see, I've got nowhere else to go."

His apartment at night was full of unfamiliar shapes, the fan wafting stale air around the room and the carpet sticky beneath her feet. Without saying a word he led her to his hall closet, putting her hand on the doorknob before sitting down at the kitchen table in his sweatpants and t-shirt. John didn't look at her, just rubbed his hands together like restless birds.

"I was waiting for you to grow up," he said.

After she flicked the lightbulb on, the closet was full of jackets and beach umbrellas, stacks of books and an old vacuum cleaner. Half-hidden beneath a parka was a freshly dead stranger in jogging shoes whose thighs had been carefully sectioned and long strips of meat taken away. There was blood underfoot. At the familiar smell of old putrefaction overlaying new putrefaction she gagged until tears came into her eyes; it filled her nostrils. It filled her mouth.

"Magicians eat," he said, looking at her with eyes the colour of ghosts. "We eat more and more and more, Cherry Murphy, of anything we can get our hands on." A careless shrug. "Just look at me. I ate your childhood."

The doorframe scored her back as she dropped to her haunches, hugging her knees tightly to her chest. Every so often she'd involuntarily gag again, rocking back and forth until John came and carried her away. She gagged into his chest and struggled when he put her in his lap, fisting her hands in his t-shirt, wadding it up into her lips so that she wouldn't scream. His hand threaded hard through her hair. Saliva filled up her mouth and overflowed in trickles down his front.

She was crying so hard she couldn't say a word. His fingers finally tugged his shirtfront away from her teeth as she drew more and more down her gullet. On her shoulders his thumbs dug deep into her collarbones, and now that he was looking at her his eyes were sunken and gleaming like the hearts of white stars. Every line in his face was deep and hard and old.

"It was never goat, was it?"

"Sweetheart, I couldn't kill a goat," said Mr. Hollis. "They're adorable."

This close up he smelled of acrid sweat and Listerine and her spittle, and her master magician had his arm around her to tether her down. He'd killed someone. He'd stashed them in his closet. He'd done it before. With an awful, dreadful surety, he slowly pressed her head into the table.

"Ball's in your court," said John.

Her stomach growled.

"I want some teriyaki sauce and a fork," said Cherry.

◄○►

KILL ALL MONSTERS

GARY McMAHON

Two or three miles south of Sheffield they pulled off the M1 motorway and into the badly lit car park of a grubby little HumChef roadside restaurant. Squat buildings huddled in the darkness, separated by narrow patches of overgrown wasteland. The road was narrow; the aged asphalt surface was cracked and blistered.

The woman glanced at the clock on the dashboard; it was two-thirty a.m. The child was asleep in the back, snoring softly. The woman reached across and clasped the man's hand on the steering wheel. Darkness pressed against the windows and the sides of the car. Metal creaked. The engine cooled.

"Here?" she said, softly. "Should we risk it?"

The man nodded. "We need to eat. Something to drink. We can't just keep driving." His gaze was locked dead ahead, focused at a point a few yards from the windscreen. There wasn't much to see but he was staring intensely: a high white-rendered concrete wall, a row of grey plastic bins, a pile of black rubbish bags with their tops knotted.

"I'll wake the child," she said, opening the car door. The interior light came on, flickered. The inrush of cold air from outside was like an unexpected kiss. It lifted her; she felt unfettered from the small, claustrophobic world inside the car. She could barely hear the traffic from the motorway; just the occasional hypnotic swish of hot rubber on smooth tarmac.

She walked around to the back of the car and opened the rear door. The child was lying across the back seat, her long, thin legs stretched out on the upholstery. Light from the small, jittery overhead bulb pooled around her face and gathered in her long blonde hair.

"Time to get up," she said, reaching inside to give the child's arm a shake. "We're here."

The child stirred. Sat up, blinking. She rubbed at her cheeks, scratched her head. "I'm hungry," she said.

"I know. You're always hungry." The woman smiled and stepped back, moving in a crouch away from the car to let the child climb out. She caught sight of her own face in the wing mirror. There were dark bags around her eyes but the bruises on her cheek had faded to look like smudges of dirt. Her long sleeves hid the scratches on her arms.

It's okay, she thought. *You're fine, now.*

The car park wasn't busy. Only a handful of vehicles sat in white-lined spaces. It was too late for the dinner traffic and too early for the breakfast crowd.

The man got out of the car, waited, and then locked the doors. He walked ahead of them, towards the island of light that was the restaurant, and paused, holding open the double doors until they caught up.

"Just be cool," said the woman. "Be cool."

The man nodded, smiling.

If he's still able to smile, she thought, *things can't be too bad.*

They walked inside and sat down at a table in the window. It always had to be in the window; the man claimed that he hated feeling hemmed in, and that being able to look outside helped to calm him.

"Is it waitress service?" He picked up a salt cellar and shook it. Tiny grains of salt made a small conical pile on the red plastic tablecloth, an unstable construction that might collapse at any given moment.

"I don't know," said the woman, afraid for some reason that the little hill of salt might crumble and provoke an outburst from the man. "I'll go and see." She stood quickly and eagerly, and walked over to the checkout. A bored young girl, barely out of her teens, was flicking through a magazine and chewing a wad of gum.

"Excuse me," said the woman. "Is it self-service?"

"Yeah," said the young girl, without even looking up. Her dark red fingernails flashed as she quickly turned the pages of the magazine.

The woman returned to the table. She didn't sit back down. She knew the man hated the kind of impatient, fuck-you attitude demonstrated by the girl. It was a trigger. "It's get-your-own. The food's over there." She used her thumb to point without looking back towards the checkout.

The man nodded. "Okay. That's fine."

"I'll get the stuff. What do you need?" She was aware that her question could be taken in one of an infinite number of ways.

The man glanced up. His lips were pressed tightly together; they were thin and pale. "I'll have a sandwich," he said. His lips regained their natural colour as he moved them. "Tuna or ham. Something like that, you know what I like. . . . And a coffee. Black. No sugar."

The woman nodded. "What about you?"

The child was staring out of the window. "Can I have a donut?"

"Yes," said the woman. "And some milk?"

"Yeah, milk."

The woman waited a few seconds, to make sure they were done, and then walked towards the food displays. She grabbed a tray from the pile—squares of thin brown plastic made to look like wood—and walked along the refrigerated display cases. She took a tuna and sweet corn sandwich on white bread for the man, a fresh cream donut for the girl, and a cheese salad for herself. She poured two cups of coffee into cardboard cups at the machine and took a carton of milk from a chiller box next to the checkout.

For a moment she felt like crying, so she stood there and waited for it to pass. There was a heavy weight in her chest, pressing against her ribs. She closed her eyes and took a deep breath. Then, once the sensation had passed, she opened her eyes again.

She paid the cashier without speaking. It was better that way; she didn't want to communicate with someone so hideously empty. She knew exactly what the man would have done, and was thankful that she'd been the one to get the food.

She returned to the table with the tray of provisions. The man tore the wrapper off his sandwich and wolfed it down. The child nibbled at her donut, slowly licking the cream from her fingers. The woman picked at her salad. It tasted flat, like fake food from a cheap window display.

There were not many other customers in the restaurant, just a few scattered diners. Most of them were alone, but two silent couples sat diagonally opposite each other across the room. The geometry of their positioning bothered the woman but she didn't know why. Her life these days was filled with such random and inexplicable fears.

"We have to go soon," she said, glancing at the man.

He was staring at the child.

"I said we'll have to go soon."

Please notice me, she thought. *Tell me I'm more than just your babysitter.*

He looked over in her direction. His eyes were wide and wet, as if he were fighting tears. "I know," he said, and smiled sadly. "We can go soon enough. Give me a minute." His lean, handsome face promised more than he could ever give.

The lighting in the place was giving her a headache. It was too bright; harsh and unrealistic. She imagined it was similar to the lighting in hospital morgues, where corpses were dissected beneath cold white bulbs.

Panic welled up inside her. She looked again at the man. He was no longer looking at the child, or out of the window; he was watching the other people in the room. One of his hands was a fist on the table. The other had balled up the wrapper from his sandwich. There were crumbs on his jacket cuff but he'd failed to notice them.

"Nearly finished?" she said to the child, a sense of urgency causing her to speak too loudly.

The child had cream smeared on her upper lip. She licked it off. "Almost," she said, distracted.

Behind her, someone got up and walked across the quiet room. The footsteps were heavy; they belonged to a man. She turned around and glanced at him. He was young—perhaps in his late twenties—and wearing fashionable clothes with designer labels. He carried an iPad in one hand. The light on the machine was flashing.

These were exactly the kind of things that tended to set the man off: people in designer clothing, flashy techno toys, a look of arrogance, a smile of dismissal, an educated accent . . . the list was endless. There were new triggers to add to the list every day.

She looked over at the man. His eyes were dry. They were hungry. It was happening again and there was nothing she could do to stop it.

"Don't," she said, reaching across the table to grab hold of his fist. "Not here. Not this time. Not in front of the child. Let's leave."

When he turned towards her, his face was flushed; his cheeks were mottled. His lips were damp with spit. He was grinding his teeth. "When?"

She squeezed his hand. "Not long now. Just hang on for a little while longer, until she's finished eating." She could see the threat of violence in his eyes, as if a moment was suspended there, frozen forever. "Just be good."

He closed his eyes and bowed his head. "Monsters," he muttered, more to himself than anyone else. "They're fucking everywhere. I see them wherever we go."

"I know, baby." She looked again at the young man who had passed by. He was vanishing into a door marked "toilets."

The man's shoulders were hitching. He was ready to blow. "Gotta stop them all . . . stop all the damn monsters."

She had to make a quick decision, to prevent the situation from becoming worse. She remembered the time when he'd assaulted two bystanders and wrecked a petrol station forecourt trying to get at a middle-aged businesswoman in the passenger seat of a Ford Mondeo. All the attention it had drawn; their blurred CCTV photographs in the paper; their mad rush to change vehicles so that the police couldn't track them down.

They'd been on the move ever since, driving at night, sleeping all day in cheap hotel rooms, eating their meals at overly lit, lonely little all-night places like this one. Crossing the country in a succession of different vehicles, each one picked up cheap at cash-only used car depots. But England was a small country; soon they would run out of road. Then what would they do, simply turn around and run the other way?

She still didn't understand how they'd never been caught.

We're riding our luck; surely it must run out soon.

Surely . . .

"Okay," she said, softly but firmly. "Do it now. Do it quickly. He's in the bathroom. Nobody will see."

The man looked up, smiled, and got to his feet.

She flinched when he moved and hated herself for it. Each time this happened another piece of herself broke away. Sometimes she thought the only reason she stayed with the man was because if she left, the rest of her would flake off like scabs of rust and there'd be nothing left. This relationship, this twisted dynamic, was the only thing keeping her alive.

The man walked quickly and soundlessly across the restaurant—it never failed to chill her; the way in which such a large man could move with that kind of quiet grace. She tried to pretend she didn't see him quickly grab a knife from the cutlery tray on his way to the bathroom.

Nobody noticed him as he followed the other man through the doorway. The door swung silently on its hinges.

"Come on," she said to the child. "Eat up now. We have to go." The thought hit her that she could stand up now and run, get away. Leave him behind. But where would she go, and who would she run to? She had nothing; there was nobody else . . . just the man and the child. Without them both she would somehow feel less complete, less of a real human being. She'd been doing this so long that it had become what defined her. She belonged here, with these people, in these places.

It didn't take long. It never did.

The man reappeared less than thirty seconds later. The door hadn't even stopped swinging. His eyes were shining, his jacket was undone, and as he approached the table she saw that his knuckles were bright red and raw. They'd be bruised in the morning. She would have to find somewhere on the road to get some ice, to stop the swelling.

He stood at the side of the table with a faraway look in his eyes, swaying ever so slightly on his heels. There were a few spots of blood on his jacket sleeve. He didn't seem able to focus, not yet. It always took a minute or two for him to snap back into the moment.

She wondered where he'd left the knife. Or had he slipped it into his pocket to carry with him? They were blunt, those knives; it would be difficult to cause any real damage. That's what she told herself. That's what she hoped.

"Back to the car. Now." She grabbed the child's arm and pulled her gently to her feet. The remains of the donut fell onto the floor. They moved towards the door, the three of them together—a family. The man was once again in front. He pushed open the glass doors and held them while the woman and the child went through, out into the night.

She raised her eyebrows as she brushed past him. He nodded, confirming that the red mist had cleared. He looked like he was about to say something—*I love you?*—but then he closed his mouth and looked away, ashamed.

Even now, after all this time, he felt shame. That was part of the reason she still loved him, and why she thought that he could be saved.

The air outside was cold; the temperature had dropped dramatically during the short time they'd been inside.

"I didn't even finish my donut," said the child, pouting.

They hurried across the car park and waited until the man unlocked the car. The woman's breath was a fine white cloud. She bundled the child onto the back seat and strapped her in. They might have to drive at speed; she didn't want to risk the child being injured if they had an accident, like last time. A few weeks ago, after a visit to an all-night supermarket, he'd run the car off the road and into a drainage ditch. She'd told the doctors in A&E that the child had fallen off her bike. She didn't think they'd believed her, but they helped the child anyway, patching her up and sending them both away with orders to return for a check-up in a week's time.

By the time she climbed into the passenger seat, the man was already at the wheel, gunning the engine.

"Will it ever end?" he said, staring through the windscreen. "I don't think I can keep doing this. There's too many of them. I have to stop putting you through this—both of you."

She placed a hand on his thigh. The muscles there were rock-hard. She rubbed the dry palm of her hand against the rough leg of his jeans. "I know," she said. "We have to keep on hoping that the next one will be the last."

He closed his hand over hers, but it didn't feel the same. It was like a ghost hand, or a chill breeze touching her fingers for a second before moving away.

They pulled out of the small car park and followed the exit road, joining the motorway about a half a mile further along from the point where they'd left it.

The child was already asleep as they crossed over into the fast lane to overtake a large truck. The woman turned her head and looked into the truck's cab. There was a light on in there; it seemed to fill the entire space, a pulsing entity. The truck driver's face was soft and kind. He had a short, neat beard and small blue eyes. He was singing along to a song on the radio. She stared at his mouth, trying to lip read the lyrics—she wished she knew the name of the tune. It seemed important somehow; the answer to a riddle that might change everything.

When the truck driver realized that he was being watched, she turned her face away from his gaze. She felt him staring at her through two layers of glass as they pulled ahead of the truck and drifted back into the slow lane. He flashed his lights but the man either didn't notice or chose to ignore the gesture.

Her hand was still resting on the man's wide thigh. He was too hot for comfort. She took her hand away and pushed it between her knees. She was cold. She was always cold. She wondered if it was warm inside the cab of that truck.

They drove on into the sodium-spattered darkness with no destination in mind. Traffic was light. The stars were silver pinpricks in the black night sky. Wherever they went the man encountered monsters, and he tried his best to wipe them out. It was what he did, what he was compelled to do. He knew of no other way to put out the fire that raged in his veins, the flame that burned him up inside.

One question had always haunted her: *what if it's true?*

What if they really were monsters?

She looked down at her lap, at her hand gripped between her knees.

I am not my husband's keeper. I'll never be able to change him.

The thought rattled around inside her head, becoming less than an echo of a truth she'd always avoided.

The woman realized that eventually she'd have to stop him rather than going along with his moods and trying to curb his violent outbursts—even if these poorly stage-managed incidents were all that stopped him from losing his mind completely and hurting her and the child, she knew that she was wrong to allow it.

One day she would have to put an end to this. She would have to, because if she failed to do so then she must surely be as insane as him.

When that day came, she hoped that she could shield the child from further harm. She loved the man but she thought she loved the child more. And on nights like this one, when the man's blood was boiling, she was certain of the task ahead of her.

She glanced over at the man.

He was looking directly into her face, as if he was able to read her thoughts. He wasn't smiling. His hands gripped the steering wheel so hard that his knuckles had turned white.

"What were you looking at back there?" His voice was steady and even.

A gun, she thought. *I'll need a gun.*

"Nothing," she said. "I was just staring into space." She braced herself for a slap but it didn't come.

"That man in the truck . . . I think he was one of them. I think he was a monster." His voice was a whisper.

She didn't say a word.

Where can I get a gun?

On the back seat, the child stirred, ready to wake. She yawned loudly.

Lights flared in the rear window; the truck she'd seen earlier was approaching at speed. When it overtook them and shifted back over into their lane just ahead of them, a strange smile crossed the man's face. He put his foot down to keep up with the truck, as if he were chasing it. His features had hardened, a likeness carved in stone.

She wondered if this would ever end, or if it would be her life forever.

The road stretched ahead of them, as if in reply to her question. They were racing towards another bright dawn and following a trail of monsters.

Maybe tomorrow, she thought, not for the first time and certainly not for the last. *Maybe tomorrow I'll stop him.*

Up ahead, the brake lights on the truck turned red.

Beside her, the man pulled the knife he'd taken from the tray in the restaurant out of his pocket.

She closed her eyes and tried to think of nothing.

◄o►

THE HOUSE ON ASHLEY AVENUE

IAN ROGERS

1

C harles and Sally pulled up to the house at a quarter of eight. They sat in the car, basking in the air-conditioning and the picture-postcard view before them. It was one of those perfect Toronto summer evenings, with the setting sun bathing everything in a rich orange glow. Ashley Avenue looked as if it had been dipped in bronze.

Charles turned off the ignition and shifted uncomfortably in his seat. Sally glanced down at the bulge in his pants pocket. "You okay down there?" she asked.

Charles ignored her. "Let's go," he said gruffly, and opened his door.

Sally smiled devilishly to herself and opened hers. The humidity hit her like a physical force; she felt invisible hands press against her chest and force the air out of her lungs. A warm breeze buffeted her bare arms and legs.

It was only the middle of June and Environment Canada had already issued half a dozen humidex warnings. A lawn-watering ban was in effect, but you wouldn't have known it to look at the verdant lawns on Ashley Avenue. The only exception was the one at number seventeen—it was dead as the people who had lived inside.

Sally looked up and down the street. According to Charles, who had become her de facto tour-guide since she had moved to the city a year ago, they were in Rosedale, one of Toronto's most affluent neighbourhoods. Occupied by the sort of personage who could get away with ignoring a city-wide lawn-watering ban without getting fined, or who could easily afford to pay it if they did.

Number seventeen stood at the end of the street, next to an overgrown lot that looked as if it might have been a Little League field once upon a time. Sally could just make out the diamond-shaped remnants of the baselines. The house itself was a large two-storey dwelling with a wrap-around porch and a tall elm in the front yard. A set of flagstones made a path to the porch. The Westons had died here four days ago, but one would never have known it to look at the place. There was nary a police cruiser or piece of crime-scene tape to be found. Sally wasn't surprised. The residents of Rosedale paid for a great many things here, but she didn't think scandal was one of them.

"Unassuming, isn't it?"

Sally shrugged. "Looks like any other house on the block. Except for the lawn."

"Just remember what it really is," Charles said. "How did Jimmy put it?"

Sally smiled thinly. "He called it the architectural equivalent of a great white shark."

Charles frowned. "Not entirely accurate, but close enough at any rate."

"It doesn't look dangerous," Sally remarked.

"Did you expect it would?"

She gave the house a long considering look, then said: "No. I... I don't know what I expected."

"Expect nothing." Charles's voice was calm and collected, but Sally thought she heard something else underneath—nervousness. "Don't allow your mind to focus on any one part of it. If you start to feel funny, close your eyes and imagine you're walking a tightrope. Think only of keeping your balance."

Sally glanced down at her shoes, a pair of high-heels she had purchased earlier that day. "That shouldn't be too hard."

Charles heard the wry note in her voice and gave her an appraising once-over. "You'll do fine. You look great. Just hang back and let me do most of the talking."

Sally nodded and looked at the house again. *One of the Eight*, she thought. *I can't believe I'm really going inside one of the Eight.*

After smoothing down his tie and checking his suit for wrinkles, Charles finally opened the waist-high gate and started up the flagstone path. Sally followed. She found it was easier to not look at the house if she was moving. She needed all of her concentration to keep from falling down and busting an ankle.

She wasn't used to wearing heels, but today's assignment required professional attire. It wasn't a problem for Charles, who had probably popped out of the womb in a suit and tie. He always referred to his clothing by their manufacturer: his Armani suit, his Saki tie, his Gucci loafers. Sally, on the other hand, wouldn't have known the difference between Donna Karan and Donna Summer. She tended to dress for comfort rather than style, and thus owned nothing that qualified as "professional attire."

Charles reached the front door, and Sally had to hurry to catch up. He knocked, and a moment later the door was opened by a young man who looked as if he had been sleeping in his business suit for the last couple of days.

"Mr. Weston?"

The young man nodded. "Ted. Ted Weston. You're with the city?"

"We're with the Mereville Group," Charles replied. "An insurance company working on behalf of the city."

Ted Weston nodded, but the vacant look in his eyes said he wasn't registering this new information. "Please come in," he said, and stepped aside.

As she followed Charles across the threshold, Sally realized she had been holding her breath, and let it out in a long exhalation. They were standing in a small foyer. Sally heard gentle sobbing to her left and looked into the dining room, where two women were sitting at a long mahogany table. The crying woman was thin with mousy hair that looked as if it hadn't seen the business end of a brush in about a week. The other woman was short and fat and draped in a ridiculous orange sarong that, in Sally's opinion, made her look like an enormous beachball. The fat woman was patting the thin woman's hand and muttering words of consolation.

" . . . s'okay . . . let it out . . . normal to feel this way. . . ."

It was hearing the fat woman's platitudes that helped Sally get over the initial shock of being inside the house on Ashley Avenue. Watching the metronomal rise and fall of her meaty paw as she patted the crying woman's hand had the effective of a hypnotist's command, snapping her out a daze she didn't remember entering.

From behind her, Ted said: "That's my sister, Dawn. She . . . she hasn't been so good."

"That's understandable," Charles said. "This is not a good time. We apologize for this intrusion."

Ted led them into the dining room, clearing his throat to announce himself to the two women. "Excuse me, Ms. Morningside."

The fat woman stood up and gave Charles and Sally a cool, appraising look. Then she reached into her pocket, took out a business card, and handed it to Charles. It said:

TANYANKA MORNINGSIDE

SPIRITUAL CONSULTATIONS AND COMMUNICATIONS

"You are also family of the departed?" Morningside inquired.

"My name is Charles Courtney, and this is my partner Sally Wakefield." Sally raised her hand and wiggled her fingers in a small wave. "We're insurance investigators with the Mereville Group. We're here on behalf of the city."

"Investigators?" the psychic said suspiciously. "I don't understand. You're investigating *me*?"

"Not at all. The police informed us of the deaths of Mr. and Mrs. Weston. One of the detectives mentioned that the children of the deceased were concerned about the circumstances surrounding the death of their parents and had decided to pursue—how shall I say—'alternative avenues of investigation'?"

The psychic seemed to inflate with rage. "If you're implying that I'm—"

Charles held up his hand, cutting off her words. "I'm not implying anything, Ms. Morningside. We're not here to interfere. Just to observe."

The psychic's face became infused with colour. "I am a . . . I have worked with the police on several occasions. . . ."

Charles's lips spread in a warm grin. "Then we shouldn't have any problems."

"I still don't understand why you're *here*."

"Ms. Morningside, if I may speak frankly." Charles raised his hand, placed the first and second fingers to his lips, and cleared his throat.

"You're here, I presume, to contact the spirits of the deceased persons in this house, in the hope of better understanding the circumstances under which they died. I will go one step further and say that you are probably operating under the assumption that this house is haunted."

The psychic started to speak, and Charles cut her off a third time with his upraised hand. "The Mereville Group has no interest in the supernatural. That includes communicating with the dead or investigating haunted houses. We are perfectly neutral in this matter.

"But one thing *our* client, the city, does care about is Rosedale. If you yell shark at a beach, everyone runs out of the water like their asses are on fire. If you yell haunted house in a neighbourhood such as this, a lot of people are going to be placing calls to their friends on the city council. Are you starting to see things from where I'm standing?"

"Yes, I think I do," Morningside said. "You're talking about covering up what happened here." She crossed her arms defiantly. "I don't care if you're here on behalf of an insurance company, the City of Toronto, or the King of Siam, *I* am here on behalf of these people." She gestured grandly to Ted and Dawn Weston.

Charles clapped his hands together like a teacher calling the attention of his class. "Fine, okay, I didn't want to do it this way, but here goes." He cleared his throat in a theatrical manner. "Since Mr. and Mrs. Weston are deceased, the house is once again the property of the city. As representatives of the city, Ms. Wakefield and myself have more right to be here than anyone. Now while I wouldn't dream of telling Ted or Dawn Weston to vacate these premises, I feel I must tell you, Ms. Morningside, that the Yellow Pages are full of psychics, and if you have a problem with us being here, then I'm sure we can find someone else in your line of work who would be more . . . accommodating."

The psychic stared into Charles's icy blue eyes for a long time. Her cheeks were very red. A thin glaze of sweat had formed on her forehead.

"I need to work in absolute silence," she said finally.

Charles exchanged a look with Sally. "We won't say a word."

The psychic looked at them both steadily.

Sally ran an invisible zipper over her lips. "Not a peep," she said.

"Fine," the psychic said. "Let's begin."

2

They sat around the mahogany dining-room table. No one said a word. They were all watching the psychic. They weren't clasping hands, but Sally figured it was only a matter of time. The table was astringently bare under the glow of the single overhead light-fixture. It made Sally think of old gangster movies, stool-pigeons sitting in bleak interrogation rooms, while grizzled, chain-smoking cops paced back and forth.

The psychic stared around the table at them with dull, heavy-lidded eyes. She looked as if she were about to go into a trance . . . or maybe she was trying to remember if she unplugged the iron before she went out. Finally, she pulled a pen and a sheaf of blank paper out of a satchel bag on the floor next to her chair and placed them on the table before her.

"Clear your minds," she intoned.

Sally thought, *That shouldn't take you very long*, and the psychic's head snapped back as if she had been slapped. She stared at Sally. Sally looked back with innocent surprise—an expression she had down pat. She practiced it in front of the bathroom mirror in her apartment. A slight widening of the eyes, a rising of the eyebrows, a gentle tilt of the head. *Oh, goodness, is something wrong?*

Charles gave her a sidelong look and kicked her foot under the table. Sally couldn't help it. She had an impish side to her personality that seemed to embody that age-old maxim, the one that said you can dress them up, but you can't take them out. She liked to think that was part of the reason she had been recruited. Besides her other, less tangible qualities.

A slight breeze blew across the table and rustled the papers in front of the psychic. "The spirits are with us," she said.

Or someone left a window open, Sally thought.

Charles was watching her intently. He shifted in his seat and the object in his pocket bumped against his groin. He groaned inwardly.

The psychic closed her eyes, picked up the pen, and began to draw a series of loops. When she came to the end of the page, she dropped down to the next line and began again, as neat and orderly as the copy from a teletype machine.

Sally had witnessed automatic writing on a few other occasions, and recognized this kind of behaviour. Drawing loops was a sort of psychic holding pattern; it was supposed to keep the writer in a trance-like state until they began to receive messages from The Other Side. The supernatural equivalent of a secretary taking dictation from her boss.

With her eyes still firmly shut, the psychic began to speak.

"I am addressing the entities residing in this house. If you are with us tonight, please give us a sign."

The house was silent for a long moment. Then, from somewhere close by, there came a loud thump. It sounded as if something heavy—like a sandbag, for instance—had been dropped on the floor.

"Good," the psychic said, satisfied. The pen in her hand continued to execute an endless series of barrel rolls.

She's certainly the tidiest automatic writer I've ever seen, Sally thought. *Much neater than the one who used crayons and construction paper.*

"Please identify yourself," the psychic said. "Tell us your name."

They all watched as the pen jerked in the psychic's hand, dropping down to the bottom of the page. It spun around in a double-loop and made a cursive letter B. This was followed by an R . . . I . . . T . . .

"Jesus . . ." Ted muttered.

Dawn crammed a fist against her mouth, stifling a cry.

Charles and Sally stared expressionlessly.

The psychic seemed oblivious to what her hand was doing; her eyes were still closed and her brow was wrinkled in deep concentration. Her hand paused for a moment, then began again, writing with a flourish, leaping from one perfectly executed letter to the next. It was like watching a spider spin a web in fast-forward.

When she was finished, the psychic dropped the pen and let out a gasping breath. The others at the table leaned over to read the final message. Charles shot Sally another sidelong glance, while Ted and Dawn looked on with matching expressions of consternation.

Charles looked up from the piece of paper to the psychic's own startled face and said, "If this is some sort of joke, Ms. Morningside, I don't think anyone at this table finds it very funny."

Four pairs of eyes bore into the psychic. She seemed to shrink under their collective glare. In her voluminous orange sarong, she looked like a gas planet undergoing some catastrophic gravitational implosion.

Finally, she looked down at the words on the paper. Her eyes sprang open and she gave out a small squeak.

"I don't understand," she said. "I . . . I . . ."

"I think your work is done here," Ted said, rising out of his chair. "Please leave."

The psychic's chubby cheeks turned red again, out of embarrassment this time rather than anger. "N-no! This isn't right. I've . . . I've consulted on dozens of police cases—*police cases! Hundreds of them!* I have an eighty-five percent accuracy rating!"

Whatever that *means*, Sally thought.

The psychic looked at Sally again as if Sally had spoken aloud. "It's not my fault," she protested. "There was interference. Yes, *interference!*" She latched onto the word like a drowning woman latching onto a life preserver. "Interference from the *house!*"

The psychic reached out to Dawn, but Charles was suddenly there, gripping the psychic's upper arm and lifting her out of her chair. She tried to pull away and the strap of her sarong slipped off her shoulder. Her chair screeched across the hardwood floor and fell over.

"You heard Mr. Weston—your work here is done." With his free hand, Charles picked up Morningside's satchel-bag. The psychic glowered at them each in turn as he directed her toward the door.

"*Sneaks!*" she hissed. "You're all a bunch of dirty, rotten *sneaks!*"

"Thank you for coming out tonight, Ms. Morningside," Charles said as he stuck the psychic's bag in her hand and ushered her out the door. "Your insight was most educational. Good night."

The psychic opened her mouth to reply, but Charles had already closed the door on her. He went back into the dining room, experiencing a momentary sensation of déjà vu as he saw Sally standing over Dawn and patting her hand. The difference was that Sally was the real deal.

"I'm so embarrassed," Dawn fretted. "I can't believe I brought that woman here, into my parents' *house!* I feel like I've polluted this place."

This place was polluted long before your parents moved in, Charles wanted to say, but didn't.

"You had questions," Sally said, "and that woman claimed to have the answers. There's nothing embarrassing about wanting to know the truth."

Dawn wiped her nose on her sleeve and nodded reluctantly.

"But sometimes you have to come to terms with the fact that the truth may not be altogether satisfying."

Dawn looked up at her with rheumy eyes. "What truth?" she asked.

"That there is no mystery." Sally gave her hand a reassuring squeeze. "As much as you might hate to admit it, your parents were the victims of a terrible accident. But accidents don't have reasons; they just happen."

"But I've heard stories about this house," Dawn said. "I've heard—"

Sally squeezed Dawn's hand again, cutting off the other woman's words. "I know," she said. "We've heard them, too. That's why we're here, remember? Every neighbourhood has its haunted house, the one where bad things happened, the one kids cross the street to avoid. Even in a place like Rosedale. But they're just stories. There are no secrets here, no hidden truths, and no answers." She picked up both of Dawn's hands and placed them in her lap. "You don't need to like it. It's a shitty deal. But you need to try and accept it."

Dawn nodded, but it was a perfunctory gesture. She wasn't going to be accepting this, not today or tomorrow, maybe not ever.

"I need some air," she said, springing out of her chair and almost knocking it over. "I'm going for a walk. Then I want to leave this place and never come back again."

Sally nodded and looked over at Ted. He stepped forward, took his sister's arm, and led her outside.

When they were gone, Sally took out the psychic's business card. "Tanyanka? Is that Russian?"

Charles said, "If she's Russian then I'm Winnie the Pooh."

Sally tore the business card in half and dropped it on the floor.

Charles wandered over to the table and turned the pile of papers around so he could read the psychic's message.

"Britney Spears?" he said dubiously.

Sally shrugged. "Projecting at that woman was like throwing rocks at the side of a barn."

"She gave you a look."

Sally shrugged. "I goosed her," she said. "To see if she was a receiver."

"Was she?"

Sally tilted her head from side to side. "Yes and no."

"Yes and no?" Charles said, pretending incredulity. "The psychic is giving me a yes-and-no answer? What a scam!"

"Fuck you," Sally said amiably.

"So was she?"

"Eighty-seven percent of the world's population are receivers, Charles. But less than point-zero-one percent are tried-and-true psychic. This particular woman was a receiver, of that I have no doubt, but beyond that, it's hard to say. I suspect she has something, or else I wouldn't have been able to influence her automatic writing. But she doesn't have much, and she doesn't know how to use it."

"An unschooled talent," Charles said, staring thoughtfully out the window at the darkening street. "Is it worth informing the Group?"

"Couldn't hurt to put her on the watch list," Sally said, "but she's too old to train. You've got to get them when they're young." She fluttered her eyes coquettishly.

"That just leaves the house, then." Charles went out to the foyer. He looked down the central hall to the kitchen, then up the stairs to the second floor. "Do you pick up anything?"

"Nope," Sally replied. "Safe as houses." She raised her eyebrows devil-ishly, but Charles ignored the comment. One time she had asked him if his sense of humour had been surgically removed as a child. Charles had looked at her blankly and said he would have to get back to her on that one.

"But I probably wouldn't feel anything anyway," she went on. "These places have triggers, right? Something that sets them off and makes them go all Amityville on people?"

"It doesn't matter," Charles said. "Things are winding down. No one's going to live here ever again."

"No one should have been living here in the first place."

"Check." He went over to the window to see if Ted and Dawn were coming back, but the street was deserted. The arc-sodium streetlights had come on, washing Ashley Avenue in a sickly jaundice colour. "Matters are being corrected as we speak. The agent who sold the house to the Westons will be found."

Sally pictured an overweight, unshaven man in a piss-yellow suit with dark circles under his eyes and sweat stains under his arms. A man on the run . . . and with good reason.

"They're going to string that bastard up by his balls when they find him," Charles said. "For starters."

"If they find him."

"They will," Charles said confidently. "They put the snoops on him, and they've never come back empty-handed."

Sally hugged herself, thinking of the snoops but not picturing them. She had never seen them and never wanted to.

"So you don't pick up anything?" Charles asked. "From the house?"

Sally placed her hands against the small of her back and stretched. "I don't know," she said. "I could take a quick look around before we leave."

"No way," Charles said firmly. "Once the Westons get back I'm locking the door and we're out of here. And if we never see the inside of this place again, we should count ourselves lucky."

"Come *on*," Sally cajoled, "this is one of the Eight. I've never been in one before. Have you?"

"No." Charles licked his lips. "There's a reason no one lives in any of these places. You'd do well to remember that this is not a house. It's a slaughterhouse masquerading as a house."

Sally wandered into the living room. It had been decorated in a style she thought of as "Toronto Trendy." Imitation antique wood furniture, Robert Bateman prints on the walls, and an honest-to-goodness wood-burning fireplace that looked as if it had never been used. A living room straight out of the Country Living section of the Pottery Barn catalogue. Designed for those who had not spent any significant amount of time in cottage country but who wanted visitors to their home to think they did.

"I can't see the harm in taking a quick walk around. I won't touch anything."

Charles shot her a look. "If you knew what this place was capable of you'd know how stupid you sound right now." He pursed his lips. "This house has been empty for over sixty years. Exactly one day—" he raised his index finger "—after the Westons moved in, they were killed."

"I'm not talking about moving in. I'm just talking about a quick tour."

Charles paced back and forth in the foyer. Through the leaded glass panes in the front door, he saw Ted Weston standing out on the porch.

"They're back," he said brusquely. "I'm going outside to have a quick smoke and get rid of them. Why don't you come out with us?"

"No thanks," Sally said. "Nicotine screws with my biorhythms."

"Bullshit," Charles said, and opened the door. "Make it quick. And don't touch *anything*."

Sally gave him a two-fingered salute and went up the stairs.

3

When Charles stepped outside, Ted was sitting on the porch steps and smoking a cigarette. He had taken off his suit jacket and loosened his tie.

"I'm worn out," he said, scrubbing one hand down the side of his face. "It's official."

"It's allowed," Charles said, sitting down next to him. He produced a gilt cigarette case from an inside pocket, took out a cigarette, tamped it. "You have my permission."

"Thanks." Ted produced a lighter and lit Charles's cigarette. Then he leaned back on his elbows and let out a deep sigh. "What a day."

Charles looked around for Dawn but didn't see her.

"She wanted to be alone," Ted said by way of explanation.

Charles stood up and went down the steps to the flagstone path. He found himself conscious of making direct contact with the house and avoided it whenever possible.

"Heading out tonight?" he asked.

"Eleven-fifteen back to Calgary," Ted said, exhaling smoke. "Would've left this morning if Dawn wasn't so set on hiring that so-called psychic."

"That was her idea?" Charles asked.

Ted looked slightly offended. "Sure wasn't mine. But it's not her fault. Not entirely. The neighbours were on her the moment we got here. Whispering about haunted houses and spooks."

Charles put his hand in his pocket. "Why do you think she was so quick to believe it?"

Ted held his cigarette between his thumb and forefinger and stared at the smouldering tip. "Your partner got it exactly right, Mr. Courtney. What happened to my parents was an accident—a strange, fluky accident—but an accident nonetheless. I can accept that, but Dawn can't. Or won't."

"But why blame the house?" Charles wondered. "Of all the possible explanations she could have gone with, why pick one with a rather unbelievable angle?"

Ted shrugged. "Because they had just moved into it, I guess. We both thought it was kind of strange, how fast they sold the old place and bought this one."

"A house in this neighbourhood is usually considered a steal," Charles offered. "They don't come up that often."

"Yeah, that's what I figured, too. But the thing is, they didn't even tell us they were looking. They never said a word to us, and Dawn and my mother talked on the phone every Sunday. Last week Dawn calls me and says our parents got a sweet deal on a house in Rosedale. They closed escrow in a week. Before I became a criminal lawyer, I used to deal in real estate law, and I never heard of anyone closing escrow in a week."

Charles said, "It's strange but not completely unheard of."

"I know," Ted said, "and that's why I'm willing to accept what happened. I don't like it, but I'm not about to blame their deaths on ghosts." He gave Charles a long, steady look. "Of course, that doesn't exactly explain why you're here, though."

"It doesn't?"

"You said you came to protect the reputation of the neighbourhood. You don't want some psychic-for-hire going to the newspapers saying a house in Rosedale is not only haunted but responsible for the deaths of two people who were living there at the time. But if that's true, then why was it the neighbours who put Dawn onto the idea in the first place? Wouldn't it have been in their own best interests to keep their mouths shut?"

Charles looked down at his shoes, pretending to give the matter serious thought. "I think some people can't help but talk. Tongues like to wag. "

Ted continued to look at Charles with that steady look in his eyes. "You might be right," he said finally. "The fact remains that only two people know what really happened in that house, and both of them are dead. I don't like that either, but that's the way it is."

Charles smoked his cigarette and said nothing.

They heard the clicking of Dawn's shoes as she came down the sidewalk. She stepped up to the front gate, but didn't pass through it. "Ready?" she asked.

"Yeah." Ted turned to Charles and offered his hand. "Thank you for stopping by. Good luck with your investigation."

"Have a good flight," Charles said.

He watched them drive off. When they were out of sight, he took the object out of his pocket.

It was an old, scuffed baseball. Part of the red waxed stitching had come loose and a flap of the nicotine-coloured rawhide hung loose. To Charles it looked like the dried scalp of a shrunken head. The letters T. R. T., faint but still legible, were printed on the side in childish block letters.

The baseball had come from the Mereville Group's private collection of paranormal artefacts. It had been found in the house after the Group took ownership in 1944. Jimmy Dumfreys, one of the whiz kids in R&D, the same Jimmy who called 17 Ashley Avenue the great white shark of haunted houses, thought it might be an "apport"—a solid object which seemingly appears out of nowhere. Its significance, if it had one, was unknown. Charles had signed it out that morning, and it was due back by midnight. If it wasn't returned, the snoops would be paying him a visit.

Right after they caught up with Dustin Haney.

Haney was the real-estate agent who had sold the house to the Westons. Except Haney was no more a real-estate agent than Charles and Sally were insurance investigators. They all worked for the Mereville Group—on the surface an ordinary multi-national insurance company, below the surface a clandestine organization with interests in paranormal research. In addition to their various projects and investigations, the Group was also the caretaker of a handful of properties that were known collectively as "the Eight." Over the years, with the assistance of individuals on the city council, they had managed to keep the properties secure, maintained, and off the real-estate markets. The house on Ashley Avenue was not the most dangerous of the Eight (that honour belonged to an old fish-processing plant on Lakeshore Boulevard), but it was certainly the most attractive. As the operative in charge of visiting the house on a weekly basis and making sure it hadn't "gone Amityville" on anyone (to use Sally's phraseology), Haney would have been familiar with the neighbourhood and known how valuable the property would be to a couple who didn't know its dark and bloody history.

The real question was why did Haney do it?

The Group was still trying to figure that part out, but Charles knew they weren't really interested in the answer. What was done was done. They had learned a few facts. That a listing for 17 Ashley Avenue had appeared on three real-estate websites over the past two weeks. That the name attached to the listing was one Dustin Haney. And that Haney stopped coming to work five days ago, which also happened to be the day the Westons closed escrow on their new home.

Charles wished he could have told Ted and Dawn the truth. He took no pride or pleasure in lying to people, though he acknowledged it as a necessary part of his duties. But the truth wouldn't give them closure; it would probably have the opposite effect. It would have acted like a battering ram to the fragile doors of perception, and once those doors were open, it was impossible to close them again. Charles knew this from personal experience.

On the other hand, he felt not even an inkling of sympathy for Haney. It was hard to feel for a man who had taken advantage of a retired couple who had wanted nothing more than a home in which to spend their twilight years—twilight years which had turned out to be twilight days. The Group's think-tank were still scratching their heads over Haney's motive, but Charles figured it was because they were looking too deeply. He was willing to bet Haney had been motivated by nothing more than simple greed. Why he thought he could outrun and outwit the snoops was the real question.

As these thoughts raced through Charles's mind, he discovered his feet had carried him around to the back of the house. From here he could see down into the Don Valley and the dark sprawling expanse of the old Brick Works. With its sooty brick and spire-like smokestacks, it would have made a better haunted house than the house on Ashley Avenue.

But looks are deceiving, aren't they, Charles, m'boy?

Oh yes. In fact, that was the first thing they taught you at the Mereville Group. It could have been their slogan.

He bounced the T. R. T. baseball in his hand and stared down into the valley of dark twining shapes and rustling leaves. He had meant to give the ball to Sally before he left the house, but Ted Weston had picked that moment to show up on the porch and then Sally was already up the stairs.

And here you are still outside while she's inside.

Charles clutched the ball in a death grip. The voice in his head had managed to do what half an hour in the house had been unable to accomplish.

It had scared him.

Here he was promenading around the yard while Sally was inside—*inside*—the house.

He started back at a quick trot.

By the time he reached the front yard, he was running.

4

Sally was twenty years old when she was recruited by the Mereville Group. On that particular day she had been standing outside the Red and White General Store in Antigonish, drinking an Orange Crush. She looked up when the car with the Hertz sticker in the corner of windshield pulled into the gravel parking lot and the man in the expensive suit stepped out. Not Charles. She didn't meet him until a month later, when she began the Group's year-long training program in Toronto. This man, who moved not toward the store but directly over to where Sally was standing, introduced himself as Edward Reed and then proceeded to ask if she had given any thought to her career.

Sally had stared at Edward Reed for a long moment. *Next he's going to ask if I ever thought of being a model.* She had heard stories about strange men who approached girls and offered them work as models. Unfortunately, most of those men turned out to be El Pervos who were interested only in girls willing to take off their clothes. Of course, they didn't tell you that up front. Oh no. First they had to butter you up, tell you how beautiful you are, and how much money you could make—and so easily!

That thought was going through Sally's mind as she reached out to shake Edward Reed's hand. The moment they touched it was jerked out of her mind (she jerked her hand back, too), and was replaced with a sudden and inexplicable amount of knowledge about the man standing before her.

His name isn't Edward Reed; it's Winter. Dan Winter. Daniel Clarence Winter. He's thirty-eight years old, he lives in Barrie, Ontario, and he's left-handed. Once, in his senior year of high school, he cheated on a trig final.

Sally dropped her Orange Crush and stared agog at Dan Winter, a.k.a. Edward Reed.

"It was a calculus final, actually," Dan Winter said. "But you were close."

Sally continued to stare. She'd had episodes like this before, but never one so strong, so *intense*.

Mr. Winter told Sally what was by then clearly evident: she was a telepath. Then he asked her again if she had given any thought to her career. Sally had replied in her mind: *My career as a telepath?*

Dan Winter grinned at her. *Yes.*

And the rest, as they say, is history.

A year later, Sally had finished the psychic's equivalent of preparatory school and was given her first assignment—bloodhound work at Pearson International Airport. Using her "wild talent," she picked out potential recruits from the crowds of people departing and arriving. She had been there only a week before the Group pulled her out. They were concerned that in the wake of 9/11, airport security would be on high alert, and that it was only a matter of time before someone noticed that Sally was never meeting anyone or taking any flights herself.

So they sent her to the mall. Five of them, to be precise, on a rotating monthly schedule. Same assignment, sniff out potential psychics for the Mereville Group. Sally did that for six months, spending her days pretending to window-shop, eating her meals in greasy food-courts (she put on fifteen pounds), and staying under the radar of mall security (who were not nearly as astute as their brethren at the airport). The Group called this sort of work "trawling." Sally called it boring.

When Charles had come to her with the Ashley Avenue assignment, Sally had done more than jump at it—she had pole-vaulted over it. Anything to get her away from the mind-numbing Muzak and the El Pervos in the food court who seemed to come not so much to eat as to ogle the teenage girls.

Looking up at the house on Ashley Avenue for the first time, Sally had wondered if she hadn't bitten off more than she could chew. But now, as she walked aimlessly through the rooms on the second floor, she found herself feeling strangely relaxed, almost at peace. It was not the sort of feeling she would have expected to feel in a place with the reputation that 17 Ashley Avenue had. Instead she was experiencing the same kaleidoscopic mix of emotions she had felt on her first few days in the Group's training facility: a heady cocktail of curiosity, excitement, and nervousness.

She wanted to do a good job here—because she took pride in her work, but more because she didn't want to go back to the mall. It was trite, but it was true. She'd had her fill of malls and was ready for something new, something marginally more exciting than "trawling." And she hoped after today, the Group would feel the same way, too.

She considered opening her mind, just a little bit, to see if she could pick anything up from the house. But that probably wasn't a good idea. In fact, it might even be a bad idea. To do such a thing in a place like this was like raising your chin to Mike Tyson and saying *Come on, big boy, gimme your best shot.* Seventeen Ashley Avenue was not the heavyweight champeen of haunted houses, but it probably still packed a wallop.

Sally wandered into the bathroom where, according to the police report, Mr. Weston had had his "accident." The mirror over the sink was gone, and she could see the contents of the medicine cabinet. This struck her as an invasion of privacy, and she averted her eyes, turning instead to the old-fashioned clawfoot tub.

It was here that Mrs. Weston had found her husband, covered in broken glass, his throat slit. The report suggested that Mrs. Weston had panicked at the sight, went to call 911, and fell down the stairs, breaking her neck.

It was a good story, but Sally had a couple of problems with it.

For starters, the report said Mr. Weston had been standing on the edge of the bathtub to hang a shower curtain and lost his balance. As he fell he reached out blindly and grabbed the mirror over the sink, pulling it off its hinges. When he landed in the tub, the mirror shattered, and a piece of it slit his throat.

Sally supposed such a thing was possible, but not very likely.

The part about Mrs. Weston going downstairs to call 911 didn't make sense, either. If that's what she was really doing, why didn't she use the phone in the master bedroom? It was closer.

She was scared. She panicked.

Yes, and in her agitated state she tripped over her own feet and fell down the stairs.

Again, it wasn't an impossible scenario, but an extremely unlikely one.

Sally went into the master bedroom. All of the furniture was draped with white sheets. Sally went over to a tall, slender piece, pulled off the sheet, and let out a frightened gasp when she saw her reflection in a gilt-framed mirror. The sheet caught on the bottom corner and rocked the mirror back on its feet. Sally reached out and caught it before it fell backwards. She didn't need seven years of bad luck, thank you very much.

As she was replacing the sheet, she heard Charles in her head admonishing her: *Don't touch anything.* She stuck her tongue out at her reflection, which responded in kind. She flung the sheet onto the bed and went over to the window that looked out on the overgrown lot next to the house. From this vantage point the diamond shape of the old baseball diamond was even more apparent.

She turned to her left and took the sheet off the piece of furniture standing next to the window. It was an old vanity bench. It was beautiful. She didn't know anything about antiques, but it looked expensive. The wood was cherry and polished to a high gloss.

Sally sat down on the bench and looked into the mirror. Another mirror. Mirrors all over the place. Two mirrors in the bedroom, a broken mirror in the bathroom.

An idea came to her then, in much the same way as the one about opening her mind to the house had come earlier. Closing her eyes, she reached out and placed her hands on the surface of the mirror. Sometimes she could pick up impressions from inanimate objects. It was called psychometry, and the Group held it in very high regard.

The glass was cool under her hands. There was an abrupt cracking sound that Sally heard not with her ears but with her mind. A psychic sound. The crack of a bat. A baseball bat.

Her eyes flew open. A whitish blur came flying in through the open window and struck the vanity mirror. There was another sound—the unmistaken crash of breaking glass—and Sally felt a sharp pain in her left eye. Her vision in that eye immediately turned red, as if a filter had been placed over it. She clamped her hand over it and felt something jagged and sharp cut into her palm. *There was a piece of glass sticking out of her eye!* She opened her mouth to scream but all that came out was a dry squeak. She stood up, her hand still clamped over her eye, and tripped over the bench in her rush to escape the room and find help.

She tried to keep her balance and probably would have succeeded if her foot hadn't come down on the baseball that had broken the mirror. Her foot went backward while the ball shot forward. Her legs were swept out from under her—prompting a sudden strange association: her airplane ride to Toronto, her first airplane ride anywhere, and the mechanical vibration as the landing-gears were pulled into the main body of the plane—and then she was falling... falling face-first onto the hardwood floor. The shard of glass sliding directly into her brain, killing her instantly.

Sally took her hands off the mirror and opened her eyes. She wasn't blind or dead, but she was crying. Suddenly she didn't want to sit here anymore. She didn't want to be in this house anymore.

She stood up abruptly, knocking the bench over. She held her arms out for balance, then walked around it, give it a wide berth, and made a beeline for the hallway.

Her attention was so focused on the bench that she didn't notice the gilt-framed mirror had inexplicably moved across the room—right into her path of travel. She saw it at the last moment, tried to dodge around it, but her foot clipped the bottom corner and sent it crashing to the floor.

Sally swore and crouched down to pick it up. The frame was empty. All the glass was on the floor. As she stared at it, something strange happened.

The pieces started to move. Not very much at first, but they *were* moving. As if the floor was vibrating and causing them to dance ever so slightly.

Then one piece flew into the air and hung there. Another piece leaped up and joined it. Then another. And another. Soon glass was flying into the air like grease on a hot-plate, joining the growing mass which hung there.

The floor was bare in a matter of seconds, and a vaguely humanoid shape constructed of broken glass stood before her. It was a flat, dwarfish form, with stumpy arms and stumpy legs. But there hadn't been that much glass to work with.

Staring at the thing which had been a mirror until a few seconds ago, Sally was reminded of another wayward girl who had wandered into a place she probably should have left well enough alone. But she didn't think Alice had ever encountered a looking-glass creature like this one in her travels through Wonderland.

It took a step toward her. Its foot made a crunching, tinkling sound on the hardwood floor. The overhead fixture sent wild flashes of light along the walls as it took another step toward her. Sally thought of Mrs. Weston and her trip down the stairs.

She hadn't gone running for the telephone, Sally realized. She had been chased.

5

Charles ran around the side of the house and up the porch steps. He experienced a brief nightmare moment when he thought the front door was locked, but then he pushed instead of pulled, and ran into the main foyer. He saw Sally lying on the floor at the top of the stairs. Her eyes and mouth were open wide in what was almost a burlesque of fright. It was an expression Charles has seen on a hundred horror-movie posters: the terrified starlet cowering before the monster. Sally was no Julie Adams, but that was okay, because the thing standing over her was no Creature from the Black Lagoon, either. It had a short, squat body that seemed to be composed entirely of broken glass.

As he watched, the creature swung one of its jagged hands in a glittering arc that opened a long red line on the palm of one of Sally's upraised hands.

Charles's heart seemed to freeze solid in his chest. He clutched at his chest, and realized he was still holding the T. R. T. baseball. Then, without realizing what he was doing or why, he turned to his side, dropping his arm as he did so, and leaned into a position he had seen a thousand times on ESPN. He adjusted his hold on the baseball, made sure he had a firm grip, and turned his head to the left (looking for the catcher's sign, he guessed). A half-second later the rest of his body started to turn; his arm came around last, snapping through the air in a whip-like motion that ended with the release of the ball.

It shot through the air like a bullet fired from a gun, striking the glass creature dead-center and exploding its strangely fragmented body into a thousand pieces. Shrapnel flew everywhere. Sally still had her hands raised and was able to protect herself from the worst of it. Charles raced up the stairs and looked her over. Three fingers on her left hand were sliced open and would require stitches; on her right hand, a piece of glass was embedded in the webbing between the thumb and index finger. Another piece was sticking out of her thigh.

"Can you walk?"

Sally nodded and took Charles's hand. He started to lead her down the stairs, but she stopped him and turned back around. She crouched down, teetering on her injured leg, and picked up the T. R. T. baseball sitting amongst the broken glass.

As her fingers made contact with the old rawhide, she saw a flash of images. *The vanity. The open window. The scratch baseball game taking place outside. Kids hollering and laughing. "Eddie's OUT, Eddie's OUT!" The crack of a bat, followed by the crash of broken glass. Then everything turns red.*

The images faded away.

Sally clutched the baseball to her chest and for a moment Charles thought she was going to start reciting the Pledge of Allegiance... or maybe a couple of verses of "Take Me Out to the Ball Game." He took her arm again and led her down the stairs and out of the house.

He put her in the car and fastened her seatbelt.

"She was trying to make herself pretty," Sally said in a low, dreamy voice. She gripped the baseball close to her chest and looked up at Charles. "But she was never pretty again. *She was never pretty again, Charles.*"

Charles closed her door and went around to the driver's side. As he slipped behind the wheel, he realized he forgot to lock the door of the house. He took the key out of his pocket and ran with it outstretched in his hand to the porch. He locked the door and ran back to the car.

As they pulled away from the house, Sally looked over at the overgrown lot. She clenched the baseball tighter. Her blood dripped across the old, cracked rawhide. The baseball didn't mind. It was like coming home.

◄◦►

DEAD SONG

JAY WILBURN

The man walked into the dark room and closed the door behind him. He put on the headphones and sat down on the stool. Images of zombies flashed on the screen in front of him. He ignored them and opened the binder on the stand. He pulled the microphone a little closer and waited.

In the darkness, a voice came over the headphones and said, "Go ahead and read the title card again for us slowly so we can set levels."

The man read with particular slowness and articulation, "Dead Doc. Productions presents *The Legend of Tiny "Mud Music" Jones* in association with After World Broadcasters and Reaniment America, a subsidiary of the Reclaiment Broadcasters Company, with permission of the Reformed United States Federal Government Broadcasters Rights Commission."

He waited silently after he finished.

The voice finally came back on, "Sounds good. We're going to get coverage on the main text for alternate takes. We're also going to have you read the quotes as placeholders until we get character actors to replace them. Read them normally without any affected voice. If we need another tone or tempo, we'll let you know and we'll take another pass at that section. There is also some new material we are adding into the documentary."

"Okay," the man answered.

The voice ordered, "When you're ready, go ahead with section one, then stop."

The man took a drink of water, swallowed, and then waited for a couple beats. He began, "Dead World Records was one of the first music companies to come online after order was restored. They were recording and signing artists during the height of the zombie plague. Tobias Baker and Hollister Z are credited with founding the company."

"They operated from a trailer and storage building on Tobias's family farm, surviving off the land, and clearing zombies from the property between recording and editing."

A black and white image of zombie pits scrolled across the screen as the guys in the booth ran the images to check timing. The man ignored it.

He continued, "They do deserve credit for recognizing the continued value of musical culture and history while everyone else was focused purely on survival. They had the vision to gather and record the unique musical evolution of the Dead Era which shaped all music that came after it."

A grainy video of the men working in their studio rolled on the screen. The man stopped and watched as he waited.

The video froze and the voice said, "Skip to section four. The text is edited from the last time you read it. Read it over once and tell us when you are ready."

The man obliged them by scanning it over. He said, "Ready."

The voice said, "We're rolling on section four."

The man took another drink before he began, "The real unsung heroes of the rise of Dead World Records Inc. are clearly the collectors that agreed to bring the recordings back to the studio. Many of them were musicians themselves and trekked hundreds of miles through zombie infested territory to find musical gatherings of the various unique pockets of survivors."

A picture of Tiny flashed on the screen with his name under it. He was wearing shorts, hiking boots, and holding a walking stick. A picture of another man wearing a helmet and carrying a bat replaced it. The name below it was Satchel Mouth Murderman.

The man continued, "Music from this period is clearly defined by both isolation and strange mixtures of people and cultures. The gatherings of these musical laboratories (many of which were destroyed and lost long before the zombies were) is the legacy of men like Tiny "Mud Music" Jones."

Stills of Tiny with arrows pointing him out passed over the screen.

The man read on, "Tiny traveled farther and gathered more than any other collector. His introverted style and musical talent won trust and entry into enclaves of people no one else could penetrate. Some historians believe much of what we know of Dead Era culture is built off the exploration of Tiny Jones."

The man stopped.

The voice ordered, "Go with section six when ready."

The man began as soon as he had the page, "Tiny was so named due to his four foot eleven inch stature. Even Tobias Baker and Hollister Z didn't know him by any other name besides Tiny. He carried a pack which looked heavier than him with more instruments and recording equipment than food and clothes. He usually played for his supper and in turn got others to play for him with tape rolling."

After a short pause, the voice said, "Section seven needs to have a foreboding tone. It's going to be over some heavy music. Articulate it well. Go when ready."

The man read, "He is also the source of the Mud Music legend making three infamous trips into Dead Era Appalachia in search of it."

The voice said, "Let's do that again. Try a little more flow, but a darker tone."

The man read it again. The voice acknowledged, "That was good. Go with section ten now when you're ready."

The man began, "Tiny discovered Donna Cash, whereabouts unknown. Donna Cash is the most quoted artist on the Tribute Wall on Survivor Book. Bootleg recordings of her work are still in the top one hundred downloads each year. Donna Cash was best known for mash-ups of Madonna and Johnny Cash on the drag queen circuit. She was touring when doing so was deadly even for individuals not in drag."

"Tiny is responsible for the only known original recordings of 'True Folsom Blues,' 'Vogue the Line,' 'When the Ray of Light Comes Around,' 'Like a Ring of Fire' and many other songs that have been covered thousands of times by both straight and drag acts in the Recovery Era. Donna Cash has also been documented more times on the missing person

Sighting Wall on Survivor Book than any other person. Mr. S. Parker, the current CEO of Survivor Book, has put a permanent block on Donna Cash sightings."

"Other popular artists on the Dead Era drag circuit that were first recorded by Tiny included Pink Orbosin, Ms. Britt Britt Rotten, and Jerri Leigh Lopper."

The man stopped again and took a drink of water. The voice said, "Let's go with section fourteen."

The man scanned the first few lines before he started, "Tiny Jones recorded examples of New Swing from Pittsburg, Philadelphia, and Cincinnati. The music was originally used as a distraction for zombies while scavengers went out into the cities for supplies. Traditionally, it is played on rooftops. New Swing is a blend of Big Band, modern Jazz, 50's Rock, and R & B. It is defined by a reverb off of buildings. Most modern New Swing musicians create the sound electronically. Tiny recorded P. City Warriors, The Big Bloods led by the late Cap Kat Krunch, and the New Philly Phunk which still plays in Las Vegas with a new lineup."

"'We let Tiny record after he fought his way to the building and knocked on the door holding two zombie heads in his hands. Would you say no to a cat that showed up like that?' – Miles Diddy, P. City Warriors original line-up."

The man paused again.

The voice asked, "Do you need a break?"

"No, I'm fine," the man answered.

The voice said, "Turn to section twenty-one and start from the third line on to the end of that section."

The man recited, "Glam Grass was discovered outside of Nashville. A tour group of old eighties metal stars ended up in a militia compound with a religious cult. After the fire, Tiny's recordings were the only record of the founders of this musical form. It was defined by electric guitars accompanied by traditional blue grass instruments. The Glam Grass artists usually sang about religious subject matter, often out of the book of Revelation. The style is described as typically heavy, but surprisingly upbeat."

The voice said, "Now section twenty-seven."

The man read, "Across the South, a style known as Death Gospel emerged from places where churches became the refuge of nonbelievers.

It was a movement where metal influence came against traditional hymns. Unlike Glam Grass, Death Gospel was darker, slower, featuring minor chords, and was usually played acoustically. This style was documented by several collectors and is still a staple of churches in the Deep South."

The voice directed, "Section twenty-nine."

The man turned one page and found his place, "Tiny was involved in spreading the music and not just recording it. This is noticed most in the style known as Cherokee R&B or Red Blues. Tiny is credited with moving the music from North Carolina all the way to Oklahoma."

"'The day he came to the fences, the zombies parted and allowed him through. He was the first white man admitted to the Cherokee Nation Compounds.' – Chief Blue Wolf Pine, rhythm guitar and vocals, The Silent Dead Players."

"With variations across the South and West, Red Blues included Native American chants combined with traditional blues instrumentation and riffs. Later, Red Blues diverged more from this original formula. The later style was sometimes referred to as Blue Sioux."

After a longer pause, the voice came back and said, "Section thirty-five has been rewritten. Start that from the beginning."

The man read it silently, then began, "Shock-A-Billy was one of Tiny Jones's favorite collections. It featured shock rocker make-up, dark subjects, and Punk/Country combinations. It was mostly advanced by touring acts. Tiny expressed that he felt a kinship with the traveling musicians. Shock-A-Billy artists that stayed in one place were looked on as cowards within the community, posers. The tour busses were often dragsters pulled by animals."

"There were competitions between the Shockers to see who could get the most elaborate dragster. At one point, my band had the three-story 'Tarmansion.' It was built on the chasse of a tractor trailer and was pulled by 26 horses. It's a wonder we didn't get eaten by zombies trying to put on a show just traveling from point A to point B. – Big Bubba Tarmancula, Big Bubba Tarmancula and the Tarmen, Rock and Roll Hall of Fame."

"Shock-A-Billy tee shirts, tour posters, and images are infused in pop culture throughout the Recovery Era."

The voice said, "Read section forty now."

The man drank the rest of his water and then read, "Several styles of urban infusion developed during the Dead Era and were all connected by and counter-influenced by one another through Tiny's travels."

"Gangster and Western was defined by rivalry as opposed to isolation. Vocals are considered more melodic than traditional B.Z. Era rap. There were often references to local blood feuds between ranches that don't make much sense to modern listeners."

"The ranchers herded animals for food and herded zombies between ranches to foil rustlers and to threaten rival ranches. The results were often quite bloody and costly to human life. Tiny was the only collector to ever go to certain sections of Texas, Arizona, and New Mexico."

"The most infamously violent ranch war was between Big Daddy Bronco and His Boys vs. the Lincoln County O.G.'s. Tiny was the only one that succeeded in recording music from both camps."

"Hip Bach is the tag given to another style of music Tiny documented where inner city orchestras and concert halls became the shelters for local populations."

"'In all the history of time, you have never heard a style as close to God and as close to the street as this. This music allowed people to transcend the situation and see the secrets of life while being surrounded by the walking dead.' – Mr. Butter Hands, Low Town Symphony."

"Tiny Jones often traced music back to its source as he did with Slam Jo. Tiny traveled all the way to the Lud Mine Camp in the Sierra-Nevada Mountains. Slam Jo featured spoken word over banjo. New Wave Slam Jo documented by Tiny and other collectors began to incorporate other instruments."

"Tiny Jones was a legend in the Zed Head community. He was deeply involved in documenting the evolution of this daring style of music which mixed techno and house music over recordings of zombies."

"The most famous story of Tiny's involvement was the two weeks he accompanied DJ RomZom out in the open in a gathering expedition through Los Angeles."

"Many fans question modern Zed Head since most D.J.'s don't gather their own moan tracks anymore."

"The recent release of the alleged 'final recording' of Tiny 'Mud Music' Jones has resulted in a rebirth of the Zed Head movement. Border Patrol forces and security have been increased to discourage Zed Head gatherers from attempting to perform unauthorized expeditions into the uncleared, gray zones."

The voice clicked back into the headphones, "You're doing a great job. Turn to section sixty-four. This is all new material."

The man turned to the page.

"Go when ready," the voice requested.

The man read, "'Tiny and the Mud Music Legend is the modern Area 51, Brown Mountain Lights, and Kennedy Assassination rolled into one. How do you tell a ghost story to a generation of people that either witnessed Z-Day and survived all the way to the Recovery or that were born in the world after the Dead Era began? What are you going to say that can scare a generation that treats the zombie drills in school like a tornado drill? You tell them about Tiny and the Mud Music. I hadn't stopped being scared since that day.' – Kidd Banjo, former Dead Music Records collector and solo artist."

A map of the B.Z. Era United States with red lines drawing themselves across it appeared on the screen and distracted the man for a split second, but he found his place in the script and continued like a professional. "The first expedition Tiny Jones made into the Appalachian territory took him into the area that today roughly constitutes the border of Gray Zone 3. This collection exposed him to traditional, mountain music not unlike recordings from the early 1920's B.Z.E. from the same area. Tiny described trailers with wooden add-ons and trinket trash, folk art he saw on the expedition that expressed the same style, character, and sentiment of the music that had managed to stay unchanged through a century and a zombie invasion."

The map now had blue lines appearing and drawing deeper into the mountains. The man read, "The second expedition into the infamous region known as Gray Zone 4 came back with a corrupted recording that could not be found later."

"'Something was different about Tiny after that second trip. He was devastated by the recording being garbled. He had me and Hollis drop what we were doing and immediately sit down in a closed, locked room to play it for us. He had whispered the words "Mud Music" like it was something akin to voodoo. When it started out, it gave me chills because the sound was all fucked up and unearthly. I thought it was the music at first because of course this was Tiny and there was no telling what he might bring back. Then, I saw him crying like he had just watched his new born child get torn apart by the zombies. He was shaking and beating his fists against his head. Hollis had to hold his hands down to stop him. Believe it or not, that's the last time I ever saw Tiny.'—Tobias Baker, co-founder Dead World Records Inc.; former CEO D. W. Farms; deceased."

"'Tiny was changed. He was the most enthusiastic lover of music I had ever known. He was tough as a block of oak. I believe every story I ever heard of him parting seas of zombies, cutting off their heads and carrying them in to impress musicians, and walking right through them to find the music. He was fearless because he loved the music so much. After that trip, he was obsessed. He sat and listened to that recording over and over and over and over and over. After he left, we never found that recording again, but I still hear that shit in my nightmares because of him repeating it and repeating it those last few nights. He sat with his ear to the speaker swearing that it was under the interference. That it was under that ruined recording. Then, he said he heard the voices of the singers speaking to him. He tried to describe the instruments they built. I can't remember now, but I wish I had recorded him talking. I didn't know that when he left that last time that that was it. I would have tried to stop him, if I had known, but he was Tiny Jones. I don't think I could have stopped him, if I had tried.' – Hollister Z, co-founder Dead World Records Inc."

The man stopped and looked up to see a blown-out, color photo of Tiny Jones leaning over with his ear to a speaker.

When his headphones crackled, it made the man jump a little. The voice just said, "Section sixty-five."

The man collected himself and began, "He did not return from his third expedition. There were no other confirmed sightings either. Only Donna Cash has more unconfirmed sightings on Internet America."

"As witnessed by Tobias Baker and Hollister Z, Kidd Banjo returned to the farm with a cassette he claimed was given to him by Tiny Jones. Kidd Banjo was a collector for Dead World and in the Recovery Era he rose to prominence as a Shock-A-Billy Revival artist. Cassettes were not in common use at the time and there are no other Tiny Jones recordings on a cassette tape. Kidd claimed he was in the Fort Guilford Colony in western Virginia near the North Carolina border. Somehow Tiny had entered his room in the fort, had awakened him without disturbing the other men in the bunks, and had given him the tape without being detected by the guards either entering or leaving the heavily secure fort."

"Kidd Banjo insisted it was Tiny and that he was covered in cuts and bruises. He told Kidd to take it directly to D. W. Farms. He said it was the only way he could record it and get out. He said he had to go back or they would know what he had done and they would come looking for him. Kidd asked who 'they' were, but Tiny shushed him and left without answering."

"The following is an excerpt of the recording that was recently released by Dead World Records and has been heavily sampled in recent Zed Head tracts. Please, be warned that the sounds are disturbing including apparent zombie attacks and human screams."

"There is only one section that has distinguishable words near the end of the 38 minute 20 second recording. The voice has not been definitively identified to be Tiny Jones. The two most common interpretations of the section you are about to hear is either 'The horror of it. They obey the mud music. Death is beautiful.' Or 'The whores they obey. The mud music death is beautiful.' "

The man stared at the words he had just read for a long moment. When he looked up, there was a black and white photo of the side of a trailer. There were painted words on the side which read, 'Don't come looking for us again or we'll come back for you.' There was an arrow superimposed over the photo pointing at something under the words.

The voice came back on and said, "Section sixty-six."

The man turned the page and read on, "The following vandalism was found on the trailer on the D. W. Farms property about a week after Kidd Banjo delivered the cassette he claimed was from Tiny Jones. Hollister Z claims the medicine bag hanging from the nail at the bottom of the photograph contained a pair of human testicles among other items such as teeth and fingernails. This was never confirmed and there was no indication of whether or not Tiny died as a result of foul play or from any other cause."

"Other collectors did go into the Appalachian region in search of the secret of the 'last recording' of Tiny Jones and the legendary Mud Music despite the sinister warning. Those that claimed to know of the Mud Music told the collectors stories of mystical powers including the power to tame or command zombies with it, of deals with the devil-god of the walking corpses, and of the fact that the source was always to be found somewhere deeper in the hills. No other collectors were able to bring back any recordings of this legendary music either."

The man stopped and saw a shot of a newspaper with a file picture of Tobias Baker under the headline: Dead World Records Exec Found butchered in Gray Zone.

The voice said, "Section sixty-seven."

The man actually said, "When did this happen?"

The voice came back on, "Stop there. I think you're in the wrong section. Sixty-seven starts with 'recently.' See if you can find the spot again."

The man turned the page, "I have it."

The voice said, "Begin when ready."

The man reached for his glass, but realized it was empty. He went ahead and started, "Recently, Tobias Baker, co-founder of Dead World Records Inc., was granted an unprecedented clearance for a manned expedition into Grey Zone 4, one of two uncleared areas deep in the Appalachian Mountains. Contact with radio and GPS were lost on the second day of the expedition. Aerial searches did not reveal the location of the expedition nor evidence to their whereabouts. Three days after the expedition was scheduled to end, Border Patrol claims seven men began approaching the gates from inside Zone 4. It wasn't until they were within ten feet and had not identified themselves that they were identified as zombies. The guards opened fire. The Border Patrol claims the zombies placed one severed head each on the ground by the gate. The seven zombies then returned to the woods despite taking heavy fire. Cameras at the gate malfunctioned before this alleged event and sources asked to remain unnamed."

"Upon inspection, the seven heads proved to be zombified and active. Officials were called in. The heads were deactivated using surgical lasers. They were then placed in secure cases using robots."

"It has been confirmed that six of the heads belonged to the members of the ill-fated D.W.R. expedition including Tobias Baker. The seventh head, which was considerably more decayed and was missing all its teeth, has not."

"An unconfirmed rumor on Internet America claims the head is that of Tiny Jones. DNA samples are unavailable and the R.U.S. agency involved has not commented."

"Hollister Z, co-founder of Dead World Records Inc., has been unavailable for comment."

"The following is an unconfirmed voice mail recording that surfaced on Internet America two days before the heads were found. Be warned that this recording contains graphic details of decapitation and dismemberment. It is quite disturbing."

The man stopped and looked up at a picture of a decayed, severed head in a thick plastic case.

The voice said, "Begin with section sixty-eight, when you are ready."

"I think I need a break. I'm out of water," the man said as he stared at the screen.

There was a long pause. He was about to repeat his request when there was a click in his headphones and a drawn out hiss of an open mic. He waited a little longer and then thought he heard distant whispers in the background. He listened as he looked at the severed head on the screen in front of him.

Then a voice came on and said, "When it is time, we will get you."

The screen went blank and the room was completely dark.

"What?" the man asked with a rush of fear.

The voice repeated, "We will break for about ten minutes. When it is time, we will come get you."

After another couple seconds, his eyes adjusted to the darkness in the room. The man removed his headphones and walked toward the door in the dark.

◄○►

SLEEPING, I WAS BEAUTY

SANDI LEIBOWITZ

The prince's eyes devour me,
in damask shawls and dancing shoes
or morning's rumpled flannel.
When my stocking tears,
he bends to buss fresh bud of ankle
flowering through the rip.

Between one bite
of saffroned pheasant and the next,
I try unsnarling the skein of words
one hundred years of sleep have knotted up.
But my husband's lips twist in distaste.
He squints each time I speak,
trying to imagine her back,
that sleeping girl he loves,
the mute.

I woke to his face dark over me,
his weight stopping my breath,
his cloak pressing thorns into my thighs,

his tongue already busy in my mouth,
and all the world rejoicing
at true love's admittance.

My throat grows dustier
than my father's cobwebbed kingdom.
Silence burns like the bonfire of wheels.
All the while, my mind spins dreams
of roses.

◄◦►

BAJAZZLE

MARGO LANAGAN

The Sheelas got on the train at Austinmer.

"Oh no," said Don softly as they filed by, six or seven of them, to take the seats the schoolkids had just left, "Bugger me gently."

"What?" Su did that old-biddy thing, tipping her head back to peer through her glasses, then forward to peer over them.

"Bloody *Sheelas*," he muttered.

Su watched them settle, their ragged, fraying layers of black clothing, their silence. All the talk had died down behind them, and Don heard the rest of the carriage notice and fall silent too. Everyone sat poised a moment in the utter quiet after the guard's whistle; then the train pooted and wrenched itself from the platform.

"Come on." He stood up and grasped the handles of the duffel bag.

Su didn't have chins, just some narrow pleats that gathered around her jaw when she pulled back like that. She raised an eyebrow, and the afternoon sunlight falling in from the top of the escarpment showed up every crinkle on her forehead. "Don't be ridiculous, Don. It's five minutes. For the bother of tracking down another seat? Another *pair* of seats? Just sit down and weather it."

Hand still on the duffel-handles, he twisted to look at the Sheelas. They perched as they always did, feet on the seats, hugging their legs. They turned their faces aside, but not with embarrassment. They just didn't give a toss about anyone else in the carriage.

Su had gone back to her Kindle. To Don's mind, there was no way to read off one of those things without looking smug. *Ooh, look at me. I've got all of Jane Austen in here, and everything Charles Dickens wrote, no bigger than a couple of CDs. I just love it!*

He sat down fuming. He wished he'd had the courage to take their bag and go. But she was right; the train was packed. They would have made fools of themselves dragging along the aisles, bumping people with the duffel, tripping over feet and baggage and children.

The Sheelas squatted motionless, all black rags and pale made-up faces. Some of them went lipless, some painted on black mouths; this one here facing away from him had blacked out more than her lips; she'd painted a bigger, toothier mouth, all the way up her cheeks.

He gave a little laugh, heard the pain in it and stopped. "I knew we should've driven."

"Yairs," said Su. God, she was a bitch sometimes. She complained about *his* tone of voice and then farted out a sour note like that right under his nose. No, he wouldn't think about where that sourness came from—the Road Rage Incident, as she called it very precisely. There was no point getting angry about that again.

He sent a vicious gaze over the Sheela he could see best, the one who was facing him between the gap in the seats. She was one of the lipless ones. He leaned closer to Su, muttered under the accelerating train-rattle, "Why would you *do* that?"

"Do what?" Su re-angled the Kindle, as if worried his breath would mist over the screen.

"Make yourself so ugly? I mean, under all that gunk you've got a perfectly nice-looking girl—' Now Su was giving him that bridling look. "What?"

"*I* don't know," she said. "Maybe you get sick of everyone expecting you to be decorative. Pervy blokes on trains included."

"I'm not being *pervy*! I'm not expecting anything! Aah, forget it."

"Yes, good idea. Why don't you sit back and enjoy the scenery *out the window*?"

Such a bitch. He was close to saying it; if she hadn't delivered that mad rant that time, against the word, and the word being used about her in particular, he would have said it out loud. It didn't matter; she heard it anyway. It burst in the air between them, spittle flying onto them both.

He tried to see some sea-view, but the foursome across the aisle had pretty much blocked the window with their *Heralds*. Only a few bits of rail-side overgrowth bounded past above their heads. No chance of *Su* being decorative, he thought, eyeing the chins on one of the Mrs-*Heralds*, the big reading specs, the bad bright lipstick, the big scallopy perm. Su had been on the way to podging up like that, but then—it was partly his fault, all those jokes about big arses—she'd *taken herself in hand,* and not in any fun, sexy way. She'd ground off the weight, lived on fricking salad, stopped joining him in the booze every night, exercised like a maniac, and now she was the scrag she'd always wanted to be. She had! She'd actually said as much. *Much rather be a scrawny old chook than a blob*, she said. And she'd topped it off with that Auschwitz haircut, so that absolutely nothing took your eye away from her haggard face.

Crikey, that's short, he'd said, when he first saw it. *Zat so you can get the nit-comb through?* Joking was all he could think of to do.

I know, she'd said, busily putting the shopping away. *I look like a bull-dyke. But better a bull-dyke than a frump.*

I didn't think you looked like a frump, he'd said cautiously, although that would have been exactly the word to express his dismay, the dismay he felt again now as he eyed this specimen in the carriage.

You didn't think anything. Bag rustle. Cupboard-bang. *You haven't looked at me with the light on for about ten years.*

The Sheelas shifted and Don steeled himself. But then they settled again, and he went back to staring at the white-faced Sheela opposite him.

Her chest, pressed out either side of her knees, was wrapped in such a mess of black *bits*, it was hard to know what was boob and what was curves of cloth. Still, there looked to be a fair bit of substance there. He uncrossed his legs and crossed them the other way.

"Keep *still*," said Su. "Wriggling around like a bloody rabbit."

He missed Su's boobs. It seemed like a horrible joke on him, that she felt good enough about herself *now* to get on top of him, just as she lost the whole reason he wanted her up there. The light might be off, but sometimes the morning light showed him the undersides of what was left of her breasts, like sad little bags of cottage cheese, all the plumpingfluid diet-and-exercised out of them. They jiggled and re-wrinkled, when they should've swung generously, towards his mouth and away. And her face above was clenched closed, as his own was when he wasn't sneaking looks—did she sneak looks at him, and think the same things? God, it was Crumple City up there, the skin slipping forward at the sides of her eyes, her lips gone to fissures. She wasn't whiskery, at least. No, she waxed her upper lip and a couple of places on her chin to down-free leather. But her tongue was scalded rough as a cat's with years of the too-hot tea she liked. And he didn't like to think about it, but there was this slight *smell* about her lately—

The Sheela straightened her back and stretched her legs wide. "Here we go," he said, *not* to Su. "All the bajazzle on display."

Sequins crowded around the girl's black tights-gusset, tiny, shiny animals fighting for a place at the eye-shaped pool that was the sequin-free patch right in her crotch. They scattered out more loosely down her inner thighs, flocked up over her pubes towards the shelter of her rucked up black skirt, roamed away along the be-tighted cleft of her bum.

That was pretty restrained, really. That time on the train after the New Year's fireworks, one girl had paved that eye-shape with pinhead-sized red lights; they'd flashed in circles, middle to rim to middle, over and over like a snake trying to hypnotise you. A lot of them did this shiny green thing, embroidered, or other cloth sewn on: a leafy face with the fanny as the mouth, and leafy arms or wings out along their thighs. Or they drew hands on, the straight fingers holding the fanny wide open, with all kinds of fancy stitching around—patterns, unreadable ancient writing.

Now that her knees were out of the way, the Sheela's bosom had fallen forward more comfortably, and now it filled with the breath she took. Noise began from her and from all of them, suddenly and softly like a foghorn, on several notes that didn't belong together. The girl he could see, she hummed out through her nose; this other one facing away from him, the curve of her cheek, with the black-and-white teeth painted on it, flattened as she opened her mouth and let the sound out of her throat, out of the depths of her.

The singing was always louder than he expected, and deeper than it should be from girls, deeper and creepier. Even though he'd been ready for it, still it sent a shock up the back of his head, and he suppressed a shiver. The two Sheelas let go their knees and dropped their hands to grasp their under-thighs. The black eye-pool widened among the sequins as the girl's fingertips, black under the nails, pulled her thighs wider apart.

In the moment her gaze flicked across him, he felt how his lip had curled. He dropped his head forward, then looked up sideways at Su. "Gawd," he said through his teeth. "How do they do that, make the whole carriage shake?" The windows would've rattled if they hadn't been sealed in place. These girls knew the exact wrong notes to put together.

Su lifted her face from the Kindle. She was one of those women, now, who go about in public with a smile half-prepared on their face, so that if they see a baby, or a dog, or they catch someone's eye, they can boost it up into a twinkle. She turned this ready expression to the girl with the painted-on teeth. She'd have a better view of that one than he had; she'd be able to tell if her chest was as good as the other one's—not that she'd look at that, of course. He didn't like how the expression settled on Su's face, as if she warmed to what she was seeing, as if she was in cahoots with them—yes, *pleased* that they were clambering into everyone's heads and vibrating there. One of the voices was so deep, he felt it through his *seat*. Had they smuggled a bloke in here with them? Was some bloke in the carriage joining in?

Across the aisle a newspaper crumpled, and a petty little voice said, "Yoohoo, people trying to *read* here." The other woman in the foursome muttered something too; *racket* was the only word he was sure he'd heard right. It was good to know someone else didn't feel as holy and patient as Su about the sacred fricking rites of the Sheelas; at the same time, how thin the women's voices sounded against the girls' song! Their little peeps had no chance against this blast, this *flooding*, this noise of old, old grudges and pain. Su had read it all out to him from the Sheelas' wiki page once; he'd half listened. *It's really interesting,* she'd said, which had put him off. Bunch of bloody whingers—he hadn't been game to say it, but he'd thought it. Miserable cows. They should just get over it, get lives.

His face was sore from holding the wince. The pitch changed and he drew up his shoulders more. A shudder took him by surprise. He hoped the bosom-girl hadn't seen, out the corner of her eye. She'd be gratified by that, tell her friends about it afterwards when they went for cappuccinos and mochas and bloody *frappés* at the Cucina in Thirroul, to congratulate themselves on giving everyone nightmares. He clung to the thought of them there, ordinary again, foolish and young in their costumes and paint; he clung because the noise of them was ancient, horrible, more than he could deal with. He wedged his hands under his own thighs because there was nothing for them to do but tremble, or cover his face.

Su had been admiring the girl all this while—was she hoping she'd look over her shoulder so Su could *smile* at her? *You go grrl?* Give her the thumbs-up? Now she twitched her mouth at Don, the tiniest bit. It didn't take much, with her near-bald head and brown lips, for her to be laughing at him. Laughing *with them* at him.

"Relax," she said, as if to a panicking child. "It'll be over soon."

"Going right through my *head*." His voice sounded as flimsy as the *Herald*-women's across the way. He could hardly hear it for the swelling and falling battle of the hums, and the shouting, in his own head, for them to stop.

"It's meant to," she said.

"Oh good, then," he squawked. "Great."

She shrugged, waited for a song-wave to ebb. "It's a free country. And this is public transport. They're not begging and they're not murdering anyone. I don't see your problem."

She might have organised this herself, so neatly were these girls punishing him for the Road Rage Incident. *Either I drive,* she'd said—knowing he wouldn't be able to stand that—*or you can drive down on your own, or you can come with me on the train.* She was *glad* they were crammed in here with the paper-flapping oldies and the mad Sheelas; she could sit here with her tidy Kindle and her tidy body and her tidied-away-to-almost-nothing hair, and look out at everyone else's suffering, and wonder why they hadn't sorted themselves out, the way she had? Really, why would you live any other way?

Nice waist you've got there, he'd said one morning, hoping she'd stop dressing and come and have sex, and because he couldn't bring himself to compliment her muscle-y bum with its under-frills of cellulite.

She'd turned to smile at him over her shoulder; one of her withered breastlets had poked out into view around her arm as she pulled up her full-brief undies. It had been a nice smile, maybe a bit tired, maybe a bit I've-got-the-measure-of-you, maybe a bit yes-well-I-worked-bloody-hard-enough-for-this-waist. It had depressed him deeply. *Cuppa?* she'd said.

One by one the Sheelas' voices eased off; there must be two of the deep-voiced ones—no one person could hold that note so long without a break. Then it ceased.

"Thank goodness," said one of the Mrs. *Heralds*, not quite under her breath. The other woman peered at Don, her eyes swimming in her glasses frames, and the two blokes gave him blank, wary looks.

"I've heard this three or four times now," he said across the aisle, trying for jocularity. "Nobody ever claps."

One bloke looked at the Sheelas again, still blank faced, the other tried for some kind of matey tilt of the head. Su's voice came faintly from behind Don. "Maybe that's 'cause it's not put on for your entertainment."

Biting back a little flare of rage, at her shaming him so casually in front of these people, he sat back, looking straight ahead, back down the tracks to Sydney. His whole fucking weekend, that he would have liked to spend getting the yard in order, and watching the MotoGP on Saturday night, had been taken over by this party of Duffs, by this obligation, and now his wife, who was supposed to be his *support*, his *helpmate*, was holding him up for these podges to laugh at, because a bunch of black-dressed *cunts* had come and poured out their great complaint into everyone's journey.

He wouldn't ask her what it *was* for, then. Either she'd explain it, calmly and with the university words that irritated him so madly, or she'd tell him to look it up himself the way *she* had—it wasn't her job to teach him Feminism For Beginners. He stared at the seat-back and the black dreadlocks on the squatting girl beyond it. The silence was easing out of the carriage, though the chat was still a bit tentative, a bit frightened, from what they'd done.

"I'm going to the Men's," he said, and got up and left.

-o-

Don's good at a party, better than Su. He goes from group to group filling glasses. *You could mingle for Australia,* says Su, anchored to the beach with a bunch of women he knows she doesn't like. He fills her glass, kisses her ear just to hear the women say *awww,* floats on by. He was *born* to circulate this way, two-fifths full himself, greeting, offering, accepting thanks. The afternoon turns blue and the stars start, hardly noticeable; then he gets enmeshed in a conversation with Terry and Denise, and the next time he looks up the black sky is thick, thick with them, the Milky Way properly milky this far from town.

The ship that is the party sails on. The fireworks come and go, the *oohs* and *aahs* at those, and after the last explosion he's marooned for a moment, smiling, by the fire, at the edge of a resumed conversation about Zumba classes. He waits for a chance to step in with his joke about things going off with a bang for the birthday boy.

She comes up to him then. Her name's Bel—she gives it to him, spells it for him, straight off. Is that a bit aggressive, or should he like her for her straightforwardness?

She's one of the very few singles here. She's pretending to be cool about it, but he can almost *smell* that she's feeling it. Tightly bound, she is, into a dress made of some stretchy cloth, big dark-bright flowers splashed onto a white background. She's got a waist, too, though not Su's sort. This one's a statement, held in with a big broad belt. Everything springs out above and below it, cunningly smoothed and sculpted by some magical under-garment. Her breasts push towards him at her neckline like a bum-crack offered on a silver tray; he feels kind and honourable, watching her eyes and animation as she talks, never letting his gaze stray down there or his finger itch to run its tip along the crack, or his palms hunger to grasp the whole, slippery-elasticised *size* of her bosom, the bolster of her bottom. She'd be the same age as Su, but full-faced she looks younger. Her thick hair curls to her shoulders, dark—with red glints, he thinks, but that might be firelight. It might not even be dyed. She's painted her face, but not so much that he's repelled; she's refreshed her lips since the buffet, and the glisten along the edge of them, well, it does what it's supposed to do. He's flattered that she's taken so much trouble, and that she laughs so willingly at everything he says. She does that thing women sometimes do when they first meet him, of asking more and more personal questions as if they've got a perfect right to know, then laughing when he hedges and squirms. She smells *great*, despite his dislike of most perfumes—or perhaps it's that the wafts take turns with gusts of bitter campfire smoke and the smell of several thousand bucks' worth of spent fireworks.

He takes a break from Bel's headiness. Look at Su over there, rocking, holding her elbows, her bored smile. She's wishing she was tucked up in bed with Mr. Kindle, as she usually is at this time of night.

"Which house are you in?" Bel asks him. Duff and Kath have rented out half this tiny beachside town to put their guests in.

"The big 'un."

"Ooh." She all but curtseys, pushing out her plummy lips. "You're one of the inner circle, are you?"

"Absolutely. I've put up with the old bugger long enough. Known him since tech. Gotta be some sort of prize for that, don't you reckon?"

"Ooh, someone's jealous."

She returns his surprised look coolly.

"Come on now, he's my mate," he says, just before the truth of her words hits him, how twisted out of shape his friendship with Duff has become, since Duff's success, and the beach house, and the happy second marriage to Kath. And he hears, in retrospect, the tightness of envy in his voice. Across the way, Duff is mid-story with the smokers, all their eyes alight and blind-looking with firelight.

"What about you?" Don almost snaps.

"Me?" she says. "Oh, which house, you mean? Just here up on Shelly Street, the corner one." She points a dark-lacquered fingernail up at the black motionless tangle of the bush behind them.

"Big green number?"

"Little yellow one. *Oceanside*," she adds witheringly. "Just in case you couldn't see or hear or smell *this*." She flings out an arm at the view. Rather than burying his face in her moonlit, fire-lit, spandex-wrapped bosom, he obligingly takes in the sea view. It sits in rows like a theatre audience, its jewellery and spectacles winking under the moon, the stars crowding in the balcony overhead.

"Haven't seen that house," he says. "Went round all the others borrowing chairs, earlier. Got to sticky-beak everywhere; it was great. All these years of coming down to Duff and Kath's, I've always wondered about the insides of these houses."

"Pop up and have a look now." She nods towards the path. "Here, take the key." She unhooks it from her bangle.

"No, no." Against unfocused breast-curve the keys shoot firelight, a sad worn Lockwood and a mortice key that must be for a back door or a laundry, swinging with a pink bulbous transparent plastic-sized ornament—maybe a fishing-float?—to make them unlosable. He holds back a joke about how much like a dildo that key-ring is. "I'll check it out tomorrow."

"We'll be gone tomorrow. We're all leaving at the crack of dawn to get back for choir and things—everyone's got Sunday rituals."

He's not quite sure what's going on, what the dynamic is, what it should be. Her eyes don't give anything away, yet this is some kind of challenge, right?

"All right, I will." He takes the key, careful not to touch her plump hand with its glossy nails. They both smile, and she nods rapidly, her eyes even brighter with that skillfully smudged dark makeup around them.

"Back in a tick, then."

Carefully he tramps up the dryer sand, the whiskery grass. Steps and a railing lead him onto the path up the slope among the tall, slender, dreamy-headed trees. It's quiet, all the usual noisy birds asleep, roosting around him disguised among the foliage like some kind of puzzle. At each turn when he glances back the fire's smaller, taking up less of the night; Bel still stands at the edge, gazing into the flames. The party's a murmur, and the wavelets fold themselves softly away along the sand. He should have asked her to come too. *Show me,* he could have said, easily. What was he frightened of?

At the top he crosses the car park, a clearing carpeted with flattened gum leaves. "*Not* the big green house," he says as it looms into view. "The little yellow one. The little yellow—?"

Surely not. It's across from the green one, right in the fringe of the bush, the dingy-looking one. He knows it well, now that he sees it. Whenever they've walked past it before, Duff or Su has shuddered or said *All it needs is police tape, that one:* fibro box, mean-looking windows, concrete porch with a sketchy '60s metal railing, roo-bitten grass all around. The garage is scared off into the back corner of the block, too little for anything more than a Morris Minor. A flat-tyred trailer is chained up to the Hills Hoist.

But *Oceanside* it is, says the beaten-copper plaque on the front.

The outer screen door is as light as cardboard. He fits and turns the key, pushes the door open across the fat nylon carpet. He stamps the sand off his shoes onto the frayed doormat before stepping in.

It smells exactly as he expected it would: of mildew, with low notes of tom-cat and dirt. He stands, heart fluttering in the darkness, then reaches to the light switch. A fluorescent strip flickers, ticks, then lights up the lounge room, cruelly and with an ongoing buzz. A black vinyl couch slumps opposite; two chairs of once-green fabric, on pivot bases, wait about. Horrid nested tables lurk, hard against the walls; on top of a low bookshelf a John Grisham and a Stephen King lean, and on the bottom shelf cables and old game consoles have fought to a deadlock. There's a laminex bar, one stool beside it with a split red vinyl seat. Perhaps as a kind of joke, someone's collected tikis large and small, hung them askew on the stained walls, stood them in every corner. Dark with age, frosted with dust, they stare past him, past each other, blind or pearly-eyed.

"Jesus."

Stiff-legged with horror, Don crosses to the kitchen. The spongy carpet gives way to sticky lino. The cupboards crowd out of the walls, each with a little plastic vent of an eye. The sink is coated with scum—did Duff and Kath not check this place out before they rented it? The counter-top stove looks as if it's only ever cooked up drugs. The fridge clunks and shudders in the corner like an ancient, startled dog.

He ventures across the curling lino of the hall, to a tiny bedroom all leaning towers of boxes; one of the closer ones has split down one seam and sprayed *National Geographics* all the way to the door.

The bathroom? Less said the better. It's like something out of a '60s mental home, icy grey-blue bath and loo, blue and white-mottle tiles on the floor. This fluoro sings a different note from the lounge room's.

With dread he creeps up to the master bedroom, pushes open the door, strokes the wall inside for the light switch. Gawd, what is that, 20 watts? The lampshade is curvaceous, crimson, fringed, some of the fringing parting from its braid. *Somebody died here,* says the chenille-covered bed with its dips either side of the centre line—or perhaps, *Two people lay here year after year, despising each other.* The pillows are so flat he could cry.

But across the bed corner lies a summery dressing-gown, dark pink and sumptuous. He can smell Bel's perfume. A pair of black mules with feather-puffs on the toes lets out a little cheer on the carpet's grey. Clothes half-pulled from their folds spill from a purple wheel-aboard on the floor to his left: something slithery and mauve-white, something flower-sprigged, a diaphanous thing that might be a sarong. He can't help but imagine Bel getting her outfit together for tonight, padding about in her underwear, bending, breathing the way Su used to breathe before she got fit.

He doesn't touch. To stop himself touching, he edges round the bed. In the mirrored nook of the wardrobe, Bel's makeup bag bulges, new, soft, agape, its zipper twinkling, a gleaming badge on its side. The things she's taken out lie like jewels around it, artifacts, gold and ebony, little cases of colour and brush, buds of foam that have stroked smoky glitter into the creases of her eyelids. His mouth waters. He picks up the nail-polish bottle. Inside is black, with only, as he holds it up to the poor light, the deepest ghost of red. He squints at the label; letter by tiny letter, *Midnight in Moscow,* it whispers.

Three footfalls on the porch, two in the hall. Sprung. He slips the bottle back in the bag, turns to the door just as she arrives.

"Haaa." She leans against the doorjamb. Her top half is darkened red by the lightshade; of her face, he can't make out more than the glitter of her eyes. Her skirt is clearer, her white curved legs, her neat-tucked ankles, her plump sandy feet, the nails painted *Midnight in Moscow*. He wants to fall on them, brush the sand off, lick away the salt.

"I thought of you up here in this room." Her voice is muffled, as if from a worn-out vinyl record. "I got so turned on."

"Jesus," he says. "Jesus, this is a horrible place. What were Duff and Kath thinking, putting you here? A woman like you—" He takes a step towards the door.

"So hot." He hears her cloth-covered hip make a little tremble against the doorpost. She takes the neck of her dress and pulls the stretchy cloth off her shoulders, off an amazing brassiere that even in this poor light goes to his head, and to his dick. Its cups curve full; the bold pattern of its lace squiggles on his brain. Not flowers—*fronds*, maybe. With thorns? He progresses to the corner of the bed, some dumb idea in his head of stopping her, but no command yet issuing from his mouth.

From the dress sleeves she draws arms so white, he startles himself with a longing to bite and mark them. She takes hold of the middle of the bra, unclicks it and spreads it wide. Her breasts release outward almost with an audible cry, that he almost cries back to. They're glorious, pale, lighting up the dimness, big brown shiny nipple-rounds on them with little mouths in the middle, pushing out from the masses that jiggle and pant in their new freedom.

"I'm a married man," he says in the smallest voice ever heard from a human throat.

She lifts the breasts and pushes them at him, her face almost swooning above them, her mouth raised and open, perfume and heat coming off her into this mausoleum of a room. "That makes it all the hotter. Oh!"

She drops them, reaches up, pulls him down and presses their lips together, thrusts into his mouth a tongue so juicy and soft that his eyes roll back in his head. He sinks forward, onto and around her. She gives—just her fleshly self yields, but then her knees give way, and in a swarming collapse he goes with her down to the bed. She *is* hot, and downy-smooth, and *soft*, great soft armloads of her, the cushion of her back warm against his wrists and the softer skin inside his forearms. Groaning, he squeezes up and down her, squeezes her arse tight-packed in its smoothing elastic, presses her to his erection. Gasping back from the kiss, he dives down her, sucks a nipple deep enough into his throat to gag. She puts her head back and makes wonderful noises, high, desperate, yearning, and she shudders and grasps and flails with her hands so much, she might already be coming.

He surfaces. Her face flings back and forth against the pink silk garment, her open lips like black sheeny pillows, breath shaking them in and out. "Oh, *look* at you," he breathes.

Muzzily she meets his eye. The lampshade lights a crimson fleck deep in her wide black pupils. She lifts her legs, hooks her ankles together behind him and pushes him hard against herself. Her underwear seams rub; he feels them very precisely through his trousers, hears the creak of her wet crotch against his tightened trouser-cloth.

"Oh man. Ohmanohmanohman. Hold on—I don't wanna go off yet—"

He lets her fling him off, push him flat onto the bed, jump aboard his thighs, attack his pants. Now would be the time to stop her, but she arches her back above her fallen dress-top, thrusts out her breasts—No, he must not look at them, so white, so wonderful, not now that he knows the feeling of that giant nipple on and in his mouth, the warmest warm, the smoothest smooth.

She gets him out of his trousers. "Aaaaah!" She beams down on his fellow leaping there, stained-looking in the crimson light. He could go off from just her watching him, her great breasts rising, falling, shaking with her speeding pulse.

She hoists up her bottom and reverses off him, stands, lets the dress drop to the floor, unfastens the dim-coloured underlayer and lets loose the rest of her full white self with a gust of perfume into the poisonous room. Trapping him in her smudged crimson gaze, she pushes her hands all over herself, kneads a breast, splays her other fingers through her black pubic hair, clutches there, closing her eyes, biting her lip, twitching her hips back and all the bottom-flesh on them.

"Come onto me," he says raspingly, propping himself on his elbows. She gets astride him again, dark-faced, glowing-breasted under the swinging light. Her wet self, all her hot slippery interleaved folds, rubs at his penis. He grasps after self-control. Her eyes might be open or closed in that shadow, her whole face might be bruised, her mouth the worst bruise of all.

She slides up, leans forward, brings her face down, shows her teeth. She presses the tip of him deep into herself, and slides back slowly, taking the rest of him in, grinning and letting out a growl. She's hot in there, scalding hot, and wet and tight and many-folded. With a low roar (it's weird, but he likes it; the change in her excites him; he loves everything about her in this moment), in a few strokes she brings him off, clenching onto him, keeping him pinned as he otherwise convulses.

It eases, but his bowels are still half in spasm when she starts again, rocking and rubbing. She's *tight*, her muscles hard as rocks in there, and the nub of her that seeks satisfaction in the jammed clammy hairs at the root of him is hard too, a nub of stone, nearly painful, rubbing and rubbing—no, *really* painful now, and she's going to *crush* him inside there. She's fierce and fast and seems to have forgotten him.

Frightened, he grabs for her, to remind her and to reassure himself. But her breasts shrink in his hands, the skin wither-and-pinching like a dying balloon's. He lets go with a shout. His hand-prints show in the flesh; one of her nipples folds into itself, blurring as she rocks, harder and faster than any woman should be able to. She's like some kind of manic monkey on him, the foolish mouth on her, wider and wider, smeared across her cheeks. All of her shrivels, and the well-filled sheen of her skin dulls, darkens; she turns crêpey, then sags to outright wrinkles, hanging, flapping in places, from the new angles of all her bones. Frazzles of greying hair thin and retreat across her spotted scalp.

The noise in her throat as she works is dry now; her tongue is white sandpaper between her teeth. Her eyes pop wide, staring at a point beside his face. She jags back and forth, digging at the base of what little is left of him. Her breasts are no more than slipped crumplings on her chest; her kneecaps are pearly in the crimson light, the fronts patched rough and white. Her limbs are bone and sinew, loosely covered with that paper skin.

Her eyes roll up. She straightens out like a praying mantis. She slides cold fingers under his arse and claws him steady while she bears down on him, mashing his penis it feels like, stabbing the base of it through with that pulsing nub-stone. A coldness spreads back around his balls, across the shrinking flesh there, across his fear-clenched bumhole. She finishes that pass, gasps forward greyly, grinds down on him again, juddering like a truck on air-brakes, beating, buckling, her breath loud in her teeth in their leather cave. The room's cheap surfaces—fibro, laminex, MDF, the thin glassed window in its aluminium frame—throw back at him the abject sounds he makes. He covers his face to blub, but she wrenches his arms aside and laughs at him. Still grinding, still pulsing, she forces her kiss into his face, the breath stuttering in her gnarled nose, her narrow lips like bands, her tongue knocking like a bone-end in his throat.

And then she's done. She springs off him, up by his head; even as she goes he's slithering out from under, checking himself. There seems to be no blood. She's dug no cavity, no gouge-marks in him. All's familiar there, bunched and dangling bedraggled, as far as he can see in this terrible light.

Smacked against the far wall he hauls up his pants. The woman squats gloating on the pillow, propped against the wall. Only her fanny and feet show uncrimsoned by the lampshade; only her teeth gleam and her eyes glitter from the shadowed part of her. His pants fastenings have never seemed so perplexing, his fingers so useless among them.

"Cover yourself up, woman!" By contrast with the black window, with the red gloom all around, the only thing bright lit is her grinning wet under-mouth. Her hands are dirt-dark and greasy-looking, her skinny thighs dirt-wiped too; the lips between, that she holds wide proudly, are fat as a grouper's, goose-fleshed, purplish, sparsely haired white and black. Between them other lips, unspeaking and unspeakable, part and show others that open on others again, in and in like the circles of a cyclone's eye, and shifting upon themselves in just that way. Don tips towards the sight of them, catches himself, fights to the door.

He falls out into the lounge room. When did she kill the light? But the song picks him up from his stagger, taking him by the head like a claw. The noise he thought was his own alarm is a real sound outside him, a roomful of humming, all dis-harmony. What he thought were tikis—hung from the walls, crouching on their perches in the gloom—have taken on flesh. He can smell it, unwashed, intimate; he can hear limbs shifting under the sound of the voices; their foul-earth breath ghosts over him in the stirred air.

They begin to turn and shine their eyes towards him, tiny white discs bobbing in the grey. Still clutching his pants closed, he dives for the open front door. He whangs up against the railing, bounds from the steps, flees across the lawn.

At the lookout above the beach, he backs up to the wooden fence and tidies himself, his eyes on the house as if to keep anything from following. The trees tower over him, hissing slightly in their sleep.

He's caught his breath. He thinks he's ready. He turns towards the stairs. The party's down there just as he left it, milling in amber firelight. At the edge of it a buxom woman, her white dress splashed with flowers, cradles a glass of wine. Pushing her dark hair back over one ear, she casts him a long look up through the trees—and then is gone, as if she never stood there, on the party-muddled sand that slopes away to the sea.

Note: Sheela-na-gigs are stone carvings, many quite crudely made, found on various medieval structures (often religious buildings) in Britain and Europe. They depict women of different ages and degrees of ugliness, with their legs spread to show their genitals. Often the woman's hands are carved to touch or hold open the vulva. No explanation for these figures or their location has survived from the Middle Ages, but it is speculated that they had significance as guardians or fertility symbols, or to avert evil or bad luck.

⊸◦⊶

THE PIKE

CONRAD WILLIAMS

Carpers further down the canal were using fishmeal and pellets to try to tempt the doubles, but Lostock wasn't interested in them. Carp might fight for longer, but they weren't as aggressive as pike. He didn't like the look of them, those bloated and gormless mouth-breathers. They turned his stomach. He'd talked to bailiffs and other fishermen about the water. Some were happy to chat with him, others hunched over their gear like poker players protecting a good hand as he approached. They'd tell him what he already knew. They suggested he find another place to fish, that this place was dead now after long years of pressure, of inexperienced anglers fouling the stock. Nothing much left. *I only fish here because it's close to home and I can't get around as much as I used to.* In their eyes: *Piss off. This is my swim. Sling your bleeding hook, or rather, don't.*

It was a deep canal; five feet in the main, sinking to six in some places. The margins were shallower and this was where most of the snags were to be found. Weed-beds, shopping trolleys, knotted drifts of ancient polythene. Over the years Lostock had lost any number of rigs to rusted, sunken bicycles or reefs of fly-tipped refuse. It wasn't ethical to lose a baited treble hook in the water—no matter that they were barbless these days—so now he tested extensively the stretches he fancied, clearing the water of obstacles, or making sure of the depth so he could cast accurately above the bed. He noticed that in some areas near the bank the depth was similar to that in the middle. Pike were known to lie up against the bank or within holes. They'd be attracted to this extra foot or so of water. He knew he might be on to something when he found one such spot near a factory. Outflow pipes flooded the canal with warm water. Fish bliss. He'd often been told by his grandad that if you ever found an area like this, you should give it some time. *Tend it like a garden, you'll reap rewards.*

So he'd bought a clean, empty paint tin from B&Q and punctured it all over with a screwdriver. He'd begged the fishmonger for a bucket of his waste and filled the tin with chopped heads, fins and guts. He'd added oil from a carton of mackerel fillets and left it by the heater in his shed all afternoon. He took the stinking tin to the canal in the evening and tied a rope to the plastic handle. It had hurt to do so, but he managed to sling it out to the swim he had his eye on. That bit of the water that roiled and rolled with the warm current from the outflow. He pegged the rope down and beat it into the packed soil of the bank and went home, checking first that nobody had seen him at work.

He ate. He bathed. He coated his skin in Imiquimod cream. He slept. There never seemed to be any great stretch between closing his eyes and opening them again. He couldn't remember his dreams any more. It was his skin, rather than the alarm clock, that brought him back. Skin so tight and dry it must belong to another body. It itched constantly, no matter how much of the cream he applied, or how often. The doctor wanted him to go for surgery, but Lostock had a thing about scars. Scars changed the way you looked. You became someone else, and he was only just coming to terms with the person that he had been shaped into. But then, maybe, it would be for the best if he did change. To be physically altered, to be at some part removed from the cast of his ancestors. The slightly prominent forehead. The downward slope of the mouth. It would help him to forget that he was the sum of a number of parts that were at best defective.

Whynt y'get 'itched, Jimmeh? Whynt y'settle down?

He turned away from the voice. He became absorbed by the routine. The flask of tea, the sandwiches—one beef paste, one ham and cheese— wrapped in greaseproof paper and tucked into the lunch-box with an apple, a Ski yogurt and half a packet of Malted Milk. His little radio, permanently tuned to TalkSport. He never listened to a word, but he needed the mutter and grumble to help distract him from more persistent voices.

A check on the tackle he'd loaded, the foldaway chair, the bait. He put the car into neutral and let the handbrake off. He coasted down the rise to the main road and only switched on the engine when he was twenty feet clear of the last house. Five a.m., and a white skin on the world. Everything shivering: the trees, the engine, the fine net of frost hanging in the air. He drove past a bungalow with a red Fiat 127 in the drive and he almost cried out. His first car had been a 127, a hand-me-down from his dad who was half-blinded by glaucoma and unable to drive. He remembered many journeys prior to that, sitting in the back seat. No radio. No seat-belts in the back. Wind-up windows. The most basic model. His mother: *Oh, it's got a ruddy engine then?* An episode leapt to the head of the queue, the one time Dad took him and his grandad fishing. Grandad hauling in breath to a pair of lungs turned to worn leather after a lifetime of heavy smoking.

He'd listened to his dad moaning about the Prime Minister, about his lack of a pay rise, about the quality, or lack of it, of the beer at The Imperial. He didn't understand a word of it. He just watched his grandad's hawkish profile, his wet blue eyes, the dry, sucking slit of his mouth. Later, when the deck chairs had been set up, his grandad sat and watched his rod. He didn't speak. He never spoke, not to Lostock, anyway. He always wore a faraway look, as if he was remembering his youth, before asbestos, or smoking, or pneumonia took it away for good. He'd never been hugged by the man, though he'd opened his arms to him when it was time to say goodbye. His grandma hugged him plenty; enough for the both of them, he supposed. What remained of his white hair curled out from beneath his cap like the barbs of a feather. Dad showed him how to thread the line through the eyes of the rod and attach a float, the lead shot, the hook. They'd brought bait in labelled Tupperware tubs: breadcrumb, sweetcorn and maggot. His Dad told him there was a trick to making a maggot wake up quickly after a night in the fridge.

"Pop one in your mouth for a few secs, warm 'im up, then hook 'im on."

But Lostock wouldn't do it. His mum had told him that a boy had done exactly that on a fishing trip, and something in or on the maggots had infected him, burned his tongue and his lips and his penis from the inside out. He was all blisters now and he would never have kids of his own.

"Y'talkin' nonsense, Barb. Don't fill the lad's 'ead wi' shite like that."

"I ruddy amn't. You let him put maggots in his mouth and I'll play holy hell, Bill Lostock. See if I ruddy don't."

His dad showed him how to keep a finger on the line while you were casting, right up until the last second. Grandad's float was orange, Dad's was yellow and his own was luminous green. He stared at it for hours. He stared for so long, that the float became superimposed on eyelids whenever he closed them.

Waterwolf. Slough shark. Old Jack.

"Jack'll take your fingers," his grandad told him, while his dad went off to take a piss. "If you don't show him some respect. Almost killed my father."

The mere lay before them like a trembling brown skin. Lostock was shocked into silence, by the suddenness of Grandad's utterance, and the way his voice sounded. It was really quite lovely: rich and liquid and touched by inflections that didn't sound like anybody he knew in his home town.

Grandad had been on a boat as a child with his father, Tom, fishing for pike, when the pike rammed them. His father and he both fell into the water. Grandad almost drowned. The pike rammed Tom in the face, scarfing down an eye. Grandad managed to pull himself back into the boat and splashed at the water with the paddle until he was sure the fish was gone. He didn't know who was screaming the most, him or Tom. Other fishermen on the bank had been roused by the commotion and waded out to them.

"Is that the worst thing you ever saw?" Lostock asked him, and his voice had been tiny in the oppressive room, under the cracked Lancashire slur of his grandad, leaning over him with his hawkish face, the grim, shark-bow mouth.

"It were the worst I ever *felt*. Watchin' me dad go into the water and see that monster try to drill itself into his head." He leaned closer. Lostock smelled tobacco and Uncle Joe's. "We all of us have a chapter like that. A black chapter. Sometimes you write it yourself. Sometimes some bastard writes it for you."

His dad came back then, face red from the sun. They stayed until dusk and packed up, empty-handed, his dad cursing the water and the idiots that were supposed to stock it. Kev Beddall had told him there were scores of perch in the mere. Big ones too, five pounders. He reckoned there might be a British record in that water. "Kev Beddall's got shite fer brains," he remembered his dad saying. His grandad resembled a fish discarded on the bank, sucking uselessly at the air, waiting for the priest to batter the life from him. He had wondered if maybe his grandad was a pike in disguise, and might be better off in the water. Lostock had stared at his dad in horror, wondering if he had read his own black chapter yet. They stopped off at the pub on the way home but he couldn't swallow his Coke for the fear that swelled in his throat.

Lostock reached the swim, his head thick and itchy with unpleasant memories that had not encroached for many years. His grandad had died maybe two or three years after that fishing trip, the only one they'd shared, and he could barely remember a conversation between them. It was as if Lostock did not exist when they were in the room together. His grandad stared straight ahead, at the wrestling on TV if it was on, or if not, at a space above it.

"Lived longer than I will, though," Lostock thought now as he set up his rig, fixing a wire leader to the line to foil the pike's teeth, attaching a circle hook, digging through the tubs of deads for some suitably tasty lure. He cast nervous glances east, to the factory, and what lay beyond. His skin trembled, as if in recognition.

The sun was a bare thin line skimming the houses in an area that had once been known as Arpley Meadows, where Thames Board Paper Mill had stood. He used to cycle up Slutcher's Lane to watch the cricket matches there in the summer, and root about in the grounds because sometimes you could find spare rolls of gaffer tape as large as a tyre. He might take some bin liners with him and fill them with the shreds and offcuts from the factory, caught in the guttering and ditches like wizards' hair. He went round the lanes near his house, selling it as bedding for rabbits and guinea pigs, a bit of pin money to keep himself stocked up on hooks and fresh line.

He'd kept that green float, for luck, and he used it now. He cast into the swirl of warm water by the outflow pipe and settled into this chair. He put on his sunglasses and cricket hat. He angled his umbrella against the coming dawn. He waited.

Basal cell carcinoma. This skin cancer was, the doctor had related to him, a result of "solar damage," as if he was no different to some kind of satellite. Plaques and lesions had formed and grown on his legs and arms, the skin becoming sore and red and even, in some places, scaly and crusted. The doctor wanted Lostock to go for surgery, had impressed upon him that this form of cancer was eminently survivable, but he didn't want any knife near him. Which left him with dawn and dusk to hide his face, and a scarf when these uninhabited acres became dotted with loners like him.

Whynt y'get 'itched, Jimmeh? Whynt y'settle down?

He closed his eyes to his dead mother's voice as if that might provide her with an answer that would satisfy her. She had, probably rightly, blamed his obsession with the fish for his inability to land what she called a proper catch, a keeper. His objections were down to his skin, but it wouldn't wash with Mam, who had always made it sound as though he was to blame for his condition. *No Lostock ever 'ad the skin cancer befowah. And we sunned ussel's daft, got sunburned and everythin'. All I can say is you 'int made of the same gristle as the rest of us. You daft get.*

He hadn't the heart to mention all the holidays they'd taken to Rhyl and Prestatyn and Aberystwyth when he was a child. Every summer in a caravan, two weeks of traffic jams, his dad pissed every night, and a diet of burgers, chips and ice cream. Dawn till dusk out in the high 70s without sunblock sucking down warm, sugary lemonade, always thirsty because of it. And when he woke up in the middle of the night in agony, his skin the colour of boiled lobsters, blisters the size of footballs on his legs, his mother had sterilised a needle with the flame from a cigarette lighter and lanced them, then squealed at him to sleep on the sofa when the lymph from within drizzled on to his sheets. That had happened so many times he couldn't count them. His GP had gone spare when he saw the scars. He ordered his mother to either keep him out of the noon day sun or slather him in factor 50.

What's that pale nobend know about suntans an' doctorin'? his mother had wanted to know. *Ant got no ruddy clue and how dare he shout at me like that? The jumped up snot-nose bastid. What is he, twelve years old? An' thinks 'e's God's gift to 'ealin'?*

Thanks, Mam. Thanks for everything.

His first memory of his mam: reaching out to her from the pram, her oval face framed with prematurely grey hair, her brown eyes wrinkling

under a brown smile. The filter between her brown fingertips. She used to
dip his dummy in rum laced with honey to get him off to sleep. She forced
it in his mouth like a plug that was slightly too small for the sinkhole.
One time, she caught a ragged fingernail on his lips and he cried so hard
his throat hurt and the breath snagged in his chest—

The green float disappeared beneath the surface of the water. He stared
at it a moment, thinking of the fake emeralds around his mother's throat
as they dipped below the scalloped neckline of her dress. He wondered
where she had bought that, or who had given it to her. Behind every
trinket, a story. She would—

Christ.

Any other fish and he'd have lost it. But it was okay, with pike, to take
your time. Most of them attacked fish acrossways, content to wait until
they arrived back at their lair to turn their meal around and eat it head first.

"Hi Jack," he said, without realising. He struck into the fish and the
immediate resistance of it corded his forearms; it was a big bastard, maybe
twenty-plus pounds. The far bank, the factory, the wedges of leaden cloud
rising on the horizon, all of this receded until his focus took in only the
tip of his rod and the boiling surface of the canal just beyond it. It was
in such moments, when the world mostly went away and he was blindly
connected to the animal on his hook, that he felt anything like alive.
His mind stopped harking back to a time when he wished he might
have been happier. It did not pick at the scab of his grandfather or mope
over the decay that drove his parents apart. His skin was just a dull sack
that contained him, rather than a complex structure that was degrading,
conspiring to pull him apart. There was a single, pure thought. How to
deliver something from one element into another.

The fish fought for a long time, longer than he was expecting. He
wondered if maybe after all he'd struck into a carp, but then the fish rose
and its duck-billed head became visible. An eye swivelled towards him
from just under the surface, with its fixed black pupil like a hammered
tack. He was granted a view of its pale belly as the fish rolled away from
him, all bronze, gold, rust. It was endless, ageless. The fish sank and
Lostock felt the tremor of its body as it flexed, finning for depth. The
line had broken. Now Lostock felt a pang of guilt through the brief
depression of his loss; fish hooked deep enough might starve to death

because the hook and wire trace couldn't be removed without damage to the delicate gut.

He put down his rod and cleaned his hands. The winter sun was finding a way through the mist, despite being unable to rise much higher than the factory roofs. Lostock got out of his chair and stretched his legs. Fighting the pike, and all that remembering had tired him but it was still too early to turn to his lunchbox. He poured out another beaker of tea and took it downstream to the hump-backed bridge. The road was cracked, studded with pot-holes. On the other side of the bridge it split into two. One branch curved left and cleaned up its act before it met the main roads on the outskirts of town. The other branch ended after a hundred yards at a steel fence locked into place with breeze-blocks. The factory beyond was out of bounds, awaiting the wrecker's ball, presumably, or a slow decay into the foaming acres of autumn hawkbit and mind-your-own-business.

There was a security poster fixed to the diamond links with nylon ties, but in all the hours Lostock had spent on the canal bank he had seen no sign of a patrol. No white vans. No dogs. He placed a foot against the fence and it bowed inwards; someone had been here before. Further along, where the fence became lost within a tangle of branches and brambles, it was torn and buckled. Lostock pushed his way through, careful not to snag his sore skin on any of the metal claws, and approached the factory entrance. The door had been recently secured with what looked like old railway sleepers bolted across the frame. The ground floor windows were boarded up with fresh panels. He took a mouthful of tea and spat it out: cold. He'd been standing on the forecourt, staring up at the building, for fifteen minutes. Cramp laced the backs of his calves. He shook it out and walked around to the side. The hair on his back and shoulders was rising but the temperature, if anything, had improved since dawn. Ducts and pipes, corroded by time and rust into metal wafers, sprawled from the factory wall like something gutted. He placed his hand against one of the less ruined conduits and felt warmth. He remembered the outflow pipe at the canal, with its constant drizzle of warm water. What had they made here? Was the factory abandoned after all?

He remembered this place from his childhood. You could see its saw-tooth roof on the bus to and from school if you sat on the top deck. His grandad had worked here, but he had no idea what he did. Dad told him he did carpentry in his spare time, and had constructed the frames for the houses that backed on to the M6 through some of the villages dotted around south Cheshire. But this didn't look like any kind of timber factory. He saw now, how, if he climbed on to the pipes that swarmed from the shattered housing, he'd be able to lever himself up to a window that was only partially obscured by chipboard. The lure of the fish was only so great now that he was in the shadow of the factory. He felt the delicious tremor of criminality, unknown for years, since minor indiscretions as an underage drunk, or shoplifting bars of chocolate from the corner shop. He placed his cup by the pipe and hoisted himself on to it, realising, too late, that if the metal gave out under his weight he would injure himself badly. His skin was in no mood for cuts or abrasions. It held, but it made plenty of distressing creaks and groans. Flakes of rust and paint fell psoriatically away. As he drew closer to the window, there was a smell of chemicals and mildew, reminding him of the bathroom at his grandad's house, before he was moved to the home. He was fond of harsh-smelling products: Vosene, Listerine, Euthymol, TCP, Dettol. He would never have touched a jar of moisturiser. It was a wonder he had not dissolved in some of the things he slathered on his own skin.

Lostock pulled at the chipboard; it broke apart under his fingers. He pushed it away and gazed through the open window-frame. The factory looked as though it had been abandoned in a hurry. There was a melamine table with a mint green surface covered in a film of grease and grime, peppered with plates and mugs. A padded jacket hung on a chair. Beyond that was a cavernous area swimming with motes. His fingers till sang with the tension from the fish and he didn't feel the dull pebbles of glass that remained in the frame as he levered himself into the factory. His boots crunched on more of that glass and the dust and dead insects of God knew how many years. The air was cold and old. It smelled of feathers and spoors. There was a rich, mushroom odour underpinning the faint chemical ghosts. Empty paint tins stood glued the floor by rust and their own leakages. In a corner, a pair of vermin-chewed boots stood facing the wall. Layers of paint and plaster peeled from the walls, revealing the lathe beneath, like rudimentary ribs in a creature that had been ignored by evolution. Much of December woman had leeched into the tiles above a bowl containing a boulder of solid sugar. Her face was smeared, her eyes accusatory. Leaflets explaining how to join a trade union were a gummed mass considering a leap from the corner of the work-top. Lostock moved through the room, hating the gritty echoes that his feet threw up. He opened a door into a corridor flanked by offices. All of them were empty, the furniture flogged, the fittings and fixtures stolen, or stripped out by renovators abruptly stymied by the plummeting economy. He found some evidence as to what the factory produced on the floor of what might have been the Human Resources base. There were yellowed dockets and invoices spilling from a file swollen with damp. They mentioned paper orders and quotas for recycled pulp. What he'd smelled all along was not the dank organic stench of mushrooms, but the ancient rot of paper. He meant to leave then, sick of the smell, and the way the air was somehow coalescing around him, the tiny fibres of cellulose tickling his nostrils and blanketing his lungs. But something about the smell was growing more familiar to him, the further along this corridor he progressed. Under the factory odours was something domestic, but not of these times. It was a mingling of notes that fled as soon as they arrived, like a word that would not sit still on the tip of the tongue. Naphthalene, suet, the hot cotton scent of antimacassars scorching by direct sunlight. Bleached hardbacks on a shelf, barely touched in fifty years. Brasso. Wright's coal tar soap. Camp coffee.

He was standing in an office without understanding how he'd reached it. Depressions in the floorboards showed where a desk and chairs had once stood. Gaps in the grille across the window allowed him to see his deck chair by the canal. What was he thinking? There was a couple of hundred pounds' worth of gear lying there, waiting to be nicked. But he was rooted. Something in the air: this smell, this peculiar mixture of smells that he'd not known for thirty years. He stared at where the desk would have been, and tried to imagine the shape of the head of the man sitting behind it. He found it hard to believe that people might have come to him to ask his advice on an aspect of work, when he was so very recalcitrant in his private life. Lostock imagined him at Christmas parties, or outings, tie off, the neck buttons undone. Handing out pints, helping women into their coats. "Thanks, Jack. Bye, Jack."

There was a large plastic rubbish bin in the opposite corner. Somebody had made a half-hearted attempt at clearing out the room but had either given in or stopped when it became clear the building was a hopeless case. He saw great clods of hoovered up dust and carpet fibres, white-board markers, broken in-trays. There was a manila file in there too, with Lostock's initials on it: J.K.L. James Kenneth Lostock. Inside were pictures drawn by a child, yellowed by time around the edges, pitted here and there by thumbtacks. Pictures of the man who had owned them, all gigantic faces and arms akimbo. Here was a picture of Grandad holding a fish in his fist. Lostock did not remember drawing them, but there was his name at the bottom of each page, with the 'e' and the 's' back to front.

He wished his grandad back for the first time, then. He thought he might be able to help him, in the way the doctors and his parents had not.

Whynt y'get itched, Jimmeh? Whynt y'settle down?

Is that the worst thing you ever saw?

Lostock was twelve when he went fishing for mirror carp with his best friend at the time, a boy from his class at school called Carl. They'd cycled to the gravel pit, mist-covered and grey this particular winter morning, with rods already set up and baited, pieces of corn infused with vanilla extract speared on their hooks. Lostock had told Carl vanilla extract was a bit gay, but Carl said the fish liked it, that they wouldn't spit the corn out because of it.

They ditched their bikes next to the pit and pitched a tent. They made their casts and sat watching the tips of their rods. Soon Lostock dug into his rucksack and started divvying up their breakfast. Morning rolls spread with peanut butter and mashed bananas, cold crispy bacon wrapped in kitchen paper, a flask of hot chocolate. Lostock was bored after a couple of hours. He wasn't the fishing nut; he'd agreed to come along with Carl, who had a passion for carp. It had sounded like an adventure. It was just cold and dull.

He told his friend he was going to do a round of the pit on his bike, maybe see if there was anywhere to do some jumps. Carl waved him off. Something made Lostock turn to look back at his friend, when he was on the opposite side of the pit. A figure, slight and pale, wearing a Lord Anthony covered in Star Trek badges and jeans so faded they were almost white.

Almost immediately he heard the sound of cows lowing. He turned toward the noise, nervous. He didn't like cows. He didn't like their thick pink tongues licking at too-wet nostrils. He didn't like their swollen udders and the caking of shit around their tails. They stank. They attracted flies. He drove his mother berserk because she was worried he wasn't getting enough calcium inside him.

There were no cows in the field. He could hear the groan of morning traffic rising from the main road, a couple of hundred metres away. And this lowing.

He scrambled through the sludge of rotten leaves and mud, splashing cold, dirty water all up the back of his cords—and his mother was going to clear his lugholes out over that when he got home—and found his way barred by a fence. Behind that was a couple of parked cars and an open door. The sound was coming from that.

He thought to go back to Carl and ask him about it; he knew his way around this place, but instead he dumped his bike and climbed over the fence. He went to the door and peeked inside. There were five men in white gowns and helmets, like a team of weird construction workers dressed up as ghosts. One of them turned around and Lostock was aghast to see an apron slicked with blood. He stepped back out into the cold air, glad of it in his chest, smacking him in the face. He thought about getting back on his bike and cycling to a phone booth, calling the police. There was murder going on here.

He had to make sure. He ran around the back of the building, where lorries were backed up against open bays. He heard the cows again. And other noises. Screams and squeals. This sounded nothing like the deaths that occurred on *Kojak*. Through a window he saw cows being led to pens. A man with what looked like a large black wand bent over them and pressed it to their heads. There was a hiss, a deep *ka-chunk* sound, and the animals dropped.

He didn't know whether what he felt then was relief or sickness. It was just another kind of murder, after all.

He was thinking of bacon sandwiches, and whether he would miss them if he decided to become a vegetarian, when he heard another scream. This one was altogether different. It was high pitched. Somehow . . . *wetter*. It suggested a knowledge of what was happening to its author.

He ran back to the windows, thinking of intelligent animals, wondering crazily when the British public had developed a taste for dolphins or octopi, and saw a long steel trench with lots of metal teeth turning within it. Someone had been piling indeterminate cuts and wobbling, shiny bits of offal from a plastic chute into one end but had got his arm trapped. His mates were running towards him and the man was screaming *shut it off, shut it off.* Thankfully, Lostock couldn't see his face. He didn't say anything else after that, because the auger ground him into the trench and he was killed. He heard the scream cut out as if he'd flicked off his own power switch. He'd heard, even at this distance, through the glass, the pulverisation of thick bone. He'd seen the teeth of the machine impacted with flesh and torn clothes. His face had risen from the trench, scooped up by a blade, like a bad horror mask on a pound shop hook.

Lostock was sick where he stood, violent and without warning. It was as if someone had punched it out of him from within.

He didn't remember climbing back over the fence, collecting his bike, or returning to Carl.

"Where have you been, you bone-on?" Carl demanded. "You nearly missed this."

He stood back to allow Lostock a look at the mirror carp lying in grass. It was enormous. It seemed deformed. Its skin was olive-coloured, there were maybe four or five scales, dotted near the tail and the dorsal fin. Its eyes protruded, its huge mouth gawped, gasping in the air. Lostock felt suddenly detached from nature. He couldn't understand how this thing could still be living, how it could have come into being in the first place. There was this sudden impact in his mind about the outrageousness of animals. He had sucked up science fiction films since the age of five and stared out at the night sky wondering if aliens truly existed without giving any thought whatsoever to the bizarre creatures that lived on his own planet. Elephants. Rhinoceroses. Squid. Mirror carp. Here was as weird as you could get. He saw Carl for what he really was, a network of organs, blood vessels, bones and nerves. A brain with ganglia. Meat. The boy in the snorkel parka was gone for ever. Everything had changed.

"I have to go home," he might have said. He didn't remember cycling back.

He returned to the canal bank and loaded a hook with bait. The skin on the back of his hands was a mass of red striations. It felt loose on his face, like a latex mask he might be able to get his fingertips under and peel away. Despite the stink of the canal, and the constant breath of the exhaust coming down from the main roads, he could smell the sweet riot of decay pulsing off him. He pushed it all away and concentrated on the green float as he cast the rig into the water. Almost immediately he saw the pale underbelly of a pike as it rolled on the surface by the far bank. Something was wrong. Lostock picked up his landing net and ensured his disgorger and his pliers were in his pocket, then hurried over the bridge to the other side. It was the same pike he'd caught that morning. He slid the net beneath it, careful not to startle it away, but this fish was going nowhere. There were ulcers all over its body, he could see now. Maybe where the fish had been fouled by careless anglers in the past, or something more serious. Struggling with the weight, Lostock brought the fish ashore and got it on to its back. It must have been forty pounds. He placed his legs either side of the body. With his gloved hand he grasped the pike's chin bone and tugged it upwards. The mouth yawned open, revealing a coral-coloured throat. Nylon line reached into the shadows. Lostock clamped the line between his pliers and wound it around the jaws; the gut rose into the mouth, revealing the embedded hook, awash with blood.

"Christ, I'm sorry," Lostock said.

With his other hand he used the disgorger to remove the hook and pushed the gut back with the blunt end while holding the head as high as he could. His muscles burned and trembled under the weight of the fish. Its eye was fixed on Lostock the whole time. There was a cold, ancient wisdom there, and despite the circumstances, and the poor condition of its flesh, Lostock, as ever when he was in such close proximity to pike, felt an immense swell of wonder. He heard his dad's voice, softened by beer, and a twelve-hour shift at the depot: *They're mean-looking buggers, and they fight hard, but they have a glass jaw, them pike. They die easy.*

He slipped into the water and drew the fish in alongside him. He tried to coax some movement from it, but it kept rolling on to its flanks. The majesty of it. The power. All potential was reduced in the end. Every spike of adrenaline was only a temporary thumbing of the flatline's nose.

Because you have nothing else. Because you want to say goodbye.

The cold crept through him, despite his exertions with the fish. His skin no longer troubled him. The pain was like something viewed through thick fog.

This fish had been around for millions of years. He wondered if it was related to the one that had attacked his grandad as a child. He wondered if, in some freak of longevity, it was the same beast. And there was a jolt of alarm as he considered the fish might be faking its sickness, and only wanted to trap him. But that passed. And he kept on with his ministrations. He got down low to the surface, close enough to smell the mud in its flesh, and he whispered to old Jack until night concealed everything.

—◦—

THE CRYING CHILD

BRUCE McALLISTER

I t was the Cold War, and my father, who worked in antisubmarine
warfare for the Navy, was stationed in Europe to help fight that war
quietly, the way it was almost always fought. My friends from school
in the little fishing village where we would live for three years weren't
afraid, of course. It wasn't like a real war. There were no planes at night,
no bombs, no radio announcements of impending invasions, and no
wounded, bleeding men—nothing like the war their parents had fought
in countless villages fifteen years earlier. And except for my own parents'
occasional mention of "nuclear missiles" and "the communist threat," I
wasn't afraid either. Why would I be? I was thirteen. We all were thirteen—young, innocent and trusting. We went about our business, which
was the business of growing up. What could there possibly be to scare us?

But there was one thing that frightened my friends—something that
had nothing at all to do with war—and it was the cobblestone path that
led from our village, little Lerici with its medieval church and castle,
up through the olive groves to the hilltop where the villas of the old
aristocratic families overlooked the Ligurian Sea. My friends, all born
in Lerici, were scared of that path, and admitted it. It wasn't that you
couldn't stay on the path and avoid the fork that took you to the even
tinier village of Magusa halfway up the hill. It was that when the path

did fork, you felt the strange pull of Magusa's olive groves and doorways
with their red hammers and sickles (or what looked like hammers and
sickles), and it felt like a spell, a trick of magic, one that left you feeling
a little sick. That's how my friends put it anyway, loving the drama of it.

The grownups saw it differently. Magusa was a communist village, they
said—if you could call something that small a village—and a communist
village angrier than most; and that (the grownups declared) was all you
needed to know. Lots of people in Italy were communists—churchgoing,
card-carrying communists who had no trouble believing both in God
and the rights of the working man, of common people shortchanged
by the aristocracy for far too long—but the residents of Magusa were
different: They were communists *so* poor and *so* angry with the world
that their comrades in other villages, no strangers to red bandanas and
shouting crowds, didn't want to be around them. The residents of Magusa
weren't even from Liguria, the grownups said. The original families,
all olive pickers, had come from the farthest south. They looked like
Southerners, too—short and darker—and that didn't help. Northerners
had always looked down on Southerners, and always would. Or, as the
grownups put it, the villagers of Magusa had never really "adjusted" to
being *Ligurians*.

But my friends knew better, they told me one day after school. Sure,
the doorways of the village were short, which said Southerners perhaps,
and certainly said poor. The houses, lined up side by side and touching
on both sides of a cobblestone path no more than a few meters wide, were
narrow and dark and damp, and the doorways were shorter than most
men. But this wasn't, my friends insisted, because the villagers of Magusa
were small, though they were indeed squat and small. *It was because the
villagers wanted to keep something out—out of their houses—something
bigger than men.*

And though (my friends insisted) the bright red slashes of paint on every
door did indeed look a little like hammers and sickles—those infamous
symbols of communism—they really weren't hammers and sickles at all.
They were something else, something much stranger.

Maybe the inhabitants of Magusa were communists, they said, and
maybe they weren't. What mattered was not what the crude design in red
paint on every doorway "represented," they said, but what it *did*.

"*Che dice?*" I said. After a year of tutoring and middle school, I spoke the language well enough. "What do you mean 'did'?"

"The doorways aren't enough," Gianluca, my best friend—the one with the long eyelashes who dreamed of working for Interpol when he grew up—said quietly. I was trying to get my friends to take the fork to Magusa that day because it was the shortest route by far to the *trattoria* in Romito—the one that had the best ice cream on the coast—and I was in a mood for ice cream. We were bored as hell that afternoon, our geography and Roman history tests behind us, and ice cream was—in my case anyway—going to break the boredom. They'd argued with me—saying that the *gelato* at Trattoria Livia or del Golfo on the waterfront was better—but I knew they just didn't want to walk all that way, especially if it meant going through Magusa.

"They've got the best pistachio," I'd said, "and you know it. You're just scared."

"No," blue-eyed Maurizio had said, turning red the way he always did when he lied. "We just don't want to walk to Romito for your damn ice cream."

No one uttered a word for a moment, and then Gianluca said what they were all feeling:

"We don't want you to go alone."

Carlo, always the bravest and cockiest, snorted, and said, "Speak for yourself, Gianluca."

"I am, Carlo."

Carlo snorted again, but didn't say anything else.

"Why not?" I asked. I knew, but wanted them to say it. I didn't believe it, and I wanted to give them a hard time.

"You know why," Maurizio said shyly.

"All of this—everything you've told me before about Magusa," I began, "you have gotten from adults who know?"

"No . . ." Maurizio said.

"You have imagined it, then?"

"No!" Gianluca frowned. "We have put it together, like detectives. We have lived here longer than you and we have had time to do detective work."

Gianluca's boast embarrassed Carlo, who looked away, but still said nothing.

"Just the three of you—you three detectives?" I teased.

"Of course not," Carlo said suddenly. "The calculations began with my uncle, Paolo, who is twenty years older. He started, with his friends, to put two and two together when he was young; and my brother, Emiliano, who is ten years older, did the same. The detective work, if you want to call it that, has been accumulating for at least twenty years, Brad."

"And how do boys know what adults do not?" I asked, a part of me *wanting* to believe, but the rest not wanting to be a fool. Why did getting ice cream have to be so complicated?

Gianluca took the condescending tone he sometimes had—the one you wanted to shoot him for, even if he was your best friend. "You are so naïve, Brad. You are an American and do not understand such things."

"Yes," Carlo agreed. "You are like the adults who want to think what they want to think, to make sense of a world that doesn't always make sense, and so they do not really think. They do not use their brains." Carlo was a little older, had the highest grades in our subjects and would be an attorney some day, we knew—maybe even city attorney of La Spezia, the port to the north.

"They do not," he went on, "really want to discover the truth."

"And so," Gianluca added, "they do not explore; they do not bother to find out—to find out important *things*."

This was getting ridiculous. "Things? Like what?"

"Like a baby crying in the night," Carlo answered.

"What's strange about that?"

My friends didn't answer. They were looking at each other now.

"This baby cries in Magusa," Carlo answered.

"There's a crying baby in *any* village," I responded, exasperated. Could this get any sillier?

"But we've all heard it," Maurizio was saying.

"So?"

"It's just one baby," Maurizio went on, "and when it cries, it doesn't stop." He was staring at me, pleading, as if to say: *Please believe us. I would not lie to you, Brad.*

And he wouldn't.

"When?"

"In the night."

"It can't just be one baby."

"But it is," Carlo insisted. "We recognized it. There are no other voices, no people, no children, no other babies. Just this one and it cries all night."

I didn't know what to say. I'd gotten a shiver, the way Carlo was telling it, but that just made me mad because I knew he *wanted* me to shiver. He loved to scare people. He'd learned it from his dad, who'd have a glass of wine and off he'd go with a ghost story until the women told him to stop. "You're scaring us all, Marco, so *zito*, please!"

"So you heard it, Carlo—"

"Yes, he did," said Gianluca. "We all did."

"How?"

"Before you and your family came to live here," Gianluca said. "Maybe two years ago. We went to Magusa, we took the fork, we stayed in the groves until night, and we waited. We had flashlights. We wanted to explore the village at night, using flashlights, but suddenly we were scared. Something scared us and we stayed in the trees all night."

"We thought dogs would smell us or hear us and we'd have to run," Maurizio said.

"*But they don't have dogs*," Gianluca said.

"What?"

"*They don't*," Gianluca said again, "*have dogs.*"

"You've never heard dogs barking at Magusa?"

"No."

"No one has. Ever."

"Even the adults say they haven't. They think it strange, but not strange enough to change how they think."

"*Bene*. I agree," I said, "that's strange, but a baby crying isn't strange. You're trying to make that village stranger than it is because you just don't want to walk to Romito."

"No," Maurizio said quietly. That Maurizio believed it—that was what was most persuasive of all. He was the clearest thinker in school, the calmest, the kindest, the most reasonable; and if *he* believed . . . I felt a chill again.

"There was just that one infant," Gianluca insisted.

"I doubt that a village has just one baby," I said, repeating myself, but not wanting to give up that easily. Finding a thing unbelievable was not the same as being afraid to believe it, I knew.

"We stayed," he went on, "in the bushes until after midnight. We knew we would get in trouble with our parents, but we were—"

"You, Gian, were afraid to move even a centimeter," Carlo interrupted smugly.

"So were you!" Gianluca glared at him.

Carlo said nothing.

Gianluca calmed down, looked at me and went on.

"All we could do was listen to that baby cry."

"Until after midnight?"

"Yes . . . all all that time."

"How many hours?"

"Six, maybe a little more."

"I don't believe you sat in the bushes not moving for six hours."

"We do not lie, Brad," Maurizio said.

"You didn't have to go to the bathroom?"

"We went to the bathroom."

"Right there? In the bushes?"

"Yes."

"Why?"

"Because we had to go . . . but we couldn't leave."

I was staring at the three of them, looking for any sign on their faces that it was a joke. There was nothing. "Mary Mother of God," I said. "You are all crazy. You got yourself scared that night like little kids. You scared each other. You couldn't even *move*? You went in the grass?"

They looked at me for a second, and it was Maurizio who spoke:

"You wouldn't have been able to move either, Brad."

"Why?"

"Because it was as if the baby were alone—that's what its crying sounded like—as if no one were there to hold it or nurse it—as if all of the people in the village were gone and only the baby was there alone—as if . . ." Maurizio ran out of words, and his mouth hung open for a moment.

"Just one baby—you're sure?"

"Yes."

"No adult voices?"

Gianluca sighed. "No adult voices anywhere."

They were standing on the path with me, and we were all silent. I'd run out of questions and they'd run out of answers. I believed them, I suppose—enough that I was still feeling the whisper of a chill—but I sure had no idea what it meant.

"So . . . let's go," I said.

"What?" they said. It was the exact opposite of what they wanted to hear. I was supposed to be scared now. I was supposed to want to go anywhere *but* Magusa.

"Let's take the fork," I went on. "Let's find out what it means. It's daytime. There are four of us. What do we have to be afraid of?"

They'd all stepped back as if I'd sprayed them with a hose.

I know why I said it. I was angry. I was angry that they'd scared me with their story, and I wanted to get back at them. I didn't really want to go to Magusa now, and they didn't either, so the last thing I expected was Carlo's next words:

"*Va bene.* Let's go."

"What?" Now it was my turn.

"You're right, Brad. The time to go there is daytime, when there are as many of us as possible. Besides...."

I didn't know what the "besides" meant, but the others did.

"Besides?"

"You're an American, and that may protect us."

"If they're communists," I countered, "they certainly won't want to see an American."

"Maybe," Carlo said. "*If* they're communists. But what may protect us—"

The others were nodding now, as if they'd all talked about it.

"—is your red hair. If they are, as our parents say, from the South, that should frighten them. *Barbarossa.* The devil's beard. The evil eye. It wouldn't frighten Northerners because they have red hair sometimes—look at Nardi—but if they're Southerners, maybe they'll think you're the devil."

I wanted to say, *And what if they are the devil?*, but didn't. I was suddenly very self-conscious of my hair.

"*We* don't think you're the devil," Gianluca said, as if I needed the assurance. "But Carlo is right—maybe *they* will."

Again I thought they were joking—how could they say such a thing with a straight face?—but they weren't smiling, they weren't laughing.

"It should," Carlo added somberly, like an old priest, "give you power over them."

"It is daylight, too," little Maurizio added brightly, "so they will see your hair better."

I wanted to laugh—to break the tension and help me breathe—but for some reason the idea of my own laughter scared me even more than Carlo's tone.

So we did it. We took the fork. Our hearts were beating louder than our footsteps on the cobbles—at least mine was—and we kept scanning the shadows of the olive groves on either side of us like soldiers looking for an enemy. The cobbles on the fork were rougher, and we tripped a lot, our eyes on the trees where things could hide, watching us. No one said a thing, as if speaking would bring the shadows to life, and it took an hour to reach the village when it should have taken half that.

I looked at innocent Maurizio, he looked back, and I knew what he was thinking: *See how much sunlight there is here, Brad! They'll be able to see your red hair perfectly. It almost glows!*

The village was about a block long. No one was on the path that led through it, or in the doorways that lined it. No voices reached us from anywhere—houses or olive groves beyond them. No one was there to watch us arrive, and no one appeared as we walked past the doorways with their red paint. I had walked this path once before, with my parents, not long after we'd arrived in Lerici. We'd been taking a Sunday walk to the Villa Mitiale on the ridge to say hello to the Contessa, who'd befriended my mother in our first weeks in the country—as the aristocracy of any country tends to do with military officers, who are, after all, the military's own aristocracy—and we'd taken the Magusa fork by accident. I hadn't paid much attention. I was chubbier then, completely out of shape, and walking that far uphill had winded me. I saw the red paint and knew what hammers and sickles were, so when my father pointed them out calling them just that, I nodded. Then he said, "Have we been here before?" and my mother said, "No, Jimmy, we haven't. And I'm really not sure we should be here." "I'm not sure either," he answered quickly. Their instant of fear made me afraid, too. An American family—a symbol of oppression, as the newspapers put it, to the downtrodden here—should not be wandering into a little village so off the beaten track and so full, we knew, of ardent communists. It wasn't that I really thought the townspeople would hurt us, clubs or knives or fists or anything like that. It was simply that I didn't want to be screamed at, which had already happened to us on a bus tour in Rome; but I also didn't want to insult them, by walking where I shouldn't walk. Their lives were hard. You could tell that from the tiny, dark and damp houses they lived in. You could tell from the size of their doorways. If you're a symbol of wealth and power—something they'd never had and never would have—why would you want to rub it in, parading up their cobblestone path, a red-haired boy, a tall blue-eyed father of military bearing, a pretty mother in a nice dress, all three so very American? If you did that, maybe you *deserved* to be shouted at, I told myself.

That day with my parents no one had come out of the houses either. It had been a Sunday afternoon and no one would be in the groves picking olives or pruning the trees or weeding under them; and yet no one was on the path or in the doorways. *What a strange little town*, I thought, but nothing more. When we mentioned it later to my tutor—that we had taken that path by accident—the *Dottore*, a dignified man from La Spezia who held his cigarettes tightly, as if they might somehow escape him, said, "Please do not do that again, *Capitano*. That is not an appropriate place for an officer and his family—American or Italian." Even he did not seem to feel it had been that dangerous an outing—only that Magusa was a place where upper-class people should not, by propriety, go. No more than that. No more dangerous than Naples in daylight. Just common sense—common sense in a world where social classes did not always get along, *Capitano*.

As my three friends and I walked through the village now, the hammers and sickles didn't look much like hammers and sickles at all. About that my friends had been right. The crude design looked more like a big crescent moon with a cross slapped over it. At first I told myself it had been easier, faster, for whoever had painted them to do it this way: You make a crescent for the sickle, leave off the handle, and paint the hammer so fast it looks like a cross. Everyone will still know what it is, right? But as we walked on, I saw that every doorway had it *exactly* the same—sickle without a handle, ends tapering like a crescent moon, and the cross definitely a cross.

Some of the designs were large, some small, and couldn't have been made by the same person; and yet the design was always the same: crescent moon and cross.

"You're right," I said at last. "Those aren't hammers and sickles."

"Of course not," Carlo answered proudly, as if I were complimenting him.

A sound farther up the path made us freeze.

Where the last houses were on the path, just up ahead, a door had started to open. My heart jumped, and I knew what the others were thinking because I was thinking it too: *Now it's going to happen. Someone is going to step from a house and start screaming at us—but isn't that better than what we'd imagined?*

But it didn't happen. Instead, from the doorway a head peered out. It was too far away to see whether it was man or woman, and it peered at us for a second even as a hand reached down to pick something up from the cobbles in front of the doorway. Then the hand stopped, withdrew, the head disappeared, and the door closed.

When the door stayed closed, we started walking again, and when we reached the front of that doorway, slowed. There, on the cobbles, was a bucket, and inside it, paint, red paint, the surface starting to harden, the paint separating into different fluids. That's what it looked like anyway as we reached the bucket, looked down in it, and found ourselves stopping to stare. We didn't want to stop. We didn't want the person inside the house to step out and start screaming at us—"Who do you think you are, *ragazzi maleducati*, sons of engineers and draftsmen, children of privilege!—with an American boy with you as well!"—but we couldn't stop looking at the paint. It was obviously the paint they used on the doors. It was what they used to make the hammers and sickles that weren't hammers and sickles at all.

Carlo, always the bravest of us, or the most full of bravado, was leaning, actually leaning, over the bucket to get a good look, saying, "What is that?"

"What is what?" I said. I could see inside the bucket from where I stood, but I certainly wasn't going to get as close as Carlo was to it.

"*That*," he said, pointing at the paint.

We looked in all directions to make sure we were safe, and then, as if given permission by God or someone, crowded around the bucket.

There were three layers of fluid in the bucket. There was the bright red paint, but also two layers on top of that—one a clear, yellowish fluid, like what comes from a cut on your finger, and the other a clotted material that was red, too, but darker than the paint below it.

We all stepped back, even Carlo. *Not everything in that bucket is paint,* we were thinking. *But if it isn't paint . . .*

In the bucket was a stick—one from an olive tree—one that had been used to mix the paint and that was covered with all three—yellow fluid, dark clots, bright red paint.

"That's blood," Carlo said, sure of himself.

No one argued.

Carlo moved suddenly and we all jumped. He was reaching down with his right hand and with his index finger touching it.

"Are you *pazzo*?" Gianluca whispered hoarsely, taking another step back, as if the bucket were going to explode and we'd all be covered with what was in it. "That's blood, Carlo!"

"I know, *idiota*," Carlo answered. He had touched the dark clots and was raising his finger to look at it. Carlo might have been the bravest of us, but he also needed to make sure we knew it—and sometimes this made him do stupid things.

"Wipe it off! Wipe it off!" Gianluca was whispering.

"Why?"

"Because—because—"

Carlo was smelling his fingertip now, and I was ready to scream, too, it was so close to his face, his eyes, his mouth.

"Wipe it off," I said. "Please, Carlo. We know you're brave."

This annoyed him. He glared at me.

"Don't you want to be brave, too?" he asked.

"No . . ." I said.

He started to wipe it on his shorts and Gianluca grabbed his arm. "Not your shorts!"

He wiped it instead on the lip of the bucket, and, as he did, the door opened. We didn't even look. We just started running.

You'd think it would take a shouting voice to make you run faster, but that day in Magusa it was the silence of whoever stood in that doorway behind us—someone we never turned to see—that made us run faster. *Just one baby crying in the night,* I remember thinking as I ran. *No one there on a Sunday . . . no one ever there . . . hammers and sickles that were moons and crosses . . . buckets that held more than paint . . .*

I heard later from Gianluca that Carlo developed a rash on his hand— the hand that had touched what was in the bucket—but who knows whether that was true. Carlo was always putting his nose (and his hands) where they didn't belong. All I know is that we ran as hard as we did from Magusa that day—on to Romito and ice cream that wasn't so great after all—because of the silence and a baby we never even heard.

It never occurred to me that the village of red paint would get me to return—and return alone—for a dog.

◦►

When the village called again, I was two years older and (I liked to think) tougher—the way that life's lessons make you tougher. One of the three old women—the "witches," *streghe*—who lived in the olive groves near our house—had poisoned my cat, *Nieve*, that first year in Lerici. I had watched the little thing die in my bathtub and then, because I was sure which witch had poisoned her, had made my way to the old woman's stone hut wearing my anger proudly, only to learn that she had lost even more, and that the poisoning, a trick of magic, had been a mistake. A year after that I'd stood up for a working-class friend, Emilio—whose family lived in a dark, tiny apartment attached to the convent down the road from us—against both my tutor's snobbery and the merciless teasing of another American boy, a bully whose father was also stationed at the center; and because I did, seen magic at work again, in the way the little metal cross on my friend's wall had glowed faintly until the bullying stopped. And throughout our stay my mother, frustrated that she couldn't teach because she didn't know the language well enough, had too much time to sit and think—to think about my baby brother who'd died when I was four from meningitis and, thinking of him, to cry and sometimes not be able to stop crying. I'd gotten stronger in two years, in other words, and was now as good as my dad at consoling her when she was feeling her darkness, when her eyes were like shadows, and her crying no longer scared me. I was able to give her what light I could—that is what love is, isn't it?—a light we give?—and sometimes it was enough.

In other words, I'd grown up a lot in two years, or at least told myself I had; and if I was older and had grown up a lot, I must be tougher—and if I was tougher, I must be on my way to becoming a man. I'd read enough stories about boys and men and their dogs to know that if I wanted to be a man, I did need a dog. Not a cat, a dog. Real men didn't have cats—everyone knew that—and so soon I was petting every dog, mongrels especially or big purebreds, I could find in the village, all the while daydreaming of my own.

Without that thought—that you couldn't be man without a dog—I'm sure I'd never have followed Ciccio to Magusa that night.

-◦-

The dog in question was a white, mid-sized mongrel with a few large black spots, the kind of coloration dairy cows sometimes have, but it was no cow. It was as skinny as a greyhound, nervous as hell, and had appeared one day in our backyard, which angled from the back patio up into the olive groves. I heard a yelp and saw our maid, Elisa, with her one blue eye and one white eye, trying to shoo it away. I said, "No, let it be," and she smiled the kind smile she always had for me, knowing how much I liked animals, and perhaps feeling, in her affection for me, that I deserved (for as long as my parents would let me keep it) a dog—even one as scrawny and mongrely as this one. "*Va bene*," she said. "*Vuoi dargli da mangiare? Would you like to feed it?*"

"Of course!"

I gave it a hotdog from the refrigerator—just the wiener—and when it had gobbled it up, another, and another.

"*Non troppo*," she said. "*Poverino, finirà per sentirsi male.*" *Poor tummy, it will get sick.*

"Yes," I said. Sometimes pity—even compassion—can hurt another, I remember thinking.

Elisa went about her business—laundry and mopping—and I sat on the flagstone stairs and petted the creature, whose coarse and dirty coat was a miracle to me. It was a *dog*, after all, and that's all that mattered.

It had no collar. It might have been a runaway from one of the villages high in the hills. And it might soon be mine.

It sat beside me for a while, hoping I might give it more, and when I didn't, it began to wander off. I called to it. It stopped, looked at me, saw nothing in my hand, and kept on, disappearing into the grove next to us. I was disappointed, sure, but what could I do? Even if I petted it until my hand was numb, the dog would be thinking of and worrying about food, and so would keep moving.

But the dog was back the next day, and around the same time. It had a cut over its right eye, and that worried me. It seemed healthy otherwise, though, and I wondered whether it was making the rounds—going from *villetta* to *villetta* on Via San Giuseppe, like a panhandler who knew who to hit up for money. Or had it come to our house—just ours—after rooting for food in the alleys down by the waterfront—because it remembered the wieners and the petting . . . and maybe even because it liked me.

I fed him for six straight days—wieners until they were gone, then old bread from the bakery near the school, then cans of cat food Nieve had never had a chance to eat, then leftovers from one dinner after another—and he returned each day in the afternoon as if he knew that on school days at least I wouldn't be home until then.

I was mustering the courage to ask my parents if I could keep him. We had no other pets; and though my mother talked constantly of getting a cat to replace "poor little Nieve," I knew it wasn't going to happen. My mother was afraid of things dying, and had good reason to be.

"Please," I rehearsed silently, "I've never had a dog before, and I'm old enough to take care of one, to be responsible for him. . . . and I . . . *really really really want one!*" My speech needed work—especially the *really*'s—and I kept working on it.

On the seventh day, he didn't return. I'd been calling him Ciccio—a joke, since "Ciccio" means "chubby—and he had started on the fourth day to answer to his name. When he didn't appear on the seventh, I wandered around the olive groves near us, calling to him, but with no luck. Back at the house, I took cardboard from the trash, put two wieners on it, and laid them on the low wall in the backyard where the olive groves began, the ones that continued up the hill to Magusa and on to the old villas of the wealthy.

The next morning, the wieners were untouched, and I gave up rehearsing my speech. I knew what it meant. I was old enough to have heard that wandering dogs usually keep wandering, and that was better than thinking he'd been hurt, or worse.

◄o►

Two days later—after a big test on Garibaldi's diary that I'd studied hard for with my friends—I was in the back yard moving the trashcans, and heard another yelp. It was from far away, up in the groves where the cobblestone path wound toward the hilltops, toward Magusa and Romito and the villas, so I thought nothing of it. A dog. Someone's dog. Not mine.

Then it yelped again, louder this time, and I went to the low wall to look over it. There, far up the hillside in the olive grove, was what certainly looked like Ciccio. He yelped again, started toward me in the grass and then stopped, as if someone had jerked him back. I blinked, trying to see. Was someone holding him on a leash? But I couldn't see any leash—I couldn't see any *someone*. Just grass, olive trees and Ciccio.

He yelped again, tried to move toward me, and again something I couldn't see jerked him back. Was he tangled in something? Had he stepped in a trap of some kind?

I climbed over the wall and began toward him. There was no tree near him. No rope, no net, no trap that I could see. His feet were free. What held him had him by the throat, jerking him again and again, but I couldn't see it.

Red doorways flashed before my eyes—even with my eyes open I could see them—and I felt a pull, the kind my friends had said they felt at the fork in the cobblestone path, the kind I'd never felt until now.

"Ciccio!" I called, feeling a chill on my skin that had nothing to do with any breeze, and walked faster. He whimpered and yelped in response, looking at me, trying to break away from what held him.

◄o►

No matter how far and fast I walked up the hillside, through the trees, the distance between us somehow remained the same. It was like a dream where your feet don't work, where you want to run but can't. He would dig in his paws, struggling against the invisible leash, and I'd get maybe twenty feet closer; but then the invisible hand would pull at him again so hard he'd be wrenched around, fall, scramble up, and be dragged farther up the hill again toward . . . toward what pulled at me, too. *The path. The fork. The doorways.*

If you don't follow him, the breeze in the trees whispered, *whatever has him will have him forever.*

I was panting hard, walking as fast as I could, jogging when the hillside flattened even for a moment, but the invisible hand was even faster.

When he disappeared suddenly over a little rise, into tall grass, I was sure I had lost him; but as I came over the rise, stopping to catch my breath, there he was, sitting as dogs sit, panting too, happy to see me, his rump on the cobblestone fork.

And then he jerked, jerked again, and the invisible leash pulled him roughly once more toward Magusa.

The sun was beginning to fade. It was probably 6 o'clock now, and if I were to save him—though I had no idea how I would do that—it would have to be soon.

As the first houses of Magusa came into view, Ciccio did what I hoped he wouldn't. He was yanked suddenly to the side, left the path, fell, got up, and began half-running and half-falling again—but to where? How would I see him in the groves without light?

He had left the path just before the village began, and so I left it too, running now, dodging back and forth to make sure I could still see his whiteness among the trees, afraid that if I lost sight of him I would not, in the wind that had come up, hear his whine or yelps.

Why he was approaching the houses from the groves—why the invisible leash wanted this—I didn't know.

I expected to see at least a few lights from the houses, but there were none. In the growing shadows of the groves I hit my head on something, slowed, looked up, squinted, and saw around me what looked like bags, burlap bags, some large, some smaller, hanging from tree limbs. I didn't stop to inspect them—I'd lose Ciccio if I did—and if they were important, wouldn't my friends have mentioned them from their night in the groves? Maybe they held olive-picking tools? Maybe they contained food that was being aged, dried? It didn't matter. What mattered was that I kept my eyes on the flashes of white that were Ciccio.

Then I lost him again. It was near the back of one of the little houses, and all of a sudden his flashes were gone. My heart flipped and began to beat hard enough that I could hear it in my ears.

Then I heard a cough—yes, a cough—and I froze. When the cough came again, I stepped behind a dark, gnarled trunk that couldn't possibly hide me if anyone really looked. I could see the back of the little house through the trees, in the deepening darkness, but I couldn't see who'd coughed. There was a wall the height of an ordinary man blocking any view of a backyard. A gate in that wall was open, but there was no one by it.

The cough came again, closer to the house, and I heard a door shut.

I stepped toward the gate, and, as I did, another bag hit me in the head. I looked up at it, but it was too dark to see clearly. I rubbed the side of my head, felt a wetness, but didn't bother looking at my hand in the dim light.

I was to the open gate in two or three strides, and there, sitting upright on the moss of a tiny walled-in yard, was Ciccio, staring straight ahead, perfectly still, making no sound.

I wanted to shout his name, but this was no place to make noise.

I took a step, expecting Ciccio to hear me, but he didn't move. He kept staring. It was as if he were deaf . . .

I was in plain sight now—he should have seen me—but he still didn't move.

. . . and blind.

I took another step, through the gate this time, and stopped breathing.

There, in the yard—two in one corner, one in the other—were three other dogs, a big black, hairy one, and two about Ciccio's size, just as mongrely.

They, too, were sitting and staring, motionless, silent.

Whatever holds them, I remember thinking, is magic, and who am I to stop magic?

There were four buckets of paint, too, in the middle of the mossy yard, and a stool beside them. Watching to make sure the other dogs didn't wake from their spells, I inched slowly into the yard. Whatever held the animals held them tightly.

Each bucket, I could see now, had a stick—just like the one in the bucket my friends and I had looked into that day in Magusa—and each bucket seemed to be full of paint, too.

And what else? I wondered. And then, as the wind picked up even more, I happened to look up at the one tree in the little yard. I don't know why I looked. There had been no sound. Nothing had moved in the tree. Perhaps I'd seen it—the bag hanging there—from the corner of my eye. Perhaps I'd even seen it dripping, like the bag that had touched my head. Whatever made me look, I squinted—

—and nearly screamed.

It wasn't a very large bag—much smaller than Ciccio—but a dog's head, its eyes closed, was sticking from the top of it, and there was something else—

I didn't want to see it, but I had to. I stepped toward the tree, squinted again and saw what was sticking from the bag just behind the head.

A dog's leg.

A leg that had been skinned.

What was dripping from the bag was blood—the dead dog's blood.

My heart thundered so loudly I couldn't think. Dog and leg and bag and blood floated in my head like snapshots, like a strange family album, and I thought I was going to faint. My hands shook, and my legs, which were cold now in my shorts, were shaking just as hard.

Can people hear it when we shake? my head asked stupidly.

Can people hear it when our hearts thunder?

I could, I knew, be killed as easily as the dog had been killed. It wouldn't even take magic to kill me. All it would take was a man or two and whatever weapons, whatever tools, they had—even bare hands. No one would hear me. Magusa was too far away. I needed to run—to get away from this place—and it didn't matter what direction I ran.

But I couldn't run—not without Ciccio.

I stepped over to him, and the instant I touched his head—I was afraid to, but more afraid not to—he looked up as if waking from a dream, whined, stood up, and began to move in little jerks, as if his legs weren't yet working.

I'd broken the spell—that was obvious. But if he yelped or whined, we might still be caught. I picked him up, hoping it would calm him, but it scared him, and he flopped and flailed in my arms. I lost my grip, he hit the ground, and all I could do was hold him by the skin of his neck and talk to him gently. "Don't make a sound, Ciccio. I'm here. *I'm here...*"

I heard the cough again inside the house, and then footsteps.

Ciccio whimpered once and for a moment the footsteps stopped, only to start again and get louder.

Telling Ciccio "Stay!", I ran to the two smaller dogs and touched them, ran to the big black dog to touch him as well, and, as their spells broke, too, the yard exploded in noise and motion—dogs running this way and that, the two smaller ones snapping at each other and the big black one woofing like a canon.

At that very moment a figure opened the back door and stepped out brandishing a big knife, one covered with something that glistened and that I knew wasn't paint.

The figure was small, but in the faint light that fell upon him he didn't look like any Southerner I'd ever seen. My father had taken us to Naples the summer before, and the summer before that we'd taken a cruise to Sicily and Libya; and this man looked nothing at all like the men I'd seen in those countries. He was squat, his head just as squat as his body, his ears like handles, his teeth too small for his mouth, and his face hairless.

I expected him to shout or scream, but, like the head that had appeared in the doorway that day with my friends, he made no sound. He moved, however, and it was toward me that he came.

The only thing that allowed Ciccio and me to escape was the two snarling little dogs and the big booming black dog, all of whom decided at the same moment to flee before the man could reach them, too. We all collided at the gate, but with a common mission—to get away from that knife—so no one snarled, no one bit, and in a moment Ciccio and I were out into the grove again.

✦

It was dark and the bags, dozens of them, hung from the trees like strange fruit. All I could do was run and try to duck them.

We had gone only a dozen yards when Ciccio stopped suddenly and began to back up. For a moment I imagined the invisible leash had gotten him again, but his legs were moving differently this time. He was whining, the way dogs do when they're afraid, and backing up, the way dogs do. I squinted into the darkness and saw something move. In the corner of my eye, even closer to us, I saw something else move, too, and a bag in a tree started swaying.

There, straight ahead of us and silhouetted by the last light of the sun, was an upright figure taller than any man; and to our left, where the bag was swaying, another figure, tall enough that its head was in the tree branches. It was pushing at a bag with its snout, snuffling, sniffing.

Other than that, the two creatures made no sound, seemingly unaware of us, though that might change.

I could *smell* them. It had to be them. The smell of dogs, but not the kind you kept on your lap or let sleep on your bed—not Ciccio's kind of dog. It was the smell of a wild animal: wet, filthy and rancid from what it ate. A dog bigger than any other dog, and upright—a creature from a dark dream.

I wanted to throw up. I wanted to scream. I wanted to lie down, cover my face, go to sleep and wake up from the nightmare of it; but Ciccio was whining next to me, backing up still, and I knew what we had to do, crazy as it was:

We had to return to the village.

Whatever was in the olive groves—and I didn't want to imagine what the faces of creatures as tall as olive branches, creatures that might sniff and swat at bags with dead dogs in them might look like—we were not going to get past them if we stayed in the grove; and frightening though the village was, it couldn't be any scarier than this.

Ciccio didn't need me to call his name. When I turned and began running, he was at my side.

I listened for heavy bodies behind us, heard nothing, but could not be sure. When they ran, did the creatures fall to four legs or did they run like men? Were their footsteps loud, or as quiet as wolves? We wouldn't be able to cut between the houses to reach the cobblestone path. The houses touched. We would have to stay in the groves until we reached the path, and this we did, stumbling from the grass and trees onto the cobblestones and into the village at last.

There was moonlight at least. I remember feeling grateful for that. Not much—a bright crescent moon, if any crescent moon could be called bright—but more light than there'd been in the groves behind the house.

Looking behind me for the creatures, I twisted my ankle on a cobble and fell. Ciccio waited for me to catch up; and when I reached him we both stopped for a moment to look up the path that ran between the houses— between the doorways with their paint and blood. *The blood of dogs.*

There was no one on the path except us, no doors starting to open, no voices in the houses.

And then I heard the baby cry.

I thought it was a whine from Ciccio, but the sound came again, and it was indeed a baby's cry.

There were no other voices. Just the baby's. And cry it did—as if there would never ever be anyone to pick it up and hold it.

As Ciccio and I stared at the empty path, we saw the creatures. We'd expected them from the groves behind us, but there they were, ahead of us somehow. I started to turn, ready to run once more, but these creatures too seemed not to see us. They'd been there on the path all along, I realized suddenly, but we just hadn't seen them. They'd been down on all fours, and now some of them were standing up.

They were looking at something on the path. The ones still on all fours were pawing at the cobbles. Those that had stood were staring and sniffing at the air.

Ciccio didn't move beside me. He didn't whimper, and for a moment I was afraid the invisible leash had gotten him once more; but he was only hypnotized, just as I was, by the sight of the creatures, their big heads and chests, their long, sinewy legs, their fur—all of it lit faintly now by the crescent moon.

Was this how an ordinary dog—the kind that men knew and loved— acted when it felt true terror? Paralyzed? The sight and smell and soundless sounds of dogs so large that their jaws could snap you in half, and yet walking upright, like your master? Was this what ordinary dogs dreamed when they kicked in their sleep, whined, in the worst nightmares of their innocent, loyal lives?

Three of the creatures—there were six in all—were down on all fours, sniffing and pawing at the cobbles, while two remained upright looking at the same spot and a sixth sniffed at the nearest doorway, but didn't touch it. It sniffed the wood, the paint, jerked back again and again from what it smelled, and finally, as if tired of the impasse, returned to the five who were so intent on the stone path and whatever was there.

The baby still cried. It wasn't in a house. It wasn't in the groves. It was as if the sound were coming from the ground, from the cobbles themselves.

I squinted, and there in the cobblestones at the creatures' feet, I saw a faint light glowing.

How could light be coming from cobbles?

I took a step, then another, ready to run if the creatures turned to look at us. I managed four steps and squinted again. The light was indeed coming from the cobbles—as if through a crack in the pavement—and the creatures hadn't noticed us yet simply because they wanted so badly to get to that light.

The baby kept crying and the crying came from the light. How was it possible?

There was something—a room, a space of some kind—under the cobblestone path, a place lit by a light, and in that space the baby cried. There was no other explanation. The creatures wanted the light because they wanted the baby. *They wanted the baby's blood.*

I don't know how I knew this, but I did. It made sense of everything.

The creatures were going crazy. They were pawing frantically at the cobbles, at the light, at the sound coming from the light. They were smelling things I couldn't imagine, and the smells were driving them crazy, too. Two had broken away from the group and were sniffing at doors, daring to touch them now, pushing hard with their snouts, pawing with long paws, then jerking back as if the paint made them sick. *And why not?* I remember thinking. *Dog's blood. The wrong blood. The blood of kin.*

The baby had stopped, but was starting again.

And then one of the creatures saw us.

Perhaps it was Ciccio. Perhaps the creature smelled him, a brother. Perhaps it was my smell, or perhaps we'd made a sound. Perhaps, in its hysteria, it had looked everywhere and its eyes had finally fallen on us.

The creature stared at us, and as it did, its brethren turned in our direction, too, stood up, and cocked their heads. It was a dog they were seeing—a cousin, skinny and white with black spots—and that was all right—but there was something else standing by that dog, something upright and hairless and not unlike the baby that cried forever in the night.

They began toward us. I wanted Ciccio to run, to run to safety; "They don't want you!" I wanted to shout—but of course he didn't run. He started barking furiously and took a step toward them.

"No, Ciccio!" I grabbed him by the skin of the neck. He turned, snarled, stopped when he saw it was me, and let me pick him up, back legs kicking as if running for us both. Barely able to carry him, I stumbled toward the nearest doorway.

Whatever was inside the house would not, I told myself, be as bad as what was coming towards us. And there was no way I could outrun them whether they dropped to all four or stayed upright.

The door was unlocked, and I remember thinking giddily: *Why not?* The villagers knew the creatures couldn't enter. The crescent moon and cross and dog's blood would stop them, and the doorways were too small anyway for them to get through. The villagers knew this because it had all been happening for a long time, the squat smooth-skinned people and the dog-creatures, the doorways and the crying baby. Perhaps at the beginning there had been no paint at all, just blood, old dark blood making the sign of the crescent moon and the cross. Perhaps (I thought giddily) the cross had been a—

I got us both inside and shut the door. Would there be a crash? Would the hinges hold? Would the creatures even try? Would there instead be a squat man in the darkness with a knife, a dog-skinning knife, who'd kill us both and put us in bags and hang us in the trees?

Nothing happened. There was no crash. No man in the dark came at us. There may have been sniffing and snuffling on the other side of the door, but how would I know, I was panting too loudly. I couldn't even tell if Ciccio was whining in my arms.

I blinked and saw a faint light near the floor. There was no light from another room. No light through windows, if there were any windows. Just that faint light near the floor.

I put Ciccio down, and he stayed.

When my eyes had adjusted as much as they were going to, I could see that the light was a crack in the floor, and, when I stepped over to it, that there was a handle on the floor, one dimly lit by that light.

There was a door in the floor—that's what it was—and the light was the same light that had been driving the creatures crazy outside.

I took the handle and started to pull up.

The baby was crying again. I could hear it now, and it wasn't coming from outside, from the path. It was coming, like the light itself, from below us, under the door in the floor. I started to pull again on the handle, and stopped. Why wasn't I afraid of what was below me, the light, the crying baby?

Because, a voice said, and it was my own, I know—the wisest one in me—*wherever the baby is, the creatures cannot be.*

So I lifted the door in the floor and found the dirt and stone stairs I somehow knew would be there, ones lit faintly by the light somewhere beyond them.

Ciccio didn't want to go. I had to pull him onto the stairs with me, quickly shutting the door over us.

◆

We followed both the baby's crying and the light, which grew brighter as we stepped from the last stone stair onto the bare earth, turned right into a passageway, and began to walk under what I knew was the front of the house, where the creatures no doubt still stood, trying to figure out how to reach the light that was driving them so crazy.

I don't know if I'm leaving things out when I say, as I always do, that we reached at last the big room, and the villagers there, and the baby in the center of them all. I have told this story—the story of Magusa—many times in my life, and, though I'm sure I have gotten some things wrong, I've remembered what matters most: The immense underground room, the villagers of Magusa filling it silently; the baby, on a stone table in the center, crying; hundreds of votive candles in the corners of the room to light it; lanterns on the dirt walls; and the light, though gentle and flickering, bright enough to shine through a crack in the cobblestone path above. Is all of this true? It must be since what we experience when we are young is burned like God's truth into our brains. What I saw that night—while my parents worried where I was—is as true as anything I have ever lived, and why I will tell this story again and again until my lips can no longer make words.

When Ciccio and I reached the great room—our noses full of dust, candle smoke, and something else—something metallic I'd smelled in the little yard where I'd saved Ciccio from the man's knife—the villagers were there, all of them, even the same squat man with the knife. And they were all there *because the baby was bleeding.*

They stood around it, watched it and did more than watch. But they were not what I was looking at. I was looking at the baby.

He was as dark-skinned as they were, but a baby like any other. He was naked on the stone table—an ancient, worn thing—and all I could think for a moment was how cold, how incredibly cold, he must be. *To be alive, to be crying for someone to hold you, and yet to lie on cold stone. What must it be like, my child, to do this forever?*

For he had indeed been doing it forever. This I knew, too.

And I recognized the metallic smell. The smell of copper. The smell of blood.

The baby was bleeding. He was bleeding slowly, and he was bleeding a lot; but this was not why he was crying. He felt nothing as he bled. He was crying for his mother, who wasn't there, and never would be, for she had died long ago.

The stone table under him, which was sloped, had little channels, and it was down these channels that his blood, red and bright, like the paint on the doors, moved like honey into little cups—some stone, some ceramic, some metal—all old and chipped and bent—as he cried and would not stop crying for someone who could not come. My brother, in the year of life he'd had, had cried that way, too, but someone had always come.

Perhaps it was the way the villagers were standing, waiting patiently, or the way the baby lay on his back, arms and legs still, no one stepping to him, as if he, the baby, had the power, and they did not, that told me how long this had been happening. Whether it happened only at crescent moons or at other times as well, it did not happen every night, I knew. It had not happened the night my friends had stayed the night in the trees, since they had met no dog-creatures.

To bleed forever . . .

He was bleeding from his hands and feet, from wounds he'd been born with that would always bleed, and the villagers knew this, as their ancestors had known it, just as they knew that all they had to do to get the blood they needed in order to live forever, too, was wait for the right moon, and keep the creatures away, and let the baby bleed. . . .

Born too soon, or too late, a voice said quietly, and whether it was a voice from the room, the village, or my own mind making sense of what should make no sense, I'll never know.

Born too soon or too late, the voice said again, and it was true. *A mistake. An infant who would never take his true place in the world—even if he lived forever.*

There were four old women standing apart from the group, and it didn't take a genius to know who and what they were. They were the women who protected the village—and the baby—from the creatures who came every crescent moon, the creatures who wanted his blood, too, for what creature does not wish to live forever? They were the *streghe* who knew the spells that could drag dogs on invisible leashes to the village, who knew how to mix a paint that wasn't a paint, who knew the design a door should have, and how big the doorway should be. They hadn't invented this magic themselves. They had learned it from old women before them, and that was enough to keep their story going.

These are the women of the moon and blood, the voice said. *These are the women who protect a child who isn't theirs and give a village what it has needed for a thousand years.*

I wanted to go to the child, and I knew why. If I did, perhaps (a part of me whispered) I would find my baby brother there, pick him up and hold him, then take him home at last.

⤙◦⤚

But he wasn't my brother—the idea was crazy—and the villagers would stop me anyway. They would have to. The squat man would produce his knife and that would be the end.

Neither I nor Ciccio had made a sound, but a little girl turned at that moment and saw us. Her mother had given her a cup. The girl had drunk from it slowly, eyes closed, as if trying to taste what could not be tasted. And when she handed the cup back to her mother, she happened to look our way. She stared for a moment, tugged at her mother's black dress, and her mother turned too.

I'd imagined a shout would go up. I was sure one would. Ciccio and I had violated this room, discovered their secret, and a shout would go up. The villagers would swarm over us, and we would be beaten, perhaps killed—and why shouldn't we be? To intrude on their story. But a shout did not go up. A dozen faces were looking at us now, then another dozen, heads turning like echoes of a thought. But there were no shouts, no mutterings, and no knives.

They just stared—at the pale, red-haired boy and his skinny dog who were standing in the archway to the great room. They stared and blinked and what I saw in their faces, their wide-set eyes that had seen the centuries pass and would see more, *world without end*, was not anger or insanity or fear.

It was a sadness and below that, a shame. I didn't understand it, and then of course did.

◂◦▸

They had no choice. They had to drink his blood—the child's—to keep living, and because they did, they would never be free.

They too are forsaken.

So the villagers stared at the boy and his dog, both of whom were free to live, love and die, and, as they did, felt their prison even more, tasting it on their lips, on the rims of battered cups, in the coppery air, in the blood of a child that would cry for them forever.

Ciccio fidgeted beside me, and I fidgeted back. We were free to go, but where? The creatures were still out there on the path and in the groves, and would be there all night.

So I headed, Ciccio beside me, toward the flickering torches that led to the stairs and to the one-room house above them. No one followed. The villagers had turned away—only the little girl and two boys kept staring at us—and were again waiting for their cups to be filled. It would take all night, and it would take forever.

The stone floor of the house—the one with the door in its floor—was cold, but there was a blanket, one I found by crawling from corner to corner, touching everything I could until I found it. It was wadded up in a corner and smelled of sweat, ordinary sweat, and of something else—something strange—but I wasn't going to be picky. I wrapped myself in it and Ciccio lay down beside me. We would keep each other as warm as we could.

We woke twice to the sounds of footsteps near us. I expected bodies to lie down beside us or voices to tell us to leave, but neither happened. The footsteps stopped both times, and the room fell silent again.

Dawn light woke Ciccio first. There was one tiny window in the wall facing the groves, and dogs always wake before men. I woke a second later and looked around the room—at the little table and chairs I'd touched in the darkness, at the stone-and-mortar walls, and at the door to another room, one I hadn't known was there. I got up, folded the blanket, put it in a corner, and led Ciccio out, closing the door behind us quietly in case people were sleeping in that other room.

There was no one on the cobblestone path, but I could hear men talking in the groves beyond the houses. Olive-picking was what they did in the day, what they did with their lives that wasn't magic, and what they'd done in every country on this sea—this olive-growing sea—since the beginning. It was the one thing, the only thing, that let them live like ordinary men and women.

When I got home, my parents were relieved, but angry, too, as all parents are when their children scare them. I lied. I told them I'd hidden in an abandoned hut in the groves all night because three boys—ones who were probably drug users from Parma, in Reggio-Emilia—had chased me at sunset when I was looking for Ciccio, and how one even had a knife, and how I'd been too scared to leave the hut, fallen asleep and woken only at dawn. But at least I'd found Ciccio, see?

They believed me. What other story would make sense? I wasn't a bad boy. I didn't drink beer with friends (how could I? my friends drank wine and only at meals), I didn't vandalize property, and no one my age in the village had a girlfriend.

My mother cried for a while, as if worrying about me had reminded her of my brother. My dad sighed—anger was never really his way—and kept patting me on the back in that gentle way of his. He even patted Ciccio to let me know man to man that everything was okay.

I didn't tell my friends what really happened. They'd have had question after question, and it would have taken days to explain, and maybe they'd have believed me, and maybe not. Mainly, they'd have been mad, feeling left out. Friends can be that way. "You almost got killed? Wonderful! Why didn't you take us with you?"

I did worry about the child, but when, a few weeks later—unable to keep quiet any longer—I started to tell my dad how I'd heard a baby crying in Magusa as if someone were hurting it, my dad said, "I'm not surprised, Brad, but there's nothing to do about it. Didn't your friends tell you? Magusa is empty. Everyone's gone. The olive trees in those groves have a blight, and the *carabinieri* think they've gone to the mountains to join the more radical communists around Montalcino. That certainly makes sense. I'm sorry about the baby. By the way, how did you hear it crying, Brad?"

I didn't answer, and he didn't press. He looked at me strangely for a few days, and then the conversation was forgotten.

My parents let me keep Ciccio, of course. He slept in my room after we bathed and de-fleaed him, and I had him for a good week before he ran away. It wasn't any invisible leash that took him. He'd been acting stir-crazy, and the last time I saw him he was down by the wharf, letting a fisherman pet him. I called to him. He looked around, saw me, but didn't come; and he didn't return home that night either. *Wandering dogs usually keep wandering*, I remembered, and that was okay. It was okay, I told myself even then, to know love and magic—to have good friends or a scrawny dog or a terrible night in a village forgotten by God—for just a moment in time, and then to move on, living your life as you needed to live it to become what you needed to become, in a world where war sometimes did not feel like war at all, and blood did not always mean dying.

◄o►

THIS CIRCUS THE WORLD

AMBER SPARKS

It was the empty Jim Beam bottle on its side in the sullen yellow shower, the fluorescent sign flickering on the roof, the bedsprings of the room next door in choruses of creaking. It was the stained beige carpet and way he shouted when he came through the door. It was the way she lay for hours, facedown on that carpet, trussed and always with the camera at her back. It was the way the room was sometimes green, was sometimes gray, was sometimes a cheap room-to-let and sometimes a cheap roadside motel and sometimes a cheap county jail cell—but always cheap, always faded and frayed as the wallpaper that sometimes lined these walls. It was the way the men in suits filed in, talking on their handsets or their earpieces and taking notes and casting eyes back and forth, fishing for visions in the close and clammy air.

It was the way she sometimes perched at the vanity, watched him enter as a tall swift triptych through the mirrors, or as a prisoner, battered. It was the way she combed her hair, the way she put on lipstick, the way she dragged mascara through her lashes while she listened to the clock tick on and on. It was the way he said he liked her better without makeup. It was the way he held her throat, the way she didn't scream, the way he called her Alice though that was not her name, had never been her name. It was the way they both signed the ledger, also not their real names, checking

239

in and out each day, heading home separately, he in his car, she in worn tennis shoes, walking three miles to the bus to her apartment where she washed her face, her arms, her legs, her feet and toes, her stomach.

It was the way she sometimes left him in the bathtub for hours, inches of water wrinkling his thin white skin, casting him in old man's costume. The way his arms and legs grew thatched and scarred as train tracks, the way she always found fresh flesh to cut. The way the men in suits would take pictures, bending down, frowning at the carpet like crime scene photographers. The way her clothes were always crumpled on that carpet. The way she sometimes wore layers of clothes, the way sometimes there were never enough clothes, the way sometimes there was never enough fabric in the world to cover her over and swallow her under.

The way they avoided eye contact but every now and then their gazes would join, would lock, would jolt them apart, the third rail of desire. The way they would sometimes forget to scratch or scream or scrape or otherwise draw blood and would instead hold each other, skin and breath and damaged heart until they fell asleep in that vibrating bed, stilled now without the meal of quarters. The way they would sometimes turn off the recording devices and stash the cat o'nine tails and the cattle prod and hide the handcuffs in the drawer next to the King James Bible. The way they would sometimes dress one another, he in a tux and she in a gown, the way they would bow to one another, the way they would sip champagne and smile politely over their prime rib. The way he would mention moonlight on the Seine. The way she would shiver.

The way they would finally say I love you and I love you too and the way alarms would shriek and the way the men in suits would invade an army of red ties and bulletproof vests. The way the room would shrink and blacken the way the room would dim the way the blood would pool and churn in the bath the way their names their real names would finally echo soft but true in tune like nothing else in this cruel circus called the world when they finally shut off the lights.

⬥

SOME PICTURES IN AN ALBUM

GARY McMAHON

The book is a slim faux leather photograph album.

The front cover is dusty and stained, and scratched crudely into the material is a circular design that matches the birthmark behind my right knee.

The very edges of the plastic pages are crumpled and torn. It's an ordinary album, something that might be stored in the loft spaces of a million family homes around the country.

Nothing strange. Nothing unusual.

Now that my father is dead, it is just another item found among his belongings . . . but for some reason I'm drawn to this particular album as I sort through his stuff to box it all up and send it to the charity shop.

I sit down on the bed in my old room and open the book.

Each of the seventeen photographs has its own page; every white-bordered Polaroid image is positioned perfectly at the center and covered in a thin plastic protective flap. Someone has taken a lot of time to put the album together. A lot of love went into the preparation.

I always called him father, not Dad. He was never that . . . he was always just a father. I can't imagine why he would take so much care in the preparation of this album, or why he would have wanted to keep the pictures I find inside.

- The first photograph shows me standing in front of a high redbrick wall. I am six years old. I recognize myself, but it's like looking into a mirror at a reflection that isn't quite right. I'm holding above my head a small silver plastic replica of the F.A. Cup with red and white ribbons tied around it. There is a long, thin shadow on the wall beside me. It is 1973; the year Sunderland beat Leeds in the cup final to produce a now legendary example of "giant killing." My face is joyous; my rosy cheeks are soft; my reddish hair almost matches the color of the bricks behind me. I am wearing a light blue shirt that looks like it has lighter blue flowers on it. My entire chest is hidden by a red and white rosette and a knitted red and white doll, both pinned to the shirt.

- The next photograph, on the adjoining page, shows simply a black door. It looks like the front door to a normal terraced house. The bricks around it are of the same shade of red as those in the previous photo, but they are more weathered. The edge of a window frame can be seen on the right of the shot. The door itself looks old, beaten. Paint is flaking off to expose patches of the cheap pale timber beneath.

- Over the page is a photograph of me on one of those mechanical animal rides that used to be outside shops on the high street in most English towns. Put in a couple of coins and let your kid ride for a few minutes. This one is a cartoon elephant. I am clutching its ears. My smile is huge. I am wearing a blue woolen hat. My mother—looking so young, so pretty—is standing to the side, smiling shyly. The arm and leg of what I assume to be my father can be seen next to her, the rest of him just clipped out of the frame. My body is slightly blurred because of the motion of the ride, but my face is perfectly still. I seem to be glimpsing something incredible. There is a light in my eyes that is difficult to define. A question occurs to me as I stare at the image: If my parents are both in the shot, who is that taking the photograph?

- Next up is the outside of a shop: a corner newsagent, Moses & Sons. Faded posters stuck up with tape in the window, a man in a white overcoat can be glimpsed behind the glass, standing at a counter. The window display is mostly sweets, with a few piles of comics and magazines. I am standing with my back to the camera, looking through the window. My face is reflected in the glass; I am not smiling. At first glance it appears that I might be crying, but it isn't clear. Perhaps I am simply concentrating on all the sugared treats in the display. There is another figure reflected in the glass window beside me, this one tall and thin, but whoever it is cannot be seen.

- The door again—at least it looks like the same one. A little older, maybe. More worn. This photograph is darker than the last one, so it could have been taken at a different time of day. Later. Closer to dark. I begin to suspect that each photograph represents a new time frame. Perhaps a year has passed since the last one.

- Over the page there are two blank sheets. No photos here, just the empty clear plastic flaps. It's as if a year has been missed, or deliberately excised.

- Me, nine years old. I know this because I can recall the scene clearly. My birthday. In the photograph I am surrounded by crumpled balls of wrapping paper and presents. A cowboy rifle, an Action man tank, several cars and an assortment of books. My father's foot can be seen at the bottom left corner of the frame. He is wearing the worn brown slippers I always remember, the pair with the hard rubber soles. The ones he used to like beating me with. He never wanted to hurt me, or so he said at the time. He always gave me a choice: the slipper or an hour spent locked up in the cubby hole under the stairs. I always chose the slipper, because it was over quickly and I didn't like the dark under the stairs—or the thought of what it might contain.

- The door again. This year it is cleaner, as if someone has given it a lick of paint. The handle has been replaced. The letter box shines. Sunlight is reflected off the golden knocker, making bright patterns on the camera lens.

- The next photograph is disturbing. It shows me sitting on the lap of a man I do not recognize. His eyes are large and empty; his creamy-white hands are massive as they drape over my shoulders, and at least some of the fingers are resting at a weird angle, as if they are in fact boneless. I look . . . well, my expression is unreadable. I am staring directly into the camera, but not smiling. There could be an element of pleading in my eyes, but that might just be the current me reading too much into a blank expression. My mother, dressed in flared pants and an ugly tie-dye blouse, stands to the side, leaning in the doorway that leads into the kitchen. She seems worried; her eyes are dull and she is biting her bottom lip. Her shoulders are slumped. I cannot remember ever seeing her look so deflated; she was always such a happy woman. The man whose lap I occupy doesn't look quite right. His hair is odd. His face is a different color to his elongated hands. Is he wearing a wig? Is that a mask?

■ The door. Soiled. Burn marks across the kickboard. The knocker is removed. The letterbox is stuffed with dead leaves.

■ In the next one, I'm ten. I'm sitting on a red Raleigh Chopper bike in the street, my legs too short to allow my feet to properly touch the ground. I'm balanced on my tiptoes, the bike leaning slightly to the right and toward a low garden wall. It must be cold because I'm wrapped up warm: a thick coat, a matching Sunderland AFC hat and scarf, woolen fingerless gloves on my hands. My smile is awkward, as if it is forced. Again, I have no recollection of this photo being taken, but I do remember the day my father brought the bike home after work—it was stolen later that same day, taken from outside our house when I left it leaning against the wall to pop inside for dinner. I got the slipper for that, too. My father carried on longer than usual, and he was crying when he finished. I have the uneasy feeling that there was someone else there, in the room, when my punishment was meted out; an unseen audience, watching silently from a corner of the back bedroom. Afterward, I couldn't sit down for hours because of the pain. I remember that part most of all.

■ The door. Hinges rusted. Wood blackened. This time it's ajar. I can see the gap, only blackness visible. I wish I could remember this door, where it was, what it led to. It certainly wasn't the door to our house: that was green, and had a lot of glass panels. The door to a family home. This door is different; less welcoming. Nobody would willingly knock on this door or want to see who lives behind it.

■ Eleven years old, in the back yard. I'm turned away from the camera, pinning young Shelley Cork to the wall with one arm on either side of her pretty face, the palms of my hands pressed hard against the bricks. We're kissing. My eyes are closed; hers are open. She looks panicked, but she doesn't seem to be struggling. I do have a memory of this, but it's much different. We were necking against the wall at the back of our house, practicing kissing like grown-ups, testing boundaries. She rested her hand against my crotch; I stuck my hand down the back of her knickers and groped her ass. There was nobody else there, so I don't know how this photograph exists. It should not be here. In my memory, Shelley wasn't panicked at all. She was excited, exhilarated. Her breathing was heavy against the side of my face; her eyes kept blinking and she pulled me tightly against her warm, soft body. The whole thing was her idea; I was the one who was afraid. I didn't want my father to come out and catch us in the act. I remember feeling a similar kind of unreasonable guilt later that same year, when Shelley Cork went missing.

- Again, we have the black door. It's half open, and this time a thin, pale hand can be seen gripping its edge. The fingers are too long, and there are only three of them but with too many joints. The knuckle bones jut out unnaturally. The skin is a sickly yellowy shade of cream.

- I'm twelve years old, sitting down by the river with my legs dangling over the rocks, the soles of my running shoes hanging mere inches above the water. Along the riverbank, on the opposite side, people are fishing. I'm not watching them. I'm staring down into the black water. My posture is strange, strained, as if I'm poised to jump. I used to go down there a lot, but this photograph seems alien, as if it isn't me there by the river, but someone else imitating me. A freakishly tall figure in the bushes directly opposite me, on the other side of the water, stands and stares.

- This time the door is wide open. The wood is rotten and splintered; the door hangs askew in its frame, the hinges damaged. Beyond the angled wooden rectangle, there is visible the rear view of someone walking along a scruffy hallway and into the interior of the house. The wallpaper is hanging in strips, the bare boards are warped and stained, and the figure is fading into the dark at the end of the hallway. The figure is naked. Its skin is the color of curdled cream. The bones of its spine stick out like a line of pebbles. The figure is tall and terribly thin, like a prisoner in one of those concentration camp photographs from WWII. Its legs are bent in the wrong place; its arms are so long that its three-fingered hands almost touch the floor. Its head—or what little of it can be seen—is smooth and almost hairless, like that of a baby.

- The next photograph is a close-up portrait shot. My face is framed nicely, centered on the page. The background is blurred, out of focus, so it could be anywhere. I am screaming. My eyes are so wide that at first I don't recognize my own face, and my mouth is stretched open to the limit. My face is pale, but my cheeks are red. I don't seem to be wearing a shirt. Someone's fingers, from the top knuckles upwards, are visible just below my neck, but the rest of the hand is cut off by the bottom edge of the photograph. The fingernails are torn and dirty. There are only three fingers on the hand. Upon closer inspection, the wall behind me is not blurred: it is ruined, the paper torn and dirtied, the uneven plaster beneath lined and raked as if by something sharp. Like nails. Or claws.

- Another blank page. But this one has small bits of adhesive dotted on the paper, as if whatever photograph was there has been hastily removed.

- The final photograph is perhaps the most disturbing of all, yet the least clear in terms of what is going on. The photographer has stepped forward, must be standing on the doorstep, so only a part of the doorframe is visible. At the end of the grimy hallway, there are two figures. Both are facing away from the black door, and from the camera. One of the figures is the familiar, thin, lanky creature from one of the previous shots. Its shoulders are hunched; its lean thighs are clenched, as if it's been caught in the act of taking a step. Holding its hand is another, smaller figure. A scrawny boy, aged perhaps fourteen years old. The boy is naked. I recognize myself from the birthmark behind my right knee: a small, dark, circular stain. The muscles in my body are tensed. I can see that even from the grainy, unfocused shot. Beyond the two figures, just about visible in the darkness at the end of the hallway, is my father. His nude body is a vague pinkish blur, but his face is a little easier to make out: a small, hazy oval in the shadows. His arms are crossed at the wrist over his pelvis. He is gripping something in his fist but I don't know what it is. His eyes are small and mean, and he is grinning.

I close the album and put it on the bed. Get up and walk to the mirror. Reflected there, in the glass, I see something other than the familiar room where I spent my childhood evenings fighting back nightmares.

I see a black door in the wall, its letterbox stuffed with dead leaves and its gold handle and knocker slightly tarnished. As I watch, the door opens. A long, thin, pale three-fingered hand bends around the frame. I stare at the ragged nails, the blood and dirt I know is crusted beneath them, and I remember.

He was always there, in my life, ever since I was six years old. For most of the time he stayed in the background, but sometimes he put on a mask and entered the frame, unable to stay out of view. I'm still not sure who he was, but my father brought him into our home, and some kind of transaction took place. My birthmark is a stamp, a barcode; it marks me out as belonging to him. Bought and paid for long ago, before the first photograph was even taken.

Each time I was taken there, to the house with the black door, I came out with something missing. The memory of what happened inside, yes, but also something else: a small part of me, sliced away. I think Shelley Cork got to see what was in there, too, but she never came back out. I suspect that my father led her through that black door and left her there, a plaything for whatever resides at the end of that dirty hallway.

I shift my gaze and stare at the door in the mirror. My face resembles that of my father, at the age that I am now. A non-identical reflection; like the left hand swapping places with the right. It does not fit. It should not be there, where it does not belong.

I glance again at the black door. It has always been waiting for me to return. The long, thin hand slips away, retreating back inside, but the door does not shut. It will never shut, not until I go back inside to take back what is mine.

To reclaim the things I left behind and stick those missing photographs back in the album.

-o-

WILD ACRE

NATHAN BALLINGRUD

hree men are lying in what will someday be a house. For now it's just a skeleton of beams and supports, standing amid the foundations and frames of other burgeoning houses in a large, bulldozed clearing. The earth around them is a churned, orange clay. Forest abuts the Wild Acre development site, crawling up the side of the Blue Ridge Mountains, hickory and maple hoarding darkness as the sky above them shades into deepening blue. The hope is that soon there will be finished buildings here, and then more skeletons and more houses, with roads to navigate them. But now there are only felled trees, and mud, and these naked frames. And three men, lying on a cold wooden floor, staring up through the roof beams as the sky organizes a nightfall. They have a cooler packed with beer and a baseball bat.

Several yards away, mounted in the back of Jeremy's truck, is a hunting rifle.

Jeremy watches stars burn into life: first two, then a dozen. He came here hoping for violence, but the evening has softened him. Lying on his back, balancing a beer on the great swell of his belly, he hopes there will be no occasion for it. Wild Acre is abandoned for now, and might be for a long time to come, making it an easy target. Three nights over the past week, someone has come onto the work site and committed small but infuriating acts of vandalism: stealing and damaging tools and equipment, spray painting vulgar images on the project manager's trailer, even taking a dump on the floor of one of the unfinished houses. The project manager complained to the police, but with production stalled and bank accounts running dry, angry subcontractors and prospective homeowners consumed most of his attention. The way Jeremy saw things, it was up to the trade guys to protect the site. He figured the vandals for environmental activists, pissed that their mountain had been shaved for this project; he worried that they'd soon start burning down his frames. Insurance would cover the developer, but he and his company would go bankrupt. So he's come here with Dennis and Renaldo – his best friend and his most able brawler, respectively – hoping to catch them in the act and beat them into the dirt.

"They're not coming tonight," says Renaldo.

"No shit," says Dennis. "You think it's 'cause you talk too loud?" Dennis has been with Jeremy ten years now. For a while, Jeremy thought about making him partner, but the man just couldn't keep his shit together, and Jeremy privately nixed the idea. Dennis is forty-eight years old, ten years older than Jeremy. His whole life is invested in this work: he's a carpenter and nothing else. He has three young children, and talks about having more. This work stoppage threatens to impoverish him. "Bunch of goddamn Green Party eco-fucking-terrorist mother*fuckers*," Dennis says.

Jeremy watches him. Dennis is moving his jaw around, working himself into a rage. That would be useful if he thought anybody was going to show tonight; but he thinks they've screwed it all up. They got here too early, before the sun was down, and they made too much noise. No one will come now.

"Dude. Grab yourself a beer and mellow out."

"These kids are fucking with my *life*, man! You tell me to mellow *out?*"

"Dennis, man, you're not the only one." A breeze comes down the mountain and washes over them. Jeremy feels it move through his hair, deepening his sense of easy contentment. He remembers feeling that rage just this afternoon, talking to that asshole from the bank, and he knows he'll feel it again. He knows he'll have to. But right now it's as distant and alien as the full moon, catching fire unknown miles above them. "But they're not here. 'Naldo's right, we blew it. We'll come back tomorrow night." He looks into the forest crowding against the development site, and wonders why they didn't think to hide themselves there. "And we'll do it right. So for tonight? Just chill."

Renaldo leans over and claps Dennis on the back. "*Mañana*, amigo. *Mañana!*"

Jeremy knows that Renaldo's optimism is one of the reasons Dennis resents him, but the young Mexican wouldn't be able to function in this all-white crew without it. He gets a lot of crap from these guys and just takes it. When work is this hard to come by, pride is a luxury. Nevertheless Jeremy is dismayed at Renaldo's easy manner in the face of it all. A man can't endure that kind of diminishment, he thinks, and not release anger somewhere.

Dennis casts Jeremy a defeated look. The sky retains a faint glow from twilight, but darkness has settled over the ground. The men are black shapes. "It's not the same for you, man. Your wife works, you know? You got another income. My wife don't do *shit*."

"That's not just her fault, though, Dennis. What would you do if Rebecca told you she was getting a job tomorrow?"

"I'd say it's about goddamned time!"

Jeremy laughs. "Bullshit. You'd just knock her up again. If that woman went out into the world you'd lose your mind, and you know it."

Dennis shakes his head, but a sort of smile breaks through.

The conversation has undermined whatever small good the beer has done for him tonight: all the old fears are stirring. He hasn't been able to pay these men for three weeks now, and even an old friend like Dennis will have to move on eventually. The business hasn't paid a bill in months, and Tara's teacher's salary certainly isn't enough to support them by itself. He realizes that their objective tonight is mostly just an excuse to vent some anger; cracking some misguided kids' heads isn't going to get the bank to stop calling him, and it isn't going to get the bulldozers moving again. It isn't going to let him call his crew and tell them they can come back to work, either.

But he won't let it get to him tonight. Not this beautiful, moonlit night on the mountain, with bare wood lifting skyward all around them. "Fuck it," he says, and claps his hands twice, a reclining sultan. "Naldo! Mas cervesas!"

Renaldo, who has just settled onto his back, slowly folds himself into a sitting position. He climbs to his feet and heads to the cooler without complaint. He's accustomed to being the gofer.

"Little Mexican bastard," Dennis says. "I bet he's got fifty cousins packed into a trailer he's trying to support."

"Hablo fucking ingles, motherfucker," Renaldo says.

"What? Speak English! I can't understand you."

Jeremy laughs. They drink more beer, and the warmth of it washes through their bodies until they are illuminated, three little candles in a clearing, surrounded by the dark woods.

⊸⊙⊶

Jeremy says, "I gotta take a piss, dude." The urge has been building in him for some time, but he's been lying back on the floor, his body filled with a warm, beery lethargy, and he's been reluctant to move. Now it manifests as a sudden, urgent pain, sufficient to propel him to his feet and across the red clay road. The wind has risen and the forest is a wall of dark sound, the trees no longer distinct from each other but instead a writhing movement, a grasping energy which prickles his skin and hurries his step. The moon, which only a short while ago seemed a kindly lantern in the dark, smolders in the sky. Behind him, Dennis and Renaldo continue some wandering conversation, and he holds onto the sound of their voices to ward off a sudden, inexplicable rising fear. He casts a glance back toward the house. The ground inclines toward it, and at this angle he can't see either of them. Just the cross-gables shouldering into the sky.

He steps into the tree line, going back a few feet for modesty's sake. Situating himself behind a tree, he opens his fly and lets loose. The knot of pain in his gut starts to unravel.

Walking around has lit up the alcohol in his blood, and he's starting to feel angry again. If I don't get to hit somebody soon, he thinks, I'm going to snap. I'm going to unload on somebody that doesn't deserve it. If Dennis opens his whining mouth one more time it might be him.

Jeremy feels a twinge of remorse at the thought; Dennis is one of those guys who has to talk about his fears, or they'll eat him alive. He has to give a running commentary on every grim possibility, as if by voicing a fear he'd chase it into hiding. Jeremy relates more to Renaldo, who has yet to utter one frustrated thought about how long it's been since he's been paid, or what their future prospects might be. He doesn't really know Renaldo, knows his personal situation even less, and something about that strikes him as proper. The idea of a man keening in pain has always embarrassed him.

When Jeremy has weak moments, he saves them for private expression. Even Tara, who has been a rock of optimism throughout all of this, isn't privy to them. She's a smart, intuitive woman, though, and Jeremy recognizes his fortune in her. She assures him that he is both capable and industrious, and that he can find work other than hammering nails into wood, should it come down to it. She's always held the long view. He feels a sudden swell of love for her, as he stands there pissing in the woods: a desperate, childlike need. He blinks rapidly, clearing his eyes.

He's staring absently into the forest as he thinks this all through, and so it takes him a few moments to focus his gaze and realize that someone is staring back at him.

It's a young man—a kid, really—several feet deeper into the forest, obscured by low growth and hanging branches and darkness. He's skinny and naked. Smiling at him. Just grinning like a jack-o-lantern.

"Oh, *shit!*"

Jeremy lurches from the tree, yanking frantically at his zipper, which has caught on the denim of his pants. He staggers forward a step, his emotions a snarl of rage, excitement, and humiliation. "What the fuck!" he shouts. The kid bounds to his right and disappears, soundlessly.

"Dennis? *Dennis!* They're here!"

He turns but he can't see up the hill. The angle is bad. All he can see through the trees is the pale wooden frame standing out against the sky like bones, and he's taking little hopping steps as he wrestles with his zipper. He trips over a root and crashes painfully to the ground.

He hears Dennis's raised voice.

He climbs awkwardly to his feet. The zipper finally comes free and Jeremy yanks it up, running clumsily through the branches while fastening his fly. As he ascends the small incline and crosses the muddy road he can discern shapes wrestling between the wooden support struts; he hears them fighting, hears the brute explosions of breath and the heavy impact of colliding meat. It sounds like the kid is putting up a pretty good fight; Jeremy wants to get in on the action before it's all over. He's overcome by instinct and violent impulse.

He's exalted by it.

A voice breaks out of the tumult and it's so warped by anguish that it takes him a moment to recognize it as Dennis's scream.

Jeremy jerks to a stop. He burns crucial seconds trying to understand what he's heard.

And then he hears something else: a heavy tearing, like ripping canvas, followed by a liquid sound of dropped weight, of moist, heavy objects sliding to the ground. He catches a glimpse of motion, something huge and fast in the house and then an inverted leg standing out suddenly like a dark rip in the bright flank of stars, and then nothing. A high, keening wail—ephemeral, barely audible—rises from the unfinished house like a wisp of smoke.

Finally he reaches the top of the hill and looks inside.

Dennis is on his back, his body frosted by moonlight. He's lifting his head, staring down at himself. Organs are strewn to one side of his body like beached, black jellyfish, dark blood pumping slowly from the gape in his belly and spreading around him in a gory nimbus. His head drops back and he lifts it again. Renaldo is on his back too, arms flailing, trying to hold off the thing bestride him: huge, black-furred, dog-begotten, its man-like fingers wrapped around Renaldo's face and pushing his head into the floor so hard that the wood cracks beneath it. It lifts its shaggy head, bloody ropes of drool swinging from its snout and arcing into the moonsilvered night. It peels its lips from its teeth. Renaldo's screams are muffled beneath its hand.

"Shoot it," Dennis says. His voice is calm, like he's suggesting coffee. "Shoot it, Jeremy."

The house swings out of sight and the road scrolls by, lurching and violently tilting, and Jeremy realizes with some dismay that he is running. His truck, a small white pickup, is less than fifty feet away. Parked just beyond it is Renaldo's little import, its windows rolled down, rosary beads hanging from the rearview mirror.

Jeremy runs fill-tilt into the side of his truck, rebounding off it and almost falling to the ground. He opens the door and is inside with what feels like unnatural speed. He slides across to the driver's side and digs into his pocket for the keys, fingers grappling furiously through change and crumpled receipts until he finds them.

He can feel the rifle mounted on the rack behind his head, radiating a monstrous energy. It's loaded; it's always loaded.

He looks through the passenger window and sees something stand upright inside the frames, looking back at him. He sees Renaldo spasming beneath it. He sees the dark forested mountains looming behind this stillborn community with a hostile intelligence. He guns the engine and slams down the accelerator, turning the wheel hard to the left. The tires spray mud in huge arcs until they find traction, and he speeds down the hill toward the highway. The truck bounces hard on the rough path and briefly goes airborne. The engine screams, the sound of it filling his head.

→◇←

"What the hell are you *look*ing at?"

"What?" Jeremy blinked, and looked at his wife.

Breakfast time at the Blue Plate was always busy, but today the noise and the crowd were unprecedented. People crowded on the bench by the door, waiting for a chance to sit down. Short order cooks and servers hollered at each other over the din of loud customers, boiling fryers, and crackling griddles. He knew that Tara hated it here, but on bad days—and he's had plenty of bad days in the six months since the attack—he needed to be in places like this. Even now, wedged into a booth too narrow for him, with the table's edge pressing uncomfortably into his gut, he did not want to leave.

His attention was drawn by the new busboy. He was young and gangly, lanky hair swinging over his lowered face. He scurried from empty table to empty table, loading dirty plates and coffee mugs into his gray bus tub. He moved with a strange grace through the crowd, like someone well practiced at avoidance. Jeremy was bothered that he couldn't get a clear view of his face.

"Why do you think he wears his hair like that?" he said. "He looks like a drug addict or something. I'm surprised they let him."

Tara rolled her eyes, not even bothering to look. "The busboy? Are you serious?"

"What do you mean?"

"Are you even *listening* to me?"

"What? Of course. Come on." He forced his attention back where it belonged. "You're talking about that guy who teaches the smart kids. What's his name. Tim."

Tara let her stare linger a moment before pressing on. "Yeah, I mean, what an asshole, right? He *knows* I'm married!"

"Well, that's the attraction."

"The fact that I'm married to you is why he wants me? Oh my God, and I thought *he* had an ego!"

"No, I mean, you're hot, he'd be into you anyway. But the fact that you belong to somebody just adds another incentive. It's a challenge."

"Wait."

"Some guys just like to take what isn't theirs."

"Wait. I *belong* to you now?"

He smiled. "Well . . . yeah, bitch."

She laughed. "You are so lucky we're in a public place right now."

"You're not scary."

"Oh, I'm pretty scary."

"Then how come you can't scare off little Timmy?"

She gave him an exasperated look. "Do you think I'm not trying? He just doesn't *care*. I think he thinks I'm flirting with him or something. I want him to see you at the Christmas party. Get all alpha male on him. Squeeze his hand really hard when you shake it or something."

A waitress arrived at their table and unloaded their breakfast: fruit salad and a scrambled egg for Tara, a mound of buttery pancakes for Jeremy. Tara cast a critical eye over his plate and said, "We gotta work on that diet of yours, big man. There's a new year coming up. Resolution time."

"Like hell," he said, tucking in. "This is my fuel. I need it if I'm going to defeat Tim in bloody combat."

The sentence hung awkwardly between them. Jeremy found himself staring at her, the stupid smile on his face frozen into something miserable and strange. His scalp prickled and he felt his face go red.

"Well, that was dumb," he said.

She put her hand over his. "Honey."

He pulled away. "Whatever." He forked some of the pancakes into his mouth, staring down at his plate.

He breathed in deeply, taking in the close, burnt-oil odor of the place, trying to displace the smell of blood and fear which welled up inside him as though he was on the mountain again, half a year ago, watching his friends die in the rearview mirror. He looked around again to see if he could get a look at that creepy busboy's face, but he couldn't spot him in the crowd.

◄◦►

The coroner had decided that a wolf had killed Dennis and Renaldo. It was a big story in the local news for a week or so; there weren't supposed to be any wolves in this part of North Carolina. Nevertheless, the bite marks and the tracks in the mud were clear. Hunting parties had ranged into the woods; they'd bagged a few coyotes, but no wolves. The developer of Wild Acre filed for bankruptcy: buyers who had signed conditional agreements refused to close on the houses, and the banks gave up on the project, locking their coffers for good. Wild Acre became a ghost town of empty house frames and mud. Jeremy's outfit went under too. He broke the news to his employees and began the dreary process of appeasing his creditors. Tara still pulled down her teacher's salary, but it was barely enough to keep pace, let alone catch them up. They weren't sure how much longer they could afford their own house.

Within a month of the attack, Jeremy discovered that he was unemployable. Demand for his services had dried up. The framing companies were streamlining their payrolls, and nobody wanted to add an expensive ex-owner to their rosters.

He never told his wife what really happened that night. Publicly, he corroborated the coroner's theory, and he tried as best he could to convince himself of it, too. But the thing that had straddled his friend and then stared him down had not been a wolf.

He could not call it by its name.

◄◦►

In the middle of all that were the funerals.

Renaldo's had been a small, cheap affair. He'd felt like an imposter there, too close to the tumultuous emotion on display. Renaldo's mother filled the room with her cries. Jeremy felt alarmed and even a little appalled at her lack of self-consciousness, which was so at odds with her late son's unflappable nature. Everyone spoke in Spanish, and he was sure they were all talking about him. On some level he knew this was ridiculous, but he couldn't shake it.

A young man approached him, late teens or early twenties, dressed in an ill-fitting, rented suit, his hands hanging stiffly at his sides.

Jeremy nodded at him. "Hola," he said. He felt awkward and stupid.

"Hello," the man said. "You were his boss?"

"Yeah, yeah. I'm, um . . . I'm sorry. He was a great worker. You know, one of my best. The guys really liked him. If you knew my guys, you'd know that meant something." He realized he was beginning to ramble, and made himself stop talking.

"Thank you."

"Were you brothers?"

"Brothers-in-law. Married to my sister?"

"Oh, of course." Jeremy didn't know Renaldo had been married. He looked across the gathered crowd, thinking for one absurd moment that he might know her by sight.

"Listen," the man said, "I know you're having some hard times. The business and everything."

Well, here it comes, Jeremy thought. He tried to cut him off at the pass. "I still owed some money to Renaldo. I haven't forgotten. I'll get it to you as soon as I can. I promise."

"To Carmen."

"Of course. To Carmen."

"That's good." He nodded, looking at the ground. Jeremy could sense there was more coming, and he wanted to get away before it arrived. He opened his mouth to express a final platitude before taking his leave, but the young man spoke first. "Why didn't you shoot it?"

He felt something grow cold inside him. "What?"

"I know why you were there. Renaldo told me what was happening. The vandals? He said you had a rifle."

Jeremy bristled. "Listen, I don't know what Renaldo thought, but we weren't going up there to shoot anybody. We were going to scare them. That's all. The gun's in my truck because I'm a hunter. I don't use it to threaten kids."

"But it wasn't kids on the mountain that night, was it?"

They stared at each other for a moment. Jeremy's face was flushed, and he could hear the laboring of his own breath. By contrast the young man seemed entirely at ease; either he didn't really care about why Jeremy didn't shoot that night or he already knew that the answer wouldn't satisfy him.

"No, I guess it wasn't."

"It was a wolf, right?"

Jeremy was silent.

"A wolf?"

He had to moisten his mouth. "Yeah."

"So why didn't you shoot it?"

" . . . It happened really fast," he said. "I was out in the woods. I was too late."

Renaldo's brother-in-law gave no reaction, holding his gaze for a few more moments and then nodding slightly. He took a deep breath, turned to look behind him at the others gathered for the funeral, some of whom were staring in their direction. Then he turned back to Jeremy and said, "Thank you for coming. But maybe now, you know, you should go. It's hard for some people to see you."

"Yeah. Okay. Of course." Jeremy backed up a step, and said, "I'm really sorry."

"Okay."

And then he left, grateful to get away, but nearly overwhelmed by shame. He'd removed the rifle from his truck the day after the attack, stowing it in the attic. Its presence was an indictment. Despite what he'd told Renaldo's brother-in-law, he didn't know why he hadn't taken the gun, climbed back out of the truck, and blown the wolf to hell. Because that's all it had been. A wolf. A stupid animal. How many animals had he killed with that very rifle?

Dennis's funeral had been different. There, he was treated like family, if a somewhat distant and misunderstood relation. Rebecca, obese and un-employed, looked doomed as she stood graveside with her three children, completely unanchored from the only person in the world who had cared about her fate, or the fates of those stunned boys at her side. He wanted to apologize to her but he didn't know precisely how, so instead he hugged her after the services and shook the boys' hands and said, "If there's anything I can do."

She wrapped him in a hug. "Jeremy," she said.

◄o►

The boy is skinny and naked. Smiling at him, his teeth shining like cut crystal. Jeremy's pants are unfastened and loose around his hips. He's afraid that if he runs they'll fall and trip him up. The kid can't even be out of high school yet: Jeremy knows he can break him in half if he can just get his hands on him in time. But it's already too late; terror pins him there, and he can only watch. The kid's body begins to shake, and what he thought was a smile is only a rictus of pain – his mouth splits along his cheeks and something loud breaks inside him, cracking like a tree branch. The boy's bowels spray blood and his body convulses like he's in the grip of a seizure.

"Jeremy!"

He opened his eyes. He was in their bedroom, with Tara standing over him. The light was on. The bed felt warm and damp.

"Get out of bed. You had a nightmare."

"Why is the bed all wet?"

She pulled him by his shoulder. She had a strange expression: distracted, pinched. "Come on," she said. "You had an accident."

"What?" He sat up, smelling urine. "What?"

"Get out of bed, please. I have to change the sheets."

He did as she asked. His legs were sticky, his boxers soaked.

Tara began yanking the sheets off the bed as quickly as she could. She tugged the mattress pad off too, and cursed quietly when she saw that the stain had already bled down to the mattress itself.

"Let me help," he said.

"You should get in the shower. I'll take care of this."

" . . . I'm sorry."

She turned on him. For a moment he saw the anger and the impatience there, and he was conscious of how long she had been putting up with his stoic routine, of the extent to which she had fastened down her own frustration for the sake of his wounded ego. It threatened to finally spill over, but she pulled it back, she sucked it in for him one more time. Her expression softened. She touched his cheek. "It's okay, baby." She pushed the hair from his forehead, turning the gesture into a caress. "Go ahead and get in the shower, okay?"

"Okay." He headed for the bathroom.

He stripped and got under the hot water. Six months of being without work had caused him to get even heavier, a fact he was acutely conscious of as he lowered himself to the floor and wrapped his arms around his knees. He did not want Tara to see him. He wanted to barricade the door, to wrap barbed wire around the whole room. But fifteen minutes later she joined him there, putting her arms around him and pulling him close, resting her head against his.

‹o›

Two months after the funeral, Dennis's wife had called and asked him to come over. He arrived at her house—a single-story, three-bedroom bungalow—later that afternoon, and was dismayed to see boxes in the living room and the kitchen. The kids, ranging in age from five to thirteen, moved ineffectively among them, piling things in with no regard to maximizing their space or gauging how heavy they might become. Rebecca was a dervish of industry, sliding through the mazes of boxes and furniture with a surprising grace, barking orders at her kids and even at her herself. When she saw him through the screen door, standing on her front porch, she stopped, and in doing so seemed to lose all of her will to move. The boys stopped too, and followed her gaze out to him.

"Becca, what's going on?"

"What's it look like? I'm packing boxes." She turned her back to him and moved through an arch into the kitchen. "Come on in, then," she called.

Sitting across from her at the table, glasses of orange soda between them, he was further struck by the disorganized quality of the move. The number of boxes seemed sadly inadequate to the task, and it seemed like things were being packed piecemeal: some dishes were wrapped in newspaper and stowed, while others were still stacked in cupboards or piled, dirty, in the sink; drawers hung open, partially disemboweled.

Before Jeremy could open his mouth, Rebecca said, "They's foreclosing on us. We got to be out by the weekend."

For a moment he was speechless. ". . . I . . . Jesus, Becca."

She sat there and watched him. He could think of nothing to say, so he just said, "I had no idea."

"Well, Dennis ain't been paid for a long time before he was killed, and he sure as shit hadn't been paid *since* then, so I guess anybody ought to of seen this comin."

He felt like he'd been punched in the gut. He didn't know if she'd meant it as an accusation, but it felt like one. It didn't help that it was true. He looked at the orange soda in the glass, a weird dash of cheerful color in all this gloom. He couldn't take his eyes off it. "What are you gonna do?"

"Well," she said, staring at her fingers as they twined around each other, "I don't really know, Jeremy. My mama lives out by Hickory but that's a ways away, and she don't have enough room in her house for all of us. Dennis ain't spoke with his family in years. These boys don't even *know* their grandparents on his side."

He nodded. In the other room, the boys were quiet, no doubt listening in.

"I need some money, Jeremy. I mean I need it real bad. We got to be out of here in four days and we don't have nowhere to go." She looked up at the clock on the wall, a big round one with Roman numerals, a bright basket of fruit painted in the center. "I'm gonna lose all my things," she said. She wiped at the corner of an eye with the inside of her wrist.

Jeremy felt the twist in his gut, like his insides were being spooled on a wheel. He had to close his eyes and ride it out.

He'd sat at this table many times while Rebecca cooked for Dennis and for him; he'd been sitting here sharing a six pack with Dennis when the call came from the hospital that their youngest had come early. "Oh, Becca," he said.

"I just need a little so we can stay someplace for a few weeks. You know, just until we can figure something out."

"Becca, I don't have it. I just don't have it. I'm so sorry."

"Jeremy, we got nowhere to go!"

"I don't have anything. I got collection agencies so far up my ass . . . Tara and I put the house up, Becca. The bank's threatening us too. We can't stay where we are. We're borrowing just to keep our heads above water."

"*I can fucking sue you!*" she screamed, slapping her hand on the table so hard that the glasses toppled over and spilled orange soda all over the floor. "*You owe us! You never paid Dennis , and you owe us! I called a lawyer and he said I can sue your ass for every fucking cent you got!*"

The silence afterward was profound, broken only by the pattering of the soda trickling onto the linoleum floor.

The outburst broke a dam inside her; her face crumpled, and tears spilled over. She put a hand over her face and her body jerked silently. Jeremy looked toward the living room and saw one of the boys, his blonde hair buzzed down to his scalp, staring into the kitchen in shock.

"It's okay, Tyler," he said. "It's okay, buddy."

The boy appeared not to hear him. He watched his mother until she pulled her hand from her face and seemed to suck it all back into herself; without looking to the doorway she fluttered a hand in the boy's direction. "It's fine, Tyler," she said. "Go help your brothers."

The boy retreated.

Jeremy reached across the table and clasped her hands in his own. "Becca," he said, "you and the boys are like family to me. If I could give you some money I would. I swear to God I would. And you're right, I do owe it to you. Dennis didn't get paid towards the end. Nobody did. So if you feel like you gotta sue me, then do it. Do what you have to do. I don't blame you. I really don't."

She looked at him, tears beading in her eyes, and said nothing.

"Shit, if suing me might keep you in your house a little while longer—if it'll keep the bank away, or something—then you *should* do it. I *want* you to do it."

Rebecca shook her head. "It won't. It's too late for that now." She rested her head on her arm, her hands still clasped in Jeremy's. "I ain't gonna sue you, Jer. It ain't your fault."

She pulled her hands free and got up. She grabbed a roll of paper towels and tore off a great handful, setting to work on the spill. "Look at this damn mess," she said.

He watched her for a moment. "I have liens on those houses we built," he said. "They can't sell them until they pay us first. The minute they do, you'll get your money."

"They won't ever finish those houses, Jer. Ain't nobody gonna want to buy them. Not after what happened."

He stayed quiet, because he knew she was right. He had privately given up on seeing that money long ago.

"A man from the bank come by last week and put that notice on the door. He had a sheriff with him. Can you believe that? A sheriff come to my house. Parked right in my driveway, for everybody to see." She paused in her work. "He was so rude," she said, her voice quiet and dismayed. "The both of them were. He told me I had to get out of my own house. My boys were standing right by me, and they just bust out crying. He didn't give a damn. Treated me like I was dirt. Might as well of called me white trash to my face."

"I'm so sorry, Becca."

"And he was such a *little* man," she said, still astonished at the memory of it. "I kept thinking how if Dennis was here that man would of *never* talked to me like that. He wouldn't of *dared!*"

Jeremy stared at his hands. Large hands, built for hard work. Useless now. Rebecca sat on the floor, fighting back tears. She gave up on the orange soda, seeming to sense the futility of it.

◄•►

It was a week before Christmas, and Tara was talking to him from inside the shower. The door was open and he could see her pale shape behind the curtain, but he couldn't make out what she was saying. He sat on the bed in his underwear, his clothes for the evening laid out beside him. It was the same suit he'd worn to the funerals, and he dreaded putting it on again.

Outside the short wintertime afternoon was giving way to evening. The Christmas lights strung along the eaves and wound into the bushes still had to be turned on. The neighbors across the street had already lit theirs; the colored lights looked like glowing candy, turning their home into a gingerbread house from a fairy tale. The full moon was resplendent.

Jeremy supposed that a Christmas party full of elementary school professionals might be the worst place in the world. He would drift among them helplessly, like a grizzly bear in a roomful of children, expected not to eat anyone.

He heard the squeak of the shower faucet and suddenly his wife's voice carried to him. "—time it takes to get there," she said.

"What?"

She slid the curtain open and pulled a towel from the shelf. "Have you been listening to me?"

"I couldn't hear you over the water."

She went to work on her hair. "I've just had a very lively conversation with myself, then."

"Sorry."

"Are you going to get dressed?" she said.

He loved to watch her like this, when she was naked but not trying to be sexy, when she was just going about the minor business of being a human being. Unselfconscious and miraculous.

"Are *you?*" he said.

"Very funny. You were in that same position when I started my shower. What's up?"

"I don't want to go."

She turned the towel into a blue turban and wrapped another around her body. She crossed the room and sat beside him, leaving wet footprints in the carpet, her shoulders and her face still glistening with beaded water.

"You'll catch cold," he said.

"What are you worried about?"

"I'm obese. I'm a fricking spectacle. I'm not fit to be seen in public."

"You're my handsome man."

"Stop it."

"Jeremy," she said, "you can't turn into a shut-in. You have to get out. It's been six months, and you've totally disengaged from the world. These people are safe, okay? They're not going to judge you. They're my friends, and I want them to be your friends too."

"They're going to look at me and think, that's the guy that left *his* friends on a mountain to die."

"You're alive," Tara said, sharply, and turned his head so he had to look at her. "You're alive because you left. I still have a husband because you left. So in the end I don't give a shit what people think." She paused, took a steady breath, and let him go. "And not everyone's thinking bad things about you. Sometimes you have to take people at face value, Jeremy. Sometimes people really are what they say they are."

He nodded, chastened. He knew she was right. He'd been hiding in this house for months. It had to stop.

She touched his cheek and smiled at him. "Okay?"

"Yeah. Okay."

She got up and headed back to the bathroom, and he fell back on the bed. "Okay," he said.

"Besides," she called back happily, "don't forget about Tim! Someone has to keep the beast at bay!"

A sudden, coursing heat pulsed through him. He *had* forgotten Tim. "Oh yeah," he said, sitting up. He watched her dress, her body incandescent with water and light, and felt something like hope move inside him.

⭒

The house was bigger than Jeremy had been expecting. It was in an upscale subdivision, where all the houses had at least two stories and a basement. The front porch shed light like a fallen star, and colored Christmas bulbs festooned the neighborhood. "Jesus," he said, turning into the parking lot already full of cars. "Donny lives *here?*"

Donny Winn was the vice-principal of the school: a rotund, pink-faced man who sweated a lot and always seemed on the brink of a nervous breakdown. Jeremy had only met him once or twice, but the man made an impression like a damp cloth.

"His wife's a physical therapist," Tara said. "She works with the Carolina Panthers or something. Trust me, she's the money."

The house was packed. Jeremy didn't recognize anybody. A table in the dining room had been pushed against a wall and its wings extended, turning it into a buffet table loaded with an assortment of holiday dishes and confections. Bowls of spiked eggnog anchored each end of the table. Donny leaned against a wall nearby, alone but smiling. His wife worked the crowd like a politician, steering newly-arrived guests toward the table and bludgeoning them with good will.

Christmas lights were strung throughout the house, and mistletoe hung in every doorway. Andy Williams crooned from speakers hidden by the throng.

Jeremy wended his way through the mill of people behind Tara, who guided him to the table. Within moments they were armed with booze and ready for action. Jeremy spoke into Tara's ear. "Where's Tim?"

She craned her neck and looked around, then shook her head. "I can't see him. Don't worry. He'll find us!"

"You mean he'll find *you*," he said.

She smiled and squeezed his hand.

He measured time in drinks, and then he lost track of it. The lights and the sounds were beginning to blur into a candy-hued miasma that threatened to drown him. He'd become stationary in the middle of the living room, people and conversations revolving around him like the spokes of some demented Ferris wheel. Tara was beside him, nearly doubled over in laughter, one hand gripping his upper arm in a vise as she talked to a gaunt, heavily made-up woman whose eyes seemed to reflect light like sheets of ice.

"He's evil!" The woman had to shout to be heard. "His parents should have strangled him at birth!"

"Jesus," Jeremy said, trying to remember what they were talking about.

"Oh my God, Jeremy, you don't know this kid," Tara said. "He's got like—this *look*. I'm serious! Totally dead."

The woman nodded eagerly. "And the other day? I was looking through their daily journals? I found a picture of a severed head."

"What? No way!"

"The neck was even drawn with jagged red lines, to show it was definitely cut off. To make sure I knew it!"

"Somebody should do something," Jeremy said. "We're gonna be reading about this little monster someday."

Tara shook her head. "Nobody wants to know anymore. 'Boys will be boys,' right?"

The woman arched an eyebrow. "People are just fooled by the packaging," she said. "Kids shouldn't be drawing severed heads!"

Tara laughed. "But it's okay for grown-ups to?"

"Nobody should draw them," the woman said gravely.

"Excuse me," Jeremy said, and moved away from them both. He felt Tara's hand on his arm but he kept going. The conversation had rattled him.

Severed heads. What the fuck!

He slid clumsily through the crowd, using his weight to help along the people who were slow in getting out of his way. He found himself edging past the hostess, who smiled at him and said "Merry Christmas," her eyes sliding away from him before the words were even out of her mouth. He was briefly overwhelmed by a spike of outrage at her blithe manner—at the whole apparatus of entitlement and assumption this party suddenly represented to him, with its abundance and its unapologetic stink of money. "I'm Jewish," he said, and felt a happy thrill when she whipped her head around as he pressed further into the crowd.

He stationed himself by the fireplace, which was, at the moment, free of people. He set his drink on the mantel and turned his back to the crowd, looking instead at the carefully arranged manger scene on display there. The ceramic pieces were old and chipped; it had clearly been in the family for a long time. He looked past the wise men and the shepherds crouched in reverent awe, and saw the baby Jesus at the focal point, his little face rosy pink, his mouth a gaping oval, one eye chipped away. Jeremy's flesh rippled and he turned away.

And then he saw Tim approaching through the crowd. Tim was a slight man, with thinning hair and a pair of silver-rimmed glasses. Jeremy decided he looked like a cartoonist's impression of an intellectual. He stared at him as he approached.

This was what he had come for. He felt the blood start to move in his body, slowly, like a river breaking through ice floes. He felt some measure of himself again. It was just as intoxicating as the liquor.

Tim held out his hand, still closing the distance, and Jeremy took it.

"Hey. Jeremy, right? Tara's husband?"

"Yeah. I'm sorry, you are?"

"Oh I'm Tim Duckett, we met last year, at that teachers' union thing?"

"Oh yeah. Tim, hey."

"I just saw you over here by yourself and I thought, that guy is frickin lost. You know? Totally out of his element."

Jeremy bristled. "I think you made a mistake."

"Really? I mean, look at these people." He shifted to stand beside Jeremy so they could look out over the crowd together. "Come on. *Tea*chers? This is hell for *me!* I can only imagine how you must feel."

"I feel just fine."

Tim touched his glass to Jeremy's. "Well here's to you then. I feel like I'm about to fucking choke." He took a deep drink. "I mean, look at that guy over there. The fat one?" Jeremy flushed but held his tongue. These people didn't think. "That's Shane Mueller," Tim continued. "Laughing like he's high or something. He can afford to laugh because he's got the right friends, you know what I mean? Goddamn arrogant prick. Not like her."

He gestured at the woman Jeremy had been talking to just a few moments ago. Where was Tara?

"Word is she's not coming back next year. She won't be the only one, either. Everybody here's scared shitless. The fucking legislature's throwing us to the wolves. Who cares about education, right? Not when there's dollars at stake." He took a drink. "*English?* Are you kidding me?"

Tim sidled up next to him, so that their arms brushed. Jeremy gave a small push with his elbow and Tim surrendered some ground, seeming not to notice.

"I always kind of envied you, you know?" he was saying.

". . . what?"

"Oh yeah. Probably freaks you out, right? This guy you barely even know? But Tara talks about you in the lounge sometimes, and it got to where I felt like I kind of knew you a little bit."

"So you like to talk to Tara, huh?"

"Oh yeah man, she's a great girl. Great girl. But what you do is real work. You hang out with grown men and build things. With your *hands.*" He held out his own hands, as though to illustrate the concept. "I hang out with kids, man." He gestured at the crowd. "A bunch of goddamn kids."

Jeremy took a drink. He peered into his glass. The ice had almost completely melted, leaving a murky, diluted puddle at the bottom. "Things change," he said.

Tim gave him a fierce, sympathetic look. "Yeah, you've been through some shit, haven't you?"

Jeremy looked at him, dimly amazed, feeling suddenly defensive. This guy had no boundaries. "What?"

"Come on, man, we all know. It's not like it's a secret, right? That fucking wolf?"

"You don't know shit."

"Now that's not fair. If you don't want to talk about it, okay, I get that. But we were all here for Tara when it happened. She's got a lot of friends here. It's not like we're totally uninvested."

Jeremy turned on him, a sudden wild heat burning his skin from the inside. He pressed his body against Tim's and backed him against the fireplace. Tim nearly tripped on the hearth and grabbed the mantel to keep his balance. "I said you don't know *shit.*"

Tim's face was stretched in surprise. "Holy shit, Jeremy, are you gonna hit me?"

Jeremy felt a hand on his shoulder, and he heard his wife's voice. "What's going on here?"

He backed off, letting her pull him away, and allowing Tim to regain his balance. Tim stared at the two of them, looking more bemused now than worried or affronted.

Tara laced her hand into her husband's. "Do you boys need a time out?"

Tim made a placating gesture. "No, no, we're just talking about—"

"Tim's just running his mouth," Jeremy said. "He needs to learn to shut it."

Tara squeezed his hand and leaned against him. He could feel the tension in her body. "Why don't we get some fresh air?" she said.

"What?"

"Come on. I want to see the lights outside."

"Don't you try to placate me. What's the matter with you?"

Tim said, "Whoa, whoa, let's all calm down a little bit."

"Why don't you shut the fuck up."

The sound of the party continued unabated, but Jeremy could sense a shift in the atmosphere around him. He didn't have to turn around to know that he was beginning to draw attention.

"Jeremy!" Tara's voice was sharp. "What the hell has gotten into you?"

Tim touched her arm. "It's my fault. I brought up the wolf thing."

Jeremy grabbed his wrist. "If you touch my wife one more time I'll break your goddamn arm." His mind flooded with images of operatic violence, of Tim's guts garlanding all the expensive furniture like Christmas bunting. He rode the crest of this wave with radiant joy.

Astonishingly, Tim grinned at him. "What the fuck, man?"

Jeremy watched Tim's lips pull back, saw the display of teeth, and surrendered himself to instinct. It was like dropping a chain; the freedom and the relief that coursed through his body was almost religious in its impact. Jeremy hit him in the mouth as hard as he could. Something sharp and jagged tore his knuckles. Tim flailed backwards, tripping on the hearth again but this time falling hard. His head knocked the mantel on the way down, leaving a bloody postage stamp on the white paint. Manger pieces toppled over the side and bounced off him.

Someone behind him shrieked. Voices rose in a chorus, but it was all just background noise. Jeremy leaned over and hit him again and again, until several hands grabbed him from behind and heaved him backward, momentarily lifting him off his feet. He was grappled by a cluster of men, his arms twisted behind him and immobilized. The whole mass of them lurched about like some demented monster, as Jeremy tried to break free.

The room had gone quiet. "Silver Bells" went on for another few seconds until someone rushed to the stereo and switched it off. All he could hear was his own heavy breathing.

He resumed a measure of control over himself, though his blood still galloped through his head and his muscles still jerked with energy. "Okay," he said. "Okay."

He found himself at the center of the crowd, most of them standing well back and staring agape. Someone was crouched beside Tim, who was sitting on the hearth, his face pale; his hands cupped beneath his bloody mouth. One eye was already swelling shut.

Tara stood to one side, her face red with anger, or humiliation, or both. She marched forward and grabbed him forcibly by the bicep, and yanked him behind her. The men holding him let him go.

"Should we call the police?" someone said.

"Oh *fuck you!*" Tara shouted.

She propelled him through the front door and out into the cold air. She did not release him until they arrived at the truck. The night arced over them both, and the world was bespangled with Christmas-colored constellations. Tara sagged against the truck's door, hiding her face against the window. He stood silently, trying to grasp for some feeling here, for some appropriate mode of behavior. Now that the adrenaline was fading, it was starting to dawn on him how bad this was.

Tara stood up straight and said, without looking at him, "I have to go back inside for a minute. Wait here."

"Do you want me to go with you?"

"Just wait here."

He did. She went up to the front door and rang the bell, and after a moment she was let inside. He stood there and let the cold work its way through his body, banking the last warm embers of the alcohol. After a while he got behind the wheel of the truck and waited. Soon, the front door opened again, and she came out. She walked briskly to the truck, her breath trailing behind her, and opened his door. "Move over," she said. "I'm driving."

He didn't protest. Moments later she started the engine and pulled onto the road. She drove them slowly out of the neighborhood, until the last big house receded into the darkness behind them, like a glittering piece of jewelry dropped into the ocean. She steered them onto the highway and they eased onto the long stretch home.

"He's not going to call the police," she said at last. "Small miracle."

He nodded. "I thought you wanted me to confront him," he said, and regretted it immediately.

She didn't respond. He stole a glance at her: her face was unreadable. She drew in a deep breath. "Did you tell Mrs. Winn that we're Jewish?"

" . . . yeah."

"Why? Why would you do that?"

He just shook his head and stared out the window. Lights streaked by, far away.

Tara sobbed once, both hands still clutching the steering wheel. Her face was twisted in misery. "You have to get a hold of yourself," she said. "I don't know what's happening to you. I don't know what to do."

He leaned his head back and closed his eyes. He felt his guts turn to stone. He knew he had to say something, he had to try to explain himself here, or someday she would leave. Maybe someday soon. But the fear was too tight; it wouldn't let him speak. It would barely let him breathe.

◄◦►

When they get home the fight is brief and intense, and Jeremy escapes in the truck, making a trip to the attic before he leaves. Now he's speeding down a winding two-lane blacktop, going so fast he can't stay in his lane. If anyone else appears on this road, everybody's fucked. He makes a fast right when he comes to the turn-in for Wild Acre, the truck hitting the bumps in the road too hard and smashing its undercarriage into the dirt. He pushes it up the hill, the untended dirt road overgrown with weeds. The truck judders around a bend, something groaning under the hood. The wheel slips out of his hands and the truck slides into a ditch, coming to a crunching halt and slamming Jeremy's face into the steering wheel.

The headlights peer crookedly into the dust-choked air, illuminating the house frames, which look like huge, drifting ghosts behind curtains of raised dirt and clay. He leans back in his seat, gingerly touching his nose, and his vision goes watery. The full moon leaks silver blood into the sky. Something inside him buckles, and acid fills his mouth. He puts a hand over it, squeezes his eyes shut, and thinks, Don't you do it, don't you fucking do it.

He doesn't do it. He swallows it back, burning his throat.

He slams his elbow into the door several times. Then he rests his head on the steering wheel and sobs. These are huge, body-breaking sobs, the kind that leave him gasping for breath, the kind he hasn't suffered since he was a little kid. They frighten him a little. He is not meant to sound like this.

After a few moments he stops, lifts his head, and stares at the closest house frame, bone-colored in the moonlight. The floor is covered in dark stains. The forest is surging behind it. In a scramble of terror he wrenches the rifle from its rack, opens the door and jumps into the road.

The gun is slippery in his hands. He strides into the house frame and raises the gun to his chin, aiming it into the dark forest, staring down the sight. The world and its sounds retreat into a single point of stillness. He watches, and waits.

"Come on!" he screams. "Come on! *Come on!*"

But nothing comes.

⟨o⟩

FINAL EXAM

MEGAN ARKENBERG

Part I - Multiple Choice

1. The first time you visited the ocean, that Fourth-of-July weekend when purple storm clouds swallowed the horizon and the great cerulean expanse below them was freckled with parti-colored sails, you looked out over the water and felt . . .

(a) the smallness of humanity in the face of a universe that is older and vaster and more full of life than any of us can imagine, much less understand.

(b) a sudden urge to jump.

(c) the awful terror of living.

(d) nothing; there was only the sea-spray on your face, salty, cold and needle-fine.

(e) all of the above.

2. At what point did you know—and I mean really *know*, in your gut, in the tautness of your heartstrings—that things had gone horribly wrong?

(a) When you ran the faucet in the motel bathroom to wash the salty tear-tracks from your face, and the water came out cold and red, staining the sink.

(b) When the equipment at work started breaking down, first the conveyor belts on the registers, then the adding machine in the office, then the registers themselves. IT had the same advice over and over again: unplug it, turn it off, and plug it in again. Of course it never worked.

(c) When Donald looked up from the papers he was correcting at the kitchen counter and said Baby girl, what do you think about couples' therapy? and you were so startled that you dropped the whole carton of orange juice.

(d) When the pink-suited reporter interrupted the inspirational drama on the television in the marriage counselor's waiting room, her hair frizzled with electricity and her left eyebrow bloodied from a shallow cut to the forehead. Tell us what you're seeing, somebody said, and she said, God . . .

(e) When you asked him to pass you a butter knife from the drawer, and he must have heard you, but he was marking something in the margin of his book and you had to ask a second time. He slammed the book shut and pulled the drawer so hard that it came off the slides. Here, he said, flinging the knife across the counter. It landed with its tongue-like blade pointed at your breast.

3. When the pink-suited reporter's station showed the first footage of the things shambling out of the water, you compared them to . . .

(a) your neighbor's dog, a blond-gray whippet with a scratched bald patch high on his left shoulder. You thought of Sultan when you saw the first shambling thing bend, drawing back its black and rubbery lips, and sink its long yellow teeth into its own thigh, biting down to the bone.

(b) fish, especially the fat, foul-smelling, tasteless white fish Donald used to bring home by the bucket-load and smoke over a charcoal fire on the patio.

(c) skinny girls, like the neighbor three blocks over who took her early morning jogs in a white tank top that, by the time she reached your house, had turned transparent with sweat, displaying her prominent ribs.

(d) Godzilla, whose movie you had never seen, but whose general shape you vaguely remembered from a commercial for a Japanese automobile.

(e) the sea-witch from a picture book your favorite teacher read to the class one day, when it was raining too hard to go outside for recess. The artist had drawn the sea-witch with a water snake wound around her shoulders like a mink; the sea-witch was offering it a taste of a tiny red crab, which she held between her own sharp teeth.

4. After several months watching them, first through the reporter's camera and then, later, through the slats in the boards you had pounded over your windows, you came to the conclusion that the shambling things had originated . . .

(a) on Mars.

(b) in an alternate dimension, where the laws of physics and geometry and merging into freeway traffic are subtly different, and it is possible to have four-sided triangles.

(c) in the nightmares of mankind, where we let our guard down and unleash the latent psychic powers of creation which, when we are awake, limit themselves to such pieces of good fortune as the perfect seat in the movie theatre, or a bra that fits.

(d) on this planet, in the natural course of evolution, which has already produced such monsters as the platypus, the hyena, and your skinny neighbor.

(e) after Chernobyl, or Three-Mile Island, or a worse disaster that a national government, or the Illuminati, had been more successful at covering up.

5. Now that it has been months since the last sighting, many people have chosen to believe that the shambling monsters are gone for good. You, however, know that they are . . .

(a) still in the ocean, huddled at the bottom of chasms too deep for sonar, waiting to rise again and feel the cold moonlight on their bulbous faces.

(b) taking on the appearance of every-day people, the cashier at the newly re-opened liquor store, the gang of skinny gun-dragging teenagers who moved into the old marriage counselor's office, the woman who walks up and down the sidewalk in the late afternoon, calling out names you can never quite understand.

(c) in our nightmares, slowly shaping us to our true forms.

(d) hiding under your bed.

(e) both c and d.

6. What could you have done to prevent all this from happening?

(a) Become a better cook, as Donald's mother always hinted with her gifts of Julia Child and Betty Crocker collections, the elaborate kitchen gadgets whose names, much less their functions, remained shrouded in mystery. Though you never really learned to love food, you did learn to cook, to boil and bubble the bacteria out of a can of condensed soup. Incidentally, your mother-in-law would be proud.

(b) Become a better liar. It is true that the pink-and-emerald tie he wanted to buy at the church flea-market was the ugliest thing you had ever seen, uglier even than the monsters from the sea, uglier even than Sultan. But it would not have hurt you to bite your lip and nod your head and say Yes, for seventy-five cents it certainly is a steal.

(c) Prayed more, and harder, and to the right people. Saint Helena is the patron of dysfunctional marriage. Saint Neot is the patron of fish.

(d) All of the above.

(e) None of the above.

7. The worst part was . . .

(a) when the first shambling thing ate the pink-suited reporter, and the camera man didn't turn away, and you sat there petrified in the marriage counselor's office, watching the flesh blossom and drip over the creature's scaly lips. Jesus Christ, you said, reaching for Donald's hand. He was gripping a magazine cover too tightly to notice.

(b) when he flung the little velvet box at you over the dinner table, and you looked at him and you asked What is this for? and he said I knew you'd forget.

(c) when you checked into the motel, and you couldn't stop licking your bottom lip even though you knew your saliva was keeping the split open, and the man at the front desk was clearly worried for you but he just as clearly didn't know what to say, so he handed you a pair of key-cards and told you, earnestly, to have a good night.

(d) later that night, when you opened the bottle of pinot grigio that the liquor clerk had recommended and drank it all in one long throat-tearing gulp. Your cell phone started to sing from its compartment in your purse, the sweet black-and-white movie love song Donald had tried to serenade you with, once, in the back seat of your car. Even drunk, your thumb found the phone's power button and turned it off.

(e) this moment, now, as you look back on all of it, and can't think of anything that you would do the same.

8. When you came home from the motel the next morning, a hangover ringing in your ears, you found his packed suitcase sitting on the coffee

table in the living room. You stumbled into the bathroom to vomit, and when you came out again, the suitcase was gone. That was, in a way, the last you ever saw of Donald. What happened to him?

(a) Shortly after he left, he was eaten by one of the shambling creatures.

(b) He met another woman on a bus to Chicago. She was taller than you are, and skinnier, and she smelled like cinnamon and vanilla.

(c) He joined that cult down in Louisiana, the one with the blood sacrifices and the idol built of concrete blocks, and he was one of the men who walked into the ocean on June 21, and became a pillar of salt.

(d) He committed suicide with a shaving razor in the bathtub of the same motel room where you hid from him, that last night. He never forgave himself for hitting you, not even when he remembered that you'd hit him first.

(e) He slipped, somehow, into an alternate dimension, where the laws of physics and geometry are subtly different, and there is a house just like yours, but the woman inside is a better liar.

9. His last thoughts were . . .

(a) incomprehensible with fear, the nauseating smell of his own blood.

(b) of you.

(c) revelations about the falseness of Euclidian geometry, the sheer *wrongness* of all human conceptions of time and history and causal relationships, that could never have been comprehended by another human being, even if Donald had lived, and admitted to himself what he had understood.

(d) of Christine Kaminski, the slender brunette who took him to junior prom, and who forged a deeper connection with him on that one night in the rented Marriott ballroom than you did in seven years of marriage. She wore pale blue, his favorite color, and only kissed him once, during the last dance of the night. If he had married her, he would have been happy.

(e) of his little brother, who died at birth, whom he never told you about. He intended to, but there was never a moment in that first year of marriage when you weren't too busy with something else—arranging furniture, organizing closets and cupboards, filing for loans, writing thank-you cards. Afterward, it seemed too late to bring it up. The closest he ever came was during that Christmas dinner at your sister's, when you teased him about being an only child.

10. Looking back on all of it, you still don't understand . . .

(a) why all the equipment at work broke down that day. You even stayed an extra fifteen minutes to play with the reset buttons and a bent paperclip; it made you late to the marriage counselor's office, which in some ways didn't matter, because her previous appointment was running over and you had to wait anyway, but in some ways it did matter, because Donald was expecting you to arrive on time. It didn't help in any case. Everything was still broken the next day.

(b) why the water in the motel bathroom turned to blood. Afterward, you asked around town, and learned that no one else had discovered blood or any other bodily fluids running through their pipes. But there was a lot going on at the time; maybe they simply hadn't noticed.

(c) why you told Donald about the Little Mermaid picture book as you collapsed drunken and giggling into your own back seat. Your throat was hoarse from swearing at your baseball team as they permitted run after humiliating run, and you had spilled beer on the sleeve of your sweatshirt. You tried to wiggle out of it and it got stuck around your hips, and you said, This reminds me of a story . . .

(d) what attracted you to Donald in the first place. Was it his eyes, his soft lips, the way he ran his fingers through his hair when he was nervous, the way all his undershirts smelled like chalkboards, the way he tightened his tie with both hands before saying something important?

(e) all of the above.

11. After that incident in Portland, when the shambling thing almost caught up to you by clinging to the bottom of your bus, your favorite shirt became stained with . . .

(a) seawater.

(b) blood (yours).

(c) ichor (its).

(d) semen.

(e) merlot.

12. Your sister, who knows these things, told you that the best technique for fighting the shambling monsters is . . .

(a) frying them with a blow torch.

(b) dowsing them with holy water.

(c) dragging them behind a truck.

(d) flinging them into a nuclear reactor.

(e) running until they tire of chasing you.

13. You most regret . . .

a) missing that shot at the fast food joint in Vancouver, when the little boy died. It was not your fault; no one had ever taught you to fire a revolver, much less where to aim on a bulbous heavy-lidded nightmare as it slivered over a drive-thru window. But it *was* your fault, because the creature had followed you, and if you hadn't stopped to eat at that particular restaurant and that particular time, it would never have killed that child.

b) not letting him buy that hideous watermelon tie at the church flea-market, when you knew it reminded him of his grandfather, and made him smile.

c) wearing your favorite shirt on the bus in Portland.

d) shaking Donald as you got into the car in the marriage counselor's parking lot, then slapping him across the face. No matter how terrified you were, no matter how much you thought he'd earned it, you should have known better than to hit him. You did know better. You knew it reminded him of his father.

e) turning into your pillow that last time he tried to kiss you goodnight, so that his lips caught you on the cheek.

14. In your dreams, the shambling monsters appear at your bedside, and their voices sound like . . .

(a) radio static, interspersed with love songs from old black-and-white movies.

(b) the screaming of the pink-suited reporter as those yellow teeth crunched through her clavicle.

(c) the marriage counselor, with her gentle eastern accent, the sharp tick of her pen against her clipboard punctuating each clause.

(d) footsteps over broken glass.

(e) the whisper of a fish's breath.

15. Now, when you look out at the sea, you feel . . .

(a) the smallness of humanity in the face of a universe that is older and vaster and more full of life than any of us can imagine, much less understand.

(b) a sudden urge to jump.

(c) the awful terror of living.

(d) his absence; there is only the sea-spray on your face, salty, cold and needle-fine.

(e) all of the above.

PART II- SHORT ANSWER

16. Is this really the end of the world? Defend your answer with evidence from the following texts: the *Apocalypse of John*, the *Collected Works of H. P. Lovecraft*, *The Shepherd of Hermas*, Ibn Al-Nafis' *Theologus Autodidactus*, Mary Shelley's *The Last Man*, the fortieth through fifty-eighth stanzas of *Völuspá*, and last week's edition of the *New York Times*.

17. Just what is it about filling in bubbles on a multiple choice test that makes you believe that every terrible decision you've made might, with luck, with sheer cussedness, have turned out right in the end?

PART III – EXTRA CREDIT

What color were Donald's eyes?

PART IV- ANSWER KEY

1. The correct answer is (e) all of the above. You were nine years old, and had wanted to see the ocean ever since the day your third-grade teacher read you a picture book with the *real* story of the Little Mermaid—Andersen, not Disney. You wore a pink-and-yellow bathing suit that you had outgrown the previous summer and carried a purple plastic pail, not because you had any intention of building sandcastles but because the children in the picture book (who appeared in the seashore-margins on every page, though they had nothing to do with the mermaid or her prince or her beautiful raven-haired rival) had carried pails and shovels, made of tin, in which they collected seashells. At that moment, standing at the edge of the pier while your parents argued through a transaction at the overpriced snack-shack behind you, you registered nothing but the caress of the waves on your face. Only later, with reflection, did you feel the smallness, the terror, the urge to jump.

On your honeymoon, Donald tried to recreate this experience (which you had shared with him in the backseat of your car, after a drunken night at the worst baseball game your team had ever played). He took you to the same pier, bought you a paper cone of roasted peanuts at the same overpriced snack-shack, but the weather was different, clean and peaceful, and your red two-piece fit your body like a second skin.

2. The correct answer is (e) when you asked him to pass you a butter knife, and he must have heard you, but he was marking something in the margin of his book and you had to ask a second time. It cost sixty-seven dollars to fix the drawer slides, sixty-seven dollars you didn't have but managed to find somewhere, probably in the old plastic KFC cup you kept by the telephone to collect money for date nights, back when you went on dates. In days to come, that cup would hold many things: pinot grigio, as you drank yourself into a stupor; vomit; distilled water for an impromptu eye wash; strips of bloody gauze.

3. The correct answer, I'm sorry to say, is (d) Godzilla. You had never done your best or most original thinking under stress. Donald would not have hesitated to point this out, but then again, when Donald saw the shambling things on the television his first thought was of the illustration of the sea-witch, which he had seen only days before as he wandered through the mall, looking for your anniversary present. He found the old picture book in a store that specialized in plush animals and greeting cards, and he thought of buying it for you, but he remembered that day on the pier by the ocean, and bought you a pearl bracelet instead.

There's an old superstition that a bride shouldn't wear pearls on her wedding day, because for each pearl she wears, her husband will give her a reason to cry.

4. The correct answer is (b) in an alternate dimension. At least, that was your theory;

the true answer is somewhat closer to (d) on this planet, in the natural course of evolution. You, however, are not expected to know this, or to retain your sanity if you had glimpsed some hint of it by mistake.

What happened between you and Donald was also by and large the result of a natural chain of events, an estrangement, a distancing of the sort that shambles into so many relationships. The truth—which you are also not expected to know—is that you never had very much in common to begin with. Your date nights stopped because you could no longer agree on a restaurant, or a movie, or a group of friends to visit. Breaking the cutlery drawer was the natural result of too many nights listening to you root for a baseball team he had never cared for in the first place.

5. The correct answer is (b) taking on the appearance of every-day people. The marriage counselor, who spoke to you briefly on the office phone when you called her during your lunch break, said that Donald thought you had trust issues. It's not paranoia if they're really out to get you, you said. Who is out to get you? asked the marriage counselor.

If your memory had a better sense of irony, it would have recalled that conversation two months later as you darted from shadow to shadow down your near-deserted block, clutching a gun you didn't know how to use, listening for the gelatinous thump of the creature's footsteps behind you. You'd learned by then that they could distinguish humans through scent, and that they gave off distinctive odors of their own; this particular creature, a female who smelled as chalky as a jar of antacid, had been trailing you for weeks. In the end, you only lost her when you packed the truck and moved up to Oregon for a few months, to stay with your sister, who'd compulsively saved canned goods and ammunition in her basement. Even later, after you worked up the courage to return home, when you cracked open the front door and slipped into the foyer, your nostrils were assaulted by the stench of mold and chalk.

6. The correct answer is (e) none of the above. Of course, you could have tried cooking, or lying, or praying; it would not have hurt to try. But you never did.

7. The correct answer is (a) when the first shambling thing ate the pink-suited reporter, and the camera man didn't turn away. You will see that scene in your nightmares for the rest of your life. You will never again look at that particular shade of pink without your stomach churning, your tongue fumbling compulsively past your lips, your ribs curling inward, your vision spotting like blood on bathroom tissue. In all of this, the reporter's death is the only thing about which you have never spoken to anyone. Sometimes, you think it is the real reason you drink.

8. The correct answer is (b) he met another woman on a bus to Chicago. Her name was Nora and she used to work in a bakery; she was not a very good baker, but her hand was perfectly steady as she drew looping cursive letters in pink gel across the smooth buttercream canvases. The last cake she decorated was for a little girl named Rebecca, who ate the

frosting in huge gobs with her fingers, but had wanted the lettering to be blue. Nora didn't care that Donald was married, and he didn't care that her last relationship had been with a woman who died of suspiciously severe food poisoning. They settled for a while in an apartment over an abandoned antique store. Then, after a year and a half, Nora joined the Louisiana blood-cult, and Donald never heard from her again.

Though he did eventually commit suicide with a shaving razor, it is too much of a coincidence to think that he did it in that same motel room where you'd sobbed over the sink all those months before.

9. The correct answer is (b) of you. For better or for worse, you were the love of his life. In the early whirlwind years, he imagined that some corner of his heart had always known and loved you, even at junior prom, when he was kissing Christine Kaminski and smelling the soapy-bubblegum scent of her shampoo. Later, when Nora disappeared, he began to write letters to you. He never sent them, which is just as well. You would never have opened them, and they would not have told you anything you didn't already know.

(Here is what the last one said:

Baby girl, I've forgotten the color of your eyes. Sorry for everything. Don.)

10. The correct answer is (e) all of the above. It's ironic, when you consider that an Apocalypse is meant to be a revelation, an unveiling, that at the end of everything so much remains veiled. No one knows why, in offices and stores around the country, computers and cash registers went down in droves that Tuesday afternoon. You were the only one to see the blood come out of the faucet, and you wouldn't even swear that it was blood. It might have been zinfandel. You will never learn why you always need to be drunk before you can share really important information with the people you love. Even this answer key won't give you all the answers.

(What first attracted you to Donald was the way he mispronounced your last name.)

11. The correct answer is (b) blood (yours). You were sitting at the window above the left rear wheel, your head jolting with each pothole against the padded headrest, when you caught the stench of chalk coming through the air conditioning. You panicked and fought your way to the front door, and the driver misinterpreted your flailing and laid you

low with a punch between the eyes. Everyone was jumpy, those first few months. You woke a half-hour later to learn that the bus had crossed six bridges while you were out, and the smell of chalk was gone, replaced by the sour-metallic taste in the back of your nostrils and gummed in your lace neckline.

12. The correct answer is, of course, (d) flinging them into a nuclear reactor, but you had to make do with (e) running until they tired of chasing you.

13. The correct answer is (e) turning into your pillow that last time he tried to kiss you goodnight. In the days and months and years to come, you would miss the taste of his mouth, miss the cool scratch of his unshaved chin across your cheek. Of course the little boy's death bothers you, and the pink-and-green tie, and the hideous satisfaction of the hard granite sound your hand made when it collided with his jaw. But none of these produced in you the same yearning, the same hunger, the deep chilling pain of a hollowness you yourself created.

14. The correct answer is (a) radio static, interspersed with love songs from old black-and-white movies. If Donald ever calls you, the ring tone will be the same: a sweet plucking of violin strings, a woman's too-mellow voice. The worst thing about these nightmares is that you often think he *is* calling you, and it pulls you out of your dream of running into the cold and poorly-lit reality of the place you ran to. And once there, in the silence, in your narrow bed, you are all alone.

15. The correct answer is (d).

16. Answers will vary.

17. Answers will vary.

◂◦▸

NONE SO BLIND

STEPHEN BACON

N ovak found an apartment in one of the districts that had remained run-down. It was an unfortunate choice, overlooking the walls of a factory, the grounds heaped with discarded shop dummies. Countless lichen-coated limbs reached out from the rusting industrial bins that littered the yard. Dismembered torsos gathered dust in stacked piles, cobwebbed together like cocooned corpses. At times the smell of chemicals and burning machinery turned his stomach. The incessant clanging frayed his nerves. The squeal of gears haunted his dreams. Often he woke with raking coughs drawing strings of blood from his lungs. The damp patches on the ceiling of his apartment resembled scar tissue. But not once did he think about finding somewhere else; the apartment's location was too convenient.

At night, the city resembled the one from his memory—a cluster of grey buildings populated by threatening shadows and screaming sirens. A place where dark figures smoked in doorways and a footstep behind you might be the last sound you'd ever hear.

But everything appeared very different by daylight. The decade and a half since he'd fled the city had seen great change. Many of the floundering industrial areas had been redeveloped. There was a heavier police presence on the streets. People strolled casually, relaxing in the recreation areas that had been created. It felt almost like the dark underbelly of the city he'd abandoned had been varnished smooth, the cracks papered over. Yet peel back the veneer of respectability and the festering decay would be revealed. Of that he was sure.

For several weeks Novak had watched the woman from a distance, noting her routines and observing her as she went about her daily life. It was obvious she was a creature of habit. At precisely 10:30 every morning she'd venture out of the gates of her walled garden and make her way to the little café on the corner. There she would enjoy two cups of coffee and a pastry. On one occasion she plumped for a toasted teacake. The café owner was accustomed to her patronage, and welcomed her warmly each morning. She even had her own table near the window.

One spring morning fate drew them together once again.

From his table in the café, Novak heard the *tap-tap-tap* of her cane seconds before the woman stepped into view, walking past the window with assured movement. She entered the café and turned instinctively towards her usual table. The owner wiped his hands on his apron and greeted her.

Novak watched the woman from behind as she took a seat and folded her white cane, placing it on the chair beside her. The server came and took her order. They chatted for a few moments about the weather. The server went into the rear of the café and the woman was alone once more. She angled her face towards the window, as if enjoying the sunlight.

The first few times he'd seen her, Novak had been unnerved by the mask. It was virtually a full overhead covering, ending where her ears protruded and the remnants of her rutted skin smoothed out into her neck. There were small apertures for the eyes, but all they did were highlight the contrasting skin-colour and reveal the furrowed scars beneath.

He considered her. She appeared happy enough. She had her pleasant habits. He felt his chest rattling so he took out his handkerchief and coughed into it, observing the speckles of scarlet as he wiped his mouth.

The woman turned in her chair and spoke in his direction: "It's such a nice table here by the window. Why don't you join me?"

For a few stunned seconds he couldn't think of anything to say. His voice was gravelled by phlegm. "Thank you—that would be lovely." He pushed the hankie into his pocket and stood sharply, causing the chair to scrape on the tiled floor. The noise sounded crude.

Novak slid into the seat beside her. His hands shook.

"You're a regular—just like me, I think." Her voice sounded breathy and soft beneath the mask.

"Regular?" He glanced towards the counter, where the manager was restocking the napkins.

She laughed. "I'm sorry—I recognized your cough. You really should get that checked out, you know." The blank expression of the mask was jarring. It was completely white, with perfectly symmetrical features. When she moved her head it looked eerie, like she was a mannequin brought to life. He looked at her arms instead.

"I'm sorry, I hope the cough hasn't bothered you," he said. "I've been ill recently."

"My name's Lyssa," said the woman. She extended a slender arm, a fragile hand.

He shook it gently, tensing as his fingers touched her cool porcelain skin. "Nice to meet you. I'm Alex."

"Alex." She rolled the name around her mouth. It sounded like a different word because the mask muffled her voice.

He didn't know what to say. He stared at her, aware that her blindness protected him.

"I like it in here. They do the most delicious pecan slice." She moved her face towards him slightly and lowered her voice. "And the owner's friendly."

He made murmurs of assent. Out on the road, several cars drove past. Sunlight blinded him momentarily.

"So—you live nearby?"

The question caught him off-guard. He blinked quickly. "Just round the corner. Quite near."

"It's a nice area. Not everyone's cup of tea but I like it because it's quiet."

He studied her perfect arms. In the sunlight there were fine hairs visible on her skin. Her fingernails were neat.

For something to say, he told her, "I lived here years ago."

"Really? I've lived here all my life." He noticed how fragile her throat looked as she swallowed. She continued. "Do you live on your own?"

"Yes. I'm divorced."

"Oh." There was a pause. He detected a slight movement of her head. A moment passed between them. She said, finally, "I'm sorry . . . I made you feel uncomfortable."

"No, not at all, it's just—"

"You're wondering about *this*, aren't you? About my face?"

"No, not at all." He suppressed the urge to say *I never noticed.*

"It's okay. Really."

"No, no." He closed his hands around hers. "Honestly, it doesn't matter."

She allowed him to clutch her hands within his. Made no move. Then she said softly: "Oh . . . your fingers."

Instinctively he pulled away.

She said quickly, "I'm sorry."

Now it was his turn. "That's okay." He returned his hands to hers. Everything was moving too quickly. He felt out of control.

"How did you lose the fingers? Were you in an accident?"

Most people never asked, but he usually noticed the looks. This woman's blindness had fooled him, buoyed him with misplaced confidence. He stared at her mask. For a long while he didn't speak. Then he said quietly, "I knew your husband."

He saw her swallow, noticed a slight shift of her head. It was only the shallow fall of her chest that betrayed the fact she was still breathing. When her voice came again it was much more brittle. "Who are you?"

"My name is Alexander Novak. I used to own a bar down by the harbour." He could see her eyelids flickering through the sockets of the mask. The left one looked like it might be able to open; the skin of the right one seemed fused to the rest of the cheek.

The mask bored into his soul. Its flat indifference seemed harsh, cruel. "Did my husband do that to you? Your hand, I mean?"

"Yes. I owed him a great deal of money. Money I could never repay." Novak was wracked by a fit of coughs again, and reached for the handkerchief. His vision blurred. A pain throbbed in the back of his chest. When the coughs finally subsided he looked up, breathless.

At that moment the server brought her order. The woman waited until the cup and saucer and the pastry had been placed down in front of her. The server asked Novak if he'd like anything else. He declined, and the server left them. Novak paused. Lyssa did not speak for a while. When she finally did, her tone was different, less harsh.

"He was a very *persuasive* man, my husband." The shape of the mask's painted lips was seductive. Her words felt like thoughts because the mask gave the impression that she wasn't speaking. "What did he do to you?"

He glanced down at his left hand. It had been so long that it felt natural, like it had always been that way. His thumb and index finger were intact, but there was just a short knuckle of skin where the other three fingers had once been. He said, "Because I couldn't pay what I owed, my hand was crushed in a vice. I lost three fingers."

"I'm sorry," she said quietly.

He raised his eyebrows. "It's not your fault."

"I know." She swallowed. "But I'm sorry all the same."

"Honestly, it's fine. I can still function normally—it's my left one anyway." He displayed his hand, flexing it in a pincer movement. Then he remembered she was blind. He returned it below the table.

"He's dead, you know."

Novak stared at her. "I heard, yes."

She angled her face to the window again. "He got what he deserved in the end."

Novak remembered reading about it in the papers. He didn't reply.

"Someone kidnapped him and chopped him up into pieces." She sniffed. Novak detected defiance in it. "Someone with the same principles as him."

Behind them, steam burst in a fierce hiss from the stainless steel milk-frothing machine. Once the final gasps had died away, Lyssa said, "He took my face, you know."

Novak stared at her. The pale mask seemed to mock the gravity of the situation. He suddenly had the feeling that he was talking to one of the mannequins from the factory; that the conversation was just taking place in his head.

"My husband discovered I was having an affair with one of his drivers. He persuaded us it wasn't in our best interests for it to continue. He could be rather forthright sometimes."

"What did he do?" Novak tried to keep his voice level.

"Marcus disappeared off the face of the earth. I never found out what happened to him. I heard rumours over the years but . . . well, I just hope it was quick, whatever it was."

"Weren't you scared?"

"Before we realized he knew about us, he'd made his move." Her voice was emotionless, steely. "I was coming home from a shopping trip. I'd just stepped out of the car when a man appeared from nowhere. At first I thought he was carrying a collection box—you know, those containers of money for charity? Anyway it wasn't one of those, it was a jar of concentrated sulphuric acid."

Novak wiped at the hollows of his eyes. His skin was hot, his cheeks burned.

"At first I thought it was just water. My eyes felt blurry, I couldn't see a thing. I tried to rub my eyes. And all the time I could hear a loud hissing, and smell a horrible smell. And then I realized it was the skin on my face dissolving."

For a while Novak fought to control the weight of emotion that threatened to burst out of his chest. His throat felt constricted.

"My face was stolen that day. And with it, my sight, my hair—everything." She shook her head and shrugged.

He clutched her hand again. The skin on her neck was flushed now, the paleness banished. He could hear her breath rattling against the inside of the mask.

"My God," Novak said at last. "I can't imagine how you must have felt . . ." He remembered those long nights when his tortured mind could think of nothing else.

"My husband always called me his little bird." She laughed hollowly. "That day he caged me forever."

Novak closed his eyes. "I'm glad he ended up dying like he did, then."

"It was a long time ago. A lifetime ago, really." She sniffed delicately.

He could hear his own heartbeat pounding in his ears. He said, "And how did you feel about the man that actually did it, the one that threw the acid?"

She hesitated, her face angled away slightly. Then she said finally, "I never saw who threw the acid. How did you know it wasn't my husband?"

Without missing a beat he said, "Men like your husband always have someone to do their dirty work, don't they?" He glanced down at his hand.

"I can still remember the two men that kidnapped me—can't forget their faces, if truth be told." He began coughing again, this time mopping at the fluid that seeped into his mouth. The handkerchief was nearly sodden.

Once he'd regained control, he swallowed loudly. "I spent night after night hating them. Wishing they would die horrible, painful deaths."

"What's the point in that?" Her tone wasn't the least confrontational. It was placatory. "It's a waste of emotion. I realize he did it under the orders of my husband. He was probably as much a victim as I was."

Novak watched an old man through the window. He was walking his dog in the morning sun, his lips pursed in the act of whistling.

"My husband denied everything. I knew he'd arranged it, though. It was so like him. That was how he handed out punishments." Her delicate fingers absently traced the shape of the fork on the table. "From that day onwards, his little bird refused to sing—at least until his death. Those eight months were the most difficult."

Novak watched her, remembering the shine of her hair that day, imagining what remained of her face; a face that was once so beautiful. "I'm so sorry for what happened to you."

"Mr. Novak, my life—since my husband's death, at least—has been pleasant enough. I have my little house, my belongings. I have my music. I can come and go as I please. My blindness hasn't stopped me doing things. On reflection, I can harbour no bitterness about what happened." She nodded firmly. "At least anymore." After a moment she added in a low voice, "I hope the men who did my husband's dirty work felt no guilt at what they were forced to do."

They sat in companionable silence for a while. Then Novak glanced at his watch and cleared his throat. "I'd better be going."

"I'm very grateful of the company this morning. Will you come here again?"

He glanced away from the mask that was angled at him expectantly. "I'm not sure. I don't know how much longer I'll be here." He stood up and took out his wallet, dropping some cash onto the table. "Like I said, I'm extremely ill. I just wanted to visit my old haunts one last time."

"Goodbye, Mr. Novak. I hope everything works out."

"Goodbye, Lyssa." He noticed her coffee and pastry had remained untouched. A skin had formed on the surface of her coffee. "It was nice talking to you."

He left the café, throwing one final glance back. Her head was tilted at an angle as if she was listening to something that only she could hear. The perfect features of her mask seared their image into his mind.

Outside on the street, dark clouds gathered on the horizon. They looked like black wings about to envelop the blue sky. Gusts of wind tore at his coat. He zipped it up and hurried along the road. At the corner he took out the sodden handkerchief and dropped it in the bin. He could feel the blood in his lungs rattling. It wouldn't be long before he'd need the use of another handkerchief.

By the time he made it back to his apartment, the rain had started to pelt the dry, dusty ground.

◄o►

THE BALLAD OF BOOMTOWN

PRIYA SHARMA

t's estimated that in 2011 there were 2,881 semi or unoccupied housing developments in Ireland.

There was a time when we put our faith in Euros, shares and the sanctity of brick. A time when we bought our books from stores as big as barns and ate strawberries from Andalusia, when only a generation before they'd been grown on farms up the road.

The wide avenues of Boomtown were named for trees when there was grand optimism for growth. Now nothing booms in Boomtown. It's bust and broken.

I miss you. You were a lick of cream. I can still taste you.

I walk to the village on Mondays. I pull my shopping trolley the three miles there and back along the lanes. I used to drive to the supermarket, just for a pint of milk, without a thought to the cost of fuel. It doesn't matter now. I like to walk.

Sheila-na-gigs look down on me from the church walls as I pass by. These stone carvings are of women with bulging eyes and gaping mouths, displaying their private parts. These wantons are a warning against lust. Or a medieval stone mason's dirty joke.

The shop's beside the church. Deceased, desiccated flies lie between the sun faded signs. There's a queue inside. I've heard all their grumbling about prices and supplies. They decry the current government, the one before, the banks and then apportion blame abroad. Despite the orderly line and polite chatter, I can imagine these women battling it out with their meaty fists if the last bag of flour in Ireland was at stake.

We're not so poor as yet that we can't afford a veneer of civilised behaviour.

I put my face to the glass as the shop owner takes the last slab of beef from the chilled counter and wraps it. I wish I'd got up earlier. I would've spent half my week's grocery allowance to smell the marbled flesh sizzling in a pan.

The bell jangles as I push the door open. A few heads turn. A woman leans towards her companion and whispers in his ear. I catch the words blow in. I'm a Boomtown interloper, buffeted by changing fortune. There's a pause before the man looks at me. His salacious glance suggests he's heard scandalous stories.

I've no doubt a few of them recall me from before, when I first came here to talk to them about my book. There was a certain glamour in talking to me.

I take my time considering the shelves' contents while the others pay and leave. There are budget brands with unappetising photos on the cans. Boxes of cheap smelling soap powder and white bread in plastic bags. I tip what I need into my basket.

"I want freshly ground coffee."

I can't help myself. I'm the Boomtown Bitch. It's cruel. The shop owner's never done me any harm. She always offers me a slow, sweet smile. It's fading now.

"We only have instant."

"Olives then." I want my city living, here in the country. I want delicatessens and coffee bars. Fresh pastries and artisan loaves.

She shakes her head.

"Anchovies, balsamic vinegar. Risotto rice." The world was once a cauldron of plenty.

"I only have what's on the shelves."

She's struggling to contain herself in the face of my ridiculous demands. I sling the basket on the counter where it lands with a metallic thud and slide. There's a dogged precision in how she enters the price of each item into the till. She doesn't speak but turns the display to show me the total, waiting as I load my shopping into the trolley. Her refusal to look at me isn't anger. There's glimmer of unshed tears. It's not her fault. It's yours. It's mine.

I feel sick. Yet another thing that can't be undone. I try and catch her eye as I hand her a note but she's having none of it. I want to tell her that I'm sorry. It's shameful that I don't even know her name and now she'll believe the worst she's heard and won't ever smile at me again. She slides my change over the counter rather than putting it into my hand.

The bell above the door jangles as I leave.

The chieftain stood before the three sisters, flanked by men bearing swords and spears, and said, "This is my land now."

"We lived here long before you came," they replied.

"By what right do you claim it? Where's your army?"

"You can't own the land, it owns you." That was the eldest sister. "Rid yourself of such foolish desires."

"No. Everything you see belongs to me."

"Do you own that patch of sky?" the middle born said.

The chieftain was silent.

"Is that water yours?" That was the youngest. "See how it runs away from you."

"I want this land." The chieftain stamped his feet. "Look at my torque. Even metal submits to my will."

"You'll be choked by that gold around your throat." The eldest stepped forward. "You're master of ores and oxen, wheat and men alike, but not us. We're like the grass. We only bow our heads to the wind."

The chieftain looked at them, pale witches in rags with swathes of dark hair and there were the stirrings of a different sort of desire.

The chieftain and his men raped the sisters, one by one.

"See," he said, "I possess everything."

"We are ancient. We are one and we are three." The youngest covered herself with the tatters of her clothes. "We were there at the world's birth. We are wedded to the earth. We don't submit. We endure."

A cold wind came in carrying rain even though it was a summer's day.

"We curse you and your greed." The middle sibling swallowed her sobs and raised her chin. "It'll grow so large that it'll devour you and your kind."

Thunderbolts cracked the sky.

"We'll dog your children's steps from womb to tomb." The eldest had the final word. "When their fortune's in decline we'll rise again. No one will be spared our wrath. Then we'll to heal what you've rent."

The eldest gathered up the other two and retreated to a place where the hills were at their backs and enfolded themselves in stone.

The Three Sisters are a group of three stones that occupy a small plateau on the eastern side of the _____ hills in County Meath. Their history has been retold for generations in the local village of _____. There are several variations of the tale. The one I've included here is the most detailed.

—*Songs of Stones: Collected Oral Traditions of Ireland's Standing Stones* by Grainne Kennedy

I drove us from Dublin. You directed. You kept glancing at my legs as they worked the pedals, which excited me. It felt like you were touching me. Sliding your hand between my knees.

"Turn right."

The indicator winked. We were on Oak Avenue.

"Does this all belong to Boom Developments?"

"Yes."

I whistled, wanting you to know I was impressed.

"Left here." Then, "This is Acacia Drive."

There were diggers, trucks, the cries and calls of men. We bumped along the unfinished road. Stones crunched under the tyres and ochre dust rose around us.

"Pull over here." You buzzed, happy amongst the evidence of your success. "I asked the lads to complete some of the houses up here first."

You ran up the road towards a group of men in jeans and T-shirts. The men looked at me when you'd turned away and I could tell they'd said something smutty from the way they sniggered.

You returned, carrying hard hats and keys. "Put this on."

I refused to be embarrassed by our audience. I piled up my hair and put my hat on, back arched in mock burlesque. You took my elbow with a light touch, as if unsure of yourself. I liked that you weren't adept with women when you seemed so proficient at the rest of life. You guided me towards a house.

"Here." You unlocked the door.

Our feet rang out on the bare boards. Fresh plaster dried in shades of pink and brown.

"This model's the best of the lot. It'll be done to the highest spec."

I followed you upstairs.

"Huge master bedroom. Nice en-suite too."

It was the view that I admired most. The hills, the open sky was spread out for us. I couldn't tell you that I'd been here before your burgeoning success scarred the land. That I'd trekked for miles under rotten skies that threatened rain, across open fields carrying my notebook, cameras and a tripod. I didn't want to spoil the moment by making it anything but yours.

You should've known though. If you'd looked at the copy of the book I'd given you, my own modest enterprise, you'd have seen. You weren't interested in history, not the ones of Ireland's standing stones, not even mine. I was a woman of the past. You were a man of the future.

"We could lie in bed together and look at this view." Your tone had changed from business to tenderness and I was beguiled by the use of we. "Don't feel pressured. Just think on it. You said you wanted to move somewhere quiet to write."

"I can't afford this."

"You're looking to buy outright. This would be yours at cost price."

"Can you do that?"

"I'm the MD," you laughed, "of course I can."

"I couldn't accept it."

"Grainne, you'd be helping me. Selling the first few will help to sell more. Things snowball. This property will treble in value over the next ten years, I promise."

I didn't enjoy this talk of values and assets. I did like the prospect of us sharing a bed that was ours.

"I'll think about a smaller one, at full price."

I'd always been careful not to take anything from you. Need's not erotic.

"It's cost price or nothing. Please, Grainne, it's the least that I can do for you."

The estate looks normal from this approach. There are cars on drives and curtains at windows. I can see a woman inside one of the houses. She bends down and comes back into a view with an infant on her hip. The portrait makes me wince. Madonna with child. She turns her back when she sees me.

I stop at Nancy's on Oak Avenue, the main artery of the estate.

"Have a drink with me." She ushers me in and shuffles along behind me.

Water rushes into the metallic belly of the kettle. I unload her groceries. UHT milk. Teabags. Canned sardines.

"Pay me next time."

Nancy snorts and forces money into my palm. "I'll come with you next week, if you don't mind taking it slow."

"It's a long walk."

"Don't cheek me." Her spark belies her age. She must've been a corker in her time. "I need to take the car out for a run. I'll drive us somewhere as a treat."

I wonder how long it'll take the village shopkeeper to forget my tantrum. Longer than a week.

Steaming water arcs into one mug, then the other.

"Grainne . . ." Her tone changes. "Lads are loitering about up here. Be careful."

When Nancy bends to add milk to the tea I can see her pink scalp through the fine white curls.

"I'm just going to come out and say this." She touches my hand. Her finger joints are large, hard knots. "You're neglecting yourself. You're losing weight. And your lovely hair . . ."

I can't recall when I last brushed it.

"You're not sleeping either. I've seen you, walking past at night."

"You're not sleeping either."

"That's my age."

Nancy sips her tea. I gulp mine down. It's my first drink of the day.

"You're all alone up at that end of the estate."

I can't answer. I've been too lonely to realise that I'm alone.

"Life's too sweet to throw away."

Then why does it taste so bitter?

She tries again, exasperated by my silence.

"What happened up there isn't my business but I can't bear to watch you punishing yourself."

I should be pilloried for my past. I should be stricken with shame but I can't tell Nancy that it's not remorse that's destroying me. It's pining for you.

"You're full of opinions." It comes out as a growl but there's no bite.

"You can stay here anytime. God knows I've room enough to spare." She opens a pack of biscuits and makes me eat one.

"Be careful out there on the hills, Grainne. You could turn your ankle and die up there and no one would know."

I kept a well made bed, dressed with cotton sheets. Worthy of the time we spent upon it. Sunlight moved across our bare bodies, which moved across one another. Hands and mouths roamed over necks, chest, breasts, stomachs, genitals and thighs, stoking a deep ache that only you could sate.

Afterward we lay like pashas on piles of pillows.

"I loved you from the first moment I saw you."

"That's a cliché." I meant to tease you but it sounded bitter.

"You don't believe me. You don't believe anything I say."

"I do."

I did believe you because I felt it too. From that first moment I wanted to open my arms to you. I wanted to open my legs to you. I promise it wasn't just lust because I wanted to open my heart to you too.

"I'm just someone you sleep with."

"Dan, don't play games to make yourself feel better."

"You don't need me, not that way I need you."

"Of course I do."

You thought yourself the more in love of the two of us. Not true. I hated sharing you. I hated not knowing when I'd see you or when you'd call.

"You've never asked me to leave her."

"Do you want me to?"

"Yes." You paused. "No." Then: "I don't know. I don't love her. I did once. I can't leave her now. Ben's still so young. But wait for me, Grainne. Our time will come. I promise."

"Don't make promises."

"I wish I'd met you first."

I wish it all the time, for so many reasons.

The shortcut to Acacia Drive goes through Boomtown's underbelly. There's a square that would've been a green but now it's the brown of churned mud. It should've been flanked by shops. Some are only foundations, others have been abandoned at hip height. A few have made it to the state of squatting skeletons. Piles of rotted timbers and broken breeze blocks litter the verges. An upturned hard hat is full of dirty rainwater. A portable toilet lies on its side and I get a whiff of its spilled contents.

I flip over a tin sign lying in the road and it lands with a clatter. I clean it with the hem of my shirt. Boom Developments, it exclaims. The symbol's a crouched tiger, its stripes orange, green and white.

I go straight to bed when I get home, leaving my shopping in the hall. The once pristine sheets are creased and grey. I push my nose against the pillowcase but can't smell you there, only my own unwashed hair. Frustrated, I strip the bed and lie down again. I touch myself in a ferocity of wanting but it's a hollow sham that ends in a dry spasm. I'll not be moved. Not without you.

I put my walking boots and coat back on. I feel the reassuring weight of my torch in my pocket. My premium property backs onto open country. I open the gate at the bottom of my garden and walk out to where the land undulates and settles into long summer grasses that lean towards the hills.

Out here, away from the estate, nothing's inert. Buzzing insects stir the grass. The wind lifts my hair and drops it. A chill settles in and I wish I'd worn another layer. I cross the stream, sliding on wet stones and splashing water up my jeans. The stream's unconcerned. It has places to go.

The sun's sinking fast. The sky is broken by a string of emerging stars as night arrives.

The ground rises and I have to work harder until I'm climbing on all fours onto the plateau. The hills crowd around to protect the Three Sisters. This trio of stones are eternal, bathed in sun and rain, steeped in the ashes of our ancestors. They're more substantial than our bricks and mortar. They'll sing long after our sagas are exhausted. They outshine our light.

The Sisters cluster together. They're not angular, phallic slabs. Their Neolithic design looks daringly modernist, each shaped to suggest womanhood. The smallest, which I think of as the youngest, has a slender neck and sloping shoulders. The middle one has a jutting chin and a swell that marks breasts. The eldest has a narrow waist and flaring hips. I touch each in turn. They're rugged and covered in lichen. I put my ear against them, wanting to hear the sibilant whispers of their myths. I kiss their unyielding faces but they don't want my apologies for ancestral wrongs. There's only silence. They wait, of course, for us to abate.

I walk back home, not looking down, playing dare with the uneven ground. My torch stays in my pocket. You could turn your ankle and die up there and no one would know.

Death comes for me. It's a white, soundless shape on the wing. A moon faced barn owl, dome headed and flat faced. I'm transfixed. It swoops, a sudden, sharp trajectory led by outstretched claws. How small have I become that it thinks it can carry me away?

I've read that owls regurgitate their prey's remains as bone and gristle. I laugh, imagining myself a mouse sized casket devoid of life.

The owl swoops low over the grass and heads for Boomtown. I press my sleeve to my cheek. Dizziness makes me lie down. The long grass surrounds me, reducing the sky to a circle. I don't know how long I'm there but cold inflames my bones. Eventually I get up and walk home, coming up Acacia Drive from the far end where the houses are unfinished. The street lamps can't help, having never seen the light. I'm convinced it's whispering, not the wind that's walking through the bare bones of the houses. Now that I've survived the menace of the hills and fields, I allow myself my torch. What should be windows are soulless holes in my swinging yellow beam. The door frames are gaping mouths that will devour me.

I don't look at the house but I feel it trying to catch my eye.

There's something akin to relief when the road curves and I see the porch light of my home. It looks like the last house at the end of the world.

You were in the shower sluicing away all evidence of our afternoon. Your clothes were laid out on the back of a chair. You were careful to avoid a scramble that might crumple your shirt or crease your trousers.

The gush of water stopped and you came in, bare, damp, the hair of your chest and stomach darkened swirls. You'd left a trail of wet footprints on the carpet. You weren't shy. I enjoyed this view of you. The asymmetry of your collarbones and the soft, sparse hair on the small of your back. My fascination for you endured, as if I'd never seen a man before.

"When will they start work again?"

By they I'd meant the builders. The estate had fallen silent. No more stuttering engines, no more drills or shouting.

You'd been drying your chest. The towel paused, as if I'd struck you in the heart. I cursed my clumsiness.

"Soon. There's been a bit of a hiatus in our cash flow. People are just a bit nervous, that's all. Everything moves in cycles. Money will start flowing again."

"Of course it will." My optimism had a brittle ring.

You wrapped the towel around your waist in a sudden need to protect yourself, even from me.

I wake in the afternoon, having lost the natural demarcations of my day. My cheek smarts when I yawn. I pick at the parallel scabs.

My mobile's by my bed. I've stopped carrying it around. You never call. It's flashing a warning that its battery is low. I ignore its pleas for power and turn it off.

I did get through to your number once. There was the sound of breathing at the other end. It wasn't you.

"Kate," I said.

The breathing stopped and she hung up before I could say I'm sorry.

You haunt me. I see your footprints on the carpet where you once stood, shower fresh and dripping. I catch glimpses of you in the mirror and through the narrow angles of partially closed doors. These echoes are the essentials of my happiness. For that fraction of a second I can pretend you're here.

It's rained while I slept. Everything drips. The ground's too saturated to take all the water in. It's not cleansed Boomtown, just added another layer of grime.

From the spare bedroom I can see the street. I put my forehead against the window, savouring the coolness of the glass. I tilt my forehead so I can see Helen's house, further along the opposite side of Acacia Drive. The other house, the one where it happened, is out of sight, at the incomplete end of the road. It's defeated me so far.

I slip on my boots and snatch up my coat. I shut my front door and freeze, the key still in the lock. Something's behind me, eyes boring into my back. It waits, daring me to turn. I can feel it coming closer. I make a fist, my door key wedged between my ring and forefinger so that its point and ragged teeth are protruding. It's a poor weapon, especially as I've never thrown a punch in my life. I turn quickly to shock my assailant, only to find it's a cat shuddering in an ecstatic arch against the sharp corner of the garage wall. It's not like other strays. The uncollared, unneutered, incestuous brood that roam around Boomtown are shy. This ginger monster's not scared of anything. It fixes me with yellow eyes and hisses. It bares it fangs and postures. I hiss back but it stands its ground, leaving me to back away down the drive.

I find myself at Helen's, which is stupid because Helen doesn't live there anymore. The For Sale sign's been ripped down and trampled on.

I walk around the house, looking through windows. It's just a shell without Helen and her family but evidence that it was once a home remains. The lounge's wallpaper, a daring mix of black and gold. Tangled wind chimes hang from a hook by the kitchen door. There's a cloth by the sink, as though Helen's last act was to wipe down the worktops.

We used to stand and chat as her brood played in the road. When they got too boisterous she'd turn and shout, "Quit your squalling and yomping, you bunch of hooligans! Just wait until your dad gets back." Then she'd wink at me and say something like, "He's in Dubai this time. Not that they're scared of him, soft sod that he is."

I used to get the girls, Rosie and Anna, mixed up. Tom squealed as he chased his sisters. Patrick rode around us on his bike in circles that got tighter and tighter.

Patrick.

I'm sick of thinking about that day.

I'm sick of not thinking about it.

Today, I decide, today I'll go inside the house where it happened.

It's about twenty doors down from Helen's. The chain link fence that was set up around it has long since fallen down and been mounted by ivy intent on having its way. The Three Sisters are reclaiming what's theirs by attrition. There are lines of grass in the guttering of Boomtown, wasps' and birds' nests are uncontested in the eaves. Lilies flourish in ditches and foxes trot about like lonely monarchs. The Sisters will reclaim us too, our flesh, blood and bones.

I stand on the threshold of the past. A breeze moves through the house carrying a top note of mould and piss, then the threatening musk lingering beneath.

The house is gutless. One wall is bare plasterboard, the rest partition frames so I can see all the way through, even up into the gloom above. There used to be ladders but they've been removed.

From the doorway I can see the stain on the concrete floor. It's a darkness that won't be moved. The blackest part gnashes its teeth at me.

I put a foot inside and then the other. I realise my mistake too late. I've already inhaled the shadows. They fill up my nose and clog my throat. I can't move. I can't breathe. My lungs seize up. Something's there. The darkness is moving.

The shadow rushes at me and takes my legs from under me. The ginger cat. It watches with yellow eyes as I land on my back. Everything goes black.

I roll onto my side and retch. Acidic vomit burns my nose and throat. When I put a hand to the back of my head I find a boggy swelling. My hair's matted and stuck to my scalp.

I stand, test my legs and find them sound. I get away from the house, to the middle of the road, but looking around I see I'm not alone. Company's coming up the street. A trio of creatures that are neither men nor boys. One throws his empty beer can away and fingers his crotch when he sees me.

"You," he says.

He's skinny, grown into his height but yet to fill out. It occurs to me that he expects me to run. His face is hard. He's gone past being abused into abusing.

"You're the Boomtown Bitch."

I turn my back and walk away at a deliberate pace.

"I'm talking to you." I know without looking that he's lengthening his stride to catch me. "Pull down your knickers and show us what all the fuss is about."

My heart's a flailing hammer. He's done this before and is looking to initiate his friends, who seem less certain of themselves. I can see him reach out to grasp my shoulder in the far corner of my vision.

I strike before he can touch me. I jab at his eyes and rake at his face with dirty claws. I'm a moon faced owl. I'll regurgitate his carcass. I'm the feral feline who'll jab his corpse with my paws. The boy's screaming now but I don't stop. Even a chink of fear will let the others in and I can't fend off all three. My would-be rapist retreats. I must put him down before he gathers his wits and tries to save face. I advance, hissing and spitting like the ginger cat.

I am crazy, scarred and unkempt, a bloodied scalp and big eyes in the dark hollows of my face. I pick up a brick and run at him and to my relief, he sprints away.

They shout from a safe distance, taunts that I'm happy to ignore. I don't look back as I walk away in case they realise I'm weak.

I saw your outline through the glass of my front door. You were wearing your suit, even though it was a Saturday.

You weren't alone. A boy stood before you. Even though you had your hands on his shoulders it took me a moment to realise it was your son. Ben. You were there in the shape of his mouth and chin. The other parts must've been your wife. I resented this child, this scrap of you and her made flesh.

"Miss Kennedy—" you mouthed sorry at me over Ben's head "—I've come to see you about your complaint over the house."

I wanted to laugh. You were a terrible actor.

"That's good of you."

"Apologies, I had to bring my son. Say hello, Ben."

"Hello." He squirmed in your grasp.

"I had to let you know I'd not forgotten you. Shall we make an appointment for next week?"

"Would you both like a drink?" I knelt before Ben, hating him because he was getting in our way. "Would you like to play outside? It's a lovely day."

I stood up and raised a hand, a plan already formed. "Patrick, over here."

Helen's brood were on their drive. Patrick cycled over. The bike was too small for him and his knees stuck out at angles.

"Meet Ben. Can he play with you?"

"Sure." Patrick sat back on the saddle. He'd no need for deference, being older than Ben and on home turf. The other children stood on the far pavement, waiting to take their cue from their brother.

"As long it's okay with your father, of course." I couldn't look at you. Please say yes. My longing was indecent. Even the children would see it.

You hesitated.

Please say yes.

"Ben—" you put a hand on his head "—stay with the other children on this road. Don't stray."

I could tell that you were proud of Ben and wanted me to see him but a dull, creeping jealousy stole over me because of the trinity of Dan, Kate and Ben.

"This way," Patrick beckoned and Ben followed, glancing back at you.

"I can't stay long," you said as I closed the door.

We raced upstairs.

"Won't your neighbours wonder when they see Ben? Won't they guess?"

"Who cares?"

I didn't. I was too busy with your belt. There was a sudden shriek of laughter and I stopped you from going to the window by snatching at your tie and pulling you into the bedroom.

"Leave them. They're enjoying themselves. So are we."

You hesitated again and then undressed, your ardour cooled by the tug of parental love. I shoved you, ineffectual considering your size. Your carefully folded clothes enraged me. You'd brought your son to my door. You'd been honest about your life when you could've lied but you'd been a coward and made the decision mine.

I shoved you again.

You picked me up and threw me on the bed. We grappled and when you understood I meant to hurt you, you held my wrists so I couldn't mark you with my nails. You didn't kiss me for fear I'd bite. I wish I'd known it was the final time. I wish we'd taken it slow. I'd have savoured the slip and slide, then the sudden sensation of you inside.

You dozed. I watched. Your breathing changed to slower, deeper tones. I treasured the minutiae of you, the banal details that made you real, like how you took your coffee, brushed your teeth, the slackness of your face in sleep.

The doorbell rang, a sudden sequence of chimes that struggled to keep up with the finger on the bell. A fist hammered at the door, followed by shouts. It went through my mind that it was your wife, that she'd followed you here spoiling for a fight. Then I recognised Helen's voice. Its urgency boomed through the hall and up the stairs.

Silence. There'd been silence during our post-coital nap. No squeals or calls.

I snatched up my blouse, fingers stumbling over the buttons.

"Dan." I reached for my skirt. "Dan, wake up."

You sat up, dazed. "What is it?"

Helen, even in panic, saw the flagrant signs. The buttons of my blouse were done up wrong and I was bra-less beneath the sheer fabric. You'd followed me down the stairs with your tousled hair and bare feet.

"You'd better come. I've called an ambulance."

You pulled on the shoes that you'd discarded by the door. You and Helen were faster than I as she led us to the empty houses. Three of the children were outside one of them. Rosie and Anna were red faced from crying. Tom sat on the step beside them, staring at the ground.

"Stay here", Helen ordered them even though it was clear they weren't about to move.

I followed you from light into the shade of the house. It took a few moments for my eyes to readjust. The coolness inside felt pleasant for a second, as did the smell of cut timber.

You and Helen squatted by the shattered body on the floor. Ben's silhouette didn't make sense and I had to rearrange the pieces in my mind. His arms had been flung out on impact but it was his leg that confused me. It was folded under him at an impossible angle that revealed bone, so white that it looked unnatural against the torn red flesh. Ben was a small vessel, his integrity easily breached.

"He must've fallen from up there."

We looked up towards the eyrie that was the unfinished loft where Patrick perched astride a joist. A ladder spanned the full height of both floors which is how they must've climbed so high. Helen's husband was at the top, reaching for the whimpering boy.

A dark stain crept out from beneath Ben's head. His eyes stared at nothing. There was an appalling sound. A dog's howl, the scream of an abandoned child. The keening of something bereft and inconsolable. It grew until it filled the room. I realised it was you. I put a hand on your shoulder and said your name.

You shook me off.

I wake up on the sofa. It's early and the grey light of dawn creeps through the parted curtains. Sleep's not healed me. I smell of spoiling meat. There's a dull throb in my head but I can't locate whether it's in my eye, my teeth, or somewhere in between. I'm cold and clammy, as if in the aftermath of a drenching sweat.

I go to the mantel mirror. There's enough light now to see that the marks on my cheek are raised, the scabs lifted by lines of pus. I touch one and it gives under gentle pressure, bringing relief and yellow ooze. The back of my head feels like it belongs to someone else.

I eat a dry cracker, drink a pint of water and then vomit in the kitchen sink. There's a pounding now, at a different rate and rhythm to my headache. A drumming that escalates.

It's outside the house.

Hooves thunder on the earth. Something's racing through the grass, running towards the rising sun as if about to engage it in battle.

I go out to the road. Someone, perhaps my failed assailants from yesterday, have spray painted filthy graffiti across the front of my house. It doesn't matter. The wind's changed and is bringing something much fouler with it. Things left too long without light or laughter. Things nursing grudges and dwelling on outrages for too long. My heart pauses and restarts. The horse's gallop makes me gasp. Its cadence changes as it hits the tarmac.

This nightmare is gleaming black. Its rolling black eyes are wild. It tosses its head about and snorts. I can't look away. The mare slows to a canter as it approaches, circling me in rings that get tighter and tighter. It's big, a seventeen hander, heavily muscled. It hits my shoulder on its next pass. When it turns and comes again I have to dodge it to avoid being knocked down.

Adh Seidh. A bad spirit. I'd be safe from its malice if I'd led an upright life.

It flattens its ears and flares its nostrils, then rears up before me and paws at the air as if losing patience. I try to edge to the safety of my open door but it kicks out again, forcing me to retreat. It follows at a trot. Each step jolts my head but I turn and run. When I shout for help my voice is faint from lack of use. There's no one to hear it anyway.

I try and dart up Helen's driveway but the horse isn't confused by my sudden change in direction. It comes around me, right, then left. Lunging at me, kicking out if I stray. Herding me.

I'm panting. My chest's tight and the stitch in my side's a sharp knife. I want to lie down and die. To let it dance on me until I'm dust beneath its hooves.

I'm at the house now. The horse waits beyond the fallen chain link fence in case I try to bolt. I've been brought here to atone for my crimes. The only place I can go is that cold, dark hole.

Broken beer bottles and rubble crunches underfoot. Kids have been in here since my last visit. I feel hot again. Sweat stings my forehead. The past is too heavy. I can't carry it anymore. The stain accuses me. It rises from the floor and spreads itself across the wall. It's absolute, sucking all the light from the room. It smells my guilt and swells, emboldened. Its waiting is over. It's Ben. It's Kate. It's you. It's all the people I can't face. It's the Sisters, taken to the wing. They have hooves and paws studded with claws. They're done with waiting. They've risen up to smother us.

They're not out there on the hills. They're not walking through the dying summer grass. They're not lingering by the streams, fingers stirring the water.

They're not out there. They're in here.

◄○►

PIG THING

ADAM L. G. NEVILL

D arkness they could taste and smell and feel came inside the house. Peaty and dewy with wet fern, it came in damp and cool as the black earth shielded by the canopy of the mighty Kauri trees, as if rising upwards from the land, rather than descending from a sinking sun. The branches in the forest surrounding the bungalow became skeletal at dusk, before these silhouettes also vanished into the black of a moonless country night. Had they still been living in England, it would have been an evening when bonfires were lit. And to the three children, although these nights were frightening, they had a tinge of enchantment in them too, and were never that bad when their parents were inside the house. But tonight, neither their mother nor father had returned from the long garden which the enclosing wilderness of bush tried to reclaim.

Dad had ventured out first, to try and get the car started in a hurry, shortly after nine o'clock. Twenty minutes later, her face long with worry, Mom had gone outside to find him and they had not heard or seen her since.

Before their mom and dad left the house the three children remembered seeing similar expressions on their parents' faces: when Mom's younger sister caught cancer and when Dad's work closed down, just before they all travelled out to New Zealand in the big ship for a fresh start on the day after the Queen's Silver Jubilee. Tonight their parents had done their best to hide their expressions. But the two brothers, Jack who was nine, and Hector who was ten, knew the family was in trouble.

Together with Lozzy, their four year old sister, Jack and Hector sat in the laundry room of the bungalow with the door shut; where Mom had told them to stay just before she went outside to find their father.

Jack and Lozzy sat with their backs against the freezer. Hector sat closest to the door by the bottles and buckets that Dad used for his home-made wine. They had been in the laundry for so long now, they could no longer smell the detergent and cloves. Only in Lozzy's eyes was there still some assurance of this situation becoming an adventure with a happy ending, and them all being back together again. They were large brown eyes, still capable of awe when she was told a story. And these eyes now searched Jack's face. Sandwiched between his sister's vulnerability and the innocence that he could still recognise in himself, and his older brother's courage that he admired and tried to copy, Jack found it his task to stop Lozzy crying.

"What dya reckon, Hector?" Jack said, as he peered at his brother while trying to stop the quiver on his bottom lip.

Hector's face was white. "We were told to stay here. They are coming back."

Both Jack and Lozzy felt better for hearing him say that, although the younger brother soon suspected the elder would always refuse to believe their Mom and Dad were not coming back. Like Dad, Hector could deny things, but Jack was more like his Mom and by making their voices go soft he and Mom would sometimes get Dad and Hector to listen.

But no matter how determined anyone's voice had been earlier that evening, their Dad could not be persuaded to stay inside the house, and had always rubbished their stories about the bush not being right; about there being something living in it, about them seeing something peer in through the windows of the two end bedrooms of the bungalow overlooking the garden and deserted chicken coup. When their dog, Schnapps, disappeared, he said they were all "soft" and still needed to "acclimatise" to the new country. And even when all the chickens vanished one night and only a few feathers and a single yellow foot were left behind in the morning, he still didn't believe them. But now he did, because he had seen it too. Tonight, the whole family had seen it, together.

For months now, the children had been calling it *the pig thing*: Lozzy's name for the face at the windows. She saw it first when playing with Schnapps at the bottom of the garden, in the dank shadows where the orchard stopped and the wall of silver ferns and flax began. *It* had suddenly reared up between the dinosaur legs of two Kauri trees. Never had her mother heard Lozzy make such a fuss: "Oh Jesus, Bill. I thought she was being murdered," she had said to their Dad, once Lozzy had been taken inside the house and quieted. Up on the hill, east of the bungalow, even the boys, who were putting a better roof on their den, had heard their sister's cries. Frantic with excitement and fear, they had run home, each carrying a spear made from a bamboo beanpole. That was the day the idea of the pig thing came into their lives. And it had returned. It was no longer a children's story.

But this was the worst visit, because earlier that evening, as they all sat in the lounge watching television, it had come right on to the sundeck and stood by the barbecue filled with rainwater to look through the glass of the sliding doors, like it was no longer afraid of their Dad. They could tell, because the pig thing had come out of the darkness beyond their brightly lit windows and momentarily reared up on its bony hind legs to display itself, before dropping and quickly moving back into the shadows of the Ponga trees at the side of their property. It could not have been on the deck for more than two seconds, which had stretched into an unbearable and unbreathable time for Jack, but the power in its thin limbs and the human intelligence in its eyes glimpsed through the glass, frightened him more than coming across one of the longfin eels in the creeks would ever have done.

"Don't. Oh, Bill don't. Let's go together, Bill, with the torch," their Mom said to their Dad, once he decided to get the car started.

They were so far from Auckland that had either of the police officers based at the nearest station been available that evening, it would have taken them over an hour to reach the bungalow. Their dad had told their mother what the police operator had told him, after he called them and reported an "intruder", some kind of "large animal or something" trying to get into their house. He couldn't bring himself to say *pig thing* to the operator, though that's what it had been. Lozzy had described it perfectly. Maybe it took a four year old to *see* it properly. It wasn't quite an animal, and was certainly not human, but seemed to have the most dangerous qualities of each in that moment it rose out of darkness, bumped the glass, and then vanished. But the two police officers had been called away to a big fight between rival chapters of bikers on the distant outskirts of the city. With *it* so close and eager to get inside with his family, because it had looked terribly keen on achieving just that, waiting was not an option even entertained by their father, or open to discussion, after he hung up the phone.

Their nearest neighbours, the Pitchfords, lived on their farm two miles away and hadn't answered their phone when the children's dad called them. They were old and had lived in the national reserve since they were both children; had spent the best part of seven decades within the vast cool depths of the bush, before much of the area was cleared for the new migrants. Mr. Pitchford even had hunting rifles as old as the Great War; he'd once shown Jack and Hector, and even let them hold the heavy cumbersome guns that stank of oil.

After the children's father ended the call, he and their mother had exchanged a look that communicated to Jack the suspicion that the pig thing had already been to visit their neighbours.

Going cold and shuddering all over, Jack believed he might even faint with fear. And all that kept appearing in his mind was the vision of the creature's long torso pressed against the window, so it's little brownish teats in the black doggish hair on its belly squished like baby's fingers on the other side of the glass. The trottery hands had merely touched the pane briefly, but that was sufficient to make it shake in the doorframe. There was nothing inside the house, not a door or piece of furniture, that could be used as a barricade. He knew it. Jack could imagine the splintering of wood and the shattering of glass, followed by his sister's whimpers, his Dad shouting and his mom's screams, as *it* came grunting with hunger and squealing with excitement into their home. He had groaned to himself and kept his eyes shut for a while after the thing disappeared back into the lightless trees. Tried to banish the image of that snouty face and the thin girlish hair that fell about its leathery shoulders.

And then their mother had said, "Bill, *please*. Please don't go outside." The children knew their Mom had put her hand on their Dad's elbow as she said this. They didn't see her do it because, by that time, they had been herded into the laundry room where they had stayed ever since, but they could tell by her voice that she had touched his arm.

"Ssh. Jan. Just ssh now. Stay with the kids," their Dad had said to their mom, but once he was outside no one heard the car engine start. The Morris Marina was parked at the bottom of the drive, under the Wattle tree where Hector once found a funny-looking bone that must have come from a cow. And they had heard nothing more of Dad since he went out to the car.

The sudden gravity introduced into their evening had increased with every passing minute as a stillness inside the house, a heaviness that made them all aware of the ticking of the clock in the hall; it was the very thickening of suspense around their bodies.

Their Mother eventually opened the laundry door to report to the kids. She was trying to smile but her lips were too tight. On her cheeks were the red lines made by her fingers when she held her face in her hands. Sometimes she did that at night, sitting alone at the kitchen table. She did it a lot when Dad was out looking for Schnapps, day after day. And Mom had never liked the new house in Muriwai or the surrounding countryside. Didn't like the whistles and shrieks of the birds, the yelps in the night that sounded like frightened children, the animal tracks in the soil beneath her washing line that spun around in the fierce winds, the fat five-foot eel they had seen by the creek with a lamb in its mouth, the large sticky red flowers that nodded at you as you walked past, the missing dog or the stolen chickens. . . . Mom didn't like any of it. Mom doubted she could ever become a Kiwi. She came here for their Dad; they knew that. And now she was missing too.

Holding Lozzy's Wonder Woman torch, because their Dad had taken the big rubber flashlight from the kitchen drawer where the matches were kept, they had heard their mother calling, "Bill. Bill. *Bill.*" in a voice with a tremble in it, as well as something else trying to smother the tremble, as she went out the front door and then walked past the side of the house toward the garden and the car. Her voice had gone faint and then stopped.

And the fact that both of their parents had vanished without a fuss—no shout, or cry, or scuffle had been heard from outside—first made the two boys hopeful with the possibility that their mom and dad would soon come back. But as the silence lengthened it made their hearts busy with a mute dread that whatever had taken them was so quick and silent, you never had a chance. Not a hope out there in the dark with *it*.

Lozzy had sobbed herself into a weary silence after seeing the pig thing on the sundeck, and had then begun whimpering after her mother's departure. For the moment, she had been placated by each of her older brother's reassurances, their lies, and their brave faces. But her silence would not last for long. Lozzy stood up. She was wearing pyjamas. They were yellow and had pictures of Piglet and Winnie the Pooh printed on the cotton. Her hair was tousled and her feet were grubby with dust. Her slippers were still in the lounge; Mom had taken them off earlier to remove a splinter from her foot with the tweezers from the sewing box. Although the soles of the children's feet were getting harder, from running around barefoot all day outside, the children still picked up prickles from the lawn and splinters from the sundeck. "Where's Mummy, boys?"

Immediately, Jack patted the floor next to him. "Ssh, Lozzy. Come and sit down."

Frowning, she pushed her stomach out. "No."

"I'll get you a Tip Top from the freeze."

Lozzy sat down. The freezer hummed and its lemon glow emitted a vague sense of reassurance when Jack opened the lid. Hector approved of the ice-cream trick. After a deep breath, Hector looked at Jack and then returned his stare to the laundry door. He sat with his chin resting on his knee and both hands gripping the ankle of that leg, listening.

Committed of face, Lozzy tucked into the cone, loaded with Neapolitan ice-cream.

Jack shuffled up beside Hector. "What dya reckon?" He used the same tone of voice before he and his brother crossed a waterfall in the creek, or explored the dark reeking caves up in the hills that Mr. Pitchford had told them to "steer clear of, lads", or shinned across a tree fallen over a deep gorge in the piny vastness of bush surrounding their house. The forest stretched all the way to the crazy beaches made from black volcanic sand, where the blowholes and riptides prevented them from swimming.

Hector had no answer for his brother about what to do now that he, the eldest, was in charge. But Hector was thinking hard. His eyes were a bit wild and watery too, so Jack knew he was about to *do* something. And that frightened him. Already, he imagined himself holding Lozzy when there were only the two of them left inside the laundry room.

"I'm gonna run to the Pitchfords," Hector said.

"But it's dark."

"I know the way."

"But . . ." They looked at each other and swallowed. Even though Jack hadn't mentioned the pig thing, they had thought of it at the same time.

Hector stood up, but looked smaller than usual to Jack.

Peering between his knees, Jack kept his face lowered until the creases disappeared from the side of his mouth and around his eyes. He couldn't let Lozzy see him cry.

Before his brother left the laundry room and then the house too, Jack longed to hold him for while but couldn't do it and Hector wouldn't want it anyway; it would make his leaving even harder. Instead, Jack just stared at his own flat toes spread on the lino.

"Where's Hegder going?" Lozzy asked, just as a bubble popped on her shiny lips.

Jack swallowed. "To get the Pitchfords."

"They have a cat," she said.

Jack nodded. "That's right." But Jack knew where Hector would have to go first before he even got close to the Pitchfords' place: he was going into the forest with the clacking branches and ocean sounds when the wind blew; along the paths of damp earth and slippery tree roots, exposed like bones, that they had run and mapped together; over the thin creek with the rowing boat smells; across the field of long grass, that was darker than English grass and always felt wet, where they had found two whole sheep skeletons and brought them home in a wheel barrow to reassemble on the front lawn. Hector was going to run a long way through the lightless night until he reached the Pitchfords' house with the high fence and the horseshoes fixed around the gate. "To keep things out," Mrs. Pitchford had once told them in a quiet voice when Hector asked why it was nailed to the dark planks.

"No. Don't. No," Jack hissy-whispered, unable to hold back when Hector turned the door handle.

On the cusp of his brother's departure, that Jack knew he could do nothing about, everything went thick and cold inside his chest. Welling up to the back of his throat, this feeling spilled into his mouth. It tasted of rain. And this time, he couldn't swallow. Inside Jack's head was the urgency of desperate prayers trying to find words. He squinted his eyes to try and push the thoughts down, to squash them down like he was forcing the lid back on a tin of paint. Did anything to stop the hysterics he could feel storming up through his entire body.

"Got to," Hector said, his face all stiff but still wild-looking.

Lozzy stood up and tried to follow Hector, but Jack snatched her hand and gripped it too hard. She winced, then stamped, was tearing up again.

"Jack, don't open the door after I'm gone. OK." They were Hector's final words.

The laundry door clicked shut behind him. They heard his feet patter across the floorboards of the hall. Then they heard him turn the catch on the front door. When that closed too, the wind chimes clinked together and made an inappropriate spacey sound. There was a brief creak from the bottom step of the porch stairs, and then the silence returned for a while, until Lozzy's sobs made an unwelcome return inside the laundry room.

After comforting her with a second ice-cream cone, Jack unplugged the freezer. Quickly but carefully, so as to make less noise, he removed the rustly bags of frozen peas, steaks, stewed apple and fish fingers. He put the food in the big laundry sink that smelled like the back of Gran's house in England. Then he stacked the white baskets from inside the freezer against the side of the sink. Around the rim of the freezer cabinet he placed plastic clothes pegs at intervals, so there would be a gap between the grey rubber seal of the freezer lid and the base. Then they wouldn't run out of air when he shut them both inside.

"Come on, Lozzy," he said, hearing some of his Mom in his voice. And he felt a bit better for doing something other than just waiting. He picked Lozzy up and lowered her into the freezer. Together, they spread Schnapps's old blanket over the wet floor of the cabinet so they wouldn't get cold bottoms and feet.

"This smells. His fur is on it. Look." She held up a tuft of the brown fur the dog used to get stuck between his claws after riffing his neck. Their Mom and Dad had been unable to throw the dog's blanket away, in case he ever came back to lie on it. So the blanket had stayed in the laundry where Schnapps had ended up sleeping at night. Their Dad's idea of dogs sleeping outside became a bad idea after Schnapps began all that barking, whimpering, and finally scratching at the front door every night. "He's soft," their Dad had said. But tonight, it all made sense.

After handing the tub of ice-cream and the box of cones to Lozzy, Jack climbed into the freezer and sat beside her. She reached for his hand with her sticky fingers. As he pulled the lid down over their huddled bodies, he secretly hoped that the cold and wet of the freezer would stop the pig thing from smelling them. He also wondered if those trotter things on the end of its front legs would be able to push the lid up when it stood up on those hairy back legs, like it had done out on the sundeck. But he also took another small comfort into the dark with him: the pig thing had never come inside their house. Not yet, anyway.

◄◦►

Mrs. Pitchford entered the house through the empty aluminium frame of the ranch-sliding door; the glass had been smashed inwards and collected in the mess of curtains that had also been torn down. She favoured net curtains behind all the windows of her own home; she didn't like the sense of exposure that the large windows gave to the new homes the government had started delivering on truckbeds for the migrants, who were settling all over the area. She also found it hard to even look at the red earth exposed beneath any more felled trees and cleared bush. The appearance of these long rectangular bungalows with tin cladding on their walls never failed to choke her with fury and grief no good for her heart. And who could now say what kind of eyes would be drawn in to these great glassy doors if you didn't use nets? *You couldn't then go blaming them who was already here.*

All of the lights were still on. It felt warm inside the house too, even though the cold and damp of the night air must have been seeping into the living room for at least an hour after that big pane of glass was put through.

She looked at the brown carpets and the orange fabric on the furniture, was amazed again with what the English did with their homes; all Formica and white plastic and patterned carpets and big garish swirls in wallpaper the colour of coffee. Shiny, new, fragile: she didn't care for it. They had a television too and a new radio, coloured silver and black: both made in

Japan. They mesmerised her, the things these soft-muscled, pale-skinned Poms brought from such faraway places and surrounded themselves with; but anyone could see they and their things didn't fit with the old bush. It had ways that not even the Maoris liked, because there were *things* here before them too.

Glass crunched under her boots as she made her way further inside the house. The kitchen and dining room were open-plan, only divided from the living room by the rear of the sofa.

Unable to resist the lure of the kitchen area, she went inside and stared, then touched the extractor fan over the stove. It was like a big hopper on a petrol lawnmower, for collecting cut grass. She marvelled again at what young mothers considered necessary in the running of a household these days. And here was the food mixer Jan had once showed her. Orange and white plastic with *Kenwood Chevette* printed along one side. A silver coffee pot with a wooden handle; what Jan had called a "percolator", beside the casserole dishes with their pretty orange flower patterns. Mrs. Pitchford ran her hard fingers across the smooth sides of all the Tupperware boxes that Jan had lined up on the counter; they were filled with cereal, rice, something called spaghetti, bran, sugar. You could see the contents as murky shadows through the sides. Everything in her own home was wood, pottery, steel, or iron. And she remembered seeing it all in use when she was a little girl and helped her mother prepare food. Hardwoods and metals lasted. Whereas plastic and carpet and "stereos" hadn't been much use to this family tonight, had they?

The sound of the car engine idling outside returned a sense of purpose to her; her Harold had told her not to get distracted. She turned and waddled out of the kitchen, but her eyes were pulled to the sideboard beside the dining table; at all of the silver and ceramic trinkets kept behind its sliding glass doors. Little sherry glasses. Small mugs with ruddy faces on the front. China thimbles. Teaspoons with patterns on their handles. She had her own things for special occasions; all a lot older than these things the family had brought with them from England.

They also had a washing machine in the little laundry room beside the "dining area", and a freezer too. Jan had been horrified to learn that Mrs. Pitchford still washed clothes in a tin bath, used a larder for food, and still preserved things in jars. *The bloody cheek.*

Mrs. Pitchford went inside the laundry room; it smelled of wine, soap powder, and urine. All of the food from the freezer was melting and softening inside the sink. The lid of the freezer was raised and there was an old blanket inside the white metal cabinet that hummed softly. It was still cold inside when she leaned over. And it puzzled her why the food was stacked in the sink, and also how the food inside the plastic bags and paper boxes was even prepared. They had no mutton, no venison, no sweet potatoes that she could see. She looked under her foot and saw that she was standing on a yellow plastic clothes peg.

Inside the unlit hallway that led down to the four bedrooms, she paused for a few moments to get her eyes used to the darkness. It was a relief to be out of the bright living area, but she would need more light to conduct a proper search. Ordinarily, she could have found a sewing pin on the floor by the thinnest moonlight, because around here there were plenty who could see better at night than others. But tonight there was no moon or starlight at all and the curtains in the bedrooms were drawn; it would be terrible if she missed something important. She found the light switch for the hallway.

The family had no rugs; they had laid carpet all the way down the passage and even inside the bedrooms. How did Jan get the dust out of them, or air them in the Spring like she did with her rugs?

Shaking her head in disapproval, she went into the first room. Jan and Bill's room. Two suitcases were open on the large bed and full of clothes. The headboard was softened with padded white plastic. Mrs. Pitchford reached out and pressed it.

The next room was for the little girl with all of that lovely thick raven hair. Dear little Charlotte. The light from the hall revealed the dim outlines of her dolls and toys, the books on all of the shelves, the bears in the wallpaper pattern. "Darlin'," she said, quietly, into the darkness. No answer. Some of the teddy bears and stuffed rabbits were on the floor; they had been pulled off the shelves. Mrs. Pitchford had a hunch a few would be missing too.

She carried on, down the passageway to the two end bedrooms: Jack and Hector's rooms. Hector was safe at their home. How he had managed to scuttle all the way to their farm in the dark had surprised her and her husband. But little Hector had come and banged on their door, then fallen inside, panting and as pale as a sheet. She and Harold hadn't wasted a moment and had swept him into their arms, before spiriting him across the yard to Harold's workshop.

"That kid was as slippery as an eel and quick as a fox," Harold had said, his eyes smiling, as he came back into the kitchen from his workshop, and removed his sheep shearing gloves and leather apron before getting their coats off the pegs. "Come on, mother. Better get our skates on."

And Hector had been so concerned for his younger brother and his sister when he arrived at their farm, that she and Harold had sped to the bungalow in the old black Rover that someone else had also once brought over from England. Harold had taught himself to drive the car, not long after acquiring it from an elderly couple with those Pommy accents that miss the *H* in every word.

Harold would dress Hector when they returned with the other two children, if they were still around. That didn't seem likely now to Mrs. Pitchford. The family's bungalow was deserted then, like all of those bungalows on Rangatera Road, waiting for other Pom families, or Pacific Islanders, or even more of those bloody Dutch Dike-Duckies. Poles were supposed to be coming too. *What next?*

The two end bedrooms were empty of life, but she smelled what all life leaves behind. Then she found it on the floor of one of the boy's rooms overlooking the wattle tree. Kneeling down, she tried to scoop it into her salt-white handkerchief. It was ruddy in colour and smelled strong; the fresh stool of excitement, the stool of too much fresh blood gulped down by a very greedy girl. There was too much of it.

She stripped a pillow case off the bed. "You've been at it here, my little joker," Mrs. Pitchford said with a rueful smile. *She* must have hunted right through the house until she'd found the other two kiddiewinks hiding; under the beds maybe, or in that hardboard wardrobe with the sliding doors on the little plastic runners. "What a rumble you've had my girl." This kind of house couldn't possibly make a family feel safe; it was like cardboard covered in thin tin. *She'd* at least had the sense to take Jack and little Charlotte outside the house first, like Harold had shown her how to do. Otherwise, they'd have to burn out another of these bungalows to incinerate the leavings, and that was always a flamin' mess. "One more and it'll smell funny," Harold had warned after the last one they lit up.

Mrs. Pitchford went back to the laundry room and found a scrubbing brush, detergent, and a bucket. She filled the bucket with hot water from the tap in the laundry, then went back to the boy's room and scrubbed the rest of the muck out of the carpet. While she was doing this, Harold had become impatient outside in the car and sounded the horn. "*Hold* your bloody horses," she'd said to Harold, who couldn't possibly have heard her.

When she was finally back inside the car and seated, a pillow case in her lap, the contents wet and heavy, plus three Tupperware containers inside a brown paper bag clutched in her other hand, she asked Harold, "You want to check the creek?"

"Nah. *She'll* be right. Long gone. *She'll* be up in them caves by now, mother."

Mrs. Pitchford smiled, wistfully. "She got carried away again, my love."

Smiling with a father's pride, Harold said, "She's a big girl, mother. You've got to let them suss their own way in this world. Be there for them from time to time, but still . . . we've done what we can for her. She has her own family now. She's just providing for them the best way she knows."

"We've been very lucky with her, Harold. To think of all them sheep Len and Audrey lost last year with their girl."

"You're not wrong, mother. But when you let a child run wild . . ." Harold rolled his eyes behind the thick lenses in the tortoise-shell frames of his glasses that he'd taken off the old Maori boy they'd found fishing too far downstream last summer. "It's all about pace, mother. We showed our girl how to pace herself. A chook or two. A dog. A cat. And if dags like these Poms are still around after that, well it comes down to who was here first. And who was here first, mother?"

"We was, dear. We was."

-◆-

THE WORD-MADE FLESH

RICHARD GAVIN

My friend Austin's distress was apparent to me before I even reached our table. His twitchy mannerisms and his mask of worry troubled me a great deal, since I knew the tragedies he'd recently endured. He was stationed in the corner, where the only light-source was the dwarfish lamp on the table. This meek, fever-yellow glow made every furrow in Austin's brow seem gorge-deep and hazed his flesh in a ghoulish pallor. I extended my hand. "Happy Christmas," I said, hoping that my somewhat saccharine tone might lift Austin's spirits. He gave my hand a limp shake and bade me to sit. "What are you drinking tonight?"

"Nothing," Austin replied.

I ordered a pint of pale for myself and nagged Austin jovially until he finally caved and requested some Darjeeling. Through the mounted speakers tabla drums tapped as rapidly as rainfall. I found myself bobbing my head to the rhythm. Austin, by contrast, seemed pained by the music. He screwed up his face and pressed his fingers into his ears.

"Should I ask them to turn down the volume?" I asked. Austin shook his head. "Are you feeling ill?"

"No" he returned. "Something . . . something's happened . . ."

"What's happened?"

Austin reached for his coat, which was hanging next to a framed painting of triple-eyed Shiva dancing raptly while he obliterates the world. From the inside pocket Austin produced a slim item.

"I found this lying in the centre of my living room when I got home from work this afternoon." He slid the item across the table.

A Tarot card. Card XVI, The Tower. The colourful illustration depicted a pair of figures falling headlong from an ominous keep whose summit was ablaze from the kiss of dead-white lightning bolts.

"I haven't used my deck in years, Elliot. It's a message"—he now spoke *sotto voce*—"a message from my cousin."

"I'm afraid I don't follow."

"My cousin's been dead for years."

The waiter's timing was impeccable; his request for my dinner order gave me a few seconds to absorb the shock of my friend's statement. I was woefully unfamiliar with Indian fare, having chosen to have my and Austin's annual pre-Christmas dinner at The Lotus Room only to appease my friend's growing interest in Eastern Mysticism. Yoga, I knew, had been one of the few pursuits he'd taken up in recent months that seemed to bring him any pleasure. I was extremely relieved that Austin undertook a discipline in order to cope rather than crawling inside a bottle—something that, if there is any truth to genetic disposition, was a sharp possibility.

I glanced over the menu and on impulse requested curried goat and another pint of pale ale. Austin asked only for saffron rice.

Once our area was again free of intruders I told Austin that he was obviously mistaken. "That card could have been lying around your room for months and just got kicked to the middle of the room. I wouldn't take it too seriously."

He was massaging his ears again. I then noticed how heavily he was perspiring. "It's him," Austin said, "no question."

"What makes you so sure?"

"The Tower," he rasped. "Only he and I knew what it means. No one else."

"And what does it mean?"

He laughed, but more from exasperation or resignation than mirth. "A long story . . ."

At my request, Austin then told me his tale.

"It won't come as any surprise to you that I used to spend as much time as I could out of my folks' house," he began. Having listened to Austin's occasional intimations about his mother's rampant alcoholism and his father's old-world ornery nature, I was able to acknowledge this sincerely. "My mother's sister and her husband were really surrogate parents to me. Every summer, as soon as school was finished, they would invite me to stay on their farm for as long as I wanted, which was usually the whole summer. I don't think I'm being too blindly nostalgic when I say that their farm was a true sanctuary for me. I think it was the year my cousin and I both turned thirteen that things began to change. That summer I only spent a few weeks on the farm, then the summer after that; just one week. Then I stopped going altogether."

"What changed?" I asked.

Austin raised his fingers to pause so that he could cradle his head in his hands.

"Maybe we should get you to a doctor," I suggested.

"No," he said, his voice meek and breathless, "it's passing. It comes in waves."

"The pain?"

"The noise. It's the same thing that plagued my cousin. That's what changed that summer, since you asked. When we were twelve or thirteen my cousin began to suffer from terrible earaches and migraines. My aunt and uncle, as you can imagine, took him for every kind of test imaginable. It took a team of specialists to finally guess that his problem was an acute form of somatic tinnitus."

"A ringing in the ears."

"Precisely. I gather the clinicians opted for somatic tinnitus because they couldn't find the problem area in the actual ear, so they assumed that the problem was somewhere else in my cousin's head or neck. It became steadily worse as he got older. He tried moving to Calgary to attend university, but it was a disaster. He collapsed on campus one morning. After that he promptly dropped out of school and moved back to his parents' farmhouse in the country. He took his own life there two years later."

I cleared my throat to crack a long silence. "Forgive me, Austin, but I'm not really seeing what any of this has to do with you feeling out of sorts tonight because you found an old Tarot card."

He exhaled sharply. "That final summer, the last time I went out to my cousin's farm, he told me that he'd heard something on the roof of the old silo, late at night."

"What did he hear?"

"The Word of God, he said. He said he'd taken the Word inside him and had taught himself how to speak it. And then that last night . . . he proved it to me. . . ." He shook his head suddenly, as if breaking a trance. I prodded for more details, but all Austin said was that he simply had to go back there.

"To your cousin's farm?"

He nodded.

"Why, for God's sake?"

"I think he's trying to tell me something with the Tower card. I think he's trying to get me back to that old silo."

A proposal, or rather a gesture of goodwill, leapt into my head, but rather than offer it straightaway I found myself wrestling with the notion, unsure whether or not I wanted to commit myself.

One look at Austin's mounting anguish inspired me to ask if he would like me to accompany him on the trip.

"Are you serious?" he asked.

"Well, I don't want to drive out there after dinner or anything like that. Tomorrow is Saturday. Why don't I pick you up at around nine?"

"The village is nearly a three-hour drive from here, even if traffic's kind," he advised me.

I told Austin he could consider the trip my Yuletide gift to him.

Austin almost smiled at this. Almost.

The next morning's sun brought much brilliance but no warmth. I left my house just after eight and the streets were already bustling. The growing throngs of holiday shoppers made me glad for Austin's and my exodus from the city.

When my first few knocks on his townhouse door went unanswered I feared that my friend had overslept, but when he finally did manage to get to the door and open it, it was obvious that he hadn't slept a wink. Dressed only in his housecoat, Austin requested I give him a moment to get cleaned up, encouraging me to sit in the dank cube that served as a living room while he went down the hall to shower and shave.

There was only the suggestion of a sofa beneath a mountain of twisted laundry, so I opted to stand.

Mingling with the room's dominant smell of a dirty furnace was the sickly-sweet perfume of incense. An end table stood in the far corner, draped in green silk and bracing a lone white taper in a brass base, a brazier, and a framed photograph of Liz holding a newborn William. The picture's background was undulating drapes of white gossamer. I remember when Austin had taken these photos of his much-adored wife and their infant son. At the time, the background had suggested purity, renewal. Seeing it now, framed within a black border, it was but a reminder of the pallor-pale face I'd seen reposing, and the second casket that sat next to it, no larger than a hope chest.

Austin emerged from the washroom with surprising suddenness. He handed me a sheet bearing what looked to be awfully scrawled directions before donning his coat.

"Let's go," was all he said.

The attempted cheer of the decorations that crowded store windows and bulged around the streetlight poles failed to pierce the morose mood within the cab of my car. Austin and I chatted intermittently about nothing in particular, and I wondered how I would survive this marathon trek with so lugubrious a passenger.

But as the city gave way to the town, and the town to a quilt of snow-padded rural expanse, I felt myself relaxing slightly, but not totally: Austin's reluctance to have even a polite chat tensed the atmosphere in the car.

The sky was beginning to darken, portending snow. I flicked on the headlights, sighed, and allowed for the mum tension for as long as I could. Eventually the pressure became unbearable, so I deliberately decided to detonate the bomb we'd both let go on ticking between us for too long.

"Can I ask you something?"

Austin shrugged.

"How have you been doing, with everything I mean?"

"Isn't it obvious?"

"Yes, actually, it is. But I'll be honest with you, I don't think Tarot cards or play-forts from your childhood are the issue here. Don't you think you feel the way you do because you are still raw from a massive loss? I mean, Christmastime can be one of the worst times for people in pain. I think you should talk about the accident, Austin, because as far as I'm concerned, *that* is what's really tearing you up inside, not anything supernatural."

"You don't know what you're talking about, Elliot," he mumbled.

"No, I'm afraid you're the one who's not seeing things clearly. That car accident tore your life out by the roots. You lost Liz, the woman you loved more than life. And you lost William, your only son."

My gaze flickered between the road ahead of me and trying to gauge Austin's reaction; but no reaction came. I inhaled slowly and deliberately cushioned my tone:

"Look, I'm not going to pretend for one moment that I can relate to what you've been put through. Your loss is... well, it's almost unthinkable. And maybe that's why you've not been able to face it. Yoga isn't going to heal your wounds."

Austin remained stoic. "Turn right here," he said.

A few moments later, the property from which my friend had drawn what might be the only august memories of his youth slouched into my field of vision. Its house and barn looked every bit as grey and spent as a pair of elephants nestling down to expire on their chosen burial grounds. A few stray splints of wood indicated where a fence had been back in the time when the land was worthy of distinguishing. Bales of soggy hay sat in loose lumps upon the dirty snow of the field. The barn door hung open, advertising the depressing absence of livestock.

I slowed the car and looked at Austin, who appeared to be holding his breath. He ran a hand over his bristly face, muttering something that sounded like "God."

I turned my head and knew precisely what had mesmerized my friend.

Whether the silo had always cast off the glamour of a castle keep or whether it had been modified over the years I of course couldn't say, but its presence was incongruous—a high Gothic set-piece in an otherwise agrarian environment.

He lowered his hand and began fishing through the pocket of his pea coat. He held up the Tower card. The similarity between its image and the structure before us was strong enough to make Austin laugh, but not smile.

"I'm going in." Austin's tone was uncharacteristically steely. "You can stay in the car if you want."

"Shouldn't you check at the house, see if anyone's home?"

"The property's abandoned," he said before exiting the car.

I watched, mute and, admittedly, timid, as Austin stepped between two crooked fence posts, long deprived of their wires, and undertook the trepid journey into his yesterdays. My fists tightened on the steering wheel as a sickening feeling overcame me, as though my gullet had suddenly been lined with grease. Intellectually I knew that Austin should be fetched back from his quest, but a strange obstruction had moved between my better judgment and my will-to-action.

My sense of unease was devoid of reason; a vague funk of disquiet. Seeing Austin stepping across the barren cropland made me regret ever carrying him out here to face his old ghosts.

Nothing good would come of this. Nothing.

At last my hand found the door handle. But before I'd even opened the door I saw Austin drop.

I stumbled out of the car and bolted across the field. The wind lashed cold and fierce. Snow swirled about me like stirred gravel. As I neared Austin I discovered that he hadn't passed out; he was curled into a foetal position, snow collecting on his hair and in the creases of his clothes. Not until I crouched to help him up did I see how agony had mangled his face.

I uttered a few consoling words and scooped him up off the earth. His legs were rag-doll-limp and he weighed much more than I'd expected.

"Don't listen!" Austin cried. *"Don't listen!"* He was pushing against me, butting me like a bull, shouting all the while. *"Focus on me! Just listen to me! Get to the car! Run! Go!"*

Austin's incessant shouting and the roar of the wind must have been muting whatever it was that Austin had been so afraid I'd hear. We reached the road and piled back into the car. No sooner had I started the engine when Austin snapped on the stereo and spun the volume dial to its limit. A blast of voices transformed the cab of my car into Babel. I slammed it into reverse and began to drive. I peered out in the hope of seeing whoever had startled Austin so, but the figure appeared to be gone.

Austin must have calculated that I'd placed a safe enough distance between ourselves and the old farm, for he finally reduced the stereo's volume to the point where I could hear the music—ironically, a children's choir singing "Hark! The Herald Angels Sing."

"What the hell happened back there?" I asked. I was so shaken that driving was taxing.

"I heard it again . . ."

"Heard what?"

"*The Word*. The one that made everything change that last summer. My cousin and I . . . we *heard* something inside the silo."

"Heard what?"

"To me, it was just sounded like a buzzing insect. It came and then it went. It startled me, but my cousin swore he heard a word being spoken."

"So?"

"I know, I know. A word, right? It's nothing. But if only you could have seen how it affected him. It *ruined* him. A mere beat of time shaped his entire life. That was when his tinnitus began. He started hearing *things* constantly.

"That last summer I went out to their farm, I realized that something was really wrong with my cousin, that his illness was only part of it.

"That final day he took me up into the silo, saying that he had something to show me. He was like a kid on Christmas. He couldn't wait to get me up to the silo's roof. Once we were there he ordered me to be quiet and listen. He kept asking me if I could hear it. But I couldn't hear anything at all, just regular noises from the farm below. My cousin looked really disappointed and bragged that he could hear the Word of God, the one that had been used to make humanity live, the Word that makes the clay dance, as my cousin said. Of course I didn't believe him and turned to leave. And that's when he did it."

"Did it?"

Austin's eyes were welling up. "He said something, the Word. It sounded like gibberish to me . . . but it changed him. Changed him right before my eyes . . ."

I went to press him further, but Austin cut me off.

"He changed right in front of me. . . . His face . . . it stretched into something big and fluid. Extra arms came sprouting out of his neck. . . .

"I ran. I went tearing down the ladder inside the silo and all the way back to the farmhouse. I insisted that my aunt drive me home that day.

I refused to stay there. She kept asking me what had happened, but I refused to tell her. I just had to leave.

"My cousin came sauntering into the farmhouse, calm as can be. His body had gone back to normal. He didn't say a word. I remember it like it was yesterday. He just walked into the kitchen and poured himself a glass of milk and then just stood at the counter and drank. He winked at me and then went off to his room.

"Before you ask, Elliot, the reason why all this is happening now is because of a stupid mistake I made. After Liz . . . after the accident, I started meditating. I thought it might be good for me, a way to quiet the storm inside my head. My instructor told me that the best way to do this was to chant and focus on the 'Om' mantra. It's said that this is the word that created the universe. Things started out okay, but then a few weeks ago, I heard It . . . the thunders. . . . It felt exactly how my cousin used to describe them; like a rumble that shakes your core. I think these thunders and the Tarot card are my cousin's attempt to get me back to that silo roof."

"For what purpose?"

"To bring Liz back to life . . ."

There was nothing else I could say.

I don't remember driving home, though I know we made it there, because I do carry vivid memories of Austin exiting my car and going up the snow-dusted steps of his townhouse. He did not look back.

When I made it back to my apartment I fell asleep right away. I slept long and deeply. My mind was likely trying to place as great a void as possible between me and the shock I'd experienced.

The next day as I sat sipping coffee in my kitchen, I felt compelled to call Austin but at the same time did not want to. I simply did not want to know.

That afternoon I received a cursory e-mail from him, telling me that "everything was okay now" and that I "shouldn't trouble my head about anything." In the last line he wished me a merry Christmas.

Hindsight makes the suspect nature of that e-mail painfully clear, but at the time I used Austin's confirmation of his well-being as a shield to cower behind. I neither called nor visited him. I avoided the coffee shops and stores I knew he frequented. I actually managed to convince myself that I was simply following my friend's advice—my head remained untroubled by him.

A full year lapsed. It took the holidays, with their insidious manipulation of emotion, to inspire me to contact Austin again. I sent him a text message in early December, suggesting that we catch up over dinner. When my query received no reply I tried to call. His number was no longer in service.

Any number of life changes could have uprooted Austin. For all I knew the bank that employed him could have relocated him to another city, indeed to an altogether different province. He could have fallen in love, moved into new quarters with his latest paramour.

On my way home from work one evening I opted to exhaust the last possibility and drop by Austin's building. I could see from the street that the windows of his apartment were dark.

I was not surprised that my knocking was futile.

Returning to my car, I saw the woman in Austin's window. Her complexion looked almost spectral against the cave-blackness of the room behind her. She faced the street, her expression emotionless. She was dressed in a short-sleeved dress that was unseasonable, given the cold snap that had recently struck.

My initial thought was that Austin must have moved and that I'd probably woken the new tenant from an evening nap.

I hadn't noticed the young boy that stood beside her, clutching her hand with its tiny fingers. He was towheaded and cute. I found myself smiling.

The mother had led the boy away from the window before the revelation erupted within me. I froze, my mind reeling to determine whether I had actually seen what I had seen, *who* I had seen in that pool of black glass.

It was Liz. The more I reflected on the features of her face, her size, the colour of her hair, the more my doubt dissipated. I was certain that the woman I'd seen was Austin's late wife. The young boy at her side could only have been William; the child now at least a year older than when his infant body had been blasted through a windshield upon impact.

I slumped behind the steering wheel of my car and remained there in a grey trance, neither puzzling out what I'd seen nor planning my next move in the game. I simply sat, thoughtless as a doll, until the frigid temperature roused me enough to start the engine and drive off.

I saw the sun crawl up the following morning, watched it through my living room window. I called in sick for work and waited until a decent hour approached for me to go back to the townhouse. By then I had *almost* convinced myself that the woman I'd seen was assuredly not Liz, any more than the toddler by her side had been Austin's son grown to his appropriate age. All that was required was confirmation. If I could just see the woman in stark daylight I knew that all the vagaries of shadow and distance and fatigue, the ones my imagination had moulded into the echo of a dead woman, would be swept away.

It was a few minutes past nine when I veered onto Austin's street.

The sight of police cruisers and a coroner's vehicle parked before the townhouse with its door wide open stunned me. I parked down the street and jogged back to join the small congregation of gawkers at the base of Austin's front stoop. Yellow tape was strewn across the townhouse entrance like Christmas tinsel. I asked if anyone knew what was happening. I was afraid that Austin had been hurt, or worse.

The details I was given by one of the onlooking neighbours *was* worse; far more than I could have fathomed.

If I knew Austin, an old man told me, I'd best tell the police. They were questioning everybody.

I slipped away from the scene and began to drive, grateful for the length and solitude of the trip because it allowed me time to sort my thoughts.

I found my way to the village with little difficulty, but got turned around on the country lanes and back roads. I squinted through the naked wood of the wintertime trees until I finally spotted the hint of the silo, which immediately became my beacon, luring me to the neglected property where my instincts told me Austin had to be. I'd known him too long to fully believe what I'd been told at the scene of the travesty. Given his anguished life circumstances these past few years, I owed him, if nothing else, a non-judgmental ear, a party that afforded him the opportunity to plead his innocence, or to explain how he'd come to be implicated in such a crime.

The daylight had begun to ashen with premature dusk by the time I finally reached the property.

The candles that sat guttering in the kitchen window were the first detail I noticed after I parked my car on the winding driveway. They glimmered like a dozen tiny suns attempting to illuminate the wormhole that was the decrepit farmhouse.

My concern over Austin's fate must have muzzled whatever anxieties I was harbouring, for I marched up to the house with a deliberate stride.

When no one responded to my rapping, I tested the door myself and found it unlocked.

Dust lay thick upon the foyer's toppled chairs. The warped floorboards were carpeted in the gaudy colours of flung junk mail. I peered through the nearest archway, observing what I presumed to be a room as vacant as it was dark.

I began feeling my way toward the swinging door where I could discern a glimmer of amber light billowing beneath the door. It stained the black floor with a suggestion of light.

But before I'd managed to push the door open someone puffed the candles out. I caught a whiff of melted wax that reminded me of birthday parties. Across the narrow kitchen, wicks smouldered like freshly cut wires. Then their tiny pinheads of light shrivelled up.

Still, there was enough of the moon leaking through the window to reveal the feminine form that was seated in the corner.

Neither of us spoke, and from what I was able to hear, I seemed to be the only one breathing; or at least breathing heavily. I swallowed but hadn't enough saliva. My voice, when I finally decided to speak, was raspy, faint:

"Liz?"

I felt a keen pain in my hands and discovered that I had dug my nails deep into the soft meat of my palms.

"*Elliott . . .*"

The voice was warbled and thick, like a phonograph spinning at an improper speed. It had the faint remnant of Liz's tone, but there was a second voice wedged in there as well—Austin's.

The woman in the corner slumped further down in her perch. Something plopped down upon the floor.

At first I thought the electric-purple glow blossoming in the corner was the flame of a novelty candle, perhaps an electric bulb. But the source of the light was the woman's head. The pulsating glimmer moved across her face in ripples and waves, gauzing her features into something indistinct, or something in a state of flux.

A whitish jelly began to leak from the woman's nostrils and the sockets of her fluttering eyes.

A strangled voice uttered "Help . . . me . . ." before the head caved in upon itself.

The shock of what I was seeing, or believed I was seeing, pressed me back against the wall. I pressed my palms against the grubby wallpaper and tried to exorcise the vision by squinting, by shaking my head to and fro, by crying out "No!" But the woman, now mute and mouthless, continued to smoulder within the cumulus of deep purple light.

When the stench of extinction crowded my nostrils and my tongue I choked and doubled over to retch. I felt my way out of the kitchen, along the foyer, and back into the chill night.

If in fact it was still nighttime.

I was blinded by an eruption of light, so immediate and harsh that I feared it would eat through my eyelids. I shielded my face with my arms, but just as quickly as it had come, the light regressed, slinking back to a concentrated source: the silo.

At the tower's summit there hovered a great orb of swirling purple, veined with searing lines of white. It pulsed and spun, and each flex emitted a cacophony of sounds. Some of these noises had all the rumble and bellow of August thunderheads; others shared the trill of young girls laughing.

I could see a figure standing just below the babbling sphere. It was holding something above its head, hoisting it like an offering. Something small.

The figure had to be Austin.

Every step I took toward the silo increased the volume and the intensity of the noises. I kept my head down and my hands clamped against the sides of my head and as I entered the silo.

The aged brick that composed the tower's shell rattled, chunks of it raining down. I made my way to the ladder and began my ascent, watching as some of the wooden rungs were shaken loose, their binding nails spat out. Collapse was the only thing on my mind, and for a beat I actually paused, wondering if my friend was worth my life.

I never gave myself time to answer, at least not intellectually. Instinct pushed me up the final rungs.

Expecting to be met with great resistance, I bashed at the trapdoor in the ceiling with all the force I could muster and was shocked when it flipped open with ease.

I crawled up, my head turned downward. The noise was a blasting wind, the force of which pinned me to the rooftop.

"Austin!"

My voice, human and puny as it was, must have startled whatever presence was there, for the light shrank more still. I looked up to see Austin turning to face me.

The light was slinking back into his gaping mouth.

It swam over his tongue like fish in a bowl. Austin's expression was emotionless, as if caging this babbling light inside his skull was as natural as drawing air.

The bundle in his arms was not a child. Not any longer. It was now as ruined as the woman in the kitchen.

"Austin . . ." I gasped, "the police . . . they found out."

He shut his mouth and swallowed, and just like that the light went out, the chorus fell silent.

"It's no good . . ." he belched. "I can't make it last."

I lifted my hands, a gesture of passivity. "Austin . . . why? You kidnapped all those women . . . those *kids*. The police can't even *identify* them, they're so mangled. Why would you *do* this?"

Austin tipped the mess he'd been cradling over the rim of the silo wall. The child would not have felt the impact after its fall.

"Oh, *God!*"

That was all my friend could manage. The sobs that tore out of him were so genuine that they were, in some ways, even more powerful than the babble of the purple light.

"I can't . . . I can't be without them, Elliott . . . I *need* them!"

I crouched down to where Austin had crumpled. The air was cold and held the reek of roofing tar. I put my hand on Austin's shoulder.

"I just wanted to use it, use the Word my cousin and I heard up here that summer. My cousin couldn't handle it; the Word ended up killing him. But I just thought . . . I just thought if I could talk their flesh in just the right way, if could speak the vessels into resembling them, I could get them back. That's all I wanted, to feel my wife again . . . to hold my little boy . . ."

"I know, Austin . . . but it's over. You understand me? It's *over*."

Austin told me no. "It can't end. As much as I'd like to believe you, it can't end because *I* can't end!"

He turned his arms over, exposing the wide rips in his wrists. Like auxiliary mouths, the wounds stretched as Austin moved his arms. Not a single drop of blood escaped the would-be-fatal gashes.

"After I failed with the first woman, trying to talk her into Liz's form, I tried to end it, Elliot. I was prepared to take the chance that I might join them in the hereafter. But it was already too late. I'd strayed too far from the scheme of things. I'm damned, Elliot. All I can do is keep on. I have to see it through in the hope that the Word will work."

"You're a wanted man," I said. "You'll be an immortal in a cell."

"I need more time."

"But it won't *be* Liz, Austin. Even if you can get body to look like her, it won't *be* her, and you know it."

Austin knitted his fingers and pressed them against his brow.

"I want out, Elliott . . ."

We talked more, and all the while a lone image haunted me: that of Austin, who had already endured more than most men could bear, being trapped inside a concrete cell; a deathless man whose body was already a prison, trapped further still. Like Job, Austin seemed born to suffer.

My suggestion for a possible solution struck me early in our conversation, but I spent a long while weighing its merits, its implications and its dangers for hours before I finally uttered:

"Teach me the Word, Austin."

He peered at me, as if trying to discover whether I was mocking him or had taken leave of my senses.

"Tell me," I repeated. "The police can't find someone who isn't here anymore, not really. And you . . . well, it's not ideal, but maybe you can keep searching for Liz. She won't need a vessel if you don't have one either."

Austin thought for a long and silent spell before shaking his head. "No, it won't work. It will never . . ."

"Then give me an alternative."

Of course, there was none.

Austin crawled down through the trapdoor.

We hunched in the cobwebbed coldness of the silo's loft. The carpet of grain and blown snow looked a thousand miles beneath us. I took in a deep breath. Austin shut his eyes, opened his mouth.

I had expected a sound—not a word in my native tongue, but something that at least *sounded*. But the Word did not sound—it pushed and blinded and burned.

The purplish light I'd seen in the sphere was now a dense ultraviolet blast that pushed into me, like a phallus puncturing a maidenhead. The air was pressed from my lungs; an electric heat fused my bones.

There was a swelling, a great mushroom cloud moving up my spine that threatened to shatter my head if I didn't vent its lethal pressure.

I opened my mouth to howl, to give voice to what I was enduring.

What came vomiting out was a serpentine finger of purple light.

The Word.

It left my mouth and shot knowingly, hungrily for Austin.

And oh how eagerly it went to work on him.

I toppled back as Austin was lifted, weightless as a windborne feather, into the electric cloud.

His flesh was the first to come apart, unravelling in an intricate grid, like threads, a skeleton of skin.

The blood must have evaporated the instant the Word kissed it, for Austin's transmutation from body to light was tidy and swift; a process that had honed itself over countless eons. Bits of light spat off the whole like globules of sperm, they landed on the loft platform, trying to infuse life into the long-dead wood.

If bliss can be known by something bodiless, there was much of it in the light's task of turning Austin into a protean Thing, an evolution I observed until my own lights went out.

That night I shovelled up the slop that had once been two human beings and buried it in the field.

I still keep my townhouse in the city, my job, the veneer of a banal life. But the majority of my time is spent here. I keep the property up as best I can, if only to show any passersby that the house is indeed inhabited. I need to avoid anyone squatting in the house, the barn, and most importantly, the silo.

Last spring I re-tarred the silo's roof and patched any holes in the mortar. The storm of purple light that lurks within is now all but invisible to the world.

I visit Austin frequently and have grown accustomed to the babbling chorus and the gooey sound of churning flesh. There are numerous faces in the violet light, but any resemblance to Austin's or Liz's or Will's is, I fear, pure projection on my part. Occasionally I can lull myself into believing that my poor friend has achieved some type of reunion in that primordial soup, but I've come to appreciate that gazing into the visible Word is like studying a vast inkblot: what one sees is what one impresses upon it.

My body ages, but I know that death is no more an option for me than it was for Austin. I hope one day to find another who is willing to take over my role as guardian. But I fear the only option left for me is to try and find a way—likely in vain—to turn the Word upon myself.

⊸◇⊸

INTO THE PENNY ARCADE

CLAIRE MASSEY

She walked down the same street every day on her way home from school. There were no houses along there, just old warehouses with boarded-up windows and rubbish-plugged holes. Red brick dust crumbled from the walls and made patterns on the pavement. Greyish-green moss grew in all the cracks.

The lorry hadn't ever been there before. It was dark blue with no writing on the side. She crossed away from it, walked faster. Her rucksack dug into her right shoulder, textbooks bounced against her spine, her heels snapped on the pavement. There were no other sounds. The street was like a tunnel; the wind sucked her along it. She emerged into the real world at the other end: cars bombing past, chip shop smell, a mum with a buggy yelling at a kid who was lagging behind.

The lorry was there again the next day. She crossed over. There were girls who got snatched. Men who did things to girls. It would be dark inside that lorry. Was it always going to be there now? Had it moved during the day whilst she was at school, or at night after she'd passed it? And then come back.

She heard him before she ever saw him. One afternoon there was hammering coming from within the lorry's blue walls; another, whistling. One morning there was a big wooden box on the pavement beside the lorry.

It was getting darker earlier, and colder. On a Monday night, when the sky was thick with clouds and the pavement coated with a dust-thin layer of snow, he was stood against the back doors of the lorry as she walked past. He smiled at her. Flicked his fag towards the drain. He wore a long black coat. He was older than her dad, his thin grey hair pulled back in a ponytail. She looked down and speeded up. The doors clanged shut.

If she hadn't left late because of helping Miss Forrest clean up the art room, she wouldn't have seen the fight. Wouldn't have heard the thud of Rachel Greenhalgh's platform shoes against the head of the girl on the pavement, or the shrieks of the girls who cheered her on. They wouldn't have seen her get her phone out and come after her instead.

"Oi, bitch, what do you think you're doing?"

"Get her."

Footsteps drummed on the pavement. She ran down the street. Icy air stung her throat, a stitch pierced her side. She slipped, scraped knees, dropped phone. Ran again. A silence opened up behind her. There was muffled laughter. Something hit her head.

"Good shot!"

Another crack. Something sharper. A trickle down the back of her neck.

He was by the back doors of the lorry again. She saw the arc of glowing ash as he flicked his fag away. She didn't cross to the other side. He stepped back up into the lorry. She thought he was going to pull the doors closed, but he turned and held out his hand to her. "I will help," he said.

She had expected to step into darkness, but the roof was full of sky. The screech of a bolt made her jump. Then the girls were outside, hammering on the doors and sides.

"What you gonna do to her in there?"

"Can we watch?"

"Paedo. Paedo. Paedo. Paedo."

"Sit down," he said, his voice muffled by the chanting.

The lorry was packed with wooden cases and cardboard boxes. She wasn't sure where she should sit so she slid into a small space on the floor. She put the tips of her fingers to the back of her head. It was wet. She pulled them away and looked at the blood.

"I will get you something," he said. He reached down a cardboard box and started rooting through it.

The blood was pooling at the base of her neck, beneath her collar. Her mum was going to kill her. He pulled down another box.

There was more stuff in the lorry than should have been possible. The wooden cases looked like machines. They had glass fronts and signs, like the arcade games on Southport pier.

He handed her a shirt. "I was trying to find you a cloth but they are all dirty."

The shirt was an off-white colour and it smelt like petrol. She held it against the back of her head and felt a strange raw numbness.

"Do you need some water? I have got that or oil." He smiled at his own joke.

She shook her head and the movement carried on after she stopped. She pressed her forehead to her knees and let her eyes close.

"They have gone now," he said.

The sky had shifted towards darkness. Huge grey clouds lay flat against the transparent roof. The lorry was full of dark shapes and shadows. Her head throbbed. She could hear a faint hammering coming from somewhere. The floor creaked as she shifted her weight to get up.

"Are you feeling better?"

She tried to find his outline, but couldn't. Above her, inside the machine she had been leant against, was a horrible pale face with a wide red smile. She crouched, fingertips splayed on the grimy floor.

"Are you scared?" His thin face appeared above her in the grey light. In his long black coat, he could have been a shadow with a mask. "Do not be scared, the streetlight will come on soon. I have candles, but they are in the box on top of the Allwin beside you. I did not want to disturb you."

He had a small hammer in one hand. As he reached over her head she curled up tighter. "I always park in a place like this. Let someone else pay for the light."

The streetlight snapped on above them.

The machines looked even stranger in the new light. Brass knobs and metal signs and slots shone. Her breath made orange clouds in the freezing air.

"I will still light some candles, so you can look properly."

He spoke slowly, as though he had to think about each word before he said it. She gently separated the damp shirt from her head; it had crusted a little and stuck to her hair in places. The blood on the shirt looked black. She didn't dare touch the wound. It pulsed with pain. "I need to go," she said. She clutched the shirt at her side. "I can wash this."

"Do not worry about it."

She kept hold of the shirt and grabbed her rucksack in her other hand. Her legs were unsteady.

He'd lit several church candles and set them out in a circle on top of an old pinball machine. "So you do not want to play on anything?"

"I need to get home," she said.

"It is not often that I have company." He stood between her and the doors. 'This one is a 1933 Allwin. The Wizard. You must have a turn. I have got a basket of pennies here, look."

She looked at the bolts. She thought she'd heard him shut one, but there were three and a padlock too. "And then can I go?"

"There are a lot of Allwins left. What makes this one special is the way it pays out. Can you see how the coins are stacked end to end in the vertical channel? If you can get the ball in a winning hole it will release one. Take a penny now, put it in."

He hadn't hurt her. He'd locked the girls out. He'd helped her. If she did as he said then surely he'd let her go. She put her bag down and took hold of a too big, too heavy penny. She pushed it into the slot. It landed somewhere inside the machine with a hollow clink.

"Now flick the lever."

She pulled at the lever with numb fingers and a small silver ball skipped into a metal spiral then dropped back down.

"Better luck next time."

"I have to go home now."

"I have one you will like. It is a special treat." He disappeared into a narrow gap between machines. "Roll up, roll up, step this way for the Shocker."

She looked back at the locked doors, then up at the sky, which seemed lighter again. It had started to snow. The floor dipped beneath her feet as she crossed to the gap and slipped in. She felt like she was walking into a wooden maze.

He beckoned her to a small machine on the wall, a little way in. It was dark and plain-looking, apart from a small brass plaque that said "Electricity is Life" and a metal handle at either side.

She took a step back and slammed into another machine.

He smiled. "No? Never mind, it is in need of some repairs, anyway." He signalled for her to turn. "We will find something else for you."

She was relieved to emerge closer to the doors, in what now felt like a larger space. She counted the bolts again, considered the padlock. She looked up into the falling snow, which made her head lurch. She steadied herself against the machine behind her.

"Now then, I have got two Catchers, a Crosset Pickwick, and a Trapper. Let us have a go on the Trapper." He held the basket out to her again. "Take one."

She took a penny and followed him into another ginnel. He stopped before a tall, narrow machine. "There are four levers to control this one. It is a 1909 machine. The balls were still made of bone then."

She pushed the penny in and pressed on the levers, which were like old typewriter keys. The sensation of being trapped between the machines was overwhelming. Her head hurt. She wanted to be sick. She wanted to close her eyes.

"Do not worry, it takes practice. Now you must go back again."

She shuffled backwards towards the doors. White specks had begun to clump together on the roof. She was quietly being buried under the snow. 'Thank you for showing me your machines, but I don't feel well, I really have to go home now.'

"But there is still so much to see, for instance you have not even asked me about this gentleman here." He rapped on the glass in front of the pale face with the wide red smile that had scared her. She could see now it was a doll with a sailor's hat and tunic on. Two limp hands rested on its bunched-up legs.

"What does it do?"

"You must put a penny in to see."

She took a penny and pushed it into the slot. There was a grinding noise. The sailor's body jerked to life. It rocked and shuddered with laughter but its glass eyes remained steady on her. She had to look away.

"Nobody likes my friend the sailor." He shook his head. He had positioned himself in front of the doors again.

She needed to get him to move so she could at least try the bolts. "What's that one, over there?" She pointed to the small pyramid that rose from the top of a machine somewhere in the middle.

He stayed where he was. "The Pharaoh's Tomb. It is a Working Model. I have several—The Iron Maiden, The Guillotine, Buried Alive—but they are delicate. Every time we have to move, it damages their mechanisms. Some are still missing figures too."

Snow had blocked out the sky and the roof shone a crystalline orange. "My head hurts. My mum's going to be getting really worried. Please will you let me go?"

"You must have your fortune told first."

Her hand shook as she took the penny he held out to her. She took deep breaths, trying to stop the panic, as she followed him back into the first passage. He stopped at a machine with a big dial on it. The sign said "The Oracle".

"You must set the pointer to the question you would like to be answered and turn the dial."

The writing was blurred, she tried to concentrate. "Will my sweetheart be rich?"; "Will I have a large family?' She hesitated over "Will I be happy?" but picked "Will my wish come true?"

"Now put the penny in."

The answer—"Yes"—appeared in white letters in a little black window at the top.

He nodded and took a key from his pocket. She turned and stumbled back towards the doors. He must have taken a different route because he arrived there before her. He unlocked the padlock and slipped back the three bolts on the door. Only one made a noise. She stepped down into the fresh snow.

She only realised she'd left her bag in the lorry when she got to the chip shop. She still had his shirt, crisp with blood, gripped in her hand.

The sound of dripping water was everywhere. The snow had gone to slush and the sky to drizzle. She'd been allowed to stay off school. She told her Mum she'd slipped on some ice and cracked her head on the kerb. She knew she would have to go back to the lorry to get her bag. Before she went to bed, she washed his shirt in the bathroom sink, thinking she could give it to him as a thank you, an exchange. The blood and grime wouldn't come out with hand soap so she put a splash of toilet cleaner in the water too. She hid the shirt under a towel on the radiator in her room. When she managed to sleep, she dreamt of being locked in a medicine cupboard full of trees.

The slush pushed in over the sides of her shoes; her socks squelched as she walked. She didn't want to have to go back inside the lorry, to get trapped looking at his machines again. She'd knock, ask for her bag, hand him the shirt and go.

Around the lorry, the slush was churned up with footsteps. The back doors were slightly ajar. They were dented and scratched too, like someone had pounded them with something. "Hello," she said.

If the girls had come back and done this it would be her fault. She pulled gently at one door and they both swung open. Inside, the floor was heaped with splintered wood and glass. Some of the machines lay on their sides with gouged wooden bodies, others had been pulled from the walls. The trailer stank of piss and smoke. Rain pattered on the roof. "Hello."

She stepped up into the debris. The lorry seemed smaller now fewer machines were standing. The passageways had disappeared. The sailor's head was at her feet. His fingers had been snapped off and pushed into his eyes and mouth. She carried on, clambered over wrecked machines, shuddered as things crunched and gave way beneath her. What if she stood on a hand or a leg? He could be underneath all this.

At first, she thought the tapping noise was just the rain on the roof, but it got louder, more insistent. It was coming from inside one of the machines, one that was still standing. "The Iron Maiden," its sign said. He hadn't shown her this one. Maybe it was a broken mechanism clicking over and over. The glass pane had gone. She could reach in and open the metal coffin in the corner, if she wanted to. There was knocking coming from somewhere else too. She followed the sound to a machine towards the back, "Buried Alive". Inside, a solitary gravestone, marked R.I.P., stood over what looked like trapdoors.

Tapping and knocking. For a second she thought she could hear muffled voices. A miniature scream.

She dropped his shirt. As she picked her way back through the shards towards the doors, her foot caught in the strap of a rucksack. It had Tipp-Ex writing on it, "Rich loves Jonas". It wasn't hers. She stepped down into the grey slush and pushed the doors to.

The next day the lorry had gone.

⋅◦⋅

MAGDALA AMYGDALA

LUCY A. SNYDER

I was bound, though I have not bound.
I was not recognized. But I have recognized
that the All is being dissolved,
both the earthly and the heavenly.
—The Gospel of Mary Magdalene

"So how are you feeling?" Dr. Shapiro's pencil hovers over the CDC risk evaluation form clamped to her clipboard.

"Pretty good." When I talk, I make sure my tongue stays tucked out of sight. I smile at her in a way that I hope looks friendly, and not like I'm baring my teeth. The exam-room mirror reflects the back of the good doctor's head. Part of me wishes the silvered glass were angled so I could check my expression; the rest of me is relieved that I can't see myself.

Nothing existed before this. The present and recent past keep blurring together in my mind, but I've learned to take a moment before I reply to questions, speak a little more slowly to give myself the chance to sort things out before I utter something that might sound abnormal. My waking world seems to have been taken apart and put back together so that everything is just slightly off, the geometries of reality deranged.

Most of my memories before the virus are as insubstantial as dreams; the strongest of them feel like borrowed clothing. The sweet snap of peas fresh from my garden. The thud of the bass from the huge speakers, and the crush of hot perfumed bodies against mine at the club. The pleasant twin burns of the sun on my shoulders and the exertion in my legs as I pedal my bike up the mountainside.

The life I had in those memories is gone forever. I don't know why this is happening to humanity. To me. I'd like to think there's some greater purpose, some meaning in all this, but God help me, I just can't see it.

"So is the new job going well? Are you able to sleep?" My doctor shines a penlight in my eyes and nostrils and marks off a couple of boxes. Thankfully, she doesn't ask to see my tongue. It's the same set of questions every week; I'd have to be pretty far gone to answer badly and get myself quarantined. The endless doctor-visits wear down other Type Threes, but I hang onto the belief that someday there might be actual help for me here.

I nod. "It's fine. I have blackout curtains; sleep's not a problem. They seem pretty happy with my work."

My new supervisor is a friendly guy, but he always has an excuse for why he can't meet with me in person, preferring to call me on his cell phone for our weekly chats. I used to bounce from building to building, repairing computers, spending equal amounts of time swapping gossip and hardware. After I got out of the hospital, I went on the graveyard shift in the company's cold network operations center. These nights, I'm mostly raising processes from the dead, watching endless scrolling green text on cryptic black screens. I'm pretty sure the company discreetly advised my quiet coworkers to carry tasers and mace just in case.

"Do you feel that you're able to see your old friends and family often enough?" Dr. Shapiro asks.

"Sure," I lie. "We meet online for games and we talk in Vent. It's fun."

For the sake of his own health, my boyfriend took a job and apartment in another state; we speak less and less on the phone. What is there to say to him now? We can't even chat about anything as simple as food or wine; I must subsist on bananas, rice, apple juice, and my meager allotment of six Bovellum capsules per day. The law says I can't go to crowded places like theaters and concerts. I only glimpse the sun when I'm hurrying from the shelter of my car's darkly tinted windows to monthly eight a.m. appointments with my court-ordered physician.

So I'm striding up the street to Dr. Shapiro's office, my head down, squinting behind sunglasses, when suddenly I hear a man in the park across the street shouting violent nonsense. Or he used to be a man, anyhow; he's wearing construction boots, ragged Carhartt's work overalls and a dirty grey T-shirt, all freshly spattered with the blood of the woman whose head he is enthusiastically cracking open against the curb. He howls at the sky, and I can see he's missing some teeth. Probably whatever he did for a living didn't pay him enough to see a dentist. But his skin looks flush and smooth, so much healthier than mine, and for a moment I envy him.

He stops howling and meets my shadowed stare, breaking into a gory, gap-toothed smile. The kind of grin you give an old, dear friend. I've never laid eyes on this wreck before, and the woman beneath him is beyond anyone's help. They both are. I don't want to be outed, not here, not like this, so I pretend I don't even see him and stride on.

A few seconds later, I hear the spat of rifle fire and the thud of a meaty body hitting the pavement, and I know that the SWAT team just took out Ragged Carhartts. They're never far away, not in this part of town. And once they've taken out one Type Three, they don't need much excuse to kill another, even if you're just trying to see your doctor like a good citizen.

"Oh, God," a lady says. She and another fortyish woman are standing in the doorway of an art gallery, staring horrified at the scene behind me. They're both wearing batik dresses and lots of handmade jewelry. "That's the third one this month."

"If this keeps up, we'll have to close." The other woman shakes her head, looking grey-faced. "Nobody will want to come here. The whole downtown will die. Not just us. The theaters, the museums, churches—everything."

"I heard something on NPR about a new kind of gel to keep the virus from spreading," the first woman replies, sounding hopeful.

I keep moving. Her voice fades away. People still talk about contagion control as if it matters, as if masks and sanitizers and prayers can stop the future.

The truth is, unless you've been living in some isolated Tibetan monastery, you've already been exposed to Polymorphic Viral Gastroencephalitis. Maybe it gave you a bit of a headache and some nausea, but after a few days' bed rest you were going out for Thai again. Congratulations! You're Type One and you probably don't even know it.

But maybe the headache turned into the worst you've ever had, and you started vomiting up blood and then your stomach lining, and when you came out of the hospital you'd lost the ability to digest most foods and to make certain proteins. And in the absence of those proteins, your body has trouble growing and healing. The enzymes your DNA uses to repair itself don't work very well anymore.

Sunlight is no longer your friend. Neither are x-rays. Even if you quit smoking and keep yourself covered up like a virgin in the Rub' Al Khali, your skin cracks and your body sprouts tumors. Your brain begins to degenerate; you start talking to yourself in second person. Sooner or later, you develop lesions on your frontal lobe and hippocampus that cause a variety of behaviors which will lead to your friendly neighborhood SWAT team putting a .308 bullet through your skull. That means you're a Type Two, or maybe a Type Three, like me.

If you're Type Four, we aren't having this conversation. Unless you're a ghost. You aren't a ghost, are you? I don't think I believe in them. But if you were a Type Four, your whole GI tract got stripped. I hope you were lucky and had a massive brain bleed right when it got really bad, and you never woke up.

I'm pretty sure I woke up.

"Do you find yourself having any unwanted thoughts or violent fantasies?" Dr. Shapiro asks.

"Of course not." I try to sound mildly indignant.

There's one upside, if it can be called that. If you lived past all the pain and vomiting, the symptoms of your chronic disease can be alleviated, if you consume sufficient daily quantities of one of a couple of raw protein sources.

If the best protein source for you is fresh human blood, congratulations, you are a Type Two! Provided you have a fat bank account, or decent health insurance, or are quick with a razor and fast on your feet, you can resume puberty or your athletic career. Watch out for HIV; it's a killer.

If, however, the best source for you comes from sweet, custard-like brains . . . you are a Type Three. Your situation is much more problematic.

And expensive. You better have a wealthy family or truly excellent insurance. Or mob connections. Otherwise, sooner or later, you'll end up trying to crack open someone's skull in public. The only question then is if you'll get that one moment of true gustatory bliss right before you die.

I have excellent health insurance. There's no bliss for me. What I and every other upstanding, gainfully-employed, fully-covered Type Three citizen gets is an allotment of refrigerated capsules containing an unappetizing grey paste. Mostly it's cow brains and antioxidant vitamins with just the barest hint of pureed cadaver white matter. It's enough to keep your skin and brains from ulcerating. It's enough to keep your nose from rotting off. It's enough to help you think clearly enough to function at your average white-collar job.

It is not enough to keep you from constantly wishing you could taste the real thing.

"I was wondering about something," I say, as Dr. Shapiro begins to copy the contents of her survey into the exam room computer.

She stops typing and gives me a wary smile. "Yes, what is it?"

"My medication. I feel okay, you know? But I think I could feel . . . better. If I could have a little more?" I'm choosing my words as carefully as possible. My tongue feels thick, twitchy.

I can't talk about the cravings I'm feeling. I can't mention wanting more energy, because nobody in charge wants someone like me feeling energetic.

I wonder if there's a sniper watching from behind the mirror on the wall; has he tightened his grip on his rifle? Are gas canisters waiting to blow in the air conditioner vent above me? My skin itches in dread anticipation.

Dr. Shapiro hedges. "Well, I know there's been a shortage of raw materials these days."

I swallow down my impatience and worry. The capsules are ninety-eight percent cow brains, for God's sake. Probably they can squeeze a single human brain for thousands of doses. There are a hundred babies stillborn every day in big city hospitals; some of the mothers have to be altruists. I can't imagine the pharmaceutical companies are running short of anything.

"Could you check, just the same? Could you ask for me?" I sound meek. Pathetic. The opposite of hostile. That's good.

She gives me a pitying look and sighs. The mirror doesn't explode in gunfire. Gas doesn't burst from the vents.

"I'll see what I can do," my doctor says.

I try to believe she'll come through for me.

I go home. I take my capsules with some Mott's apple juice. I rinse my mouth out with peroxide and don't look at my tongue. I rub salve on the places my clothes have rubbed raw, and I climb naked into my bed. Sometime later, the alarm goes off, and I rise, shower, dress, and drive to work in darkness.

My shift is dull-clockwork, until just after grey drizzling dawn, when one of the new tech leads comes in to talk to my coworker George about some of the emergency server protocols. I haven't seen this young man before; he's wearing snug jeans and the sleeves of his black polo shirt are tight over biceps tattooed with angels and devils. His blond hair is cut close over a smooth, high-browed skull. He starts talking about database errors, but he's thinking about a gig he has with his band on Friday night, and it suddenly hits me not just that I know what he's thinking but that I know because I can smell the sweet chemicals shifting inside his brain. The chemicals tell me his name is Devin.

I am filled with Want in the marrow of my bones. I am filled with Need from eyeballs to soles. I excuse myself and hurry out into the mutagenic morning and punch Betty's number into my cell. Soon after we met, she made me promise not to save her details in my phone, just in case anything went wrong.

It's early for her. But she answers on the third ring. Speaking in the casual code we've used since we met online, we agree to meet that evening. It's her turn to host.

I sleep fitfully. When my alarm goes off, I call in sick, shower, dress, and check my phone. Betty's texted a cryptic string of letters and numbers for my directions. And so I drive out to a hotel we've never visited before, drinking Aquafinas the whole way. It's a dark old place, once grand, now crumbling away in a forgotten corner of downtown. I wonder if she's running short of money or if the extra anonymity of the place was crucial to her.

Still, as I get out my car and double-check my locks in the pouring rain, I can't help but peer out into the oppressive black spaces in the parking lot, trying to figure out if any of the shadows between the other vehicles could be lurking cops or CDC agents. The darkness doesn't move, so I hurry to the front door, head down, hands jammed in my raincoat pockets, my stomach roiling with worry and anticipation. I avoid making eye contact with any of the damp, tired-looking prostitutes smoking outside the hotel's front doors. None of them pay any attention to me.

My phone chimes as Betty texts me the room number. I take the creaking, urine-stinking elevator up four floors. My pace slows as I walk down the stained hallway carpet, and I pause for a moment before I knock on the door of Room 512. What if the watchers tapped Betty's phone? What if she's not here at all? My poised hand quivers as my heart seems to pound out "A trap—a trap—a trap."

I swallow. Knock twice. Step back. A moment later, Betty answers the door, wearing her Audrey Hepburn wig and a black cocktail dress that hangs limply from her skeletal shoulders. It's appalling how much weight she's lost; her eyes have turned entirely black, the whites permanently stained by repeated hemorrhages.

But she smiles at me, and I find myself smiling back, warmed by the first spark of real human feeling I've had in months. I have to believe that we're still human. I *have* to.

"You ready?" Her question creaks like the hinge of a forgotten gate.

"Absolutely." My own voice is the dry fluttering of moth wings.

She locks the door behind me. "I'm sorry this place is such a pit, but the guy at the Holiday Inn started asking all kinds of questions, and this was the best I could do on short notice."

"It's okay." The room isn't as seedy as the lobby and exterior led me to expect it to be, and it's got a couch in addition to the queen-sized bed. Betty has already covered the couch and the carpet in front of it with a green plastic tarpaulin. Her stainless steel spritzer bottle leans against a couch arm.

"Want some wine?" She gestures toward an unopened bottle of Yellow Tail Shiraz on the dresser.

"Thanks, but no . . . I couldn't drink it right now. Maybe after."

She nods. "There's a really good Italian restaurant around the corner. Kind of a Goodfellas hangout, but everything's homemade. Great garlic bread."

Betty pulls off the wig. Before she got the virus, she could grow her thick chestnut hair clear down to her waist. I've never seen it except in pictures; her bare scalp gleams pale in the yellow light from the chandelier.

The scar circumscribing her skull looks red, inflamed; I wonder if she's been seeing other Type Threes. I quickly tamp down my pang of jealousy. We never agreed to an exclusive arrangement. And maybe she just had to go to the hospital instead; she told me she's got some kind of massive tumor on her pituitary.

She looks so frail. I can't possibly begrudge her what comfort she can get. I should just be grateful that she agrees to see me when I need her.

And, oh sweet Lord, do I need her tonight.

Betty pulls me down to her for a kiss. Her hands are icy, but her lips are warm. She slips her tongue into my mouth, and I can taste sweet cerebrospinal fluid mingled in her saliva. The tumor must have cracked the bony barriers in her skull. Before I have a chance to try to pull away, my own tongue is swelling, toothed pores opening and nipping at her slippery flesh.

She squeaks in pain and we separate.

"Sorry," I try to whisper. But my tongue is continuing to engorge and lengthen, curling back on itself and slithering down my own throat; I can feel the tiny maws rasping against my adenoids.

"It's okay." Her wan smile is smeared with blood. "We better get started."

She kisses the palm of my hand and begins to take my clothes off. I stare up at the tawdry chandelier, watching a fly buzz among the dusty baubles and bulbs. When I'm naked, she slips off her cocktail dress and leads me to the tarp-covered couch.

"Be gentle." She presses a short oyster knife into my hand and sits me down, the plastic crackling beneath me. I nod, barely keeping my lips closed over my shuddering tongue, and spread my legs.

With slow exhalation, Betty settles between my thighs, her back to me. She's a tiny woman, her head barely clearing my chin when we're seated, so this position works best. Her skin is already covered in goose bumps. The anticipation is killing both of us.

I carefully run the tip of the sharp oyster knife through the red scar around her skull; there's relatively little blood as I cut through the tissue.

Betty gives a little gasp and grips my knees, her whole body tensed. The bone has only stitched back together in a few places; I use the side-to-side motion she showed me to gently pry the lid of her skull free.

She moans when I expose her brain; it's the most beautiful thing I could hope to see. Her dura mater glistens with a half-inch slick of golden jelly. Brain honey. When I breathe in the smell of her, I feel my blood pressure rise hard and fast.

I set the bowl of skin and bone aside and present the knife to her in my outstretched left hand. With a flick of her wrist, she slits the vein in the crook of my arm and presses her mouth against my bleeding flesh. I wrap my cut arm around her head and pull her tight to my breast.

I open my mouth and let my tongue unwind like an eel into her brainpan. It wriggles there, purple and gnarled, the tiny maw sucking down her golden jelly. It's delicious, better than caviar, better than ice cream, better than anything I've had in my mouth before. Sweet and salty and tangy and perfect.

The jelly gives me flashes of her memories and dreams; she's been with other Type Threes. She's helped them murder people. I don't care. I keep drinking her in, my tongue probing all the corners of her skull and sheathed wrinkles of her brain to get every last gooey drop.

I can control my tongue, but just barely. It's hard to keep it from doing the one thing I'd dearly love, which is to drive it through her membrane deep between her slippery lobes. But that would be the end of her. The end of us. No more, all over, bye bye.

A little of what my body and soul craves is better than nothing at all. Isn't it?

My arm aches, and I'm starting to feel lightheaded on top of the high. We're both running dry. I release her, spritz her brain with saline and carefully put the top of her head back into place. She's full of my blood, and already her scalp is sealing back together. We've done well; we spilled hardly anything on the tarp this time. But my face feels sticky, and I've probably even gotten her in my hair.

She daintily wipes my blood from the corners of her mouth and smiles at me. Her skin is pink and practically glowing, and her boniness seems chic rather than diseased. "Want to go to that Italian place after we get cleaned up?"

"Sure." I'm probably glowing, too. My stomach feels strong enough for pepperoncinis.

I head to the bathroom to wash my face, but when I push open the door—

—I find myself in Dr. Shapiro's office. She's staring down at an MRI scan of somebody's chest. The monochrome bones look strange, distorted.

"There's definitely a mass behind your ribs and spine. It's growing fast, but I can't definitely say it's cancer."

I'm dizzy with terror. How did I get here? What mass? How long have I had a mass?

"What should we do?" I stammer.

She looks up at me with eyes as solidly black as Betty's. "I think we should wait and see."

I back away, turn, push through her office door—

—and I'm back in a rented room. But not the downtown dive with the dusty chandelier. It's a suburban motel someplace. Have I been here before?

The green tarp on the king-sized bed is covered in blood and bits of skull. There's a body wrapped in black trash bags, stuffed between the bed and the writing desk. Did I do that? What have I done?

Oh, God, please make this stop. I have to lean against the wall to keep myself from tumbling backward.

Betty comes out of the bathroom, dressed in a spattered silk negligee. I think it used to be white. There's gore in her wig. Her eyes go wide.

"I told you not to come here!" She grabs me by my arm, surprising me with her strength. In the distance, I can hear sirens. "They'll be here any minute—get away from here, fast as you can!"

She presses a set of rental car keys into my palm, hauls me to the door and pushes me out into the hallway—

—and I'm stepping into the elevator at work.

Handsome blond Devin is in there. A look of surprised fear crosses his face, and I know the very sight of me repels him. His hand goes to his jeans pocket. I see the outline of something that's probably a canister of pepper spray. It's too small to be a taser.

But then he pauses, smiles at me. "Hey, you going up to that training class?"

I nod mechanically, and try to say "Sure," but my lungs spasm and suddenly I'm doubled over, coughing into my hands. When did simply breathing start hurting this much?

"You okay?" Devin asks.

I try to nod, but there's bright blood on my palms. A long-forgotten Bible verse surfaces in the swamp of my memory: *Behold, I am vile; what shall I answer thee? I will lay mine hand upon my mouth.*

I look up and see my reflection in the chromed elevator walls—my face is gaunt, but my body is grotesquely swollen. I've turned into some kind of hunchback. How long have I had the mass?

Instead of the pepper spray, Devin's pulled his cell phone out. I can smell his mind. He's torn between wanting to run away and wanting to help. "Should I call someone? Should I call 911?"

The elevator is filled with the scent of him. Despite my pain and sickness, the Want returns with a vengeance. Adrenaline rises along with my blood pressure. My tongue is twitching, and something in my back, too. I can feel it tearing my ribs away from my spine. It hurts more than I can remember anything ever hurting. Maybe childbirth would be like this.

Betty. I need Betty. How long has it been since I've seen her? Oh God.

"Call 911," I try to say, but I can't take a breath, can't speak around the tongue writhing backward down my throat.

"What can I do?" Devin touches my shoulder.

And the feel of his hand against my bony flesh is far too much for me to bear.

I rise up under him, grab him by the sides of his head, kissing him. My tongue goes straight down his throat, choking him. He hits me, trying to shake me off, but as strong as he is, my Want is stronger.

When he's unconscious, I let him fall and hit the emergency stop button. The Want has me wrapped tightly in its ardor, burning away all my human qualms. The alarm is an annoyance, and I know I don't have as much time as I want. Still. As I lift his left eyelid, I take a moment to admire his perfect bluebonnet-iris.

And then I plunge my tongue into his eye. The ball squirts off to the side as my organ drills deeper, the tiny mouths rasping through the thin socket bone into his sweet frontal lobe. After the first wash of cerebral fluid I'm into the creamy white meat of him, and—

—Oh, God. This is more beautiful than I imagined.

I'm devouring his will. Devouring his memories. Living him, through and through. His first taste of wine. His first taste of a woman. The first time he stood onstage. He's at the prime of his life, and oh, it's been a wonderful life, and I am memorizing every second of it as I swallow down the contents of his lovely skull.

When he's empty, I rise from his shell and feel my new wings break free from the cage of my back. As I spread them wide in the elevator, I realize I can hear the old gods whispering to me from their thrones in the dark spaces between the stars.

I smile at myself in the distorted chrome walls. Everything is clear to me now. I have been chosen. I have a purpose. Through the virus, the old gods tested me, and deemed me worthy of this holiest of duties. There are others like me; I can hear them gathering in the caves outside the city. Some died, yes, like the ragged man, but my Becoming is almost complete. Nothing as simple as a bullet will stop me then.

The Earth is ripe, human civilization at its peak. I and the other archivists will preserve the memories of the best and brightest as we devour them. We will use the blood of this world to write dark, beautiful poetry across the walls of the universe.

For the first time in my life, I don't need faith. I know what I am supposed to do in every atom in every cell of my body. I will record thousands of souls before my masters allow me to join them in the star-shadows, and I will love every moment of my mission.

I can hear the SWAT team rush into the foyer three stories below. Angry ants. I can hear Betty and the others calling to me from the hollow hills. Smiling, I open the hatch in the top of the elevator and prepare to fly.

◄⊙►

FRONTIER DEATH SONG

LAIRD BARRON

Night descended on Interstate-90 as I crossed over into the Badlands. Real raw weather for October. Snow dusted the asphalt and picnic tables of the deserted rest area. The scene was virginal as death.

I parked the Chevy under one of the lamp posts that burned at either end of the lot. A metal building with a canted roof sat low and sleek in the center island, most of its windows dark. Against the black backdrop it reminded me of a crypt or monument to travelers and pioneers lost down through the years. Placards were obscured by shadows and could've pronounced warnings or curses, could've said anything in any language. Reality was pliable tonight.

I loosed Minerva and watched her trot around the perimeter of the sodium glow. She raised her graying snout and growled softly at the void that surrounded us, poured from us. Her tracks and the infrequent firefly sparks on the road were the only signs of life for miles. Snow was falling thick and those small signs wouldn't last long. Periodically a semi chugged along the freeway, its running lights tiny and dim. Other than that, this was the Moon. It was back to the previous ice age for us, the end for us. I kind of, sort of, liked the idea that this might be the end, except for the fact sweet, loyal Minerva hadn't asked for any of it, and my nature, my atavistic shadow, was, as usual, a belligerent sonofabitch. My shadow exhibited the type of nature that causes men to weigh themselves with stones before they jump into the midnight blue, causes them to mix the pills with antifreeze, trade the pistol bullet to the brain for a shotgun barrel in the mouth, just to be on the safe side. My shadow didn't give a shit about odds, or eventualities, or pain, or certain death. It just wanted to keep shining.

So, Minerva pissed in the snow and I ticked off the seconds until the ultimate showdown.

My ear was killing tonight, crackling like a busted radio speaker and ringing with good old tinnitus. The sensation was that of an auger boring through membrane and meat. My back and knee ached. I lost the ear to a virus upon contracting pneumonia in Alaska during a long ago Iditarod. The spine and knee got ruined after I fell off a cliff into the Bering Sea and broke just about everything that was breakable. Resilience was my gift and I'd recovered sufficiently to limp through the remainder of a wasted youth, to fake a hale and hearty demeanor. That shit was surely catching up now at the precipice of the miserable slide into middle age. All those forgotten or ignored wounds blooming in a chorus of ghostly pain, reminders of longstanding debts, reminders that a man can't always outrun provenance.

I checked my watch and the numbers blurred. I hadn't slept in way too long, else I never would've pulled over between Bumfuck, Egypt and Timbuktu. Since suicide by passivity was off the table, this was an expression of stubbornness on my part, probably. Grim defiance, or the need to reassert my faith in the logical operations of the universe if but for a moment.

What a joke, faith. What a sham, logic.

A hunting horn sounded far out there in the darkness beyond the humps and swales and treeless drumlin that went on basically forever, past the vast hungry prairies that had swallowed so many wagon trains.

Oh, yes. The horn of the Hunt bugling my death song.

Not simply a horn, but one that could easily be imagined as the hollowed relic from a giant, perverted ram with blood-specked foam lathering its muzzle and hellfire beaming from its eyes. A ram that crunched the bones of Saxons for breakfast and brandished a cock the girth of a wagon axle;

the kind of brute that tribes sacrificed babies to when crops were bad and mated unfortunate maidens to when the chief needed some special juju on the eve of a war. Its horn was the sort of artifact that stood on end in a petrified coil and would require a brawny Viking raider to lift. Or a demon.

That wail stood my hair on end, slapped me wide awake. It rolled toward the parking lot, swelling like some Medieval air raid klaxon. Snowflakes weren't melting on my cheeks because all the heat, all the blood, went rushing inward. That erstwhile faith in the natural universe, the rational order of reality, wouldn't be troubling me again anytime soon. Nope.

I whistled for Minerva and she leaped into the truck, riding shotgun. Her hackles were bunched. She barked her fury and terror at the night. Sleep, O blessed sleep, how I longed for thee. No time for that. We had to get gone. The Devil would be there soon.

⌐o⌐

Years ago when I raced sled dogs for a living, I knew a fellow named Steven Graham, a disgraced lit professor from the University of Colorado. He'd gotten shitcanned for reasons opaque to my blue collar sensibilities— something to do with privileging contemporary zombie stories over the works of the Russian masters. His past was shrouded in mystery and like a lot people, he'd fled to Alaska to reinvent himself.

Nobody on the racing circuit cared much about any of that. Graham was charming and charismatic in spades. He drank and swore with the best of us, but he'd also get three sheets to the wind and recite a bit of *Beowulf* in Olde English and he knew the bloodlines of huskies from Balto onward. Strap a pair of snowshoes to that lanky greenhorn bastard and he'd leave even the most hardened back country trapper in the proverbial dust. All the girlies adored him, and so did the cameras. Like Cummings said, he was a hell of a handsome man.

Too good to be true.

Steven Graham got taken by the Hunt while he was running the 1992 Iditarod. That's the big winter event where men and women hook a bunch of huskies to sleds and race twelve hundred miles across Alaska from Anchorage to Nome. There's not much to say about it—it's long and grueling and lonely. You're always crossing a frozen swamp or mushing up an ice-jammed river or trudging over a mountain. It's dark and cold and mostly devoid of sound or movement but for one's own breath and the muted panting of the huskies, the jingle and clink of their traces.

Official records have it that Graham, young ex-professor and dilettante adventurer, took a wrong turn out on Norton Sound between Koyuk and Elim and went through the ice into the sea. Ka-sploosh. No trace of him or the dogs was found. The Lieutenant Governor attended the funeral. CNN covered it live.

The report was bullshit, of course; I saw what really happened. And because I saw what really happened, because I meddled in the Hunt, there would be hell to pay.

◂◦▸

Broad daylight, maybe an hour prior to sunset, mid March of 1992.

All twelve dogs in harness trotted along nicely. The end of the trail in Nome was about two days away. Things hadn't gone particularly well and I was cruising for a middle of the pack finish and a long, destitute summer of begging corporate sponsors not to drop my underachieving ass. But damn, what a gorgeous day in the arctic with the snowpack curving around me to the horizon, the sky frozen between apple-green and steely blue, the orange ball of the sun dipping below the Earth. The effect was something out of *Fantasia*. After days of inadequate sleep I was lulled by the hiss of the sled runners, the rhythmic scrape and slap of dog paws. I dozed at the handlebars and dreamed of Sharon, the warmth of our home, a cup of real coffee, a hot shower, and the down comforter on our bed.

When my team passed through a gap in a mile-long pressure ridge that had heaved the Bering ice to an eight-foot tall parapet, the Hunt had taken down Graham on the other side, maybe twenty yards off the main drag. This I discovered when one of Graham's huskies loped toward me, free of its traces yet still in harness. The poor critter's head had been lopped at mid-neck and it zig-zagged several strides and then collapsed in the trail. You'd think my own dogs would've spooked. Instead, an atavistic switch was tripped in their doggy brains and they surged forward, yapping and howling.

Several yards to my right so much blood covered the snow I thought I was hallucinating a sunset dripped onto the ice. The scene confused me for a few seconds as my brain locked down and spun in place.

The killing ground was a fucking mess like there'd been a mass walrus slaughter committed on the spot. Dead huskies were flung about, intestines looped over berms and piled in loose, steaming coils. Graham himself lay spread-eagle across a blue-white slab of ice repurposed as an impromptu sacrificial altar. He was split wide, eyes blank.

The Huntsman had most of the guy's hide off and was tacking it alongside the carcass as one stretches the skin of a beaver or a bear. Clad in a deerstalker hat surmounted by antlers, a blood-drenched mackinaw coat, canvas breeches, and sealskin boots, the Huntsman stood taller than most men even as he hunched to slice Graham with a large knife of flint or obsidian—I wasn't quite close enough to discern which.

Meanwhile, the Huntsman's wolf pack ranged among the butchered huskies. These wolves were black, and gaunt as cadavers; their narrow eyes glinted, reflecting the snow, the changeable heavens. When several of them reared on hind legs to study me, I decided they weren't wolves at all. Some wore olden leather and caps with splintered nubs of horn; others were garbed in the remnants of military fatigues and camouflage jackets of various styles, gore encrusted and ingrown to the creatures' hides. They grinned at me and their mouths were . . . Very, very wide.

Nothing brave in what I did, or at least tried to do. My befuddled intellect was still processing the carnage when I sank the hook and tethered the team, left them baying frantically in the middle of the trail. I wasn't thinking of a damned thing as I walked stiff-legged toward the Hunt and the in-progress evisceration of my comrade. Most mushers carried firearms on the trail. There were moose to contend with and frankly, a gun is pretty much just basic equipment in any case. We toted rifles or pistols like folks in the Lower 48 carry cell phones and wallets. Mine was a .357 I stowed inside my anorak to keep the cylinder from freezing into a solid lump. The revolver was in my hand and it jumped twice and I don't recall the booms. No sound, only fire. The closest pair of dog men flipped over and a small part of my mind celebrated that at least the fuckers could be hurt, it wasn't like the legends or the movies; no silver required, lead worked fine.

The Huntsman whirled when I was nearly upon him, and Jesus help me I glimpsed his face. That's probably why my hair went white that year. I squeezed the trigger three more times, emptied the gun and even as the bullets smacked him, I had the sense of shooting into an abyss—absolute hopeless, soul-draining futility. The Huntsman swayed, humungous knife raised. The blade was flint, by the way.

Worst part was, Graham blinked and looked right at me and I saw his skinned hand twitch. How he could be alive in that condition was no more or less fantastical than anything else, I suppose. Even so, even so. I still get a sick feeling in my stomach when I recall that image.

Apparently, the gods of the north had seen enough. Wind roared around us and everything went white and I was alone. Hurricane force gusts knocked me off my feet and I barely managed to crawl to the team, almost missed them, in fact. Visibility was maybe six feet. Easily, easily could've kept going into the featureless maelstrom until I found the lip at the edge of a bottomless gulf of open water and joined Graham, wherever he'd gone.

That storm pinned the dogs and me to Norton Sound for three days. Gusts of seventy knots. Wind chill in excess of negative one hundred degrees Fahrenheit. You wouldn't understand how cold that is. I can't describe it. It's like trying to explain how far away Alpha Centauri is from Earth in highway miles. The brain isn't equipped. Froze my right hand and foot. Froze my face so that it hardened into a black and blue mask. Froze my dick. Didn't lose anything important, but man, there are few agonies equal to thawing a frostbitten extremity.

I actually managed to cripple across the finish line. Suffering through the aftermath of physical therapy and counseling, the memory of what I'd seen out there was wiped clean from my mind with the efficacy of a kid tipping an Etch A Sketch and giving it a shake. Seven or eight years passed before the horrible event came back to haunt me and by then it was too late to say anything, too late to be certain whether it had happened or if I'd gone round the bend.

◄◦►

Snow drifted both lanes and the wind buffeted the Chevy, and goddamn, but I was reliving that blizzard of '92. The fuel gauge needle fell into the red and I drove another half an hour, creeping along in four wheel hi. Radio reception was poor and I'd settled for a static-filled broadcast of '80s rock. Hall & Oates, The Police, a block of Sade and Blue Oyster Cult, all that music our parents hated when we were bopping along in mullets.

"Godzilla" cut in and out during the drum solo and a distorted animal growl that had nothing to do with heavy metal issued from the speakers. My name snarled over and over to the metronome of the wipers.

A truck stop glittered on the horizon of the next off ramp. Exhausted, frazzled, pissed, and afraid, I pulled alongside the pumps and got fuel. Then I hooked Minerva to a leash and brought her inside with me. I patted her head as we went through the door, and wished that I possessed more of her canine equanimity in the face of the unknown.

She curled at my boots while I drank a quart of awful coffee and ate a New York steak with all the trimmings. The waitress didn't say anything about my bringing a pit bull to the table. Maybe the folks in Dakota were hip to that sort of thing. Didn't matter; I'd gotten the little card that proved Minerva was a service dog and of vital importance should I experience an "episode" of depression or mania.

Depression had haunted me since my retirement from mushing and a friend who worked as counselor at the University of Anchorage suggested that I adopt a shelter puppy and train it as a companion animal. The local police had busted a dog fighting ring and one of the females was pregnant, so Sharon and I eventually picked Minerva from a litter of eleven. A decade later, after my world burned to the ground, career in ashes, wife gone, friends few and far between, Minerva remained steadfast. A man and his dog versus the Outer Dark.

The diner was doing brisk trade. Two burly truckers in company jumpsuits occupied the next booth, but most of the customers were gathered at the counter so they could watch weather reports on TV. Nothing heartening in the reports, either. The storm would definitely delay me by half a day, possibly more. My ardent hope was that I could just bull through it and be in the clear by the time I crossed Minnesota tomorrow. I also prayed that the pickup would hang together all the way to Lamprey Isle, New York, my destination at the end of the yellow brick road. My plan was to reach the home of an old friend named Jack Fort, a retired English professor and fellow author. Jack claimed he could help. I had my doubts. The pack and its leader were eternal and relentless. A man could plunk a few, sure. In the end, though, they simply reformed and kept pursuing. The Devil's smoke demons on the hunt.

Be that as it may, I'd decided to go down swinging and that meant a hell-bent for leather ride into the east. Currently, my worries centered on weather and equipment. The drive from Alaska via the Alcan Highway had been rough and I suspected the old engine was fixing to give up the ghost. I could say the same thing about my heart, my sanity, my luck.

Sure enough. Minerva snarled and bolted from her spot under the table. She crouched beside me, shivering. Foam dribbled from her jaw and her eyes bulged.

Graham strolled in, taller and happier than I remembered. Death agreed with some people. He loomed in Technicolor while reality bleached around him. His long black hair was feathered with snowflakes and the lights hit it just right so he appeared angelic, a movie star pausing for his dramatic close-up. He lugged the ivory hunting horn in his left (indeed a ram's horn, albeit much more modest than its report); he carried a faded cowboy hat with a crimson and black patch on the crown. He wore the Huntsman's iceberg-white mackinaw, ceremonial flint knife tucked into his belt so the bone handle jutted in a most phallic statement. He ambled over and slid in across from me. I noticed his sealskin boots left maroon smears on the tiles. I also noticed puffs of steam escaping our mouths as the booth cooled like a meat locker.

I cocked the .357 and braced it across my thigh. "You must not be heralding the great zombie invasion. Lookin' great, Steve. Not chalk white or anything. The rot must be on the inside."

He flipped his hair in a Fabio imitation. His trophy necklace of wedding rings, key fobs, dog tags, driver licenses, and glass eyes clinked and rattled. "Likewise, amigo. You've lost weight? Dyed your hair? What?"

"This and that—diet, exercise. Fleeing in terror has the bonus effect of getting a man in shape. Divorce, too. My wife used to fatten me up pretty good. Since she split . . . you know. TV dinners and Johnnie Walker. I got it going on, huh?" I gripped Minerva's collar with my free hand. Her growls were deep and ferocious. She strained to lunge over the table, an eighty pound bowling bowl; rippling muscle and bone crushing jaws and, at the moment, bad intentions. My arm was tired already. Tempting to let my girl fly, but I loved her.

"I'm yanking your chain. You look like crap. When's the last time you slept? There's a motel a piece up the trail. Why not get room service, watch a porno, drink some booze and fall into peaceful slumber? You won't even notice when I slip in there and slice your fucking throat ear to ear." Graham's smile widened. It was still him, too. Same guy I'd gotten drunk with at Nome saloons. Same perfect teeth, same easy manner, probably sincere. He'd not intimated any malice regarding his intent to skin me alive and eat my beating heart. This was business, mostly. He inclined his head slightly, as if intercepting my thought. "Not so much *business* as tradition. The Hunt is a sacred rite. I gave you the head start as a courtesy."

He was telling the truth as I understood it from my research of the legends. To witness the Hunt, to interfere with the Hunt, was to become prey. I'd wondered why the emissaries of the Horned One waited so long to come after me, especially considering the magnitude of my transgression. "Well, I reckon that was sporting of you. Twenty years. Plenty of time for Odysseus to screw his way home from the front."

"Yep, and you're almost there too," Graham said. "Crazy ass scene on the ice, huh? Sergio Leone meets John Landis and they do it up right with razors. Man, you were totally Eastwood, six gun blazing. Wounded the Huntsman in a serious way. Didn't kill the fucker, though. Don't flatter yourself on that score. Might be able to smoke the hounds with regular bullets. That shit don't work so well on the Huntsman. We're of a higher order. Nah, when that storm hit, some sort of force went through me, electrified me. I tore free of that altar and jumped on the bastard's back, stuck a hunting knife into his kidney. Still wouldn't have worked except the forces of darkness were smiling on me. Grooved on my style. The Boss demoted him, awarded me the mantle and the blade, the hounds, more bitches in Hell than you can shake a stick at. I've watched you for a while, bro. Watched you lose your woman, your career, your health. You're an old, grizzled bull. No money, no family, no friends, no future. It's culling time, baby."

"Shit, you're doing me a favor! Thanks, pal!"

"Come on, don't be sarcastic. We're still buds. This is going to be super-duper painful, but no reason to make it personal. Your hide will be but one more tossed atop a mountainous pile beside a Chthonic lagoon of blood and the Horned One's bone throne. The muster roll of the damned is endless and the next name awaits my attentions."

"Okay, nothing personal. Here's the deal since I'm the one with the hand cannon. You hold still and I'll blow your head off. Take my chances with whomever they send next. No hard feelings." I debated whether to shoot him under the table or risk raising the gun to aim properly.

Graham laughed. "Whoa, chief. This isn't the place. All these hapless customers, the dishwasher, the fry cooks. That sexy waitress. If we turn this into the O-K Corral, the Boss himself will be on the case. The Horned One isn't a kindly soul. He comes around, *everybody* gets it in the neck. Them's the rules, I'm afraid."

A vision splashed across the home cinema of my imagination: every person in the diner strung from the rafters by their living guts, the hounds using the corpses for piñatas and the massive, shadowy bulk of the Horned God flickering fire in the parking lot as he gazed on in infernal joy. Like as not this image was projected by Graham. I glanced out the window and spotted one of the pack, a cadaverous brute in a threadbare parka and snow pants, pissing against the wheel of a semi. In another life he'd been Bukowski or Waits, or a serial killer who rode the rails and shanked fellow hobos, a strangler of coeds, a postman. I knew him for a split second, then not. Other hounds leaped from trailer to trailer, frolicking. Too dark to make out details except that the figures flitted and fluttered with the lithe, rubbery grace of acrobats.

I said, "Tell me, Steve. What would've happened to you if I hadn't interrupted the party? Where would you be tonight?"

He shrugged and his movie star teeth dulled to a shade of rotten ivory. "Ah, those are the sort of questions I try to let lie. The Boss frowns on us worrying about stuff above our pay grade."

"Would you have become a hound?"

"Sometimes a damned soul gets dragged over to join the Hunt. Only the few, the proud. It's a rare honor."

Cold clamped on the back of my neck. "And the rest of the slobs who get taken? Where do they go after you're done with them?"

"Not a clue, amigo. Truly an ineffable mystery." His grin brightened again, so white, so frigid. He put on the cowboy hat. The logo was a red patch with a set of black antlers stitched in the foreground. Sign of the Horned God who was Graham's master on the Other Side.

Minerva's snarls and growls escalated to full-throated barks as she bristled and lunged. She'd had her fill of Mr. Death and his shark smirk.

One of the truckers set down his coffee cup, pointed a thick finger at me, and said, "Hey, asshole. Shut that dog up."

Graham's eyes went dark, monitors tuned to deep space. A stain formed on the breast of his lily-white mackinaw. Blood dripped from his sleeve and the stink of carrion wafted from his mouth. He rose and turned and his shoulders seemed to broaden. I caught his profile reflected in the window and something was wrong with it, although I couldn't tell what exactly. He said in a distorted, buzzing voice, *"No, you shut your mouth. Or I'll eat your tongue like a piece of Teriyaki."*

The trucker paled and scrambled from his seat and fled the diner without a word. His buddy followed suit. They didn't grab their coats or pay the tab, or anything. Other folks had twisted in their seats to view the commotion. None of them spoke either. The waitress stood with her ticket book outthrust like a crucifix.

Graham said to them, "Hush, folks. Nothing to see here." And everyone took the hint and went back to his or her business. He nodded and faced me, smile affixed, eyes sort of normal again. "I better get along, li'l doggie. Wanted to say hi. So hi and goodbye. Gonna keep trucking east? Wait, forget I asked. Don't want to spoil the fun. See you soon, wherever that is." Yeah, he grinned, but the wintry night was a heap warmer.

"Wait," I said. "You mentioned rules. Be nice to know what they are."

"Sure, there are lots of rules. However, *you* only need to worry about one of them. Run, motherfucker."

⋯

So, how did I wind up on the road with the hounds of hell on my trail?

I never fully recovered from the incident in '92; not down deep, not in the way that counts. Nightmares plagued me. Oblique, horror-show recreations as seen through the obfuscating mist of a subconscious in denial. Neither me nor the shrink could make sense of them. He put me on pills and that didn't help.

I sold the team to a Japanese millionaire and moved to the suburbs of Anchorage with Sharon, took a series of crummy labor jobs and worked on the Great American horror novel in the evenings. She finished grad school and landed a position teaching elementary grade art. Ever fascinated with pulp classics, when the novel appeared to be a dead end I tried my hand at genre short fiction and immediately landed a few sales. By the early Aughts I was doing well enough to justify quitting the construction gig and staying home to work on stories full-time.

These were supernatural horror stories, fueled by the nightmares I didn't understand until it all came crashing in on me one afternoon during a game of winter golf with some buddies down at the beach. I keeled over on the frozen sand and was momentarily transported back to Norton Sound while my friends stood around wringing their hands. Normal folks don't know what to do around a lunatic writhing on the ground and babbling in tongues.

A week on the couch wrapped in an electric blanket and shaking with terror followed. I didn't level with anyone—not the shrink, not Sharon or my parents, not my friends or writer colleagues. I read a piece on the Wild Hunt in an article concerning world mythology and it was like getting socked in the belly. I finally knew what had happened, if not why. All that was left was to brood.

Life went on. We tried for children without success. I have a hunch Sharon left me because I was shooting blanks. Who the fuck knows, though. Much like the Wild Hunt, the Meaning of Life, and where matching socks vanish to, her motives remain a mystery. Things seemed cozy between us; she'd always been sympathetic of my tics and twitches and I'd tried to be a good and loving husband in return. Obviously, living with a half-crazed author took a greater toll than I'd estimated. Add screams in the night and generally paranoid behavior to the equation . . .

One day she came home early, packed her bags, and headed for Italy with a music teacher from her school. Not a single tear in her eye when she said adios to me, either. That was the same week my longtime agent, a lewd, crude alcoholic expat Brit editor named Stanley Jones, was indicted on numerous federal charges including embezzlement, wire fraud and illegal alien residence. He and his lover, the obscure English horror writer Samson Marks, absconded to South America with my life savings, as well as the nest eggs of several other authors. The scandal made all the industry trade rags, but the cops didn't seem overly concerned with chasing the duo.

I depended on those royalty checks as my physical condition was deteriorating. Cold weather made my bones ache. Some mornings my lumbar seized and it took twenty minutes to crawl out of bed. I hung on for a couple of years, but my situation declined. The publishing climate wasn't friendly with the recession and such. Foreclosure notices soon arrived in the mailbox.

Then, last week, while I was out on a nature hike, after all these bloody years, Graham reappeared to put my misery into perspective. We'll get to that in a minute.

You see, prior to this latter event, my colleague, the eminent crime novelist Jack Fort, theorized that Sharon didn't run off to Italy because she was dissatisfied with the way things were going at home. Nor was it a coincidence that Jones robbed me blind and left me in the poorhouse (Jack also employed the crook as an agent and from what I gathered the loss of funds contributed to his own divorce). My friend became convinced dark forces had aligned against me in matters great and small. Figuring he might not dismiss me as a nutcase out of hand, I recounted my brush with the Hunt on the ice in 1992, how that particular chicken had come home to roost. He wasn't the least bit surprised. Unflappable Jack Fort; the original drink-boiling-water-and-piss-ice-cubes guy.

The other night when I called him we were both drunk. I spilled the story of how Graham had returned from the grave and wanted to mount my head on a trophy room wall in hell.

Instead of expressing bewilderment or fear for my sanity, Jack just said, "Right. I figured it was something like this. From grad school onward, Graham was headed for trouble, pure and simple. He was asshole buddies with exactly the wrong type of people. Occultism is nothing to fuck with. Anyway, you're sure it's the Wild Hunt?"

I gave him the scoop: "Last Wednesday, I was hiking along Hatcher Pass to photograph the mountain for research. Heard a god-awful racket in a nearby canyon. Howling, psycho laughter, screams. Some kind of Viking horn. I knew what was happening before I saw the pack on the summit. Knew it in my bones—the legends vary, of course. Still, the basics are damned clear whether it's the Norwegians, Germans, or Inuit. The pack wasn't in full chase mode or that would've been curtains. They wanted to scare me; makes the kill sweeter. Anyway, I beat feet. Made it to the truck and burned rubber. Graham showed up at the house later in a greasy puff of smoke, chatted with me through the door. He said I had three days to get my shit in order and then he and his boys would be after me for real. Referred to himself as the Huntsman. So. It happened almost exactly like the legends."

Yeah, I knew all about the legends. I'd done my due diligence, you can bet on that. Granted, there were variations on the theme. Each culture has its peculiarities and so focus on different aspects. Some versions of the Hunt mythology have Odin calling the tune and the exercise is one of exuberance and feral joy, a celebration of the primal. Odin's pack travels a couple of feet off the ground. Any fool that stands in the way gets mowed like grass. See Odin coming, you grab dirt and pray the spectral procession passes overhead and keeps moving on the trail of its quarry.

The gang from Alaska seemed darker, crueler, dirtier than the story-book versions; Graham and his troops reeked of sadism and madness. That eldritch psychosis leached from them into me, gathered in effluvial dankness in the back of my throat, lay on my tongue as a foul taint. The important details were plenty consistent—slavering hounds, feral Huntsman, a horned deity overseeing the chase, death and damnation to the prey.

Jack remained quiet for a bit, except to cough a horrible phlegmy cough—it sounded wet and entrenched as bronchitis or pneumonia. Finally he said, "Well, head east. I might be able to help you. Graham and I knew each other pretty well once upon a time when he was still teaching and I got some ideas what he was up to after he left Boulder. He was an adventurer, but I doubt he spent all that time in the frozen north for the thrill. Nah, my bet is he was searching for the Hunt and it found him first. Poor silly bastard."

"Thanks, man. Although, I hate to bring this to your doorstep. Interfere in the Hunt and it's you on the skinning board next."

"Shut up, kid. Tend your knitting and I'll see to mine."

Big Jack Fort's nonchalant reaction should've startled me, and under different circumstances I might've pondered how deep the tentacles of this particular conspiracy went. His advice appealed, though. Sure, the Huntsman wanted me to take to my heels; the chase gave him a boner. Nonetheless, I'd rather present a moving target than hang around the empty house waiting to get snuffed on the toilet or in my sleep. Graham's flayed body glistening in the arctic twilight was branded into my psyche.

"You better step lively," Jack warned me in that gravelly voice of his that always sounded the same whether sober or stewed. A big dude, built square, the offspring of Raymond Burr and a grand piano. Likely he was sprawled across his couch in a tee shirt and boxers, bottle of Maker's Mark in one paw. "Got complications on my end. Can't talk about them right now. Just haul ass and get here."

I didn't like the sound of that, nor the sound of his coughing. Despite a weakness for booze, Jack was one of the more stable guys in the business. However, he was a bit older than me and playing the role of estranged husband. Then there was the crap with Jones and dwindling book sales in general. I thought maybe he was cracking. I thought maybe we were *both* cracking.

Later that night I loaded the truck with a few essentials, including my wedding album and a handful of paperbacks I'd acquired at various literary conventions, locked the house, and lit out.

In the rearview mirror I saw Graham and three of his hounds as silhouettes on the garage roof, pinprick eyes blazing red as I drove away. It was, as the kids say, game on.

-o-

Rocketing through Indiana, "Slippery People" on the radio, darkness all around, darkness inside. The radio crackled and static erased the Talking Heads and Graham said to me, "Everybody on the lam from the Hunt feels sorry for himself. Thing of it is, amigo, you're dialed to the wrong tune. You should ask yourself, *How did I get here? What have I done?*"

The pack raced alongside the truck. Hounds and master shimmered like starlight against the velvet backdrop, twisted like funnels of smoke. The Huntsman blew me a kiss and I tromped the accelerator and they fell off the pace. One of the hounds leaped the embankment rail and loped after me, snout pressed to the centerline. It darted into the shadows an instant before being overtaken and smooshed by a tractor trailer.

I pushed beyond exhaustion and well into the realm of zombification. The highway was a wormhole between dimensions and Graham occasionally whispered to me through the radio even though I'd hit the kill switch. And what he'd said really worked on me. What *had* I done to come to this pass? Maybe Sharon left me because I was a sonofabitch.

Maybe Jones screwing me over was karma. The Wild Hunt might be a case of the universe getting Even-Steven (pardon the pun) with me. Thank the gods I didn't have a bottle of liquor handy or else I'd have spent the remainder of the long night totally blitzed and sobbing like a baby over misdeeds real and imagined. Instead, I popped the blister on a packet of No-Doze and put the hammer down.

⟶◦⟵

I parked and slept once in a turnout for a couple of hours during the middle of the day when traffic ran thickest. I risked no more than that. The Hunt had its rules regarding the taking of prey in front of too many witnesses, but I didn't have the balls to challenge those traditions.

The Chevy died outside Wilkes-Barre, Pennsylvania. Every gauge went crazy and plumes of steam boiled from the radiator. I got the rig towed to a salvage yard and transferred Minerva and my meager belongings to a compact rental. We were back on the road before breakfast and late afternoon saw us aboard the ferry from Port Sanger, New York, to Lamprey Isle.

What to say about LI West (as Jack Fort referred to it)? Nineteen miles north to south and about half that at its widest, the whole curved into a malformed crescent, the Man in the Moon's visage peeled from Luna and partially submerged in the Atlantic. Its rocky shore was sculpted by the clash of wind and sea; a forest of pine, maple, and oak spanned the interior. Home of hoot owls and red squirrels; good deer hunting along the secret winding trails, I'd heard. Native burial mounds and mysterious megaliths, I'd also heard.

The main population center, Lamprey Township (population 2201), nestled in a cove on the southwestern tip of the island. Jack had mentioned that the town had been established as a fishing village in the early nineteenth century; prior to that, smugglers and slavers made it their refuge from privateers and local authorities. A den of illicit gambling and sodomy, I'd heard. Allegedly, the name arose from a vicious species of eels that infested the local waters. Long as a man's arm, the locals claimed.

Lamprey Township was a fog-shrouded settlement hemmed by the cove and spearhead shoals, a picket of evergreens. A gloomy cathedral fortress reared atop a cliff streaked with seagull shit and pocked by cave entrances.

Lovers Leap. In town, everybody wore flannel and rain slickers, boots and sock caps. A folding knife and mackinaw crowd. Everything was covered in salt rime, everything tasted of brine. Piloting the rental down Main Street between boardwalks, interior of the car flushed with soft blue-red lights reflecting from the ocean, I thought this wouldn't be such a bad place to die. Release my essential salts back into the primordial cradle.

Jack's cabin lay inland at the far end of a dirt spur. Built in the same era as the founding of Lamprey Township, he'd bought it from Katarina Veniti, a paranormal romance author who'd become jaded with all of the tourists and yuppies moving onto "her" island during the last recession. A stone and timber longhouse with ye old-fashioned shingles and moss on the roof surrounded by an acre of sloping yard overgrown with tall, dead grass. An oak had uprooted during a recent windstorm and toppled across the drive.

Minerva and I hoofed it the last quarter of a mile. The faceless moon dripped and shone through scudding clouds and a vault of branches. The house sat in darkness except for a light shining from the kitchen window.

"Welcome to Kat's island," Jack said, and coughed. He reclined in the shadows on a porch swing. Moonlight glinted from the bottle in his hand, the barrel of the pump-action shotgun across his knees. He wore a wool coat, dock-worker's cap snug over his brow, wool pants, and lace-up hiking boots. When he stood to doff his sock hat and shake my hand, I realized his clothes hung loose as sails, that he was frail and shaky.

"Jesus, man," I said, shaken at the sight of him. He appeared more of an apparition than the bona fide spirit pursuing me. I understood why he didn't mind the idea of the Hunt invading his happy home. The man was so emaciated he should've been hanging near the blackboard in science class; a hundred pounds lighter since I'd last seen him, easy. He'd shaved his head and beard to gray stubble; his pallid flesh was dry and hot, his eyes sparkled like bits of quartz. He stank of gun oil, smoke, and rotting fruit.

"Yea. The big C. Doc hit me with the bad news this spring. Deathwatch around the Fort. I sent the pets to live with my sister." He smiled and gestured at the woods. "Just you, me, and the trees. I got nothing better to do than help an old pal in his hour of need." He led the way inside. The kitchen was cheerily lighted and we took residence at the dining table where he poured me a glass of whiskey and listened to my recap of the trip from Alaska.

"I hope you've got a plan," I said.

"Besides blasting them with grandma's twelve gauge?" He patted the stock of his shotgun where it lay on the table. "We're going out like a pair of Vikings."

"I'd be more excited if you had a flamethrower, or some grenades."

"Me too. Me too. I got a few sticks of dynamite for fishing and plenty of ammo."

"Dynamite is good. This is going to be full on Hollywood. Fast cars, shirtless women, explosions. . . ."

"Man, I don't even know if it'll detonate. The shit's been stashed in a leaky box in the cellar for a hundred years. Honestly, my estimation is, we're hosed. Totally up shit creek. Our sole advantage is, prey doesn't usually fight back. Graham's powerful, he's a spirit, or a monster, whatever. But he's new on the job, right? That may be our ray of sunshine. That, and according to the literature, the Pack doesn't fancy crossing large bodies of open water. These haunts prefer ice and snow." Jack coughed into a handkerchief. Belly-ripping, Doc Holliday kind of coughing. He wiped his mouth and had a belt of whiskey. His cheeks were blotched. "Anyway, I brought you here for another reason. This house belonged to a sorcerer once upon a time. Type they used to burn at the stake. An unsavory guy named Ewers Welloc. The Wellocs own most of this island and there's a hell of a story in that. For now, let me say Ewers was blackest in a family of black sheep. The villagers were scared shitless of him, were convinced he practiced necromancy and other dark arts on the property. Considering the stories Kat told me and some of the funky stuff I've found stashed around here, it's hard to dismiss the villagers' claims as superstition."

I could only wonder what he'd unearthed, or Kat before him. Jack bought the place for a dollar and suddenly that factoid assumed of ominous significance. "What were you guys up to? You, Kat, and Graham attended college together. Did you form a club?"

"A witch coven. I kid, I kid. Wasn't college. We met at the Sugar Tree Hill writers' retreat. Five days of sun, fun, booze, and hand jobs. There were quite a few young authors there who went on to become quasi-prominent. Many a friendships and enmities are formed at Sugar Tree Hill.

The three of us really clicked. Me and Kat were wild, man, wild. Nothing on Graham's scale, though. He took it way farther. As you can see."

"Yeah." I sipped my drink.

"Me and Graham were pretty tight until he schlepped to Alaska and started in with the sled dogs. Communication tapered off and after a while we fell out of touch. I received a few letters. Guy had the world's shittiest penmanship; would've taken a cryptologist to have deciphered them. I thought he suffered from cabin fever."

"Seemed okay to me," I said. "Gregarious. Popular. Handsome. He was well-regarded."

"Yea, yea… The rot was on the inside," Jack said and I almost spilled my glass. He didn't notice. "As it happens, my hole card is an ace. Lamprey Isle was settled long before the whites landed. Maybe before the Mohawk, Mohican, Seneca. Nobody knows who these people were, but none of the records are flattering. This mystery tribe left megaliths and cairns on islands and along the coast. A few of those megaliths are in the woods around here. Legend has it that the tribe erected them for use in necromantic rituals. Summon, bind, banish. Like Robert Howard hypothesized in his Conan tales—if the demonic manifests on the mortal plane, it becomes subject to the laws of physics, and cold Hyperborean steel. Howard was on to something."

"Fairy rocks, huh?" I said. The whiskey was hitting me.

"Got any problem believing in the Grim Reaper with a hunting knife and a pack of werewolves chasing you from one end of the continent to the other?"

I tried again. "So. Fairy rocks."

"Fuckin' A, boy-o. Fairy rocks. And double aught buckshot."

⟶

We took shifts at watch until dawn. The Hunt didn't arrive and so passed a peaceful evening. I slept for three hours; the most I'd had in a week. Jack fried bacon and eggs for breakfast and we drank a pot of black coffee. Afterward he gave me a tour of the house and the immediate grounds. Much of the house gathered dust, exuding the vibe particular to dwellings of bachelors and widowers. Since his wife flew the coop,

Jack's remit had contracted to kitchen, bath, living room. Too close to a tomb for my liking.

Tromping around the property with our breath streaming slantwise, he showed me a megalith hidden in the underbrush between a pair of sugar maples. Huge and misshapen beneath layers of slime and moss, the stone cast a shadow over us. It radiated the chill of an ice block. One of several in the vicinity, I soon learned.

Jack wasn't eager to hang around it. "There were lots of animal bones piled in the bushes. You'll never catch any animals living here. Wasn't the two decks of Camels I smoked every day since junior high that gave me cancer. It's these damned things. Near as I can figure, they're siphons. Let's pray the effect is magnified upon extra-dimensional beings. Otherwise, Graham will just eat our bullets and spit them back at us."

The megalith frightened me. I imagined it as a huge, predatory insect disguised as a stone, its ethereal rostrum stabbing an artery and sucking my life essence. I wondered if the stones were indigenous or if the ancient tribes had fashioned them somehow. I'd never know. "Graham's an occultist. Think he's dumb enough to walk into a trap?"

"Graham ain't Graham anymore. He's the Huntsman." Jack scanned the red-gold horizon and muttered dire predictions of another storm front descending from the west. "Trouble headed this way," he said and hustled me back to the house. We locked and shuttered everything and took positions in the living room; Jack with his shotgun, me with my pistol and dog. Seated on the leather Italian sofa, bolstered by a pitcher of vodka and lemonade, we watched ancient episodes of *The Rockford Files* and *Ironside* and waited.

Several minutes past 2:00 p.m. the air dimmed to velvety purple and the trees behind the house thrashed and rain spattered the windows. The power died. I whistled a few bars of the *Twilight Zone* theme, shifted the pistol into my shooting hand.

He grinned and went to the window and stood there, a blue shadow limned in black. The booze in my tumbler quivered and the horn bellowed, right on top of us. Glass exploded and I was bleeding from the head and both hands that I'd raised to protect my face. Wood splintered and doors caved in all over the house and the hounds rolled into the living room; long, sinuous figures of pure malevolence with ruby-bright eyes, low to the floor and moving fast, teeth, tongues, appetite. I squinted and fired twice from the hip and a bounding figure jerked short. Minerva pounced, snarling and tearing in frenzy, doggy mind reverting to the swamps and jungles and caves of her ancestors. Jack's shotgun blazed a stroke of yellow flame and sheared the arm of a fiend who'd scuttled in close. Partially deafened and blinded, I couldn't keep track of much after that. Squeezed the trigger four more times, popped the speed loader with six fresh slugs, kept firing at shadows that leaped and sprang. The Riders of the Apocalypse and Friends galloped through the house; our own private Armageddon. More glass whirled and bits of wood and shreds of drapery; a section of ceiling collapsed in a cascade of sparks and rapidly blooming white carnations of drywall dust. Now the gods could watch.

Thunder of gunshots, Minerva growling, the damned, yodeling cries of the hounds, and crackling bones, wound around my brain in a knotted spool. I got knocked down in the melee and watched Minerva swing past, lazily flying, paws limp, guts raveling behind her. I'd owned many dogs, Minerva was my first and only pet, my dearest friend. She was a mewling puppy once more, then inert bone and slack hide, and gone, gone, the last pinprick of my old life snuffed.

Something was on fire. Oily black smoke seethed through a vertical impact crater where the far wall had stood. Clouds and smoke boiled there. A couple of fingers were missing from my left hand and blood pulsed forth; a shiny, crimson bouquet thickening into a lump, a wax sculpture from the house of horrors, an object example of Medieval torture. It didn't hurt. Didn't feel like anything. My jacket had been sliced, and the flesh beneath it so that my innards glistened in the cold air. That didn't hurt either. Instead, I was buoyed by the sense of impending finality. This wouldn't take much longer by the looks of it. I pulled the jacket closed as best I could and began the laborious process of standing. Almost done, almost home.

Jack cursed through a mouthful of dirt. The Huntsman had entered the fray and caught his skull in one splayed hand and sawed through his throat with the jagged dagger, that dagger hewn from Stone Age crystal. The Huntsman sawed with so much vigor that Jack's limbs flopped crazily, a crash test dummy at the moment of impact. Graham let Jack's carcass thump to the sodden carpet among the savaged bodies of the pack. He pointed at me, him playing the lead man of a rock band shouting out to his audience. Yeah, the gods were with us, and no doubt.

"So, we meet again." He chuckled and licked his lips and wiped the Satan knife against his gory mackinaw. He approached, shuffling like a seal through the smoldering gloom, lighted by an inner radiance that bathed him in a weird, pale glow as cold and alien as the Aurora Borealis. The death-light of Hades, presumably. His eyes were hidden by the brim of his hat, but his smile curved, joyless and cruel.

I made it to my feet and scrambled backward over the flaming wreckage of coffee tables and easy chairs, the upended couch, and into the hall. All but dead, but still fighting, an animal to the end. Blood came from me in ropes, in sheets. Graham followed, smiling, smiling. Doorframes buckled as his shoulders brushed them. He swiped the knife in a loose and easy diamond pattern. The knife hissed as it rehearsed my evisceration. I wasn't worried about that. I was long past worry. Thoughts of vengeance dominated.

"You killed my dog." Blood bubbles plopped from my lips and that's never good. Another dose of ferocious, joyful melancholy spurred me onward. I pitched the empty revolver at his head, watched the gun glance aside and spin away. My tears froze to salt on my cheeks. Arctic ice groaned beneath my boots as the sea swelled, yearned toward the moon. The sea drained the warmth from me, taking back what it had given in the beginning.

"*You* killed your dog, mon frère. You did for our buddy Jack, too. Bringing me and my boys here like this. Don't beat yourself up. It's a volunteer army, right?"

I turned away, sliding, overbalancing. My legs folded and I slumped before a fallen timber, its charred length licked by small flames. The blood from my ruined hand sizzled and spat. I rubbed my face against the floor, painting myself a war mask of gore and charcoal. By the time he'd crossed the gap between us and seized my hair to flip me onto my back, at the precise moment he sank the blade into my chest, the fuse on the glycerin-wet stick of dynamite was a nub disappearing into its burrow.

Graham's exultant expression changed. "Well, I forgot Jack was a fisherman," he said. That fucking knife kept traveling, the irresistible force, and I embraced it, and him.

The Eternal Footman clapped.

◦

After an eon of vectoring through infinite night, the door to the tilt-a-whirl opened and I plummeted and hit the earth hard enough to raise dust. Mud instead. An angelic choir serenaded me from stage left, beyond a screen of tall trees and fog. Wagner as interpreted by Homer's sirens. The voices rose and fell, sweetly demanding my blood, the heat of my bones. That sounded fine. I imagined the soft, red lips parted, imagined that they glowed as the Huntsman glowed, but as an expression of erotic passion rather than malice, and I longed to open a vein for them…

I came to, paralyzed. Pieces of me lay scattered across the backyard. For the best that I couldn't turn my neck to properly survey the damage.

Graham sprawled across from me, face-down in the wet leaves. Wisps of smoke curled from him. He shuddered violently and lifted his head. Bones and joints snapped into place again. The left eye shimmered with reflections of fire. The right eye was black. Neither were human.

He said, "Are you dead? Are you dead? Or are you playing possum? I think you're mostly dead. It doesn't matter. Hell is come as you are." He shook himself and began to crawl in my direction, slithering with a horrible serpent-like elasticity.

Mostly dead must've meant 99.9 percent dead, because I couldn't even blink, much less raise a hand to forestall his taking my skull for the mantle, my soul to the bad place. A red haze obscured my vision and the world receded, receded. The sirens in the forest called again, louder yet. Graham hesitated, his glance drawn to the voices that came from many directions now and sang in many languages.

Jack staggered from the smoking ruins of the house. He appeared to have been dunked in a vat of blood. He held his shotgun in a death grip. "The bell tolls for you, Stevie," he said and blew off Graham's left leg. He racked the slide and blasted Graham's right leg to smithereens below the kneecap. Graham screamed and whipped around and tried to hamstring his tormentor. Not quite fast enough. Jack proved agile for an old guy with a slit throat.

The siren choir screamed in pleasure. Blam! Blam! Graham's hands went bye-bye. The next slug severed his spine, judging by the ragdoll effect. His body went limp and he screamed some more and I'm sure he would've happily leaped on Jack and eaten him alive if Jack hadn't already dismembered him with that fancy shotgun work. Jack said something I didn't catch. Might've uttered a curse in a foreign tongue, a Latin epithet. He stuck the barrel under Graham's chin and took his head off with the last round.

I cheered telepathically. Then I finished dying. The score as the curtains closed was so fucking beautiful.

-⚬-

This time I emerged from eternal night to Minerva kissing my face. I was lying on my back in the kitchen. There was a hole in the ceiling and gray daylight poured through along with steady trickles of water from busted pipes.

Jack slouched at the table, which was stacked with various odds and ends. His shoulders were wide and round as boulders and he'd gained back all the weight cancer had stolen; his old self, only far more so. He clutched a bottle of Old Crow and watched me intently. He said, "Stay away from the light, kid. It's fire and lava."

I spat clotted blood. Finally, I said, "He's dead?"

"Again."

"Singing . . ." I managed.

"Oh, yeah. Don't listen. That's just the vampire stones. They're fat on Graham's energy."

"How'd I get in here?"

"I dragged you by your hair."

The world kept solidifying around me, and my senses along with it. Me, Minerva, and Jack being alive didn't compute. Except, as the cobwebs cleared from my mind, it made a sinister kind of sense. I laid my hand on Minerva's fur and noticed the red sparks in her eyes, how goddamned long and white her teeth were. "Oh, shit," I said.

"Yeah," Jack said. He set aside the bottle and shrugged into the Huntsman's impeccable snow white mackinaw. Perfect fit. Next came the Huntsman's hat. Different on Jack; broader and of a style I didn't recognize. The red and black crest was gone. Real antlers in its stead. A shadow crossed his expression and the light in the room gathered in his eyes. "Get up," he said. Thunder rumbled.

And I did. Not a mark on me. I felt quite alive for a dead man. Hideous strength coursed through my limbs. I thought of my philandering ex wife, her music teacher beau, and hideous thoughts coursed through my mind. I must've retained a tiny fragment of humanity because I managed to look away from that vista of terrible and splendorous vengeance. For the moment, at least. I said, "Where now?"

Jack leaned on a long, barbed spear that had replaced his emptied shotgun. "There's this guy in Mexico I'd like to visit," he said. He handed me the flint knife and the herald's horn. "Do the honors, kid."

"Oh, Stanley. It'll be good to see you again." I pressed the horn to my lips and winded it, once. It tasted cold and sweet. The kitchen wall disintegrated and the shockwave traveled swiftly, rippling grass and causing birds to lift in panic from the trees. I imagined Stanley Jones, somewhere far to the south, seated on his veranda, tequila at hand, *The Sun* balanced on his rickety knee, ear cocked, straining to divine the origin of the dim bellow carried by the wind.

Minerva bayed. She gathered her sleek, killing bulk and hurtled across the yard and into the woods. I patted the hilt of the knife and followed her.

◄◦►

HONORABLE MENTIONS

Barron, Laird "A Strange Form of Life," *Dark Faith: Invocations*.

Barron, Laird "DT," *A Season In Carcosa*.

Barron, Laird "Hand of Glory," (novella) *The Book Of Cthulhu II*.

Bell, Peter "A Midsummer's Ramble in the Carpathians," (novella) *Strange Ephiphanies*.

Bestwick, Simon "The Churn" Black Static 27

Brownworth, Victoria A. "Ordinary Mayhem," (novella) *Night Shadows*.

Campbell, Ramsey "The Moons," *The Devil's Coattails: More Dispatches*.

Chaon, Dan "How We Escaped Our Certain Fate," *21ˢᵗ Century Dead*.

Clark, Simon "The Shakespeare Curse," *Terror Tales of the Cotswolds*.

Coleman, Emma "Home," *Dark Currents*.

Demory, Sean "The Ballad of the Wayfaring Strange & the Dead Man's Whore," kindle

Dowling, Terry "Nightside Eye," Cemetery Dance #66.

Ford, Jeffrey "Blood Drive," *After*.

Ford, Jeffrey "The Wish Head," Crackpot Palace.

Gaiman, Neil "Click-Clack the Rattlebag," Audible.

Grabinski, Stefan "On the Hill of Roses," *On the Hill of Roses*.

Hempel, Amy "A Full-Service Shelter," Tin House 52.

Ingold, Jon "Cracks" Black Static 28.

Johnstone, Carole "The Pest House," Black Static 28.

Jones, Stephen Graham "After the People Lights Have Gone Off," Phantasmagorium

Jones, Stephen Graham "Notes From the Apocalypse," Weird Tales #359.

King, Stephen and Hill, Joe "In the Tall Grass," Esquire June/July/August.

Langan, John "Bloom," *Black Wings II*.

Lansdale, Joe R. "The Tall Grass," *Dark Tales of Lost Civilizations*.

Leslie, V.H. "Skein and Bone," Black Static 31.

Link, Kelly "Two Houses," *Shadow Show*.

Littlefield, Sophie "Jimmy's Legacy," Cemetery Dance #66.

Littlewood, Alison "In the Quiet and in the Dark," *Terror Tales of the Cotswolds*.

Littlewood, Alison "The Swarm," *The Screaming Book of Horror*.

Livings, Martin "Birthday Suit," *Living with the Dead*

Marshall, Helen "Blessed," *Hair Side, Flesh Side*.

McDougall, Sophia "Bells Ringing Under the Sea," *Dark Currents*.

McMahon, Gary "Cinder Images," *Darker Minds*.

Moore, Alison "Small Animals," Nightjar Press Chapbook.

Morris, Mark "Biters," *21ˢᵗ Century Dead*.

Nahrung, Jason "The Last Boat to Eden," *Surviving the End*.

O'Driscoll, Mike "Eyepennies," chapbook.

Oliver, Reggie "Charm," *Terror Tales of the Cotswolds*.

Ruby, Jacob "The Little Things," Black Static 27.

Russell, Karen "Reeling for the Empire," Tin House 54.

Ryan, Alan Peter "Amazonas," Cemetery Dance Chapbook.

Ryan, Carrie "After the Cure," *After*.

Sedia, Ekaterina "A Handsome Fellow," Asimov's Science Fiction Oct/Nov.

Sharma, Priya "Pearl, Bourbon Penn 4.

Shearman, Robert "Bedtime Stories for Yasmin," Shadows & Tall Trees 4.

Shearman, Robert "Blue Crayon, Yellow Crayon," *Remember Why You Fear Me*.

Tem, Steve Rasnic "Saguaro Night," *Ugly Behavior*.

Thomas, Lee "The Hollow is Filled With Beautiful Monsters," *Night Shadows*.

Warren, Kaaron "The Lighthouse Keepers' Club," *Exotic Gothic 4*.

ABOUT THE AUTHORS

MEGAN ARKENBERG lives and writes in Wisconsin. Her work has appeared in *Asimov's Science Fiction Magazine, Strange Horizons, Lightspeed*, and dozens of other places. In 2012, her poem "The Curator Speaks in the Department of Dead Languages" won the Rhysling Award in the long form category. She procrastinates by editing the fantasy e-zine *Mirror Dance*.

"Final Exam" was originally published in *Asimov's Science Fiction Magazine* edited by Sheila Williams.

◄○►

STEPHEN BACON lives in Rotherham, South Yorkshire, UK, with his wife and two sons. His short stories have appeared in various magazines and anthologies including *Black Static, Shadows & Tall Trees, The Willows, Crimewave, Murmurations: An Anthology of Uncanny Stories About Birds*, edited by Nicholas Royle, *Where the Heart Is,* edited by Gary Fry, and the final three editions of *Nemonymous,* edited by DF Lewis.

His debut collection *Peel Back the Sky* was published in 2012. Forthcoming is a chapbook from Spectral Press called *The Allure of Oblivion*.

"None So Blind" was originally published in *Shadows and Tall Trees 3*, edited by Michael Kelly.

◄○►

NATHAN BALLINGRUD was born in Massachusetts but spent most of his life in the Deep South. He worked as a bartender in New Orleans and a cook on offshore oil rigs; currently he's a waiter in a fancy restaurant.

His stories have appeared in several anthologies and year's best collections. He won the Shirley Jackson Award for his short story "The Monsters of Heaven." His first book, *North American Lake Monsters: Stories*, is due from Small Beer Press in 2013. He lives in Asheville, NC, with his daughter.

"Wild Acre" was originally published in *Visions Fading Fast*, edited by Gary McMahon, Pendragon Press.

◄o►

LAIRD BARRON is the author of several books, including *The Imago Sequence, Occultation, The Croning*, and *The Beautiful Thing That Awaits Us All*. His work has appeared in many magazines and anthologies. An expatriate Alaskan, Barron currently resides in Upstate New York.

"Frontier Death Song" was originally published in *Nightmare Magazine* edited by John Joseph Adams.

◄o►

The *Oxford Companion to English Literature* describes **RAMSEY CAMPBELL** as "Britain's most respected living horror writer". He has been given more awards than any other writer in the field, including the Grand Master Award of the World Horror Convention, the Lifetime Achievement Award of the Horror Writers Association and the Living Legend Award of the International Horror Guild. Among his novels are *The Face That Must Die, Incarnate, Midnight Sun, The Count of Eleven, Silent Children, The Darkest Part of the Woods, The Overnight, Secret Story, The Grin of the Dark, Thieving Fear, Creatures of the Pool, The Seven Days of Cain, Ghosts Know* and *The Kind Folk*. Forthcoming are *The Last Revelation of Gla'aki* (a novella), and *Bad Thoughts*. His collections include *Waking Nightmares, Alone with the Horrors, Ghosts and Grisly Things, Told by the Dead,* and *Just Behind You*, and his non-fiction is collected as *Ramsey Campbell, Probably*. His novels *The Nameless* and *Pact of the Fathers* have been filmed in Spain. His regular columns appear in *Prism, Dead Reckoning,* and *Video Watchdog*. He is the President of the British Fantasy Society and of the Society of Fantastic Films.

Ramsey Campbell lives on Merseyside with his wife Jenny. His pleasures include classical music, good food and wine, and whatever's in that pipe. His web site is at www.ramseycampbell.com.

"The Callers" was originally published in *Four for Fear*, edited by Peter Crowther.

⟶⟨○⟩⟶

Author most recently of the 2012 short story collection *Stay Awake*, **DAN CHAON** wrote the national bestseller *Await Your Reply*, which was named one of the ten best books of 2009 by *Publisher's Weekly*, *Entertainment Weekly*, Janet Maslin of *The New York Times*, and Laura Miller of *Salon. com*, as well as being named among the year's best fiction by the American Library Association and others.

He is also the author of the short story collections *Fitting Ends* and *Among the Missing*, which was a finalist for the 2001 National Book Award, and the novel *You Remind Me of Me*. Chaon's fiction has appeared in *Best American Short Stories*, *The Pushcart Prize Anthologies*, *The Year's Best Fantasy and Horror*, and *The O. Henry Prize Stories*. He has been a finalist for the National Magazine Award in Fiction, and he was the recipient of an Academy Award in Literature from the American Academy of Arts and Letters.

Chaon lives in Ohio and teaches at Oberlin College, where he is the Pauline Delaney Professor of Creative Writing and Literature.

"Little America" was originally published in *21ˢᵗ Century Dead* edited by Christopher Golden.

⟶⟨○⟩⟶

STEPHANIE CRAWFORD had her first publishing credit with "Tender as Teeth", and continues to work on short stories, a novel, and screenplay while living among the wild Elvi in their natural habitat of Las Vegas. She can be reached on Twitter via @scrawfish

"Tender as Teeth" was originally published in *21ˢᵗ Century Dead*, edited by Christopher Golden.

⟶⟨○⟩⟶

TERRY DOWLING is one of Australia's most respected, versatile and awarded writers of science fiction, dark fantasy and horror, and author of the internationally acclaimed Tom Rynosseros saga. His collection Basic Black won the 2007 International Horror Guild Award for Best Collection and is regarded as "one of the best recent collections of contemporary horror" by the American Library Association. *The Year's Best Fantasy and Horror* series featured more horror stories by Terry in its twenty-one year run than any other writer, while London's *Guardian* compared his novel *Clowns at Midnight* to John Fowles's *The Magus*.

Terry's homepage is at www.terrydowling.com

"Mariner's Round" was first published in *Exotic Gothic 4* edited by Danel Olson.

⟨◦⟩

GEMMA FILES was born in London, England but is a Canadian citizen, and has lived in Toronto, Ontario for her entire life. She has been a film critic and a teacher of screenwriting and Canadian film history. in addition to publishing two collections of short stories: *Kissing Carrion* and *The Worm in Every Heart*, and two chapbooks of poetry.

Five of her short stories were adapted for the US/Canadian horror television series, *The Hunger* and she wrote two screenplays for the series.

Her short story "The Emperor's Old Bones" won the International Horror Guild Award for Best Short Story of 1999. Her first novel *A Book of Tongues: Volume One in the Hexslinger Series* won the 2010 Black Quill award for "Best Small Press Chill" (both Editors' and Readers' Choice) and made the 2010 Over The Rainbow Reading List. The trilogy has since been completed with *A Rope of Thorns* and *A Tree of Bones*. She has is currently working on her first stand-alone novel.

"Nanny Grey" was originally published in *An Anthology of the Esoteric and Arcane Magic* edited by Jonathan Oliver.

⟨◦⟩

JEFFREY FORD is the author of eight novels, most recently *The Shadow Year*, and four collections of short stories (his most recent, *Crackpot Palace*, was published in 2012. He is the recipient of the World Fantasy Award, Shirley Jackson Award, Edgar Allan Poe Award, and Nebula. His story, "The Drowned Life" was recently included in *The Oxford Book of American Short Stories, 2nd ed.* He lives in Ohio with his wife and sons.

"A Natural History of Autumn" was originally published in *The Magazine of Fantasy and Science Fiction* edited by Gordon Van Gelder.

RICHARD GAVIN is one of Canada's most acclaimed authors of horror fiction. His books include *Charnel Wine, Omens, The Darkly Splendid Realm,* and *At Fear's Altar.* His critical writings on the genre have appeared in Rue Morgue and *Dead Reckonings.*

For more information check out his website: www.richardgavin.net.

"The Word-Made Flesh" was originally published in *At Fear's Altar.*

KIJ JOHNSON is a winner of the Hugo, Nebula, World Fantasy, Sturgeon, and Crawford Awards. Her books include two novels, *The Fox Woman* and *Fudoki,* and a short-story collection, *At the Mouth of the River of Bees.* She splits her time between Seattle and Lawrence, Kansas, where she teaches writing and is the associate director for the Center for the Study of Science Fiction.

"Mantis Wives" was originally published in *Clarkesworld Magazine* edited by Neil Clarke and Sean Wallace.

MARGO LANAGAN has published five collections of short stories (*White Time, Black Juice, Red Spikes, Yellowcake,* and *Cracklescape*) and two dark fantasy novels, *Tender Morsels* and *The Brides of Rollrock Island* (published as *Sea Hearts* in Australia). She is a four-time World Fantasy Award winner, and her work has also won and been nominated for numerous other awards. Margo lives in Sydney, Australia, maintains a blog at *www.amongamidwhile.blogger.com* and can be found on Twitter at @margolanagan.

"Bajazzle" was originally published in *Cracklescape.*

SANDI LEIBOWITZ'S works have appeared or are forthcoming in magazines such as *Strange Horizons, Mythic Delirium, Jabberwocky, Apex, Niteblade,* and *Cricket.* She sings classical and folk music with Cerddorion and New York Revels, and plays recorders, medieval harp, and even more obsolete instruments with the early music trio Choraulos.

"Sleeping, I Was Beauty" was originally published in *Goblin Fruit* edited by Amal El-Mohtar, Jessica P. Wick, and Oliver Hunter.

◄◦►

CLAIRE MASSEY'S short stories have been published in *Best British Short Stories*, *Murmurations: An Anthology of Uncanny Stories About Birds*, *A cappella Zoo*, *Unsettling Wonder*, and elsewhere. Two of her stories are available as chapbooks from Nightjar Press. Claire lives in Lancashire, England, with her two young sons.

"Into the Penny Arcade" was originally published as a chapbook by Nightjar Press.

◄◦►

BRUCE McALLISTER'S fantasy and science fiction have appeared over the year's in the field's major magazines and in "year's best" anthologies (including *Best American Short Stories 2007*, guest-edited by Stephen King); and been a finalist for the Hugo and Nebula awards. His new novel, *The Village Sang to the Sea: A Memoir of Magic*—of which "The Bleeding Child" is a section—will be published by Aeon Press in 2013. His previous novels are *Dream Baby* and *Humanity Prime*. Two of his short stories—the Hugo finalist "Kin" and "Moving On"—have been optioned for film.

"The Bleeding Child" was originally published in *Cemetery Dance Magazine* edited by Richard Chizmar.

◄◦►

KEVIN McCANN has published seven collections of poems for adults and has had poems included in over thirty children's anthologies to date. He has also published a collection of new and original ghost stories called *It's Gone Dark*.

His website is www.kevinmccann.co.uk

"Two Poems for Hill House" were originally published in *Here and Now/7beats*.

◄◦►

GARY McMAHON is the acclaimed author of seven novels. His short fiction has been reprinted in several "Year's Best" volumes. He lives with his family in Yorkshire, where he trains in Shotokan karate and likes running in the rain.

Read more about Gary here: *www.garymcmahon.com*

"Kill All Monsters" was originally published in *Shadows & Tall Trees* edited by Michael Kelly.

◆

TAMSYN MUIR is based in Auckland, New Zealand, where she divides her time between writing, dogs, and teaching high school English. A graduate of the Clarion Writer's Workshop 2010, her work has previously appeared in *Fantasy Magazine, Weird Tales,* and *Nightmare Magazine.*

"The Magician's Apprentice" was first published in *Weird Tales #359* edited by Ann VanderMeer.

◆

ADAM NEVILL was born in Birmingham, England, in 1969 and grew up in England and New Zealand. He is the author of the supernatural horror novels *Banquet for the Damned, Apartment 16, The Ritual, Last Days,* and *House of Small Shadows.* In 2012 *The Ritual* was the winner of The August Derleth Award for Best Horror Novel.

Adam lives in Birmingham, England, and can be contacted through www.adamlgnevill.com.

"Pig Thing" was originally published in *Exotic Gothic 4,* edited by Danel Olson.

◆

IAN ROGERS is a writer, artist, and photographer. His short fiction has appeared in several publications, including *Cemetery Dance, Supernatural Tales,* and *Shadows & Tall Trees.* He is the author of the dark fiction collection *Every House Is Haunted* and *SuperNOIRtural Tales,* a series of stories featuring supernatural detective Felix Renn. Ian lives with his wife in Peterborough, Ontario. For more information, visit ianrogers.ca.

"The House on Ashley Avenue" was originally published in *Every House Is Haunted.*

◆

PRIYA SHARMA is a medical doctor in the UK, where she spends as much time as she can devouring books and writing speculative fiction. She has a computer but prefers a fountain pen and notebook. Her short stories have appeared in publications such as *Black Static*, *Interzone*, *Albedo One*, *On Spec*, *Fantasy Magazine* and *Bourbon Penn*, as well as at *Tor.com*. She is currently working on a historical fantasy novel set in North Wales, not far from where she lives. More information can be found at www. priyasharmafiction.wordpress.com

"The Ballad of Boomtown" was originally published in *Black Static* edited by Andy Cox.

◄◦►

LUCY A. SNYDER is the Bram Stoker Award-winning author of the novels *Spellbent*, *Shotgun Sorceress*, *Switchblade Goddess*, and the collections *Sparks and Shadows*, *Chimeric Machines*, and *Installing Linux on a Dead Badger*. Her writing has appeared in *Strange Horizons*, *Weird Tales*, *Hellbound Hearts*, *Dark Faith*, *Chiaroscuro*, *GUD*, and *Lady Churchill's Rosebud Wristlet*.

She currently lives in Worthington, Ohio with her husband and occasional co-author Gary A. Braunbeck. You can learn more about her at www.lucysnyder.com.

"Magdala Amygdala" was originally published in *Dark Faith: Invocations*, edited by Maurice Broaddus and Jerry Gordon

◄◦►

AMBER SPARKS'S short story collection, *May We Shed These Human Bodies*, was published by Curbside Splendor in 2012. Her short fiction has appeared in many journals and magazines. She lives in Washington, DC with her husband and two cats.

"This Circus the World" was originally published in *Corium Magazine* edited by Lauren Becker.

◄◦►

DUANE SWIERCZYNSKI is the author of the Edgar-nominated and Anthony Award-winning *Expiration Date*, as well the Shamus Award-winning Charlie Hardie series (*Fun & Games, Hell & Gone*), which is currently being developed by Sony Pictures Television.

He currently writes the monthly comic series *Judge Dredd* for IDW, *Bloodshot* for Valiant, and has written various bestselling comics series for Marvel, DC, and Dark Horse. Duane has also collaborated with *CSI* creator Anthony E. Zuiker on a series of bestselling "digi-novel" thrillers.

In a previous life, he worked as an editor and writer for *Details, Men's Health* and *Philadelphia* magazines, and was the editor-in-chief of the *Philadelphia City Paper*. He lives in Philly. You can say "yo" to him at www.secretdead.com or twitter.com/swierczy.

"Tender as Teeth" was originally published in *21ˢᵗ Century Dead*, edited by Christopher Golden.

◄◦►

LUCY TAYLOR is the author of seven novels, including *Nailed, Dancing with Demons, Eternal Hearts*, and the Stoker-award-winning *The Safety of Unknown Cities*. Her stories have appeared in over a hundred magazines and anthologies, including *Best of Cemetery Dance, The Mammoth Book of Historical Erotica, Century's Best Horror Fiction, Twentieth Century Gothic, Danse Macabre*, and the Exotic Gothic anthology series.

New editions of four earlier collections: *Painted in Blood, Close to the Bones, The Flesh Artist*, and *Unnatural Acts and Other Stories*, will be published by the Overlook Connection Press in 2013 followed by a new collection, *Fatal Journeys*, later the same year.

Taylor lives in Pismo Beach, CA, where she attends the White Heron Sangha and volunteers with the Feline Network, a cat rescue group.

"Nikishi" was originally published in *Exotic Gothic 4* edited by Danel Olson.

◄◦►

JAY WILBURN taught public school for sixteen years, but left to care for his younger son and to pursue a career as a full-time writer. He has published many horror and speculative fiction stories including his novels *Loose Ends: A Zombie Novel* and *Time Eaters*. Follow his many dark thoughts on Twitter @AmongTheZombies and at JayWilburn.com.

"Dead Song" was originally published in *Zombies for a Cure* edited by Angela Charmaine Craig.

◀◦▶

CONRAD WILLIAMS is the author of seven novels, four novellas and over 100 short stories, some of which are collected in *Use Once, then Destroy* and *Born with Teeth*. In addition to his International Horror Guild Award for his novel *The Unblemished*, he is a three-time recipient of the British Fantasy Award, including Best Novel for *One*. He's also editor of the acclaimed anthology *Gutshot*.

He is currently working on a novel that will act as the prequel to a major video game from Sony, as well as a novel of supernatural horror.

ACKNOWLEDGMENT IS MADE FOR REPRINTING THE FOLLOWING MATERIAL

"The Callers" by Ramsey Campbell. © 2012 by Ramsey Campbell. First published in *Four for Fear*, edited by Peter Crowther. PS Publishing. Reprinted by permission of the author.

"Two Poems for Hill House" by Kevin McCann. © 2012 by Kevin McCann. First published in *Here and Now/7beats*, July 2012. Reprinted by permission of the author.

"Mariner's Round" by Terry Dowling. © 2012 by Terry Dowling. First published in *Exotic Gothic 4*, edited by Danel Olson, PS Publishing. Reprinted by permission of the author.

"Nanny Grey" by Gemma Files. © 2012 by Gemma Files. First published in *An Anthology of the Esoteric and Arcane Magic* edited by Jonathan Oliver, Solaris Books. Reprinted by permission of the author.

"The Magician's Apprentice" by Tamsyn Muir. © 2012 by Tamsyn Muir. First published in *Weird Tales* #359. Reprinted by permission of the author.

"Kill All Monsters" by Gary McMahon. © 2012 by Gary McMahon. First published in *Shadows & Tall Trees* #3, spring. Reprinted by permission of the author.

"The House on Ashley Avenue by Ian Rogers. © 2012 by Ian Rogers. First published in *Every House is Haunted*, Chizine Publications. Reprinted by permission of the author.

"Dead Song" by Jay Wilburn. © 2012 by Jay Wilburn. First published in *Zombies for a Cure*, edited by Angela Charmaine Craig, Electrik Milk Bath Press. Reprinted by permission of the author.

"Sleeping, I Was Beauty" by Sandi Leibowitz. © 2012 by Sandy Leibowitz. First published in *Goblin Fruit*, winter. Reprinted by permission of the author.

"Bajazzle" by Margo Lanagan. © 2012 by Margo Lanagan. First published in *Cracklescape*, Twelfth Planet Press. Reprinted by permission of the author.

"The Pike" by Conrad Williams. © 2012 by Conrad Williams. First published in *Born with Teeth*, PS Publishing. Reprinted by permission of the author.

"The Crying Child" by Bruce McAllister. © 2012 by Bruce McAllister. First published in *Cemetery Dance*, #68 as "The Bleeding Child." Reprinted by permission of the author.

"This Circus the World" by Amber Sparks. © 2012 by Amber Sparks. First published in *Corium Magazine,* summer. Reprinted by permission of the author.

"Some Pictures in An Album" by Gary McMahon. © 2012 by Gary McMahon. First published in *Chiral Mad: An Anthology of Psychological Horror* edited by Michael Bailey, Written Backwards. Reprinted by permission of the author.

"Wild Acre" by Nathan Ballingrud. © 2012 by Nathan Ballingrud. First published in *Visions Fading Fast*, edited by Gary McMahon, Pendragon Press. Reprinted by permission of the author.

"Final Exam" by Megan Arkenberg. © 2012 by Megan Arkenberg. First published in *Asimov's Science Fiction Magazine*, June 2012. Reprinted by permission of the author.

"None So Blind" by Stephen Bacon. © 2012 by Stephen Bacon. First published in *Shadows & Tall Trees* #3, spring. Reprinted by permission of the author.

"The Ballad of Boomtown" by Priya Sharma. © 2012 by Priya Sharma. First published in *Black Static* 28. Reprinted by permission of the author.

"Pig Thing" by Adam L.G. Nevill. © 2012 by Adam L. G. Nevill. First published in *Exotic Gothic 4*, edited by Danel Olson, PS Publishing. Reprinted by permission of the author.

"The Word-Made Flesh" by Richard Gavin. © 2012 by Richard Gavin. First published in *At Fear's Altar*, Hippocampus Press. Reprinted by permission of the author.

"Into the Penny Arcade" by Claire Massey. © 2012 by Claire Massey. First published by Nightjar Press. Reprinted by permission of the author.

"Magdala Amygdala" by Lucy A. Snyder. © 2012 by Lucy A. Snyder. First published in *Dark Faith: Invocations*, edited by Maurice Broaddus and Jerry Gordon, Apex Publications.

"Frontier Death Song" by Laird Barron. © 2012 by Laird Barron. First published in *Nightmare Magazine* #1. Reprinted by permission of the author.